POKÉMON THE MOVIE

Pokémon™ Hoopa and the Clash of Ages

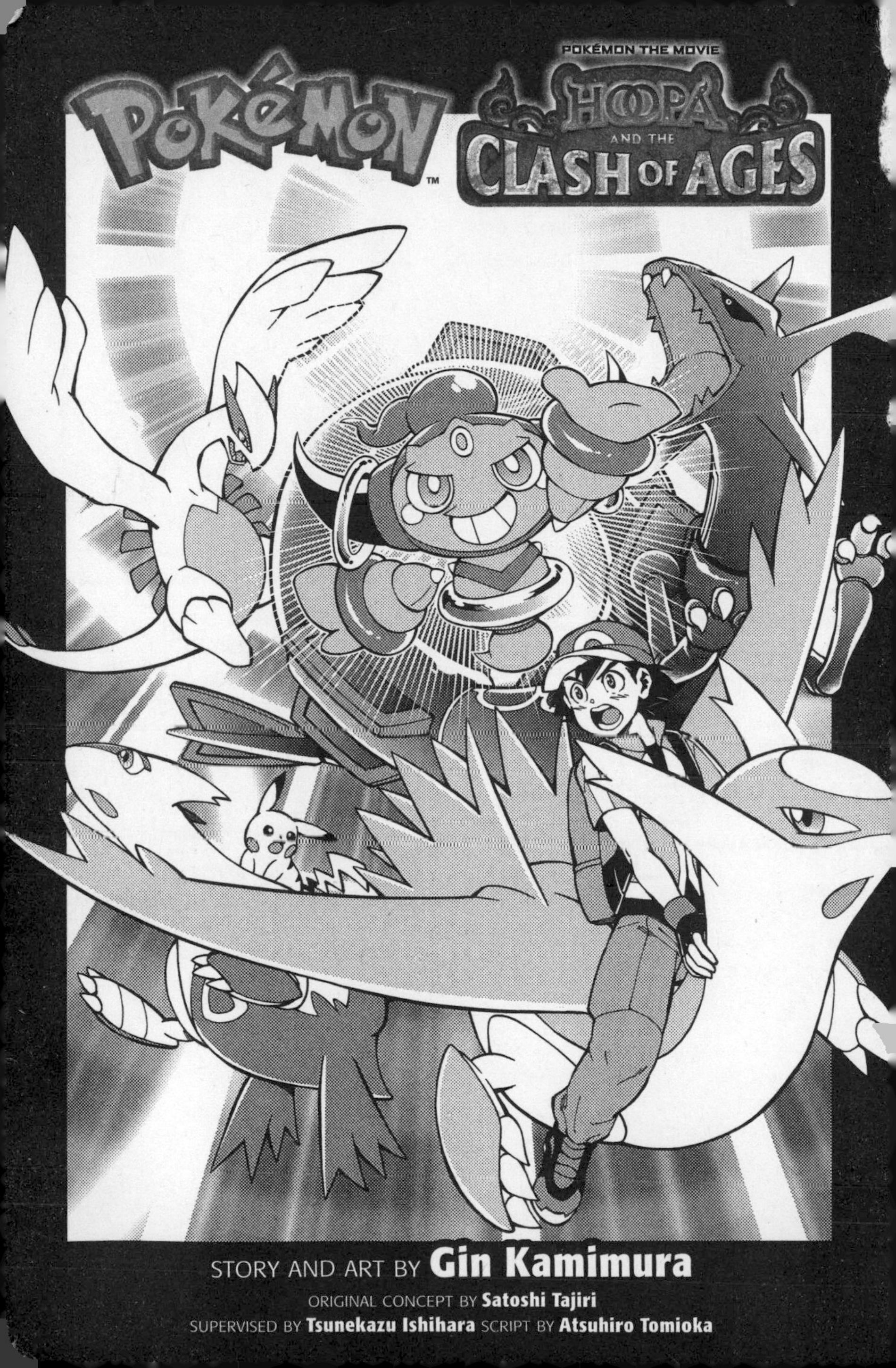

STORY AND ART BY **Gin Kamimura**

ORIGINAL CONCEPT BY **Satoshi Tajiri**

SUPERVISED BY **Tsunekazu Ishihara** SCRIPT BY **Atsuhiro Tomioka**

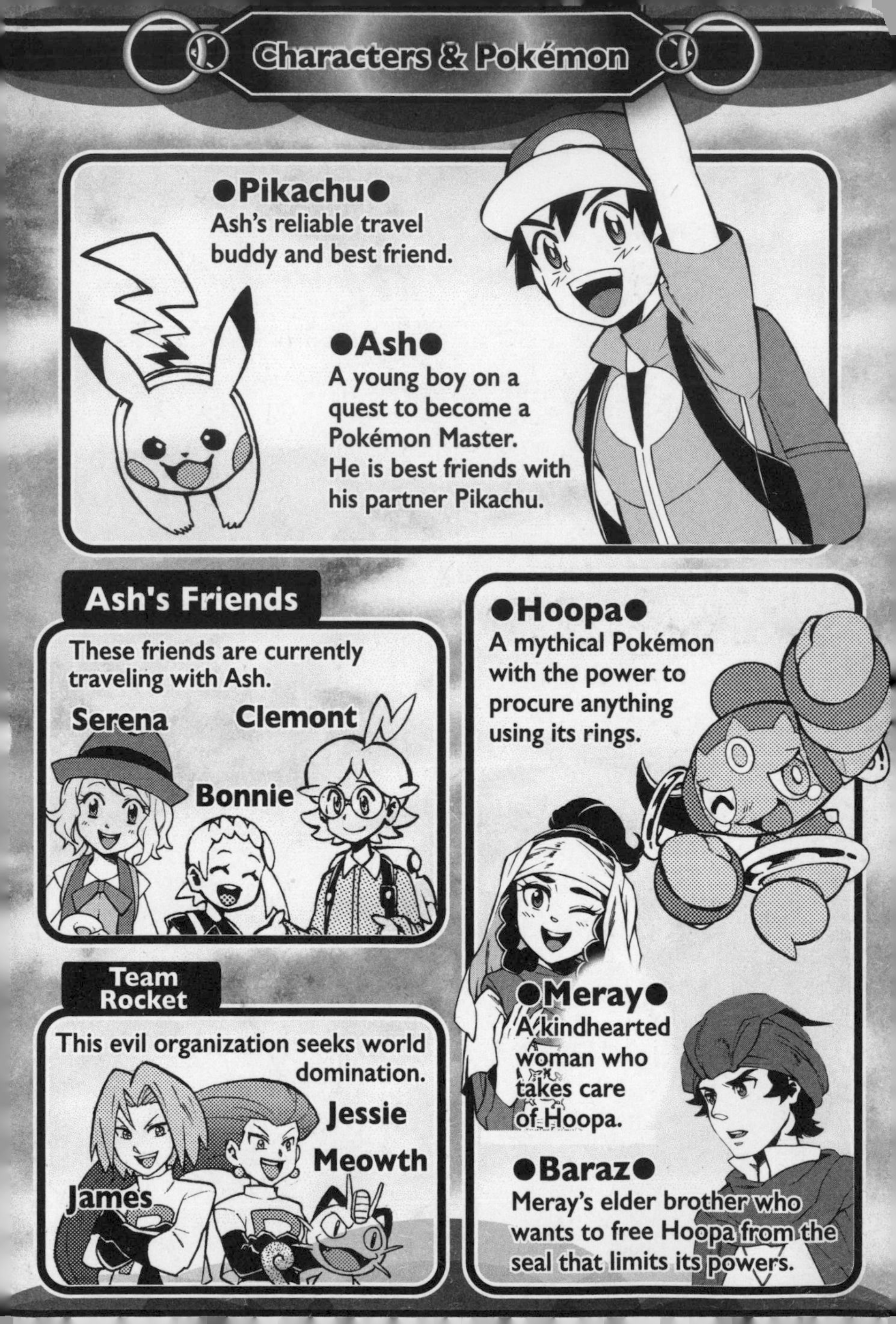
Characters & Pokémon
●Pikachu●
Ash's reliable travel buddy and best friend.
●Ash●
A young boy on a quest to become a Pokémon Master. He is best friends with his partner Pikachu.
Ash's Friends
These friends are currently traveling with Ash.
Serena
Clemont
Bonnie
●Hoopa●
A mythical Pokémon with the power to procure anything using its rings.
Team Rocket
This evil organization seeks world domination.
Jessie
Meowth
James
●Meray●
A kindhearted woman who takes care of Hoopa.
●Baraz●
Meray's elder brother who wants to free Hoopa from the seal that limits its powers.

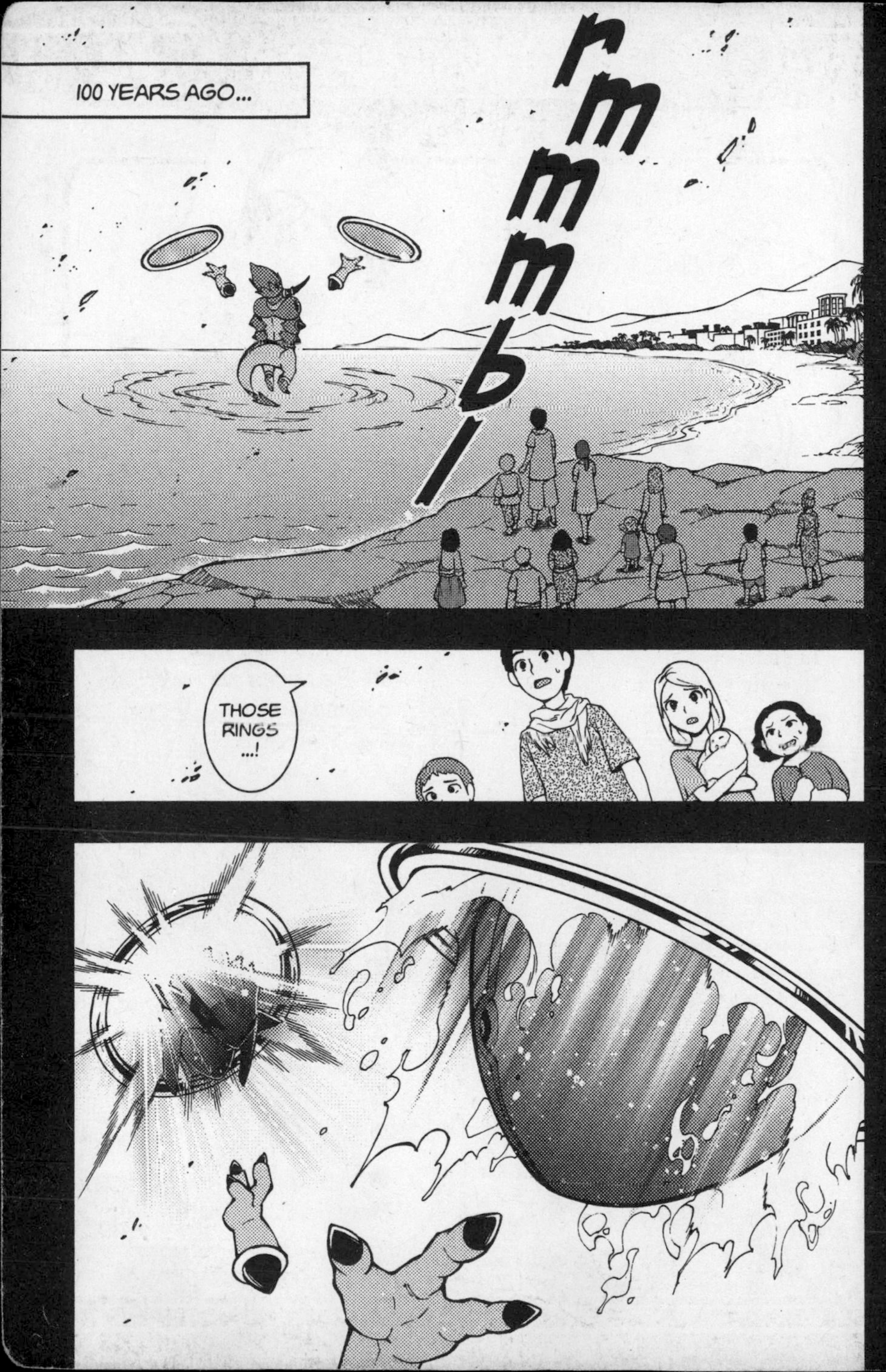
100 YEARS AGO...
rmmmbl
THOSE RINGS ...!

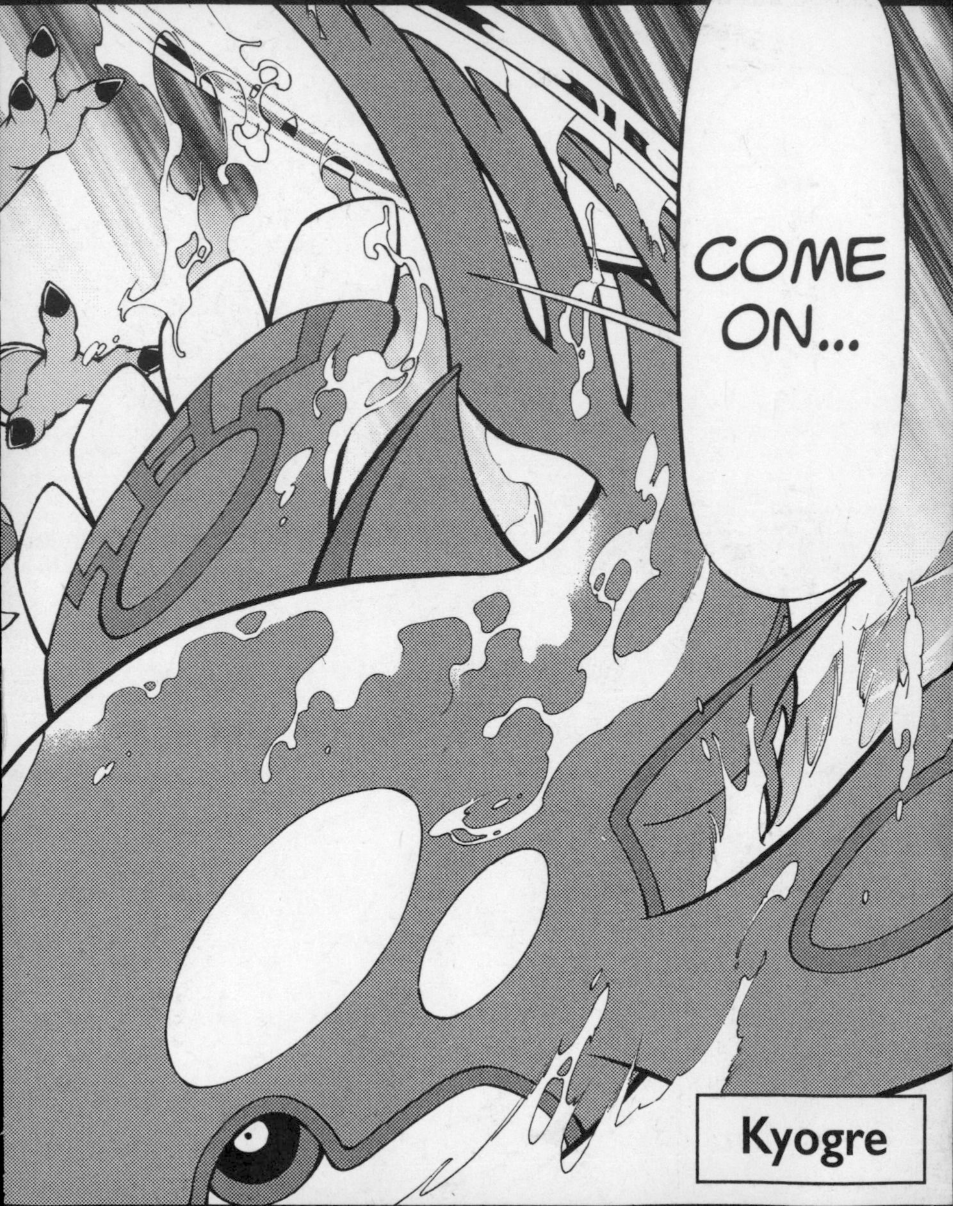
COME ON...
Kyogre

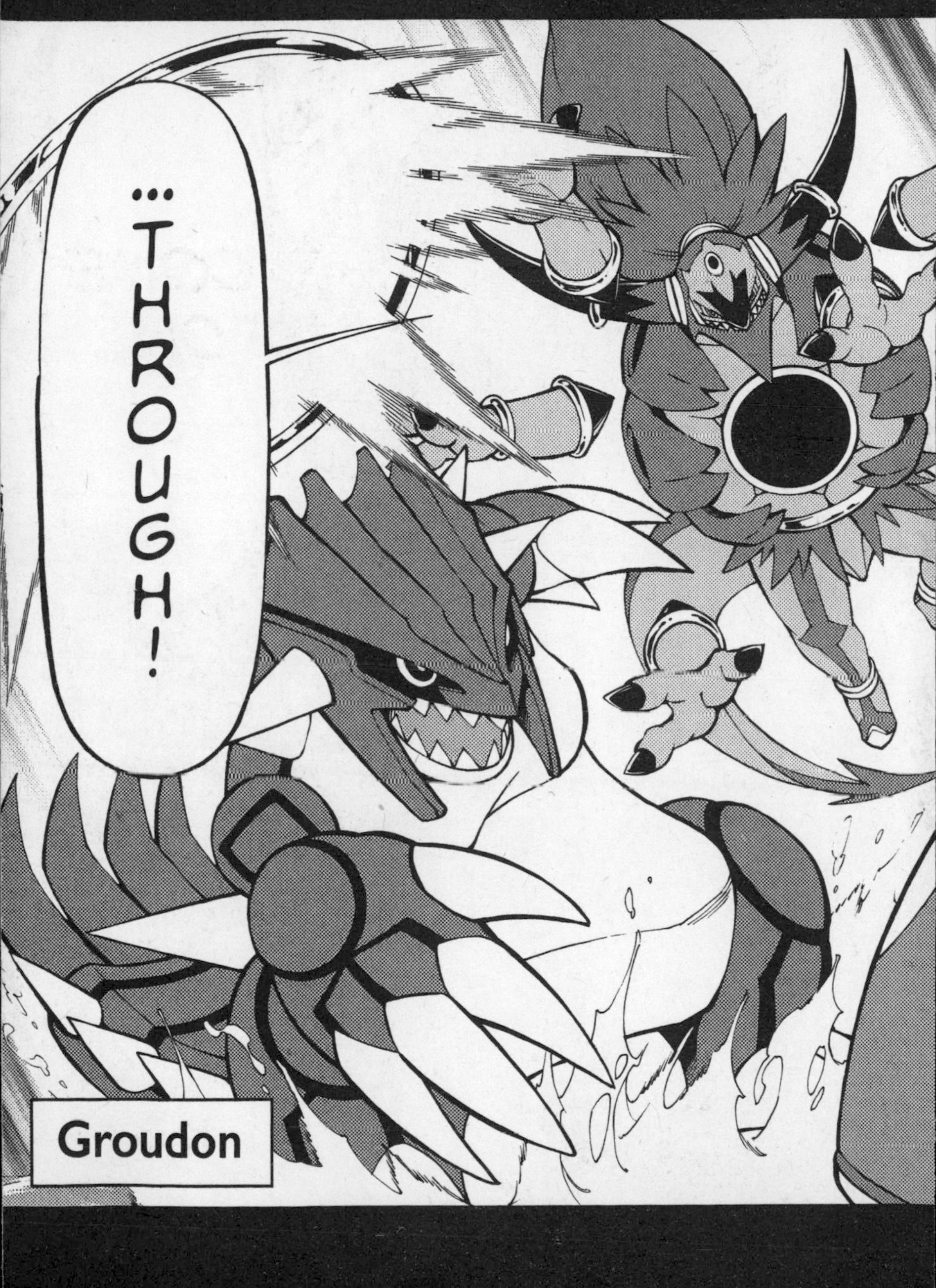
...THROUGH!
Groudon

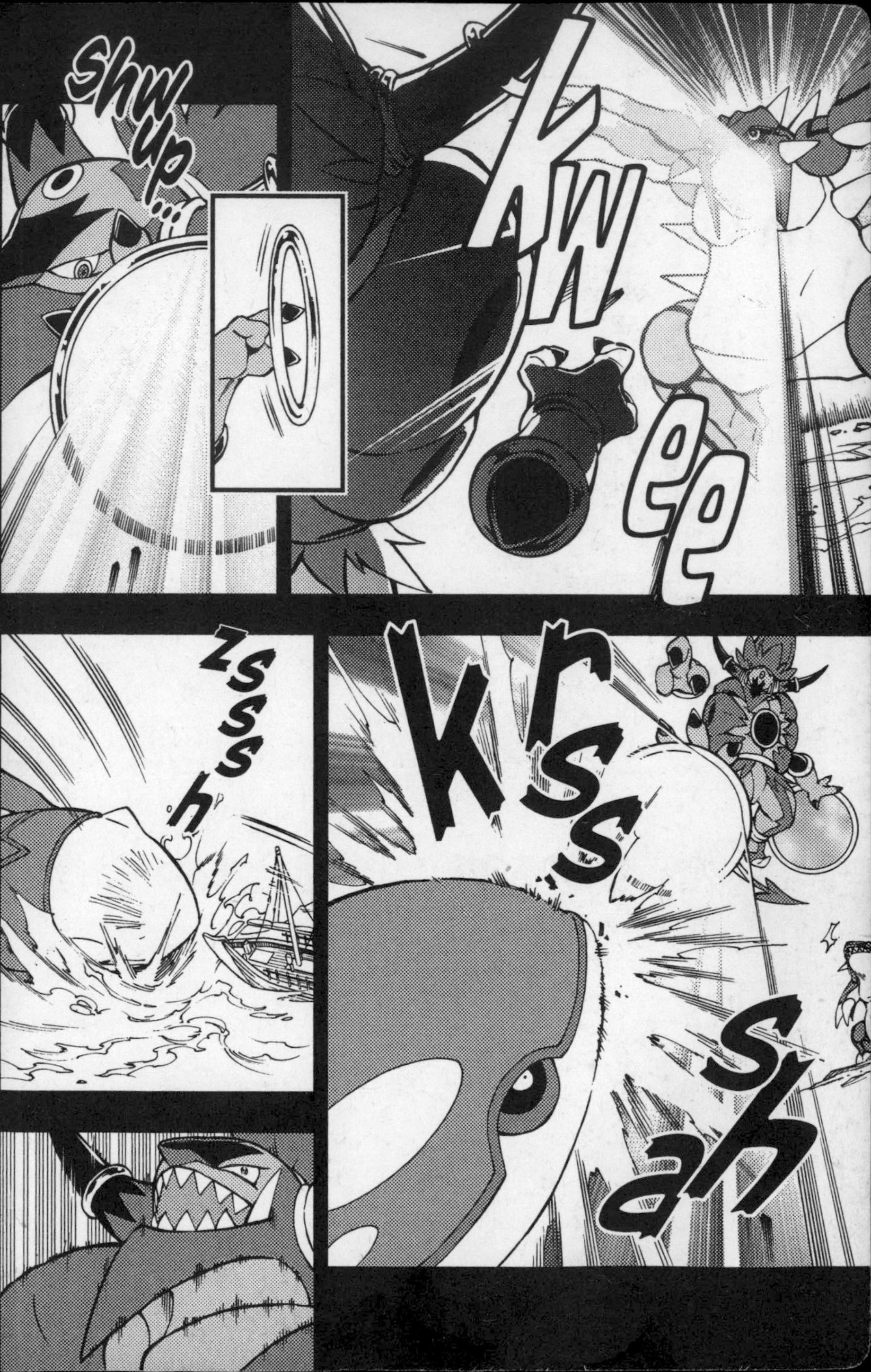
kAWeee
Shwup...
Krss
Shah
zsssh

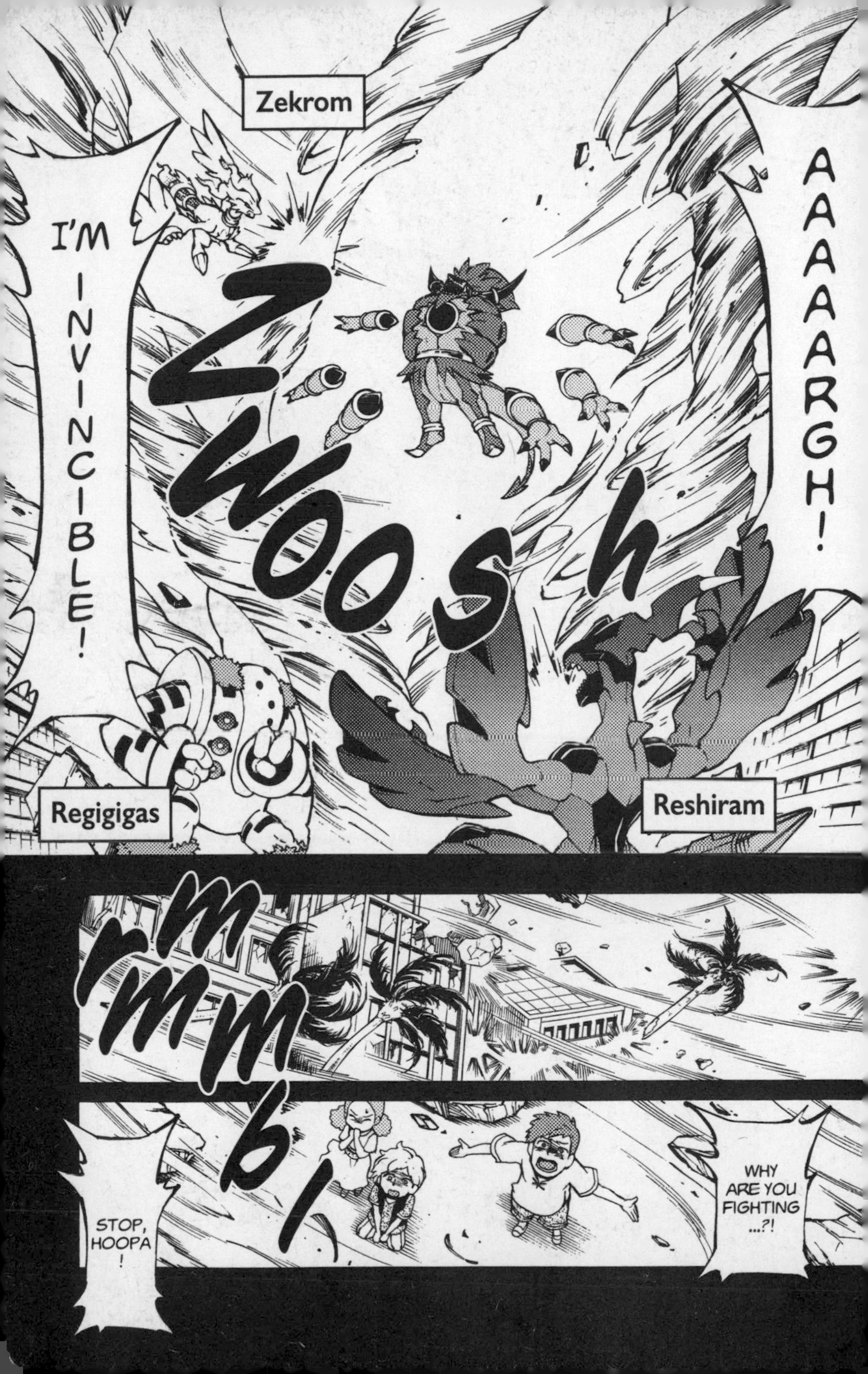

AAAAARGH!
Zekrom
ZWOOSH
I'M INVINCIBLE!
Reshiram
Regigigas
rrmmmmbl
WHY ARE YOU FIGHTING ...?!
STOP, HOOPA!

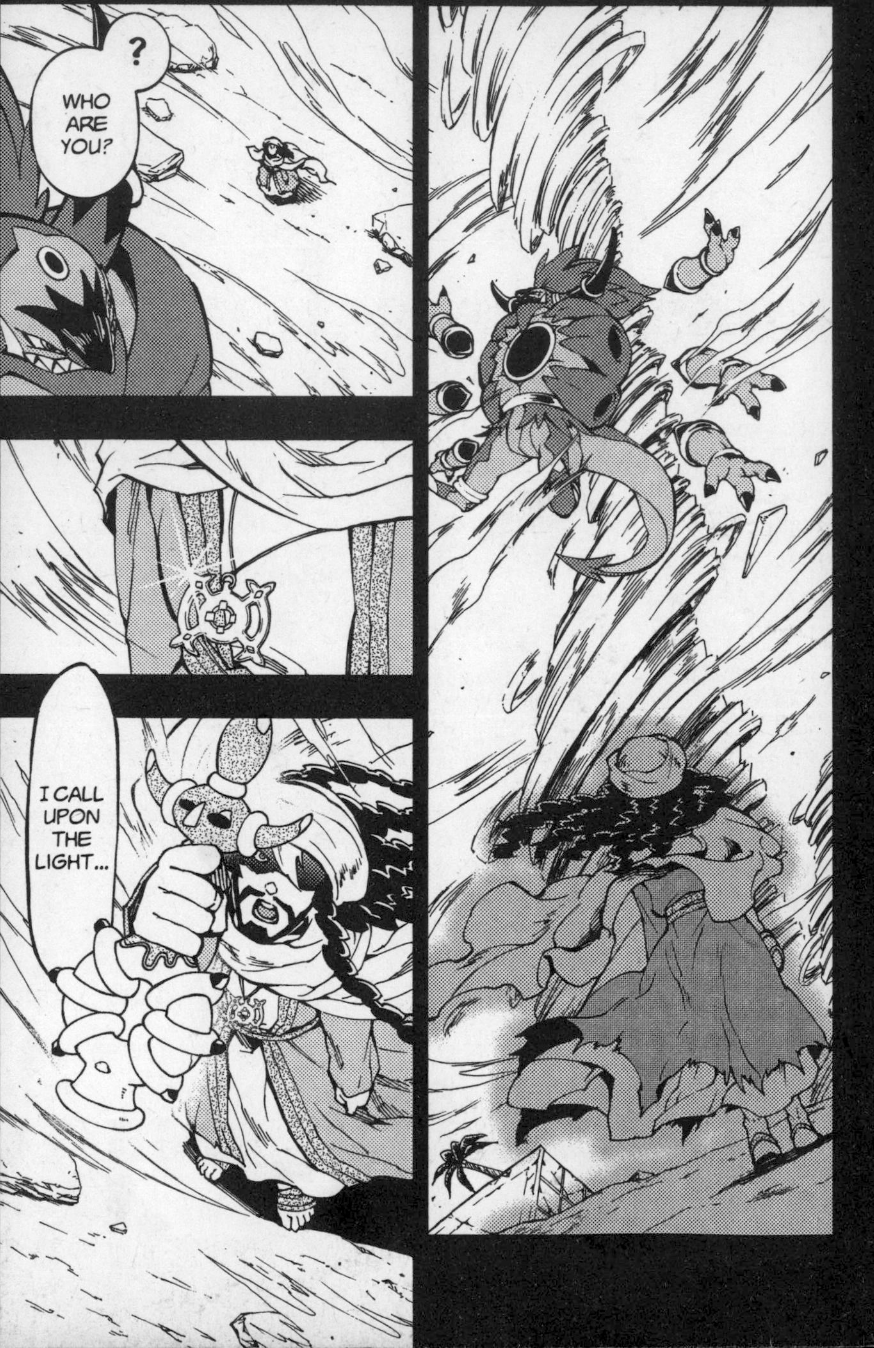
?
WHO ARE YOU?
I CALL UPON THE LIGHT...

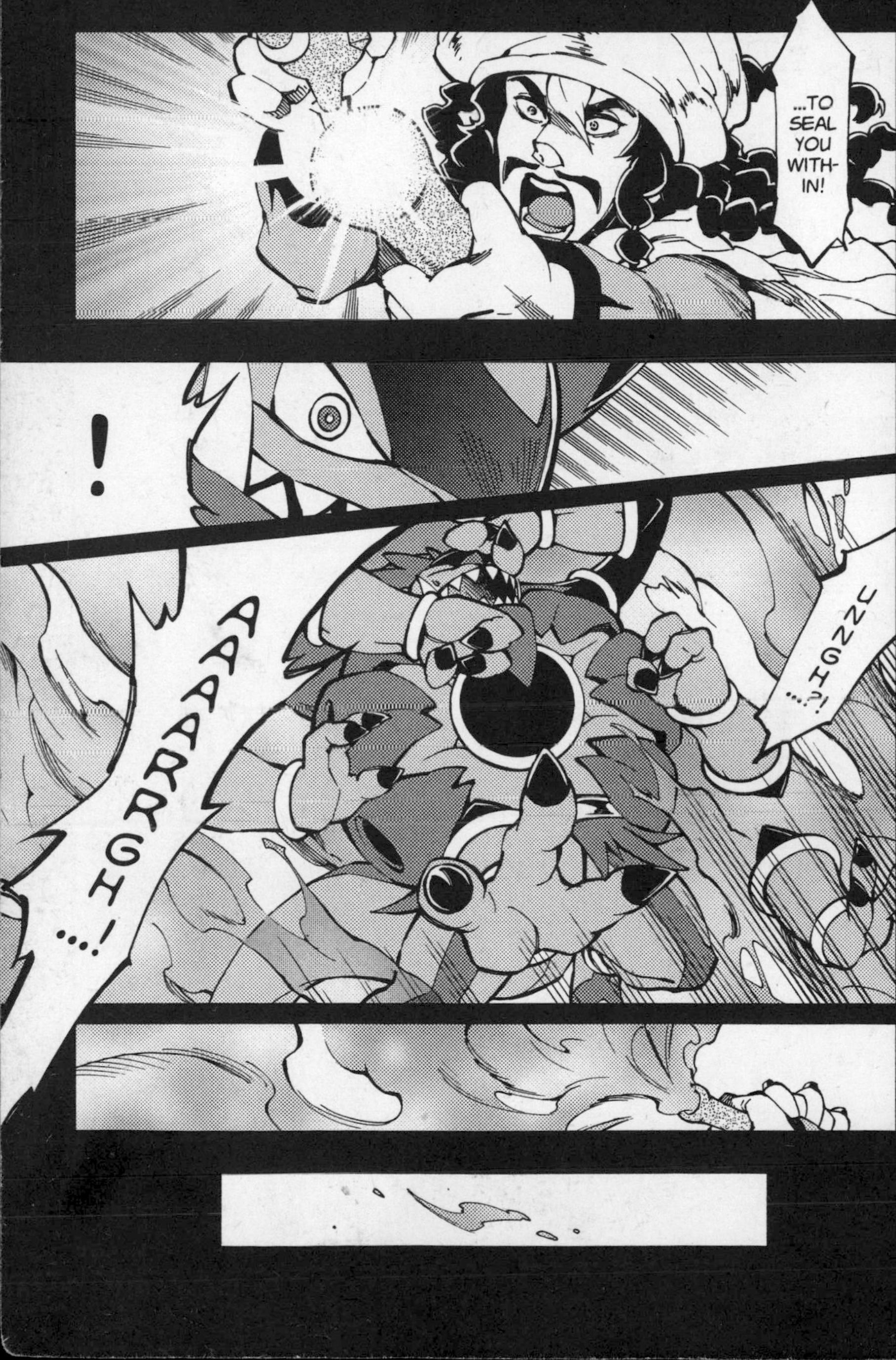
...TO SEAL YOU WITH-IN!
!
UNNGH...?!
AAAAARRRGH...!

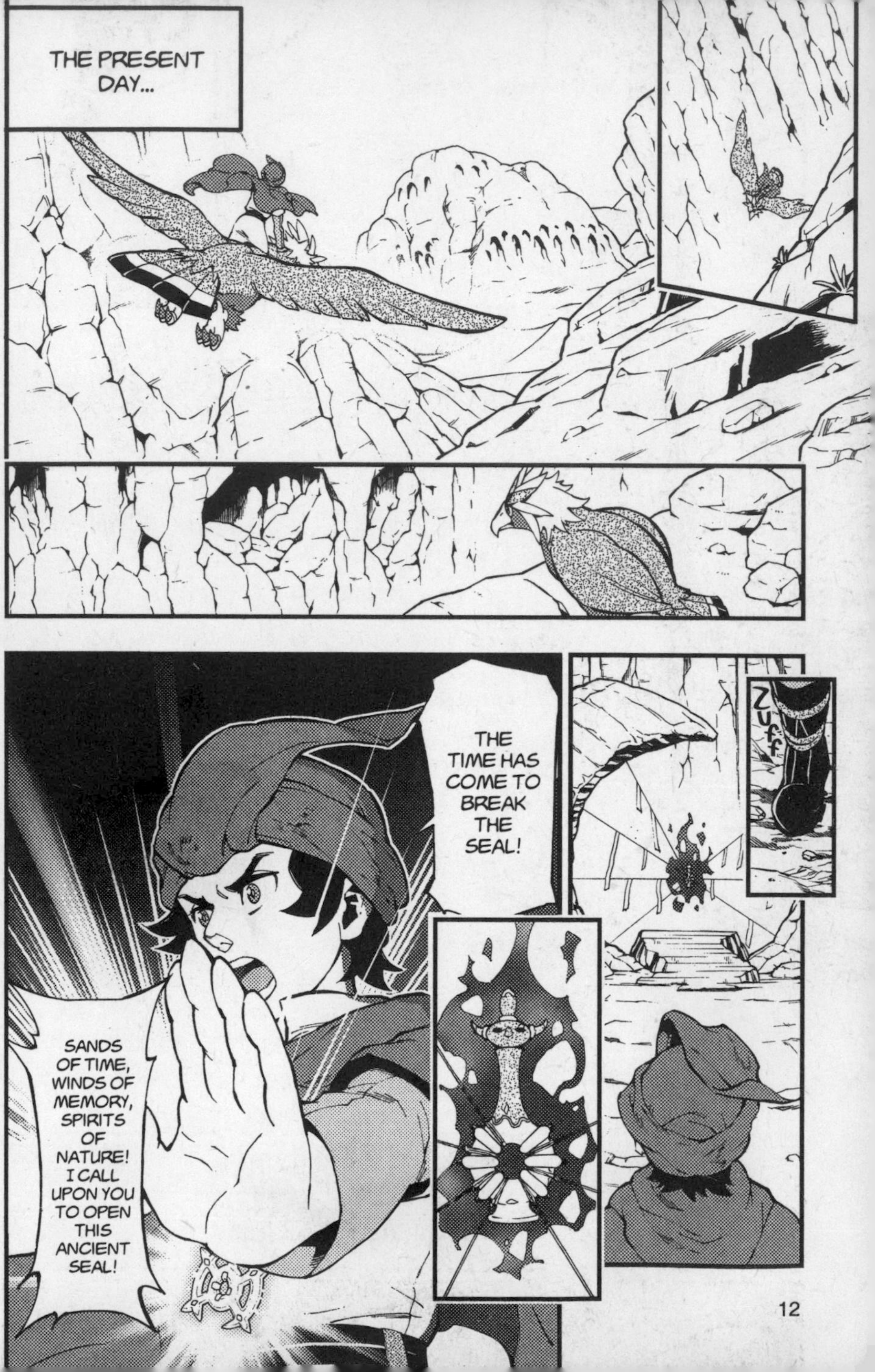
THE PRESENT DAY...
ZUFF
THE TIME HAS COME TO BREAK THE SEAL!
SANDS OF TIME, WINDS OF MEMORY, SPIRITS OF NATURE! I CALL UPON YOU TO OPEN THIS ANCIENT SEAL!

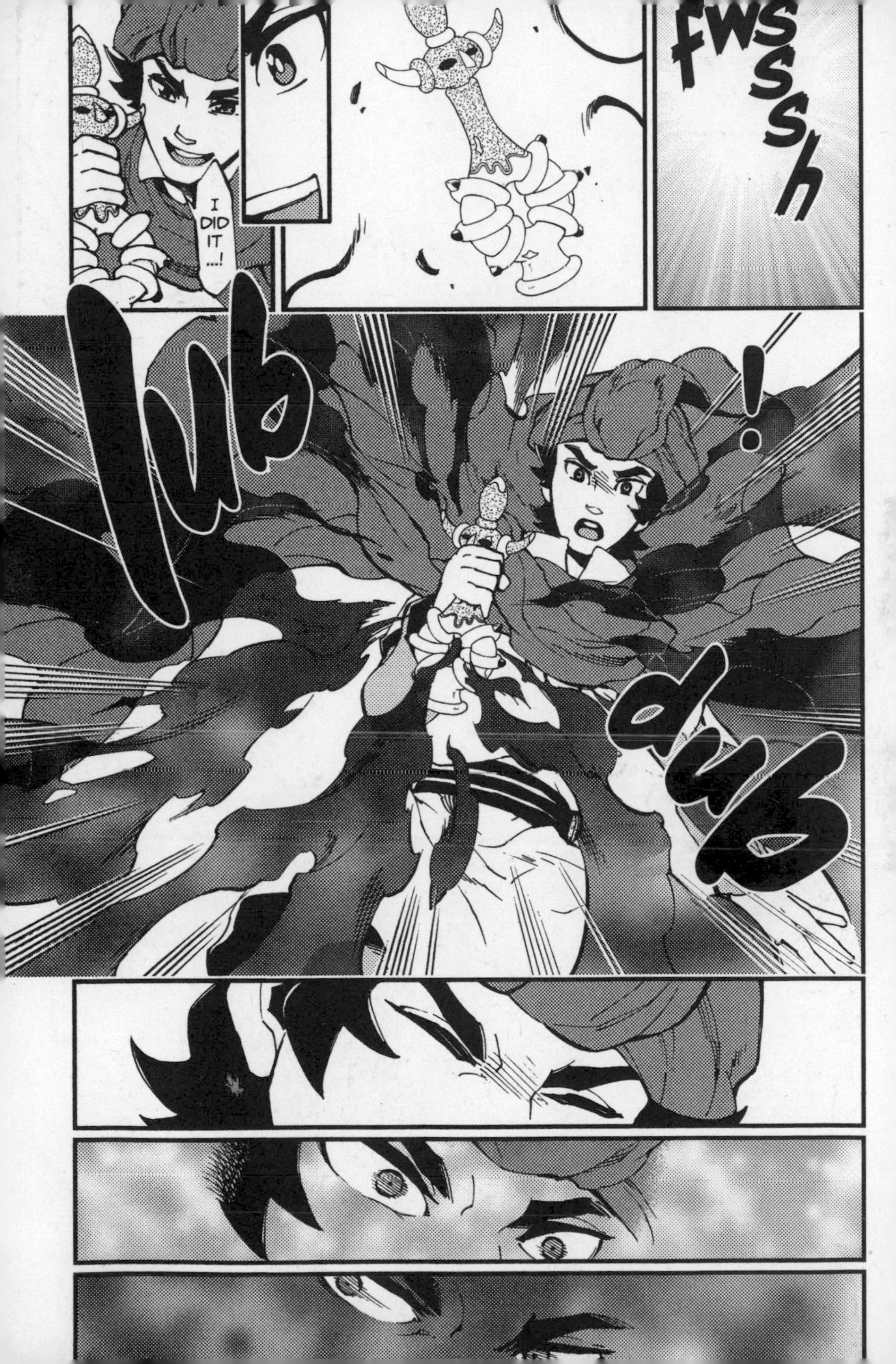
fwsssh
I DID IT ...!
!
lub
dub

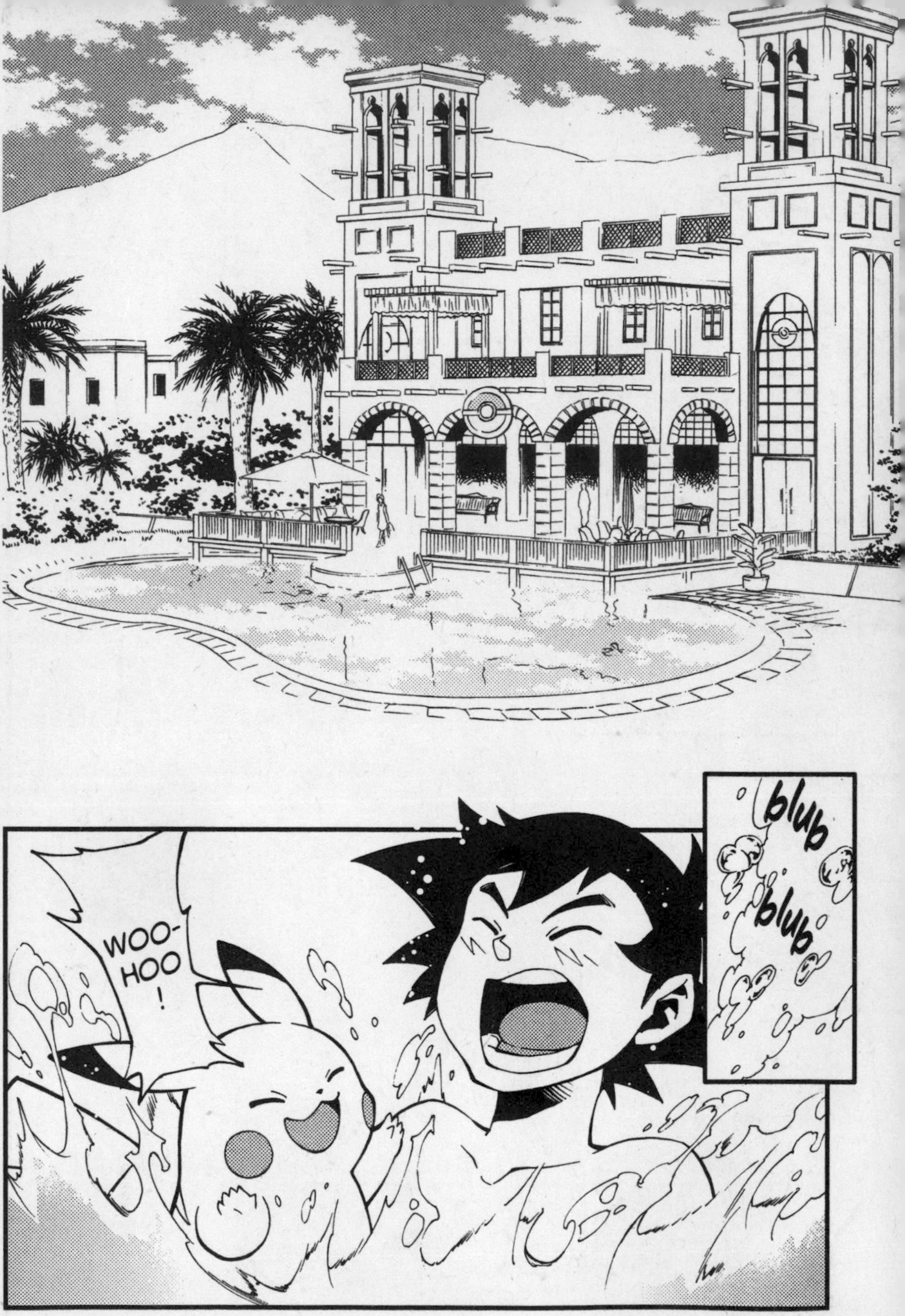
blub blub
WOO-HOO!

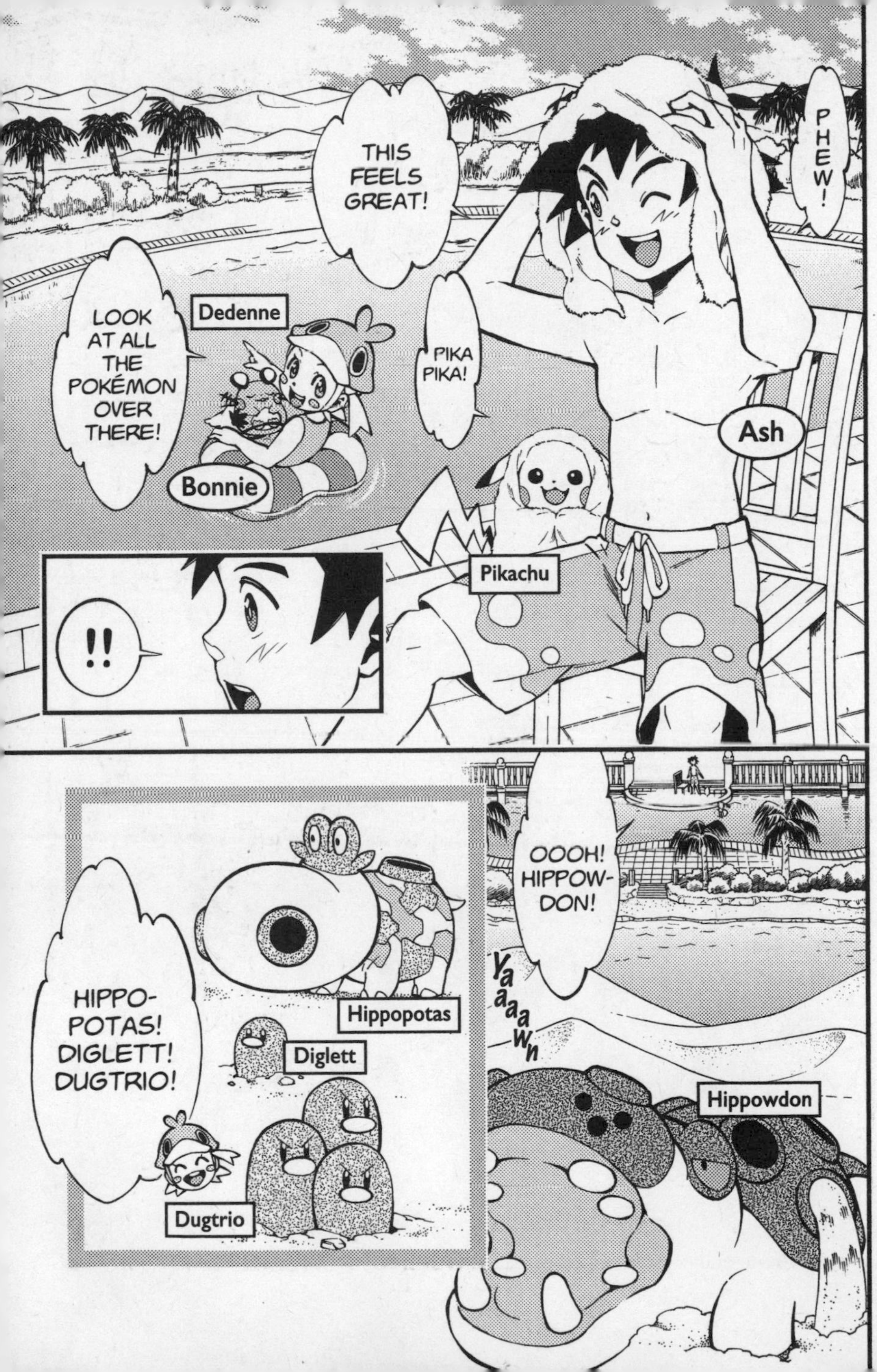
PHEW!
THIS FEELS GREAT!
Ash
PIKA PIKA!
Pikachu
LOOK AT ALL THE POKÉMON OVER THERE!
Dedenne
Bonnie
!!
OOOH! HIPPOW-DON!
Yaaaawn
Hippowdon
HIPPO-POTAS! DIGLETT! DUGTRIO!
Hippopotas
Diglett
Dugtrio

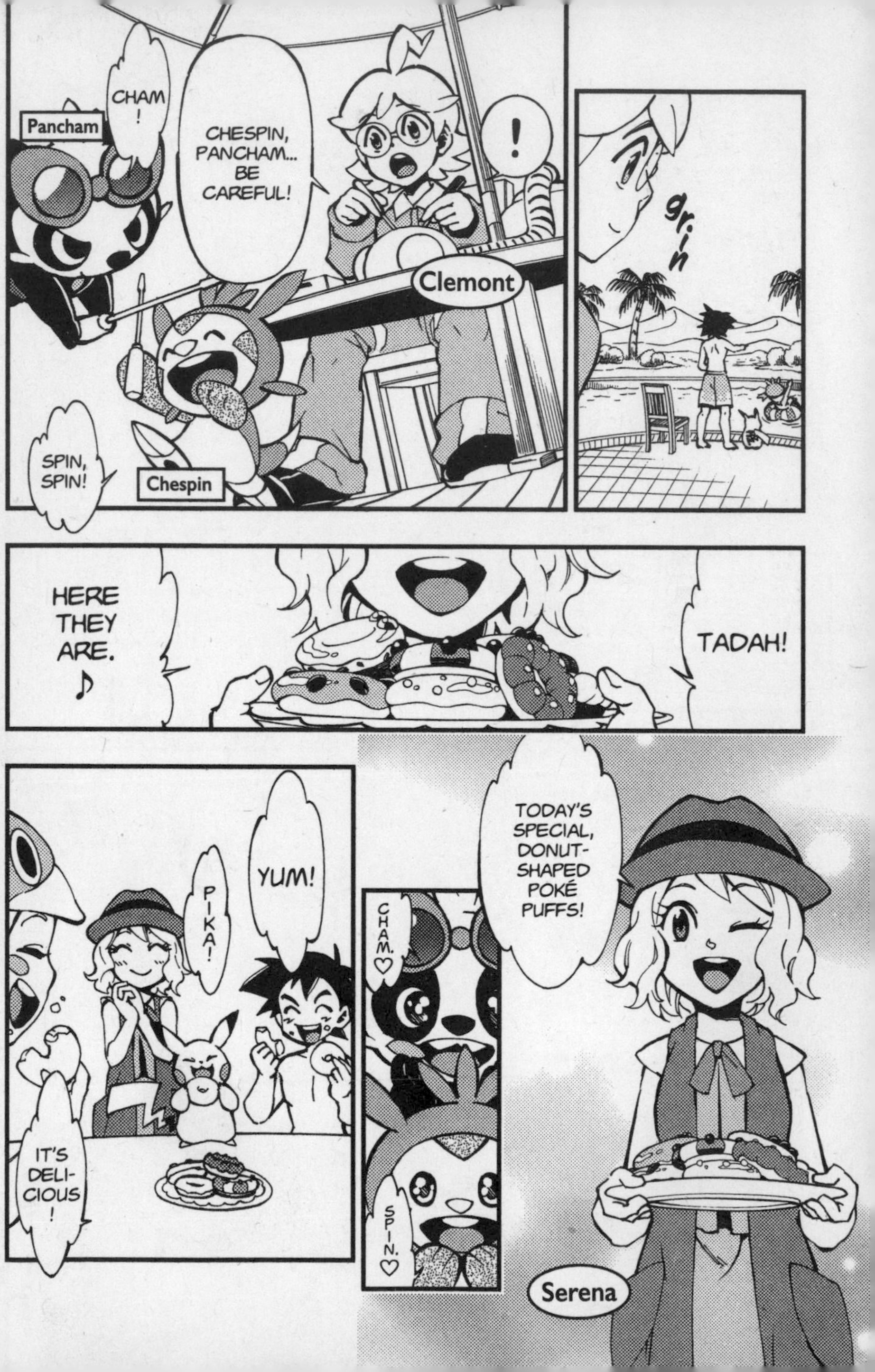

grin
!
CHESPIN, PANCHAM... BE CAREFUL!
Clemont
CHAM!
Pancham
SPIN, SPIN!
Chespin
TADAH!
HERE THEY ARE. ♪
TODAY'S SPECIAL, DONUT-SHAPED POKÉ PUFFS!
Serena
CHAM. ♡
SPIN. ♡
YUM!
PIKA!
IT'S DELICIOUS!

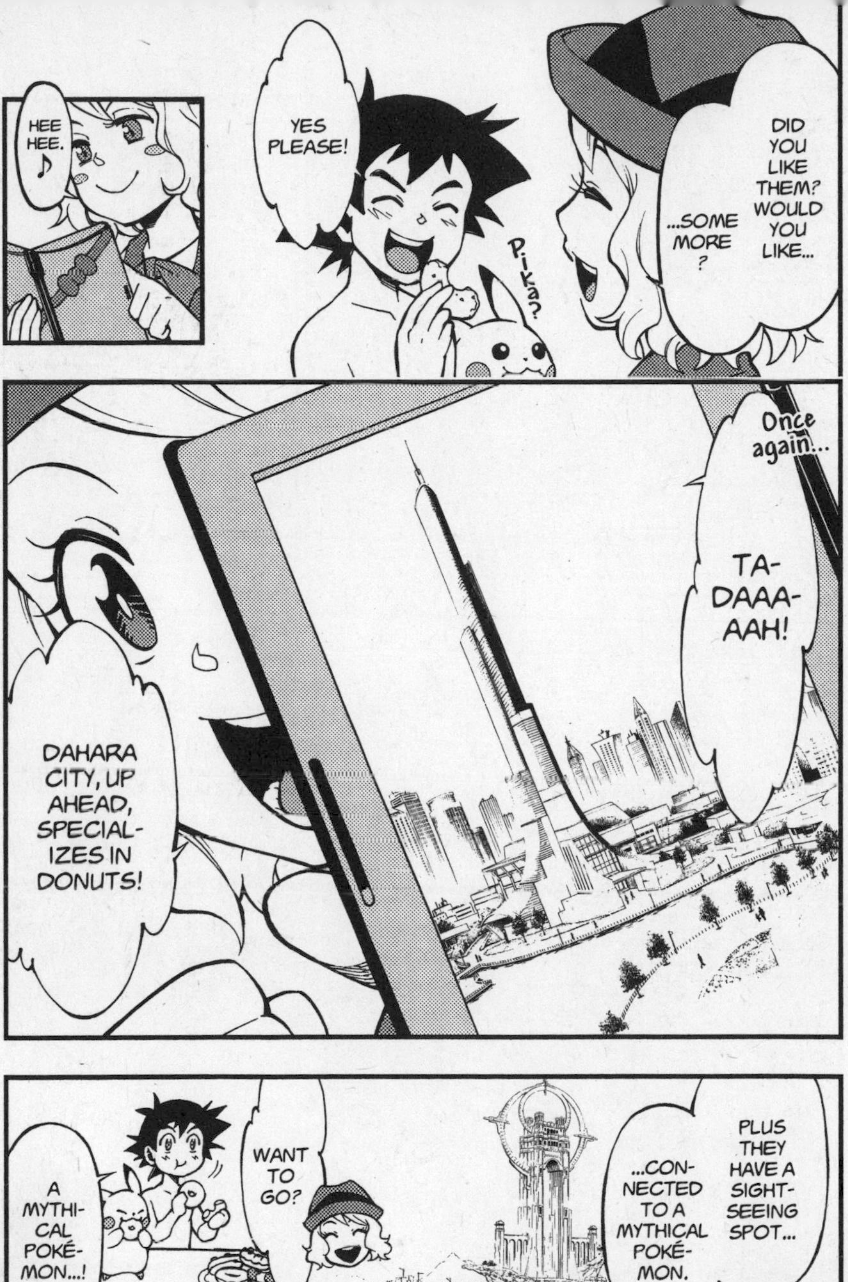
DID YOU LIKE THEM? WOULD YOU LIKE...
...SOME MORE?
YES PLEASE!
Pika?
HEE HEE. ♪
Once again...
TA-DAAAA-AAH!
DAHARA CITY, UP AHEAD, SPECIALIZES IN DONUTS!
PLUS THEY HAVE A SIGHT-SEEING SPOT...
...CONNECTED TO A MYTHICAL POKÉMON.
WANT TO GO?
A MYTHICAL POKÉMON...!

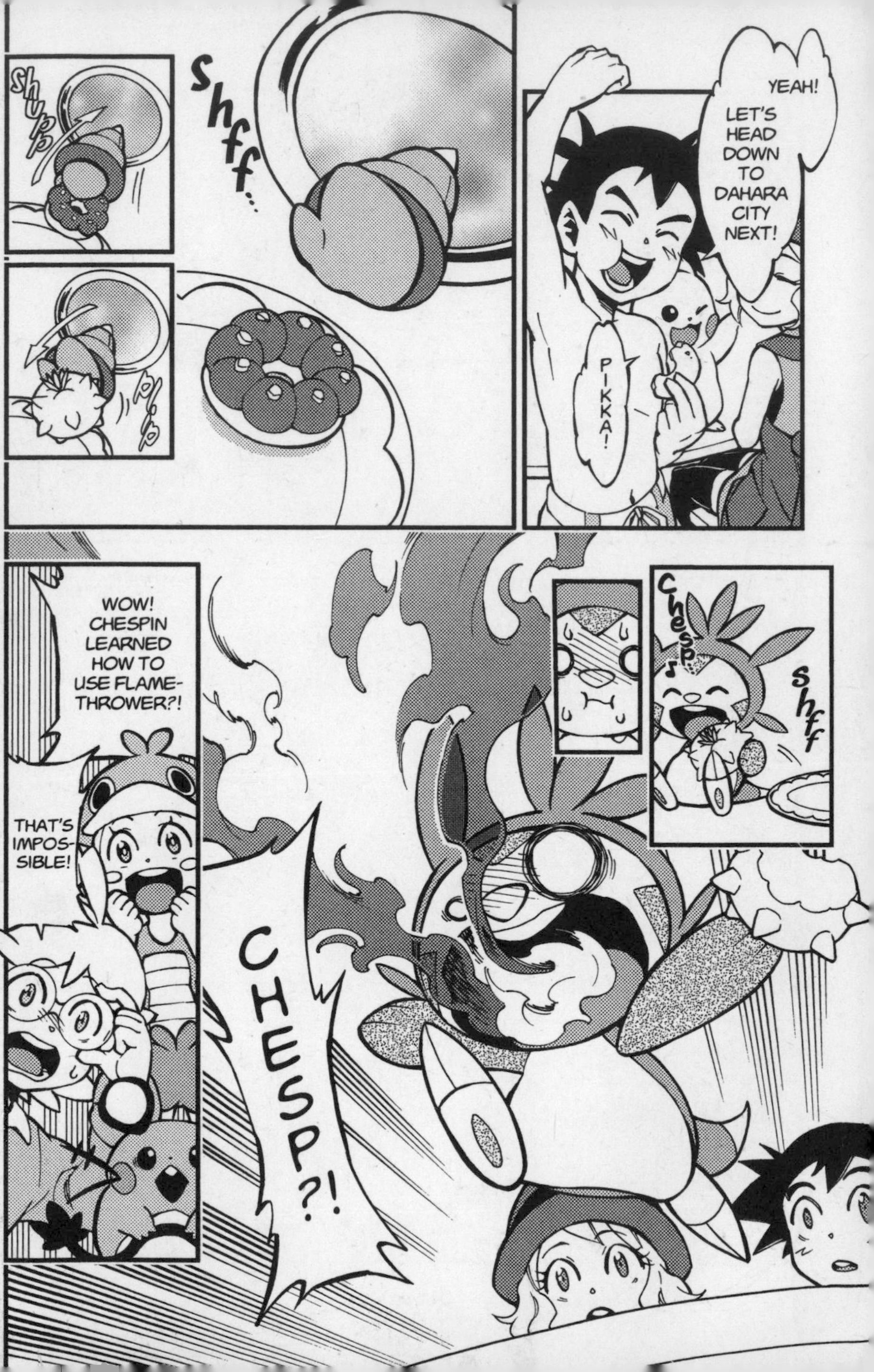
YEAH!
LET'S HEAD DOWN TO DAHARA CITY NEXT!
PIKKA!
shff...
shupp
plop
Chesp♪
shff
CHESP?!
WOW! CHESPIN LEARNED HOW TO USE FLAME-THROWER?!
THAT'S IMPOSSIBLE!

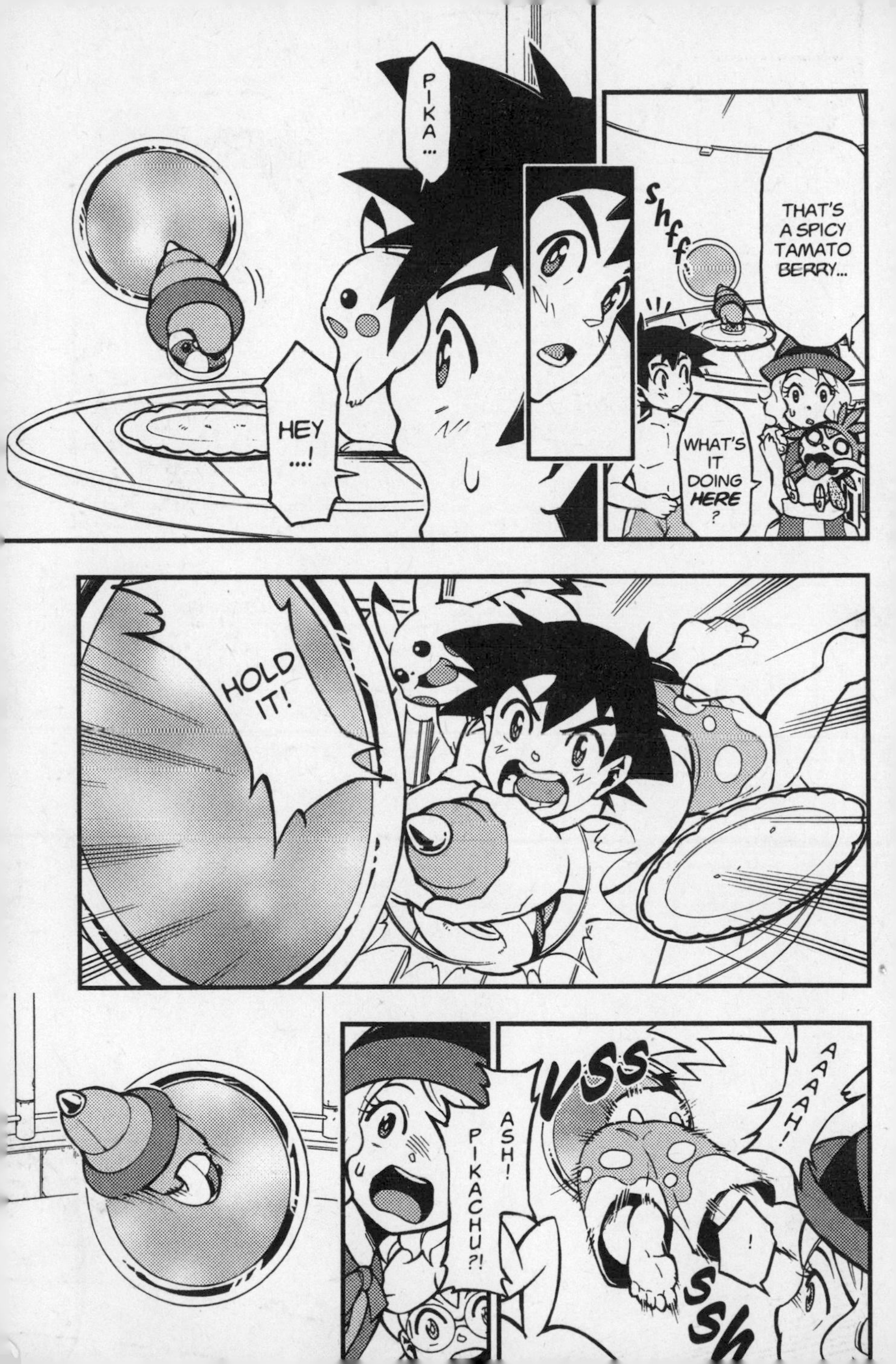

THAT'S A SPICY TAMATO BERRY...
shfff
WHAT'S IT DOING HERE?
PIKA...
HEY ...!
HOLD IT!
AAAAAH!
VSS
!
SSH
ASH! PIKACHU?!

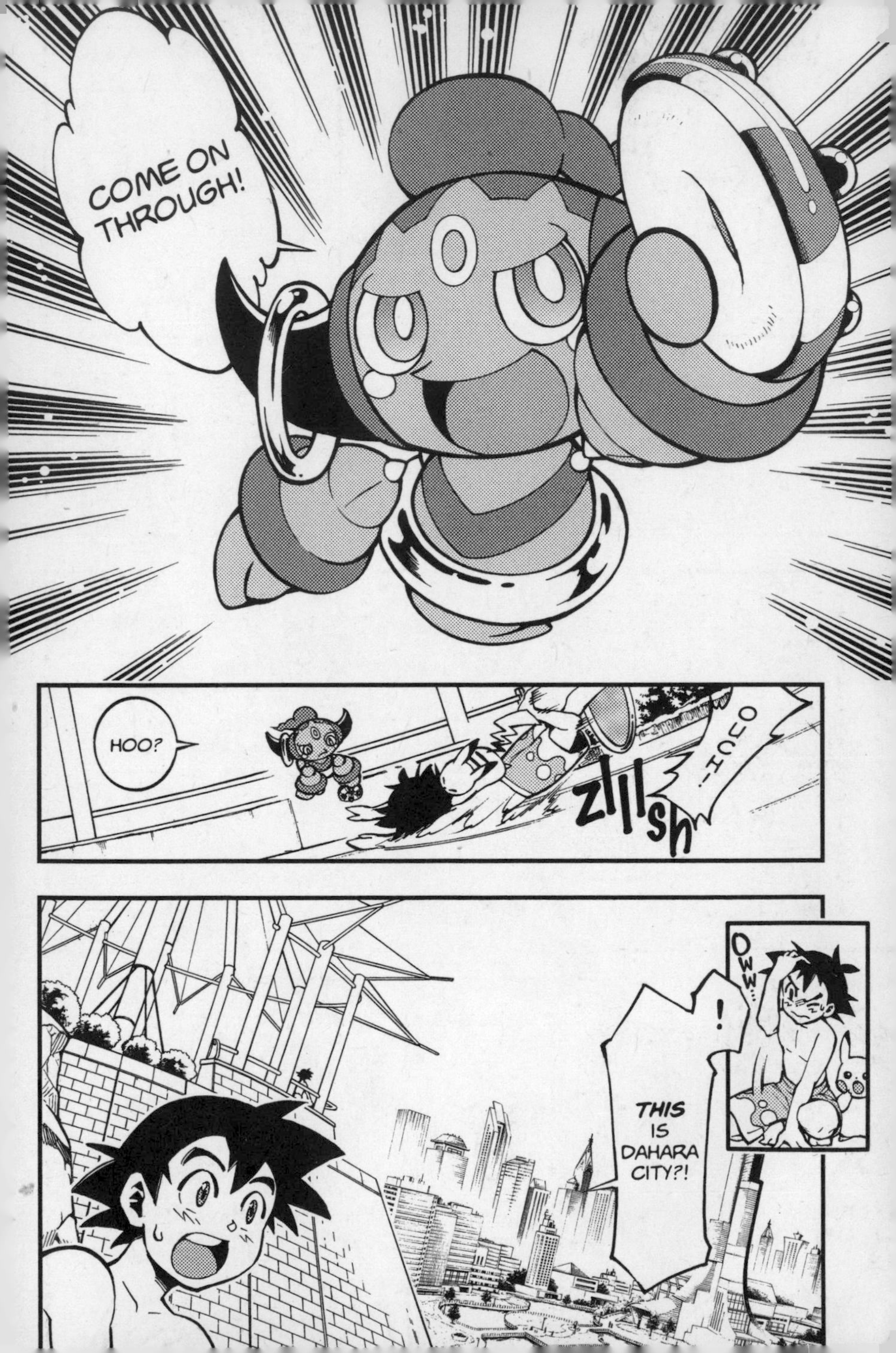
COME ON THROUGH!
OUCH-!
zlllsh
HOO?
OWW...
!
THIS IS DAHARA CITY?!

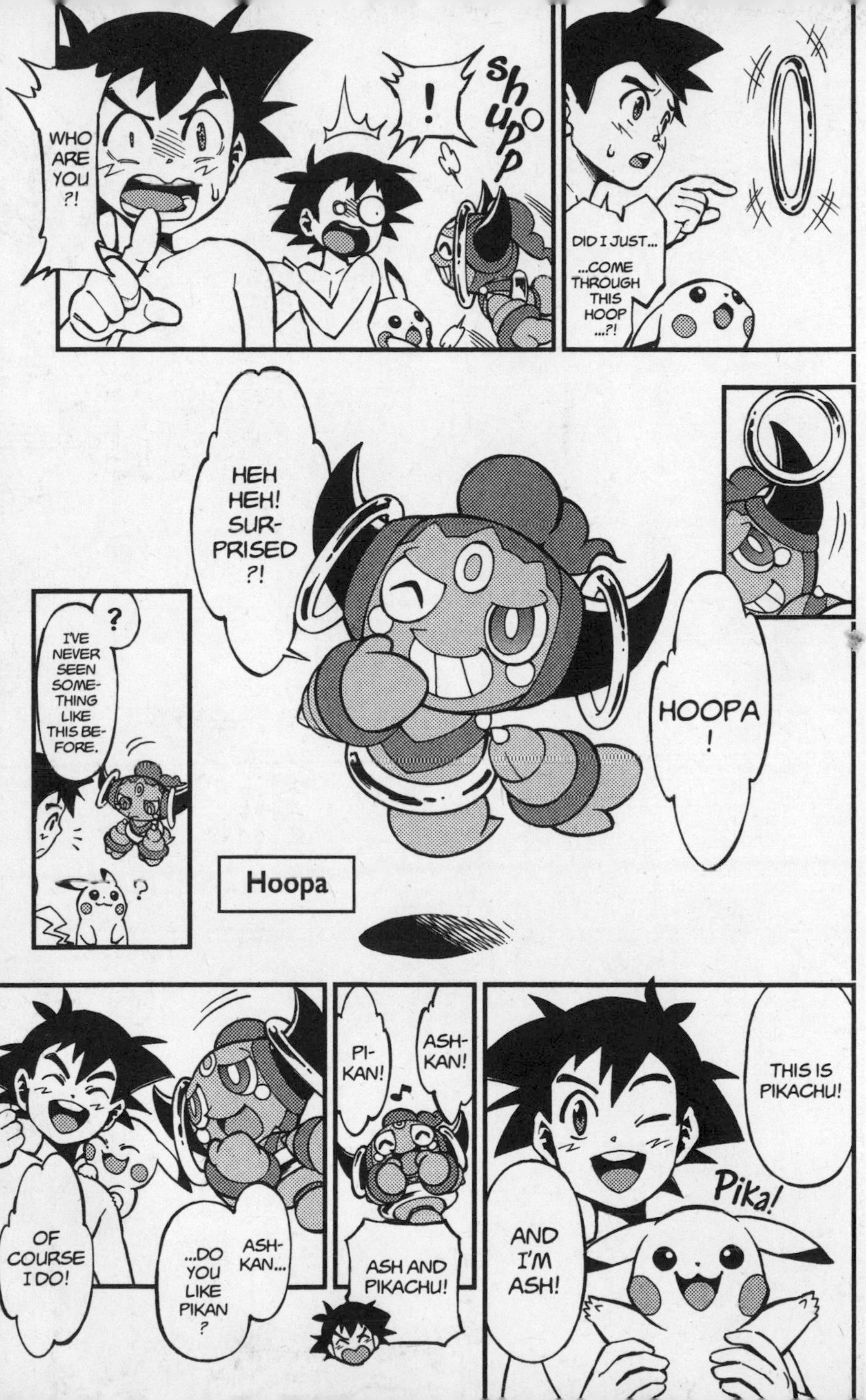

DID I JUST...
...COME THROUGH THIS HOOP ...?!
shoupp
!
WHO ARE YOU ?!
HOOPA !
HEH HEH! SUR-PRISED ?!
Hoopa
?
I'VE NEVER SEEN SOME-THING LIKE THIS BE-FORE.
?
THIS IS PIKACHU!
AND I'M ASH!
Pika!
ASH-KAN!
PI-KAN!
ASH AND PIKACHU!
ASH-KAN...
...DO YOU LIKE PIKAN ?
OF COURSE I DO!

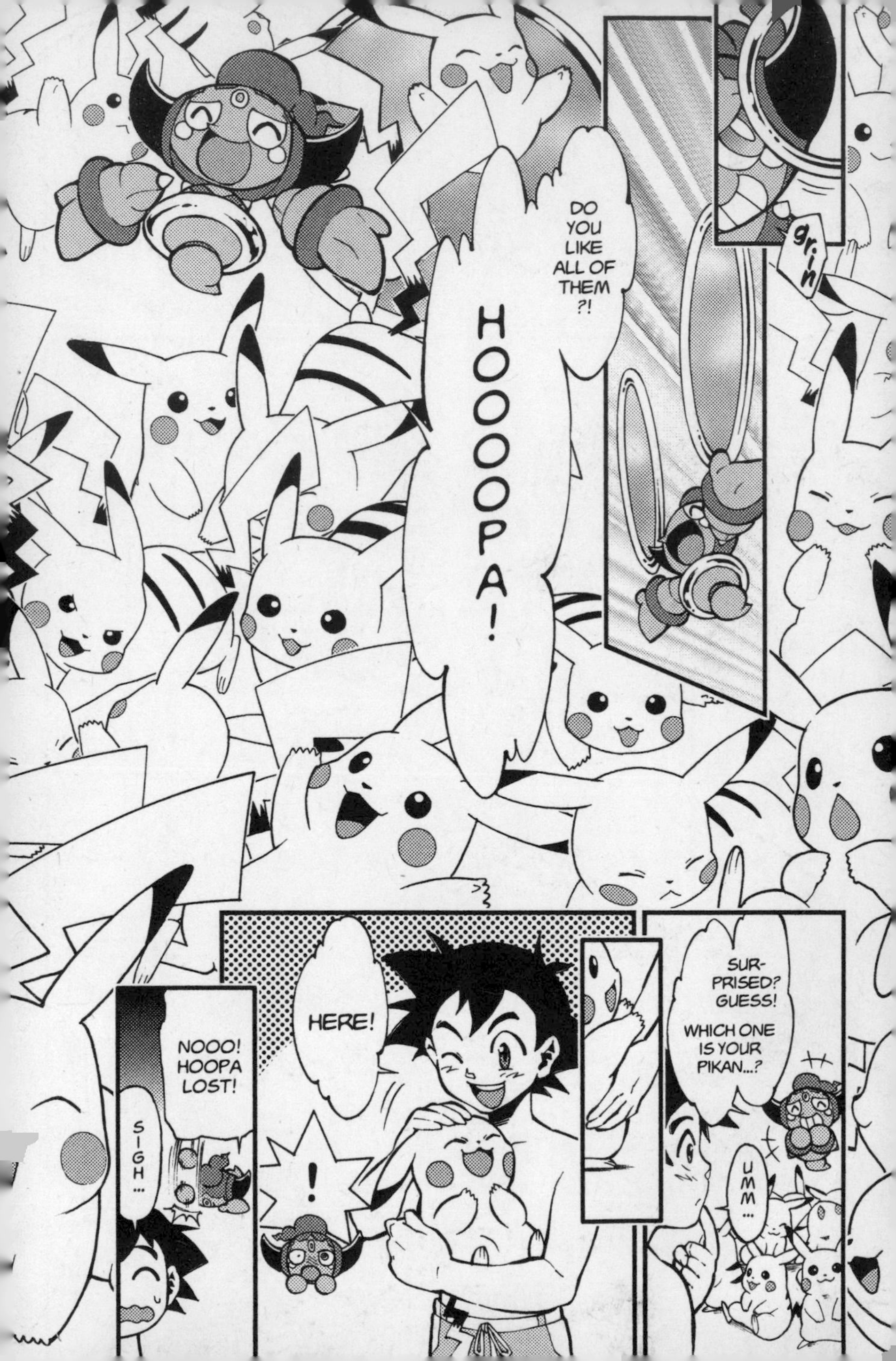
grin
DO YOU LIKE ALL OF THEM?!
HOOOOPA!
SUR-PRISED? GUESS!
WHICH ONE IS YOUR PIKAN...?
UMM...
HERE!
!
NOOO! HOOPA LOST!
SIGH...

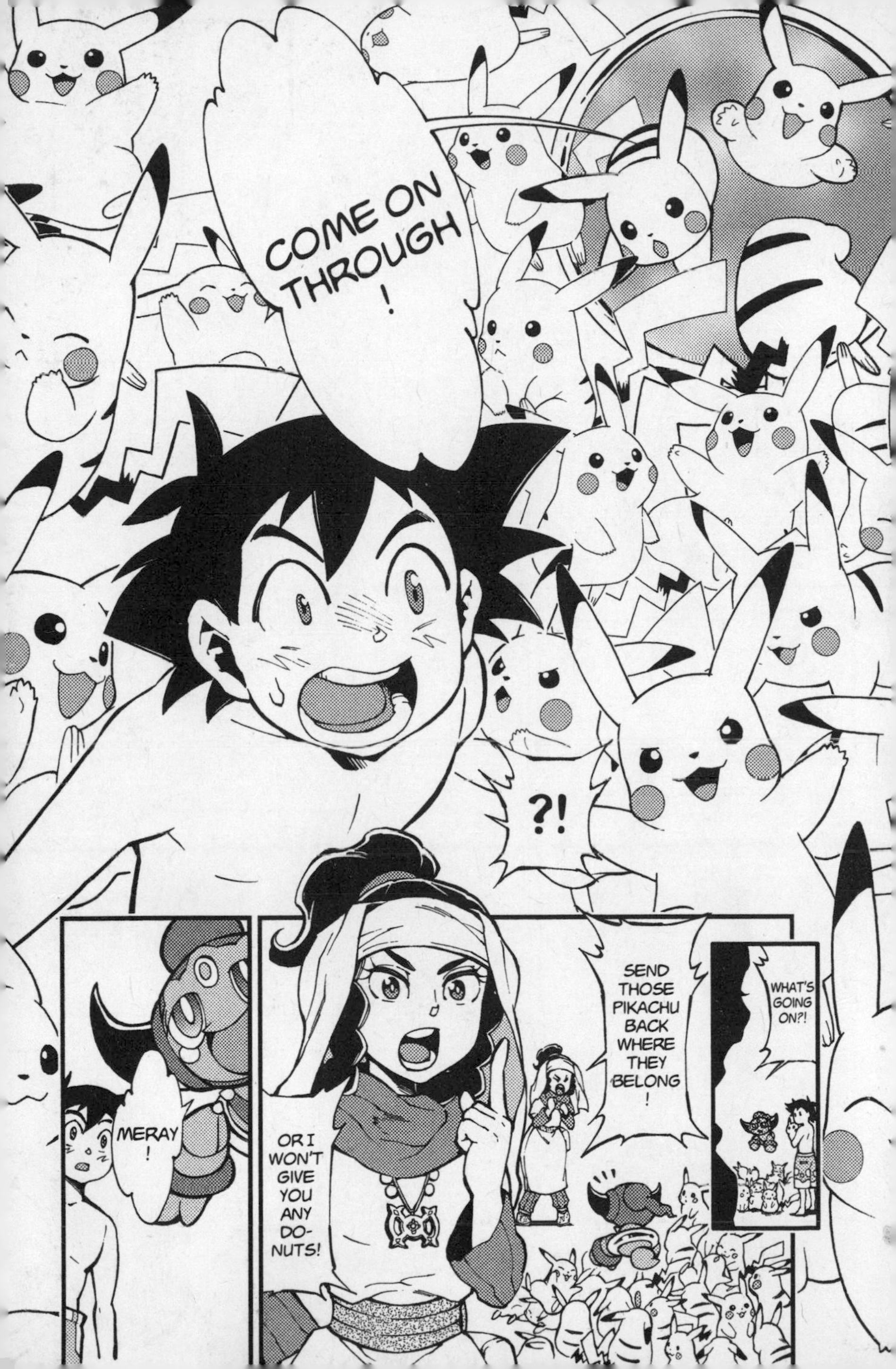
COME ON THROUGH!
?!
WHAT'S GOING ON?!
SEND THOSE PIKACHU BACK WHERE THEY BELONG!
OR I WON'T GIVE YOU ANY DO-NUTS!
MERAY!

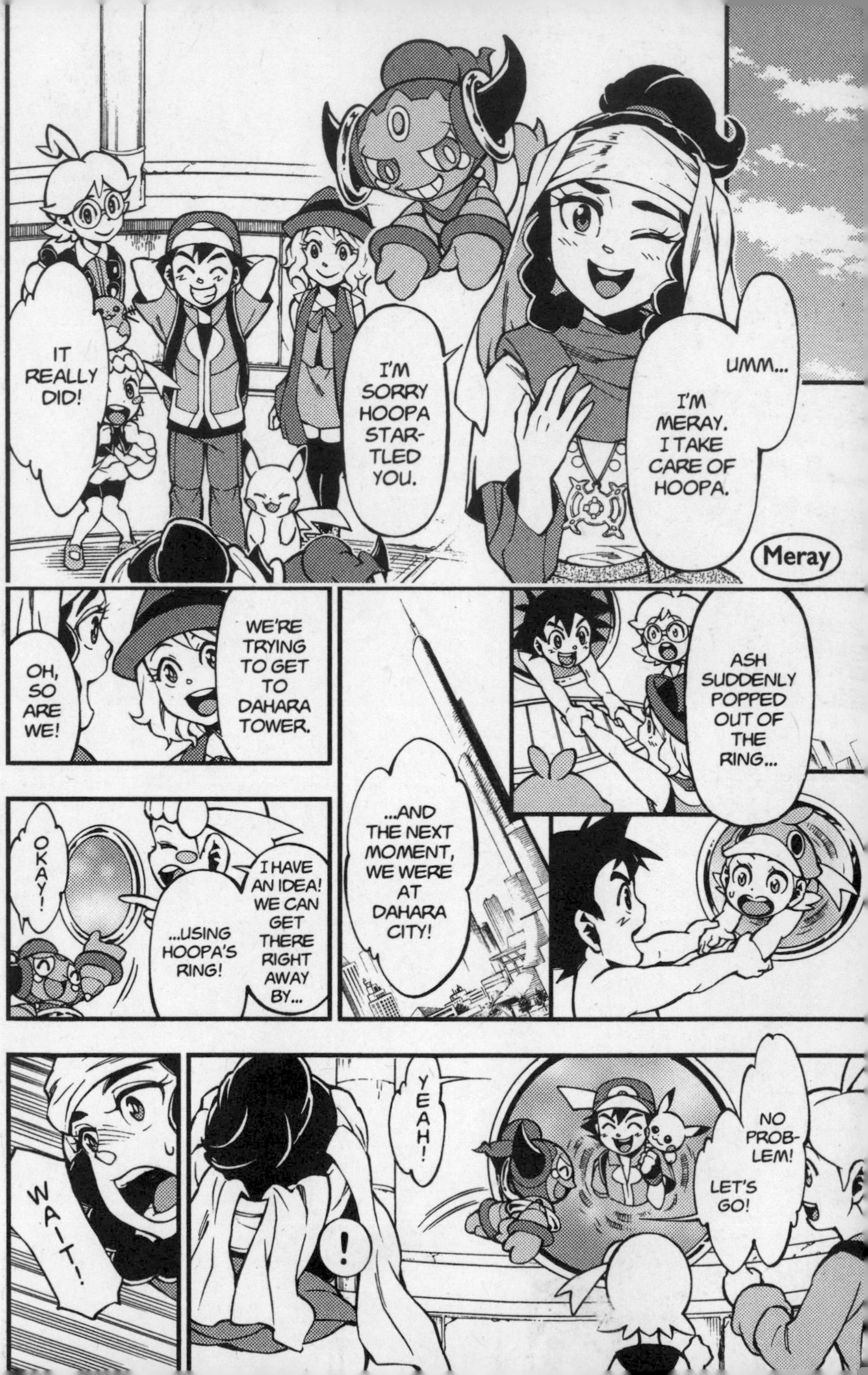
Meray
UMM... I'M MERAY. I TAKE CARE OF HOOPA.
I'M SORRY HOOPA STARTLED YOU.
IT REALLY DID!
ASH SUDDENLY POPPED OUT OF THE RING...
...AND THE NEXT MOMENT, WE WERE AT DAHARA CITY!
WE'RE TRYING TO GET TO DAHARA TOWER.
OH, SO ARE WE!
I HAVE AN IDEA! WE CAN GET THERE RIGHT AWAY BY...
...USING HOOPA'S RING!
OKAY!
NO PROBLEM!
LET'S GO!
YEAH!
!
WAIT!

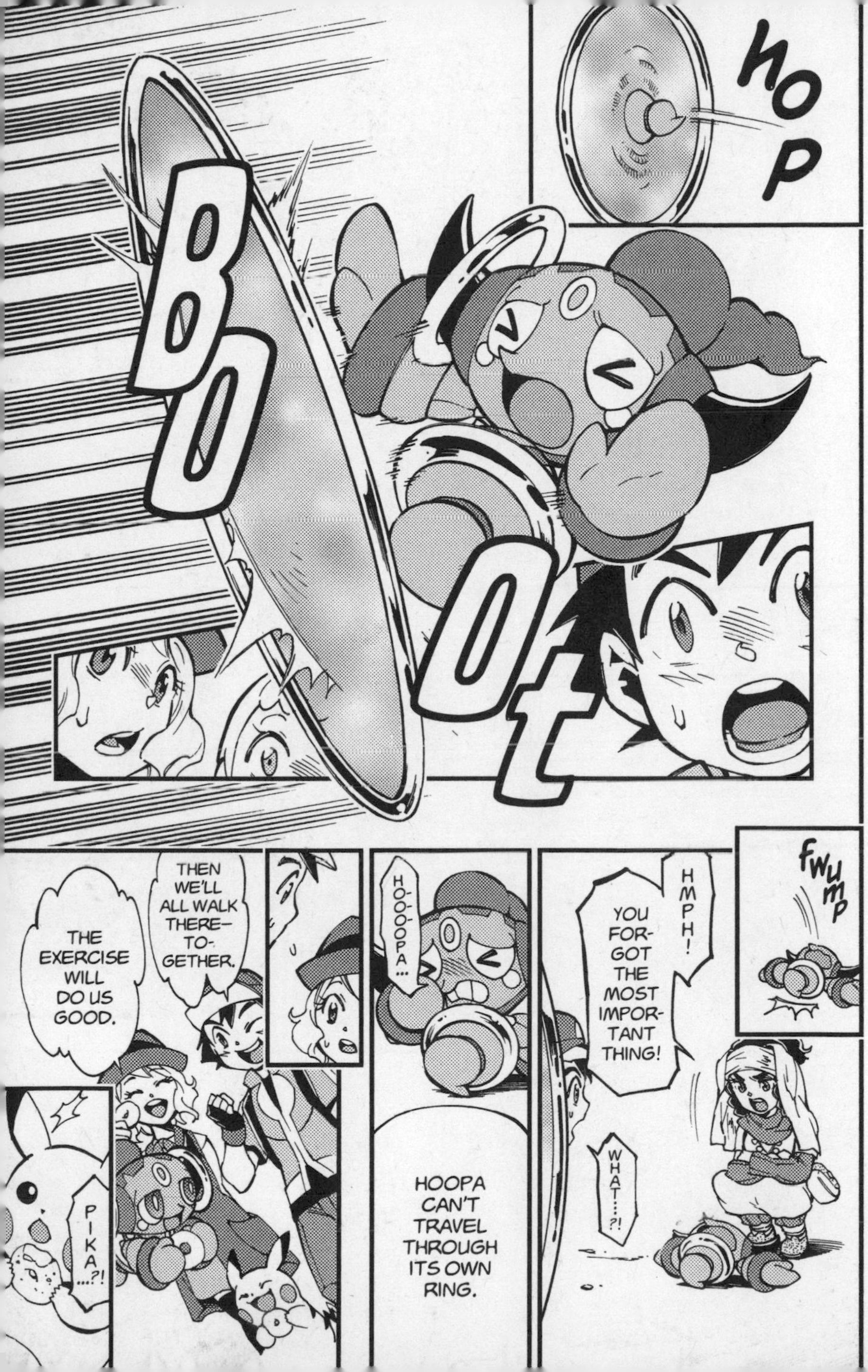

HOP
BOOT
FWUMP
HMPH!
YOU FOR-GOT THE MOST IMPOR-TANT THING!
WHAT...?!
HO-O-O-OOPA...
HOOPA CAN'T TRAVEL THROUGH ITS OWN RING.
THEN WE'LL ALL WALK THERE—TO-GETHER.
THE EXERCISE WILL DO US GOOD.
PIKA...?!

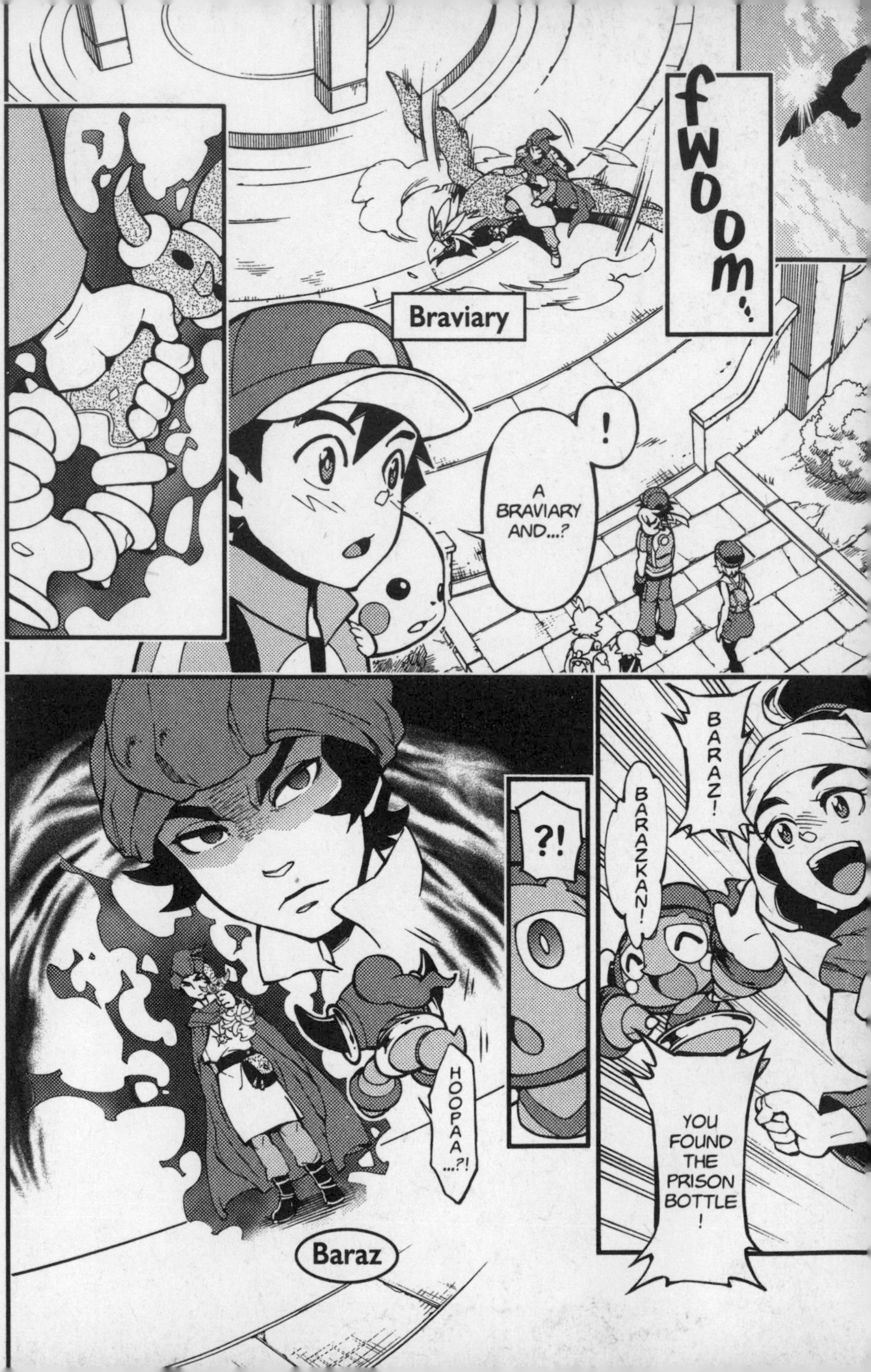
FWOOM...
Braviary
!
A BRAVIARY AND...?
BARAZ!
BARAZKAN!
YOU FOUND THE PRISON BOTTLE!
?!
HOOPAA...?!
Baraz

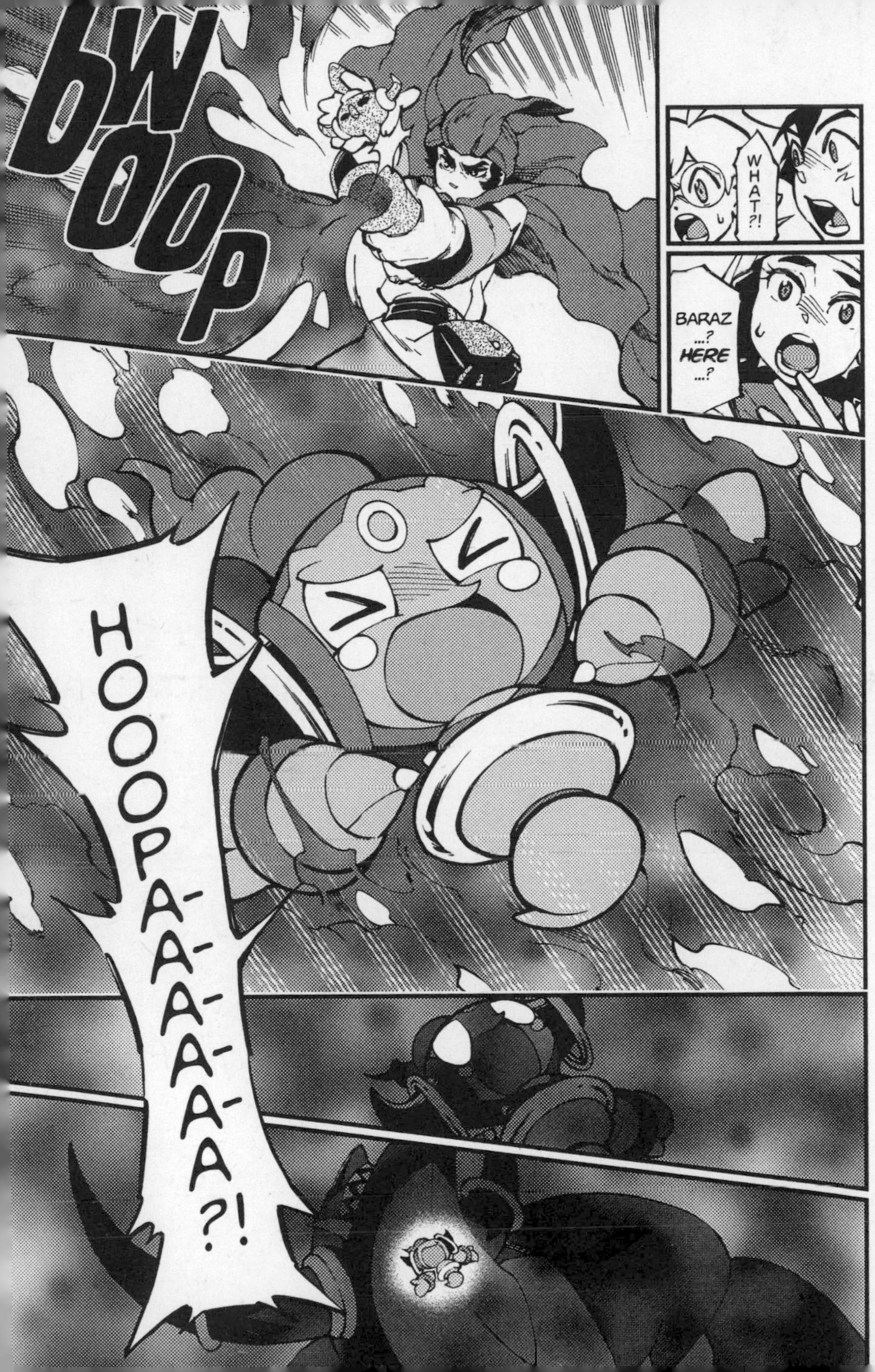

WHAT?!
BARAZ...? HERE...?
BWOOOP
HOOOPA-A-A-A-A-A?!

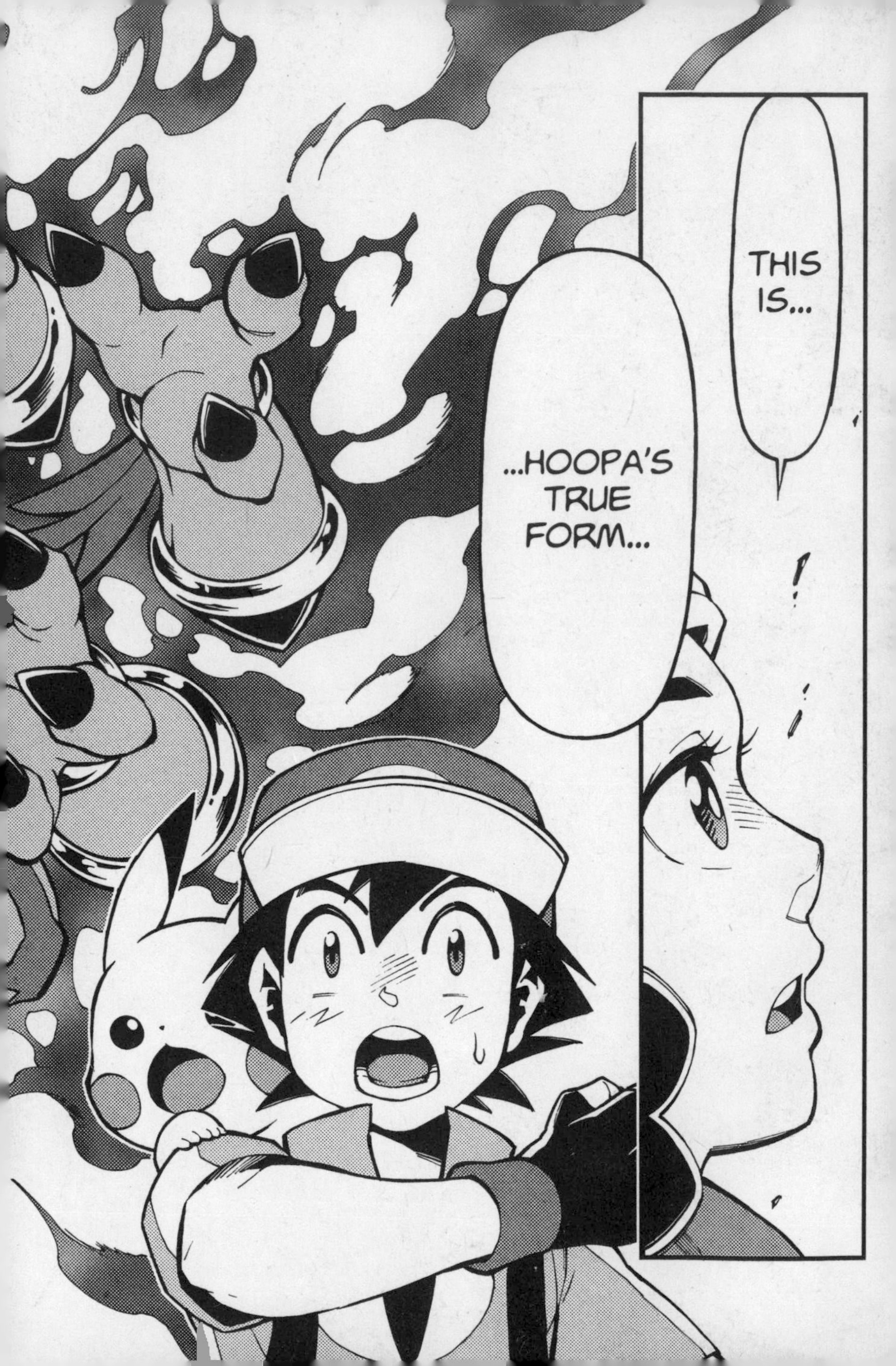
THIS IS...
...HOOPA'S TRUE FORM...

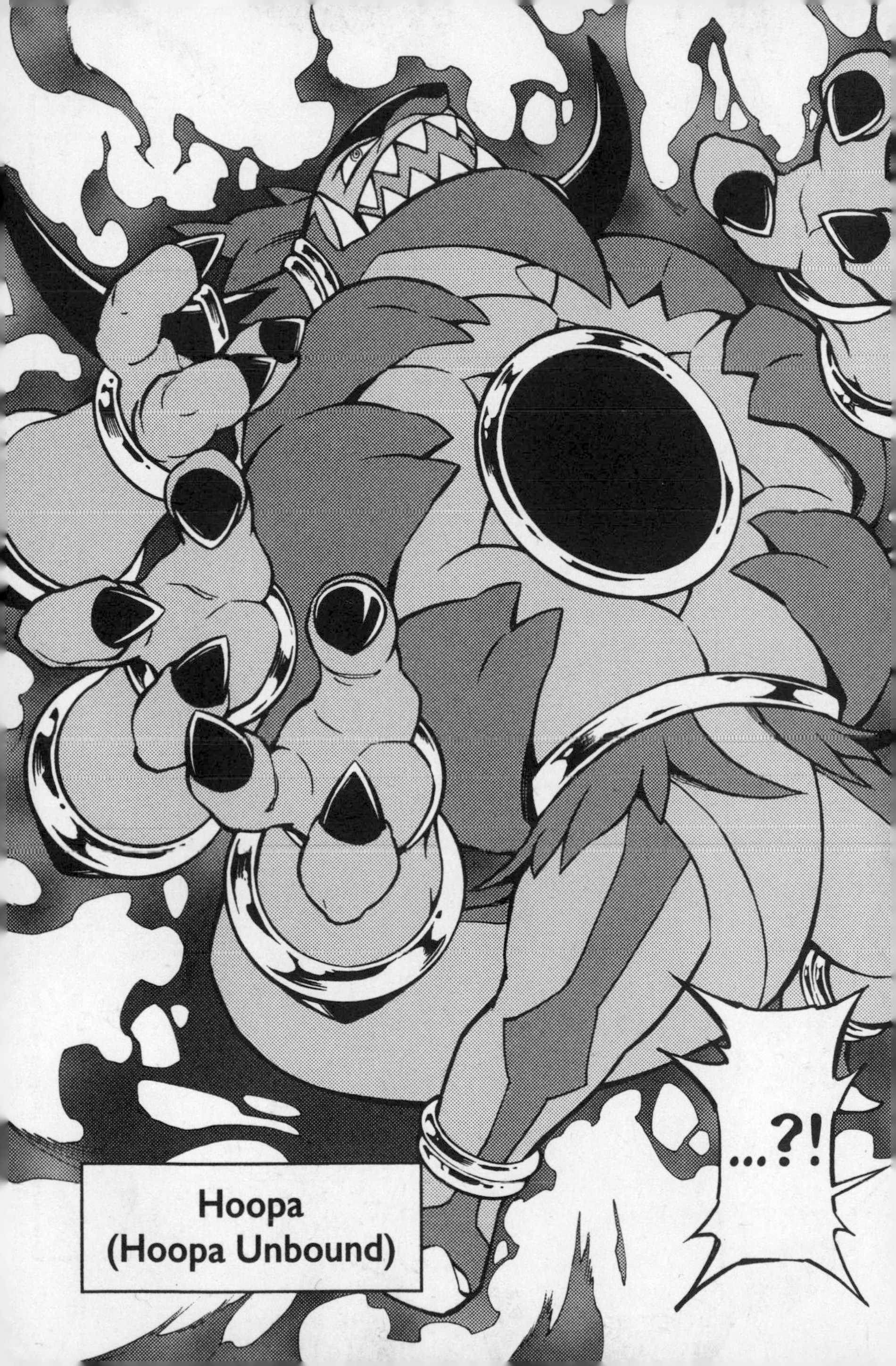
...?!
Hoopa
(Hoopa Unbound)

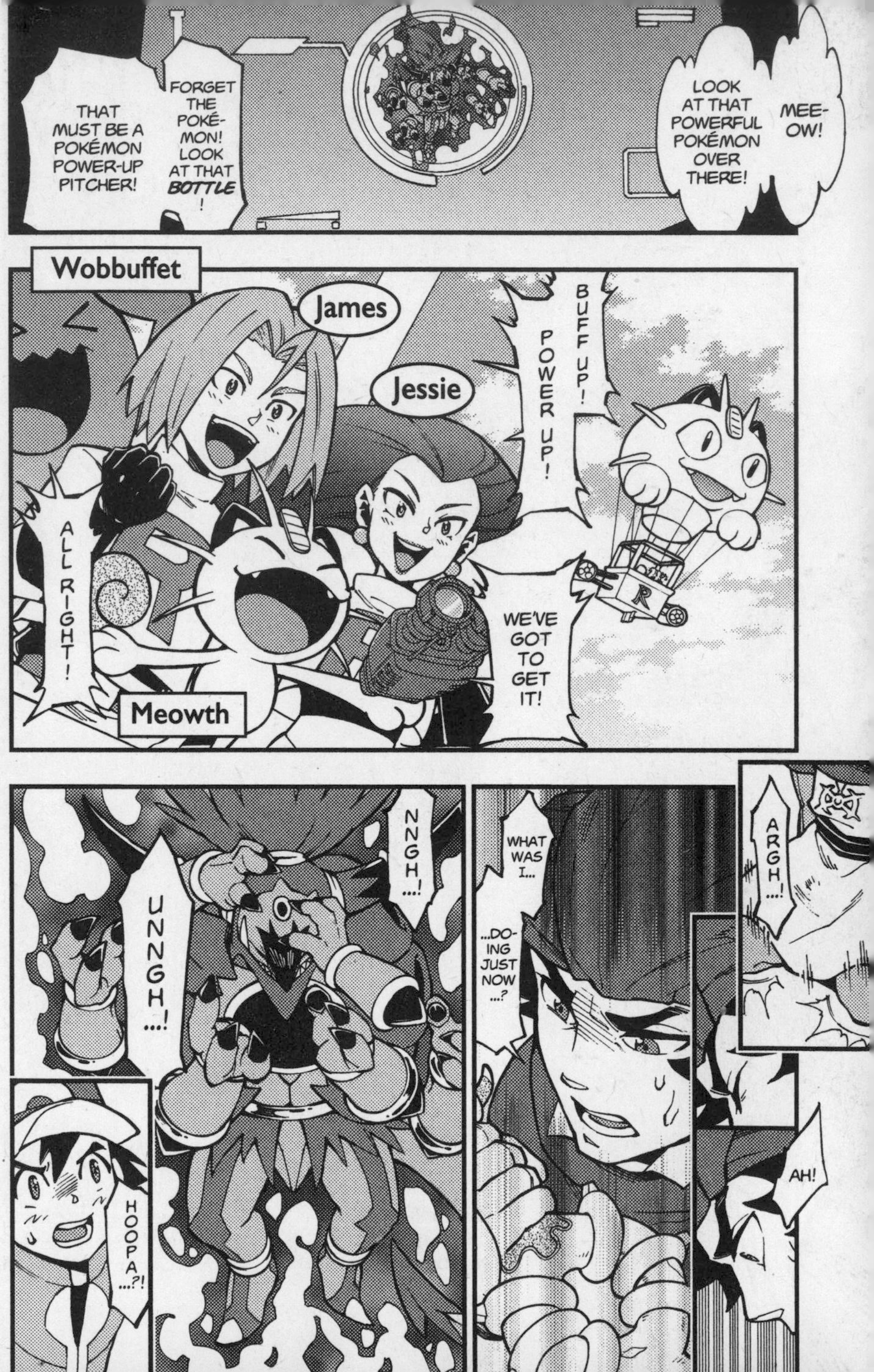
MEE-OW!
LOOK AT THAT POWERFUL POKÉMON OVER THERE!
FORGET THE POKÉ-MON! LOOK AT THAT BOTTLE!
THAT MUST BE A POKÉMON POWER-UP PITCHER!
BUFF UP! POWER UP!
James
Wobbuffet
Jessie
WE'VE GOT TO GET IT!
ALL RIGHT!
Meowth
ARGH...!
AH!
WHAT WAS I...
...DO-ING JUST NOW...?
NNGH...!
UNNGH...!
HOOPA...?!

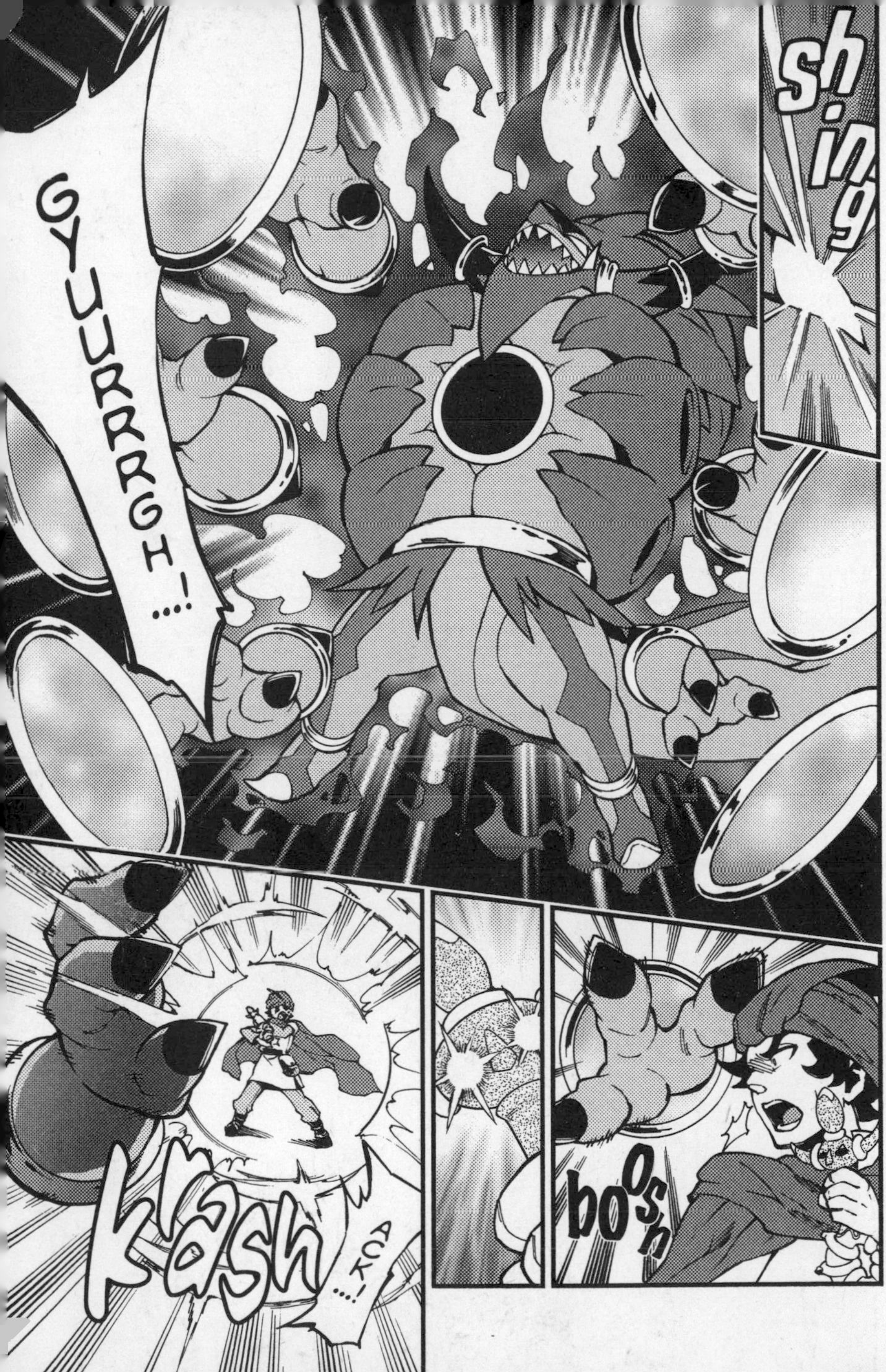
shing
GYUURRRGH...!
boosh
k'ash
ACK...!

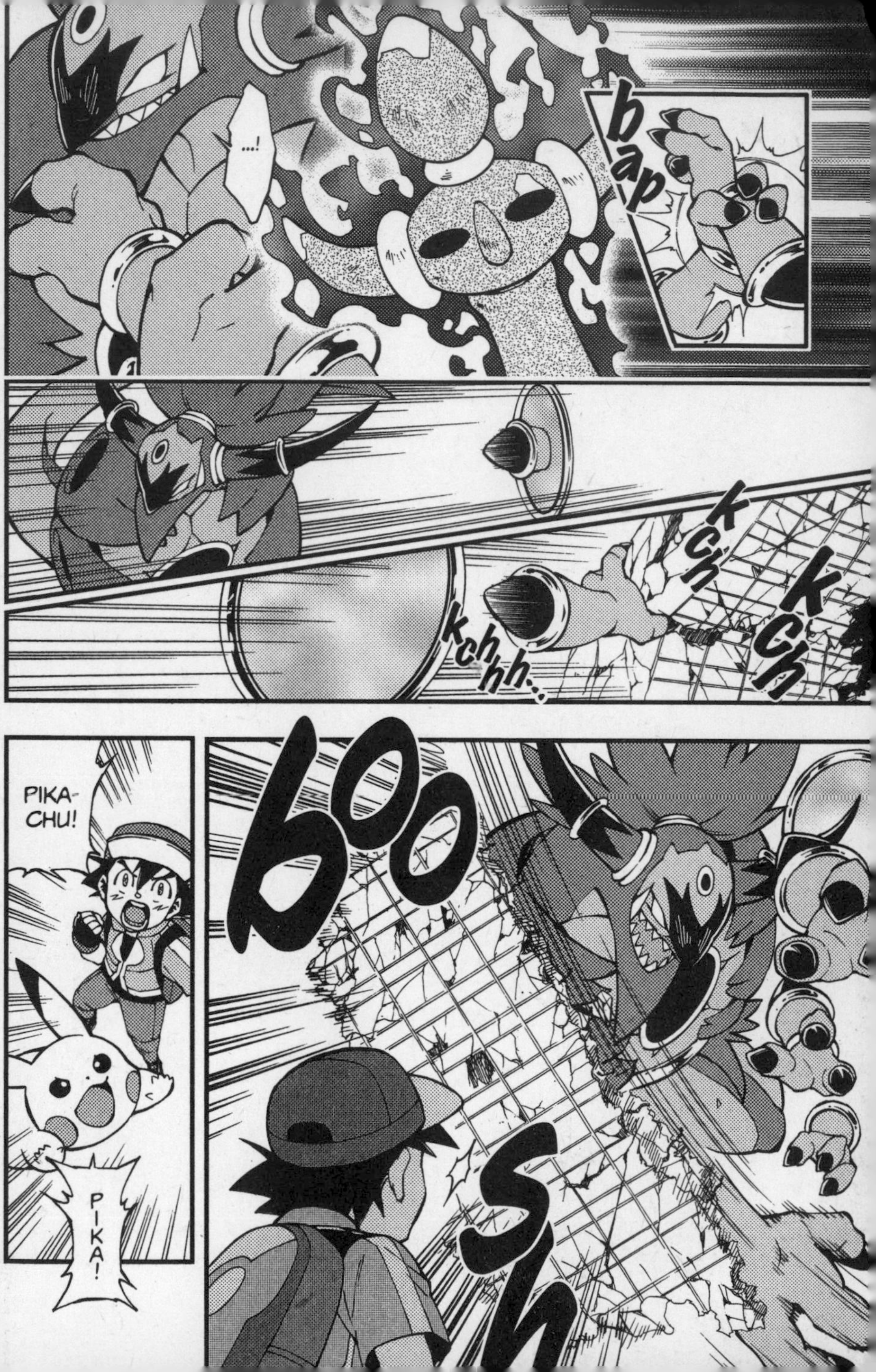
bap
...!
kch
kch
kchhh...
boosh
PIKA-CHU!
PIKA!

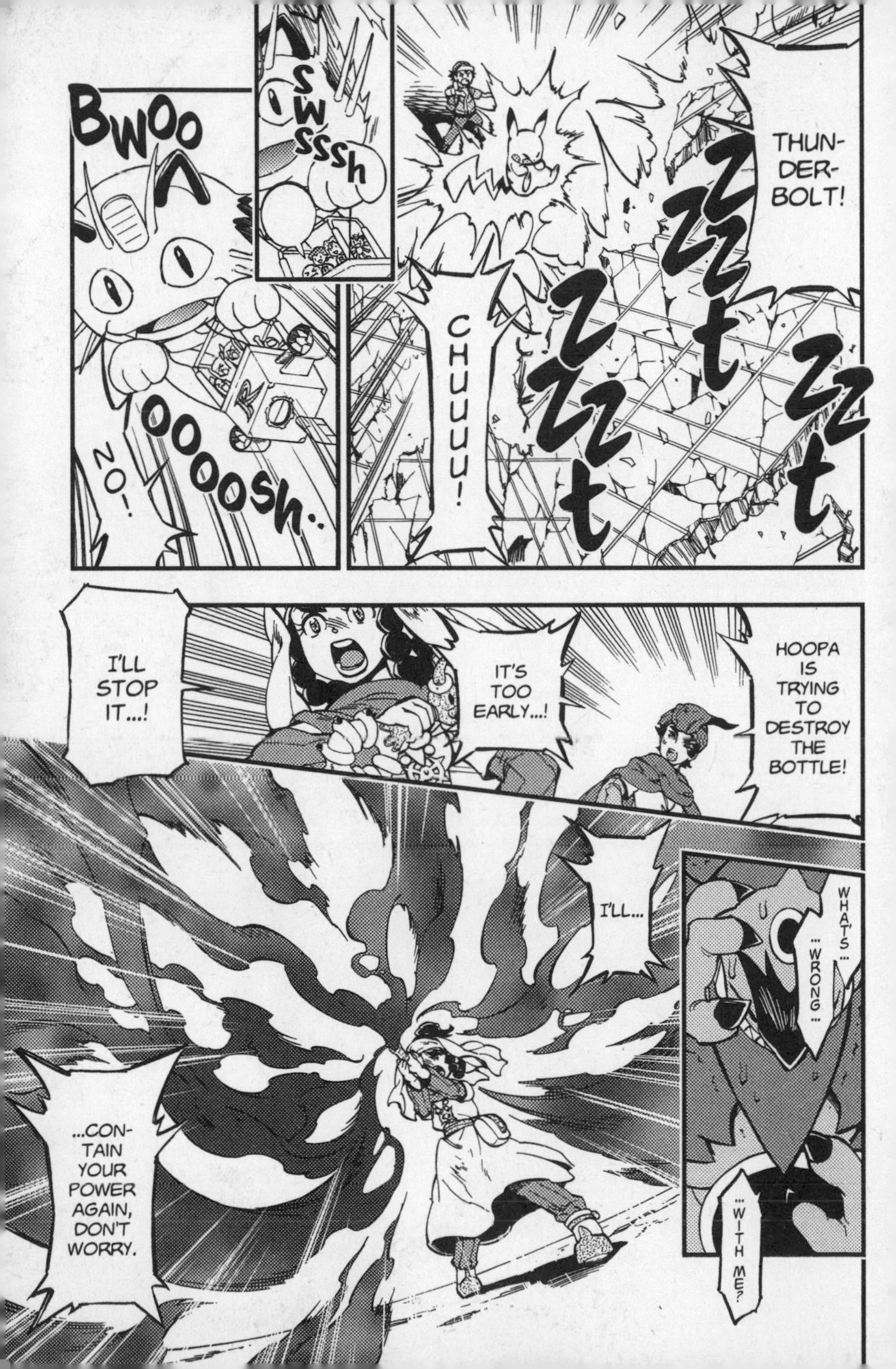
THUN-
DER-
BOLT!
ZZZt
ZZZt
ZZZt
CHUUUUU!
SWSSSh
BWOO
OOOOOOSh..
NO!
HOOPA IS TRYING TO DESTROY THE BOTTLE!
IT'S TOO EARLY...!
I'LL STOP IT...!
WHAT'S... ...WRONG... ...WITH ME?
I'LL...
...CON-TAIN YOUR POWER AGAIN, DON'T WORRY.

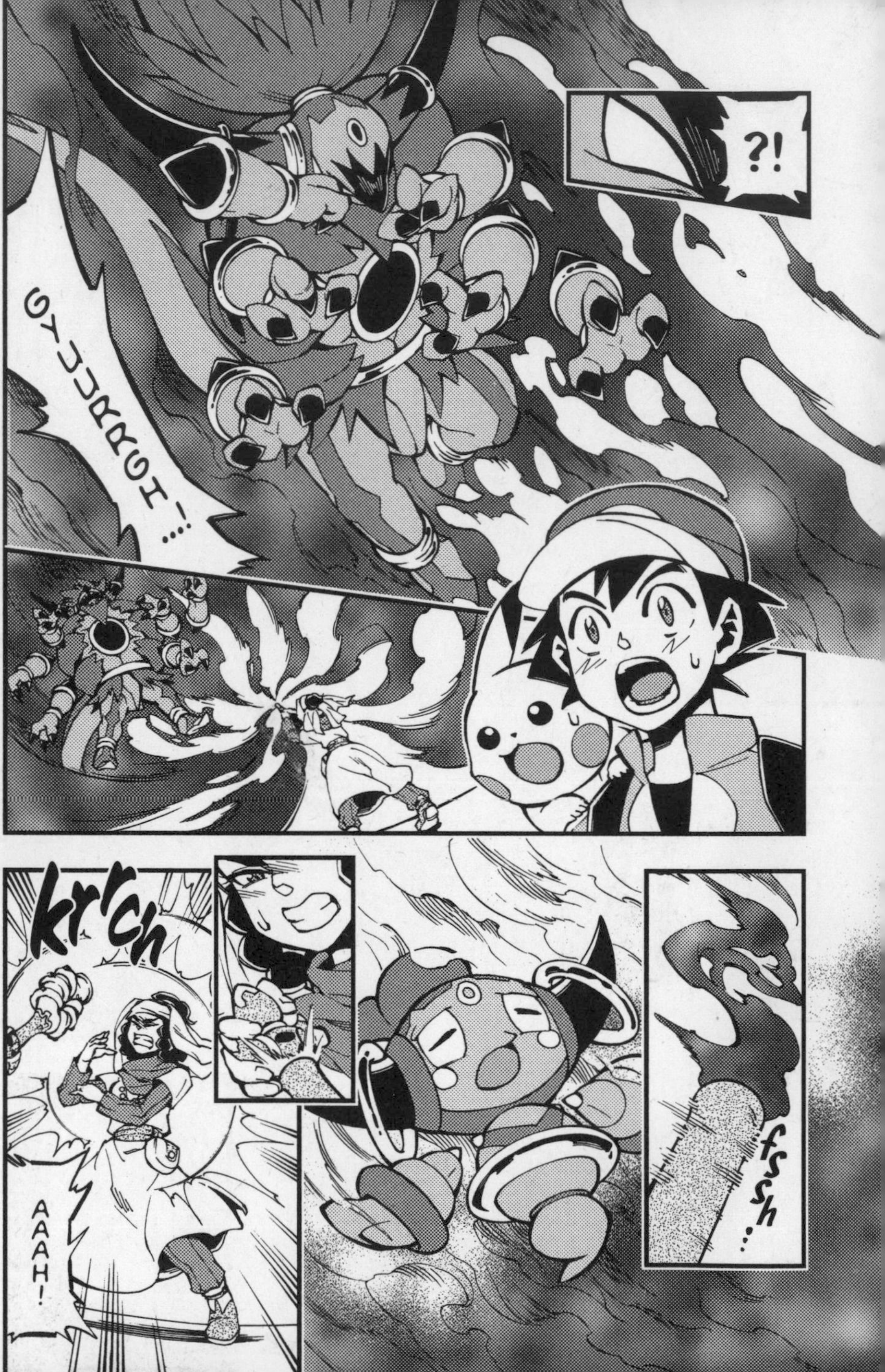
?!
GYUJJRRGH...!
fssh..
krrch
AAAH!

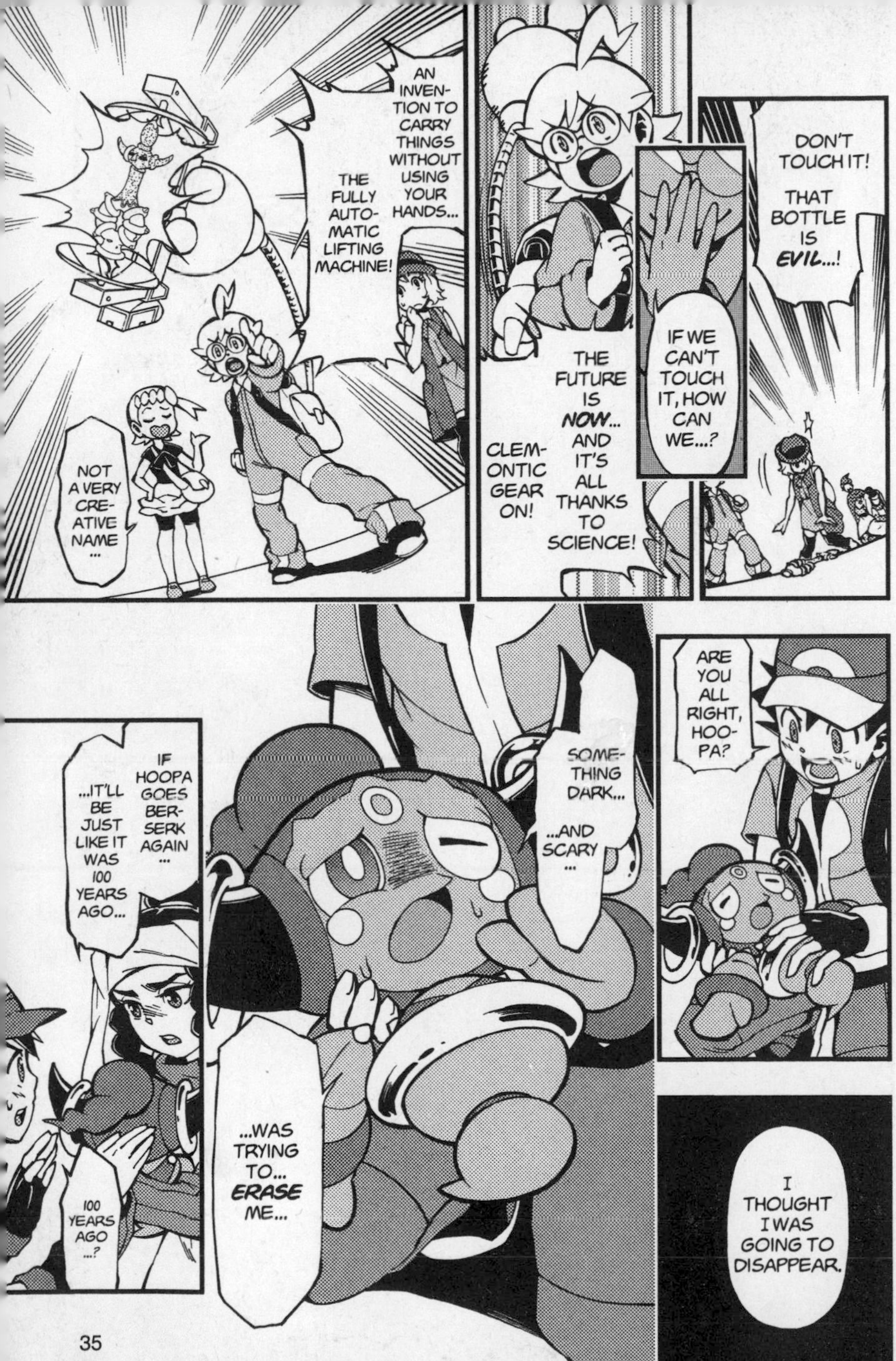
DON'T TOUCH IT!
THAT BOTTLE IS *EVIL*...!
IF WE CAN'T TOUCH IT, HOW CAN WE...?
THE FUTURE IS *NOW*... AND IT'S ALL THANKS TO SCIENCE!
CLEMONTIC GEAR ON!
AN INVENTION TO CARRY THINGS WITHOUT USING YOUR HANDS...
THE FULLY AUTOMATIC LIFTING MACHINE!
NOT A VERY CREATIVE NAME...
ARE YOU ALL RIGHT, HOOPA?
I THOUGHT I WAS GOING TO DISAPPEAR.
SOMETHING DARK...
...AND SCARY...
...WAS TRYING TO... *ERASE* ME...
IF HOOPA GOES BERSERK AGAIN...
...IT'LL BE JUST LIKE IT WAS 100 YEARS AGO...
100 YEARS AGO...?

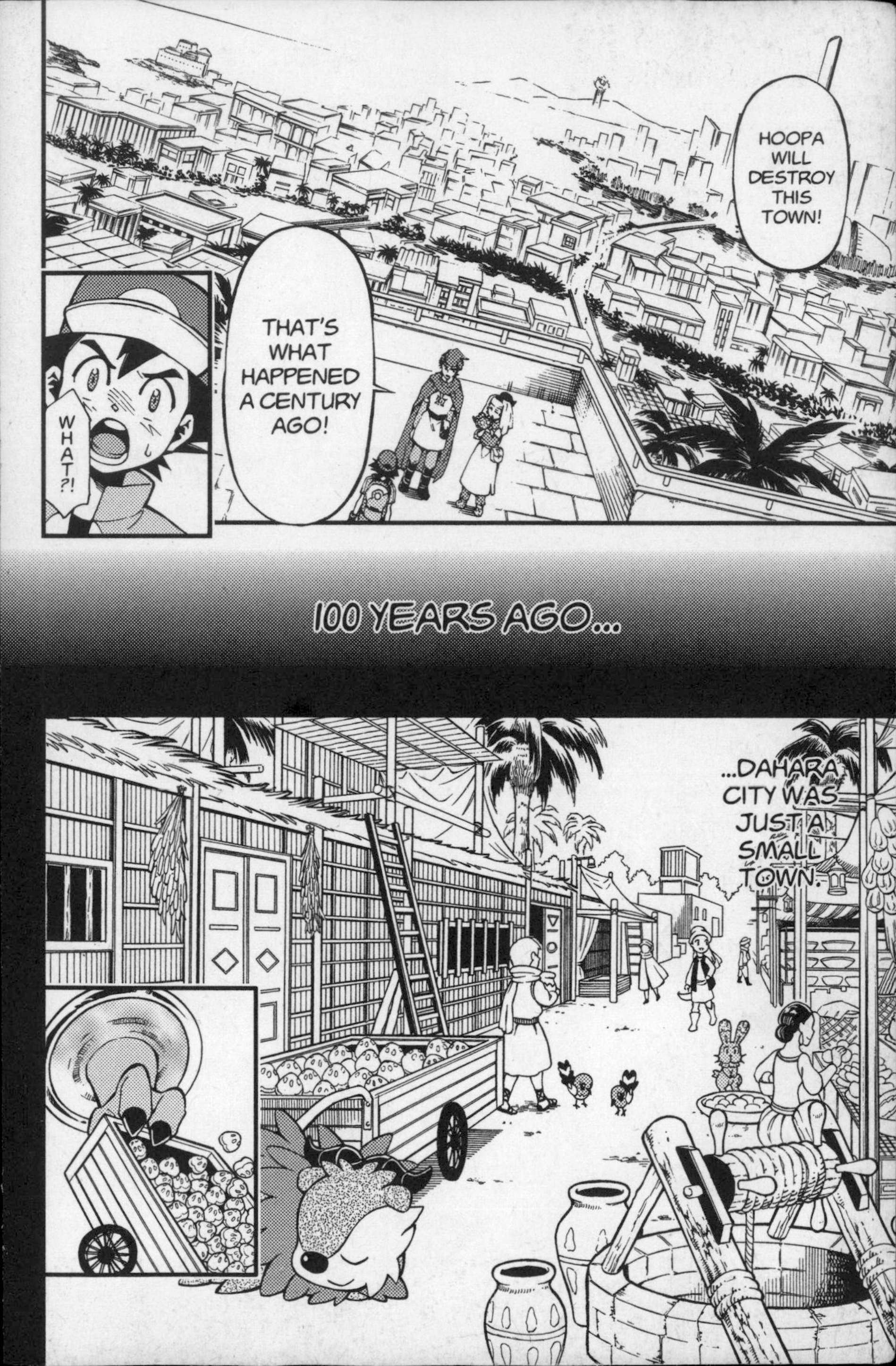
HOOPA WILL DESTROY THIS TOWN!
THAT'S WHAT HAPPENED A CENTURY AGO!
WHAT?!
100 YEARS AGO...
...DAHARA CITY WAS JUST A SMALL TOWN.

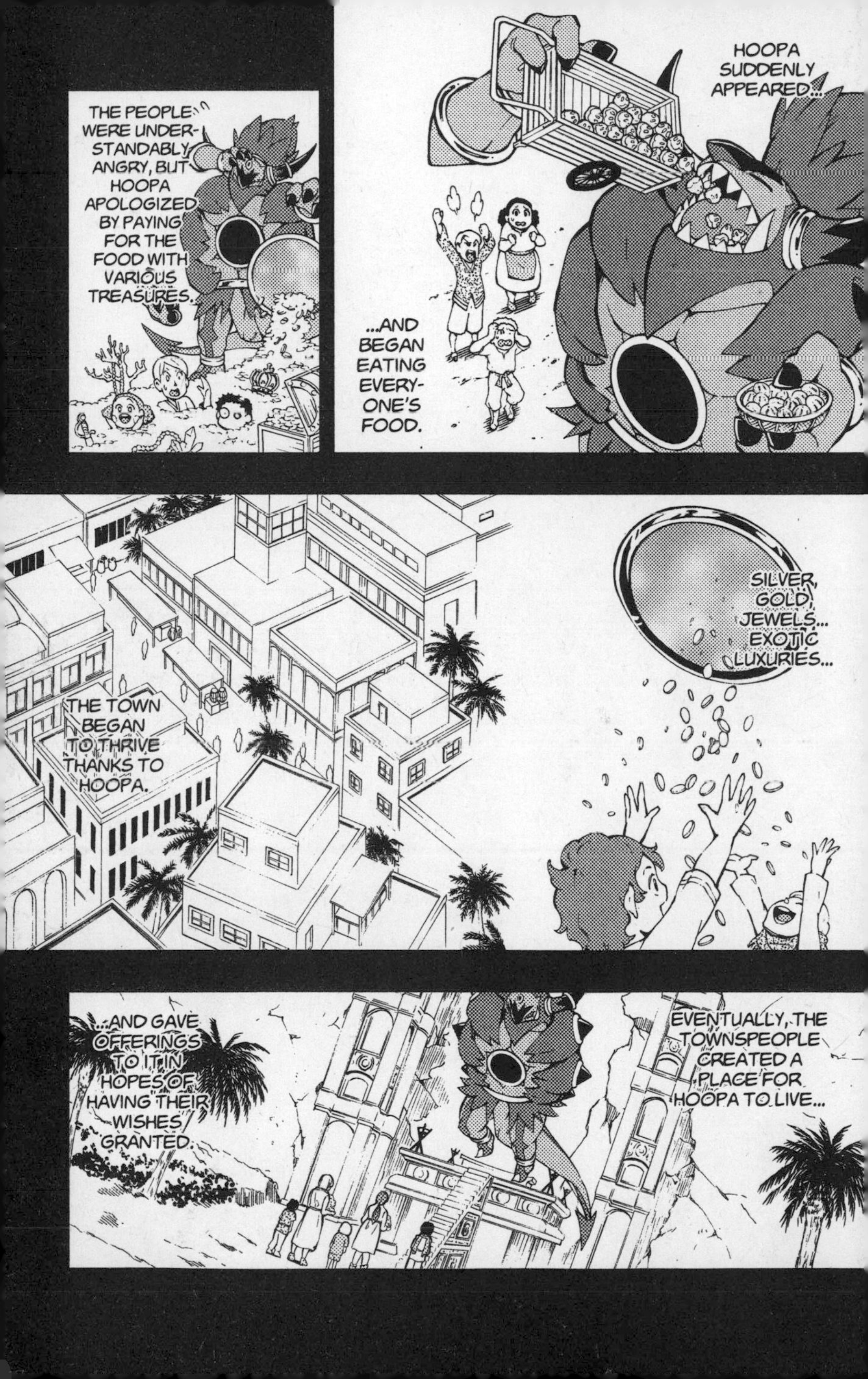
HOOPA SUDDENLY APPEARED...
...AND BEGAN EATING EVERYONE'S FOOD.
THE PEOPLE WERE UNDERSTANDABLY ANGRY, BUT HOOPA APOLOGIZED BY PAYING FOR THE FOOD WITH VARIOUS TREASURES.
SILVER, GOLD, JEWELS... EXOTIC LUXURIES...
THE TOWN BEGAN TO THRIVE THANKS TO HOOPA.
EVENTUALLY, THE TOWNSPEOPLE CREATED A PLACE FOR HOOPA TO LIVE...
...AND GAVE OFFERINGS TO IT IN HOPES OF HAVING THEIR WISHES GRANTED.

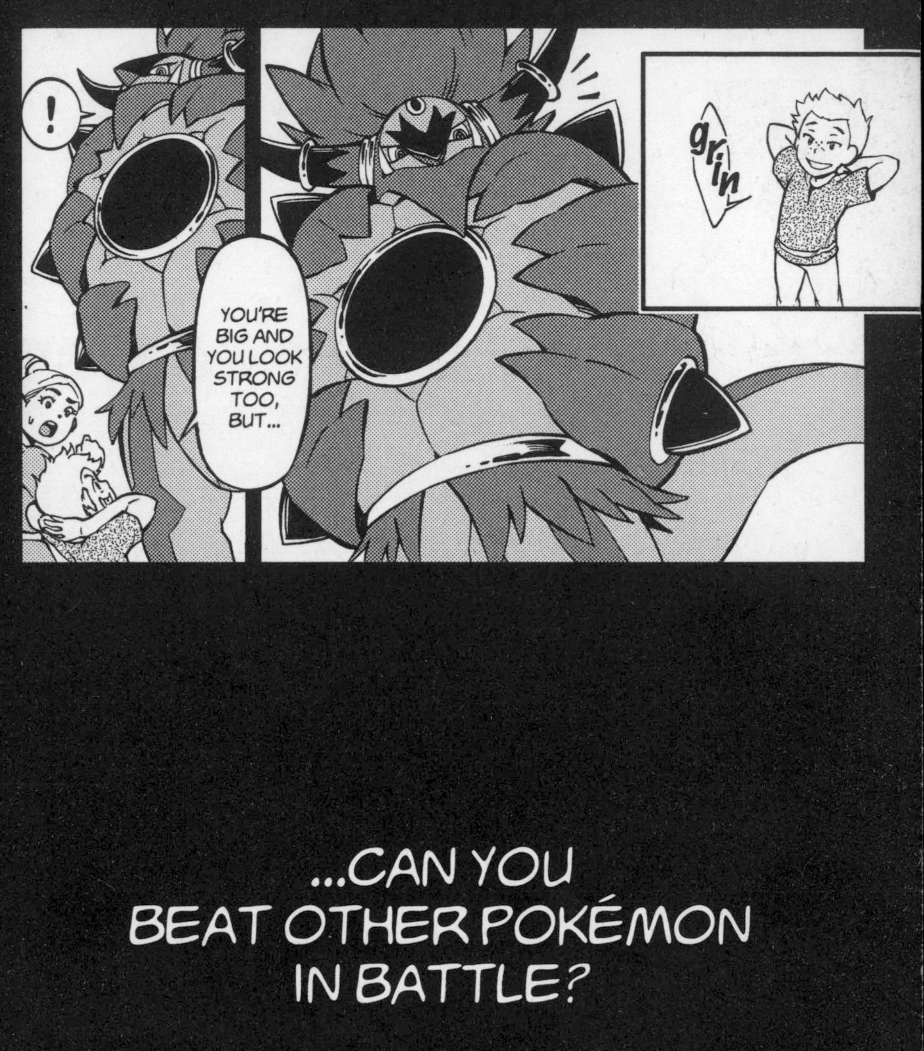
grin
YOU'RE BIG AND YOU LOOK STRONG TOO, BUT...
!
...CAN YOU BEAT OTHER POKÉMON IN BATTLE?

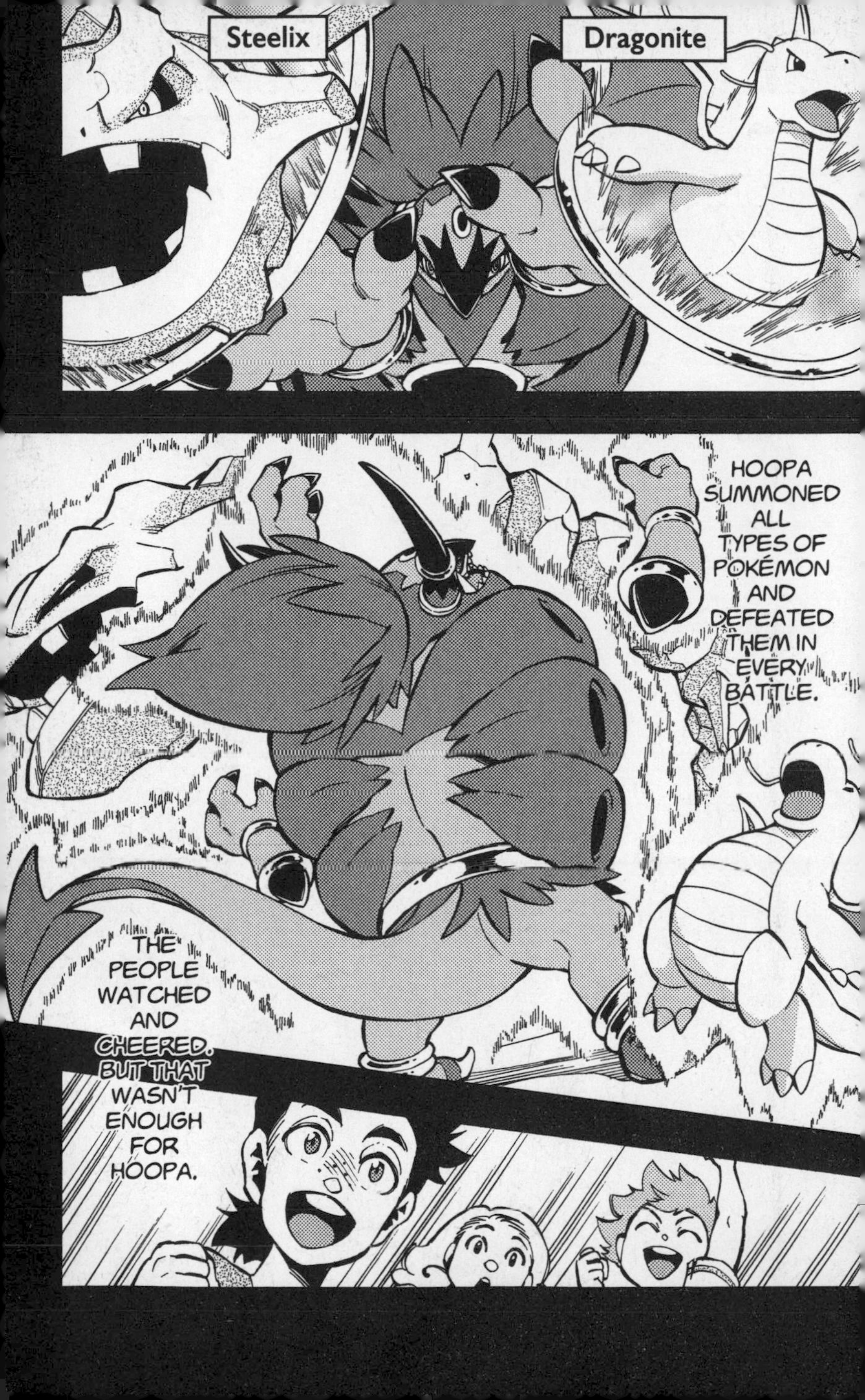
Dragonite
Steelix
HOOPA SUMMONED ALL TYPES OF POKÉMON AND DEFEATED THEM IN EVERY BATTLE.
THE PEOPLE WATCHED AND CHEERED. BUT THAT WASN'T ENOUGH FOR HOOPA.

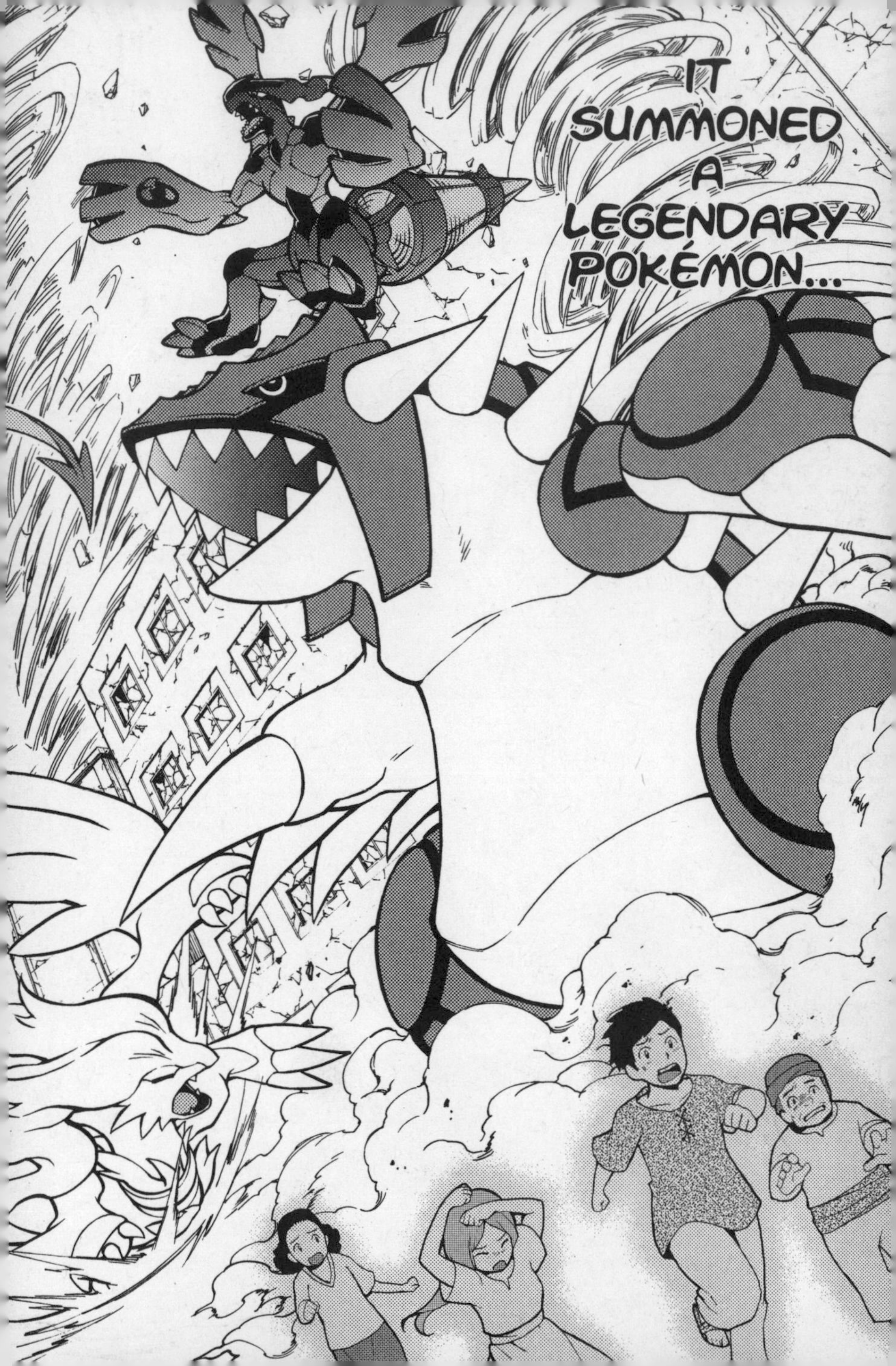
IT SUMMONED A LEGENDARY POKÉMON...

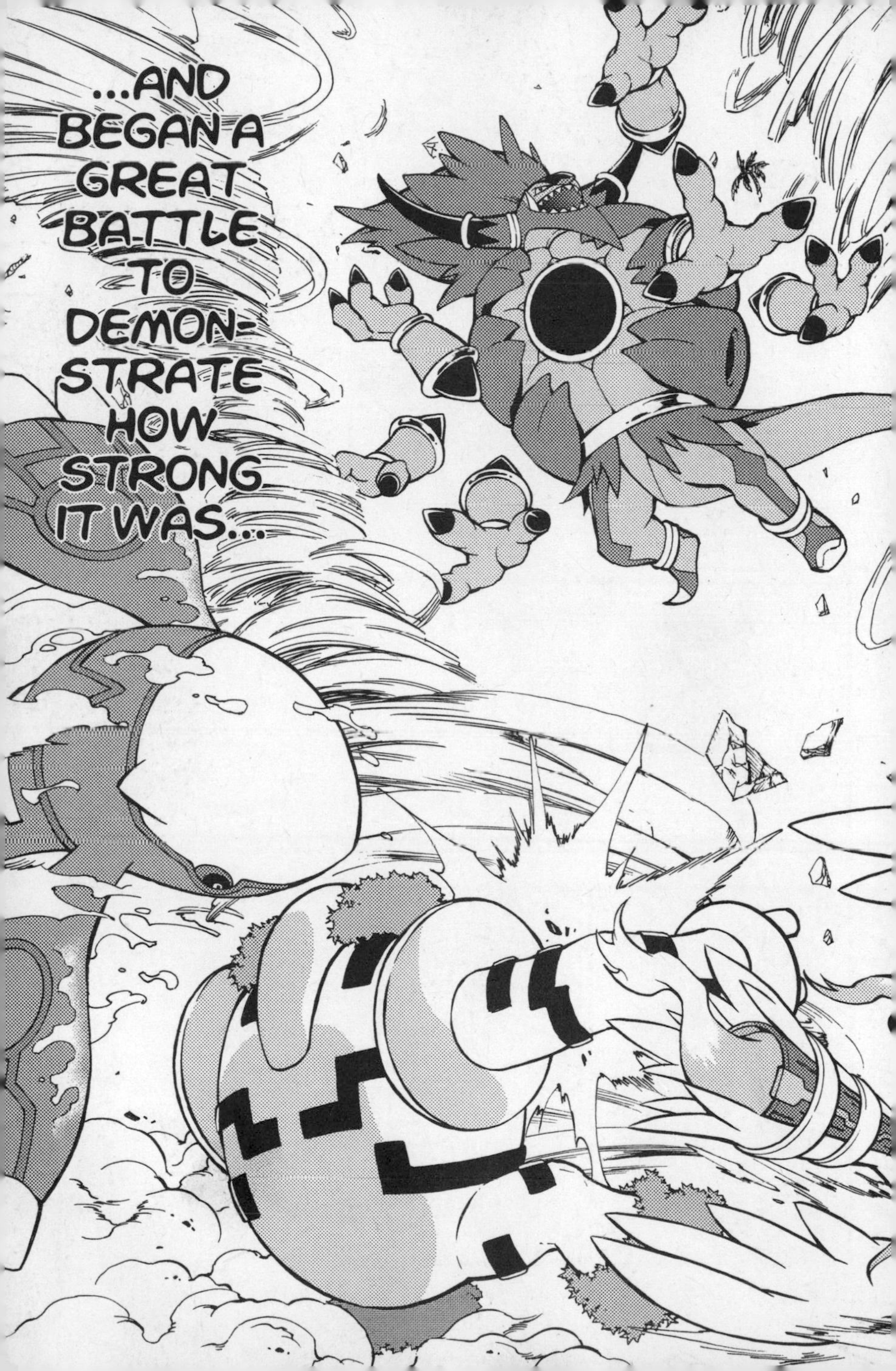
...AND BEGAN A GREAT BATTLE TO DEMON-STRATE HOW STRONG IT WAS...

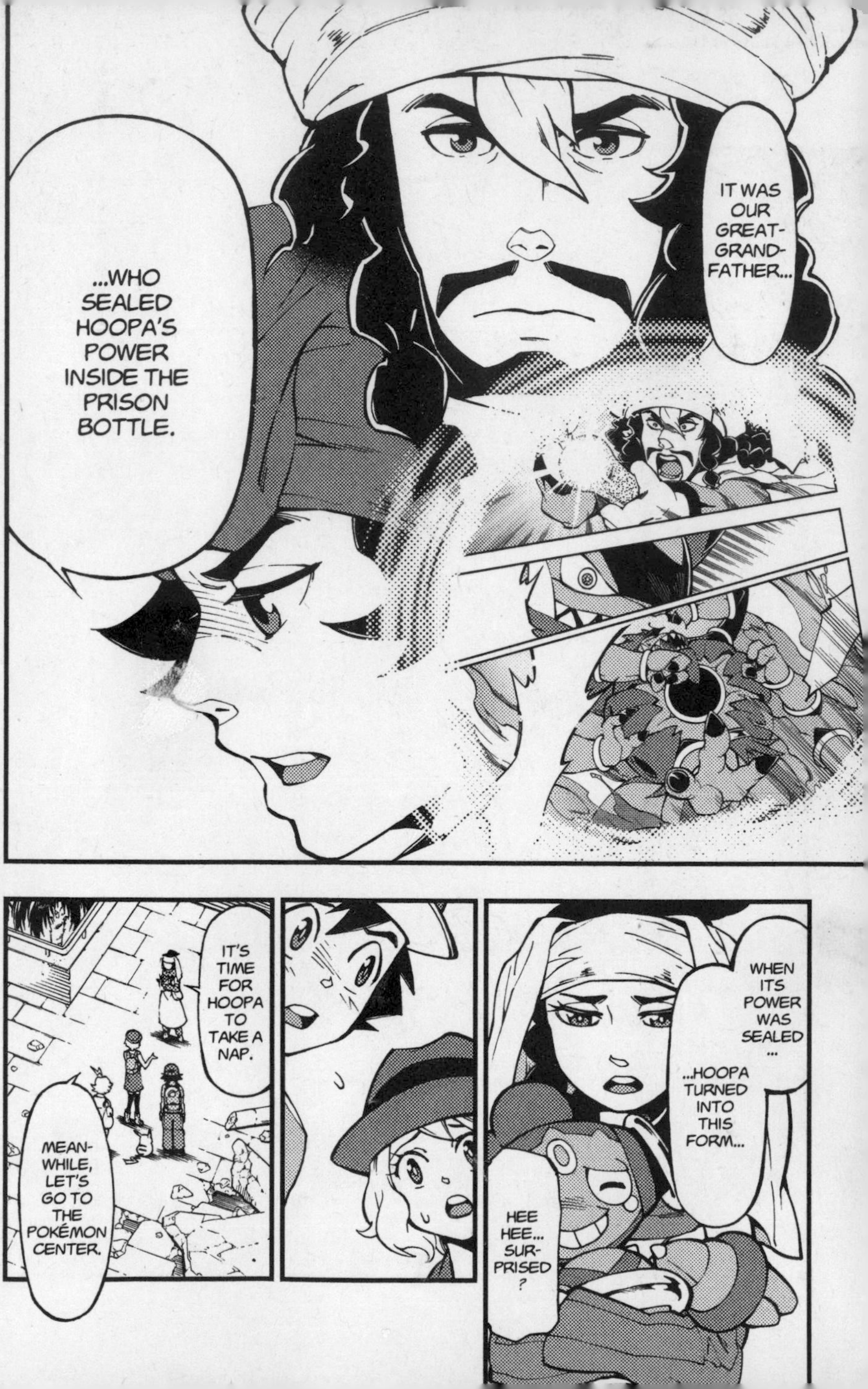

IT WAS OUR GREAT-GRAND-FATHER...
...WHO SEALED HOOPA'S POWER INSIDE THE PRISON BOTTLE.
WHEN ITS POWER WAS SEALED...
...HOOPA TURNED INTO THIS FORM...
HEE HEE... SUR-PRISED?
IT'S TIME FOR HOOPA TO TAKE A NAP.
MEAN-WHILE, LET'S GO TO THE POKÉMON CENTER.

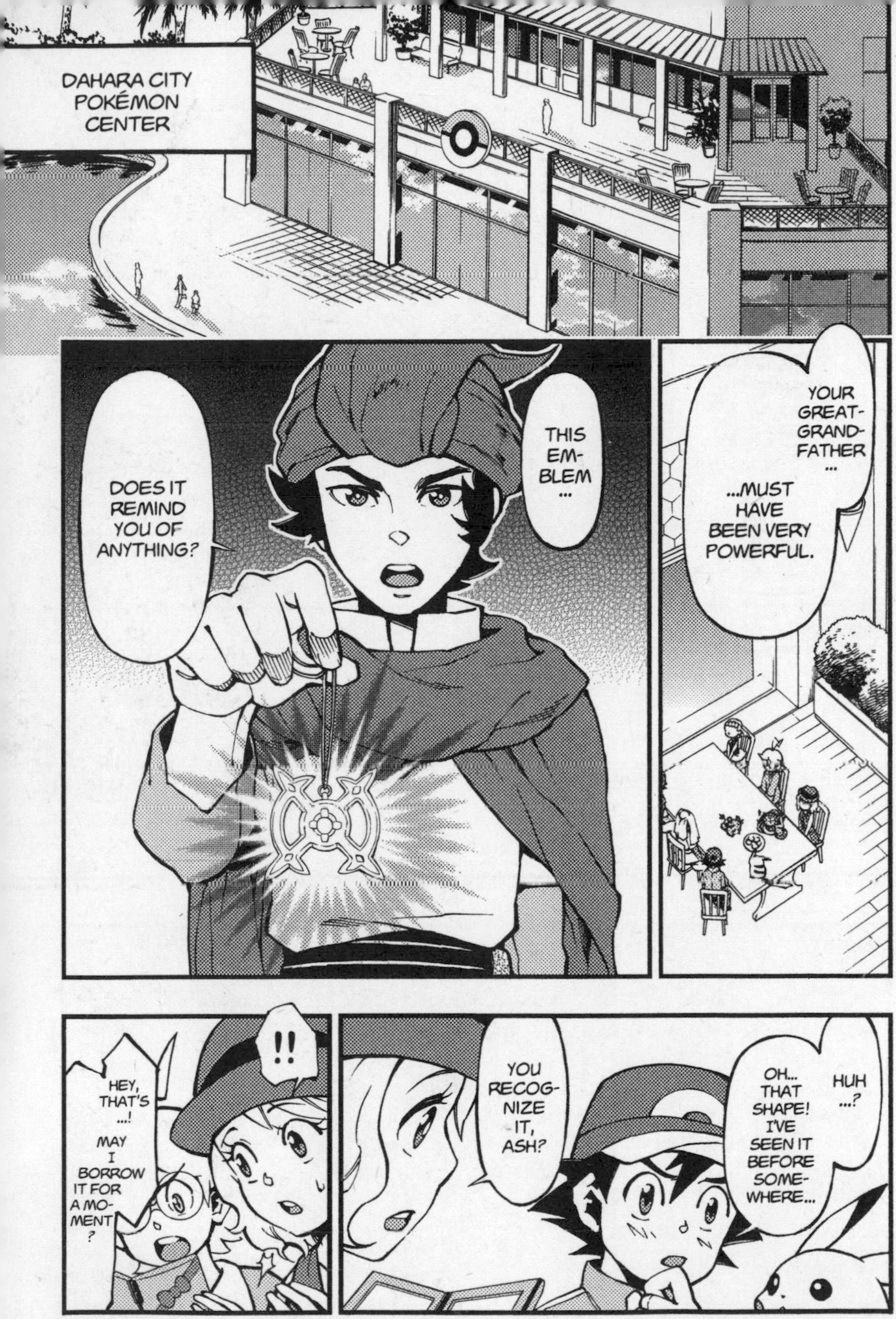
DAHARA CITY POKÉMON CENTER
YOUR GREAT-GRANDFATHER ...
...MUST HAVE BEEN VERY POWERFUL.
THIS EMBLEM ...
DOES IT REMIND YOU OF ANYTHING?
HUH ...?
OH... THAT SHAPE! I'VE SEEN IT BEFORE SOMEWHERE...
YOU RECOGNIZE IT, ASH?
!!
HEY, THAT'S ...! MAY I BORROW IT FOR A MOMENT?

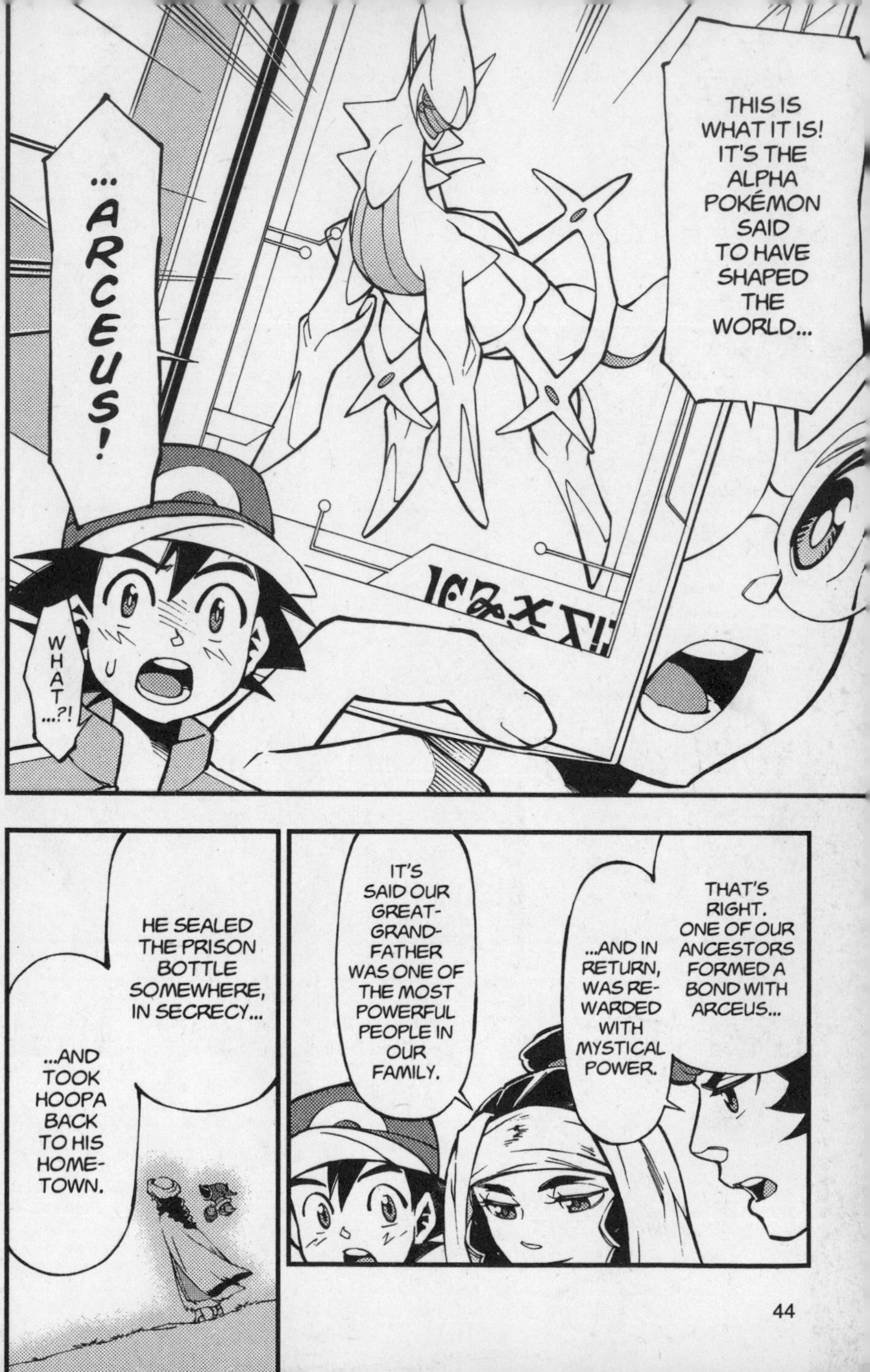
THIS IS WHAT IT IS! IT'S THE ALPHA POKÉMON SAID TO HAVE SHAPED THE WORLD...
...ARCEUS!
WHAT...?!
THAT'S RIGHT. ONE OF OUR ANCESTORS FORMED A BOND WITH ARCEUS...
...AND IN RETURN, WAS RE-WARDED WITH MYSTICAL POWER.
IT'S SAID OUR GREAT-GRAND-FATHER WAS ONE OF THE MOST POWERFUL PEOPLE IN OUR FAMILY.
HE SEALED THE PRISON BOTTLE SOMEWHERE, IN SECRECY...
...AND TOOK HOOPA BACK TO HIS HOME-TOWN.

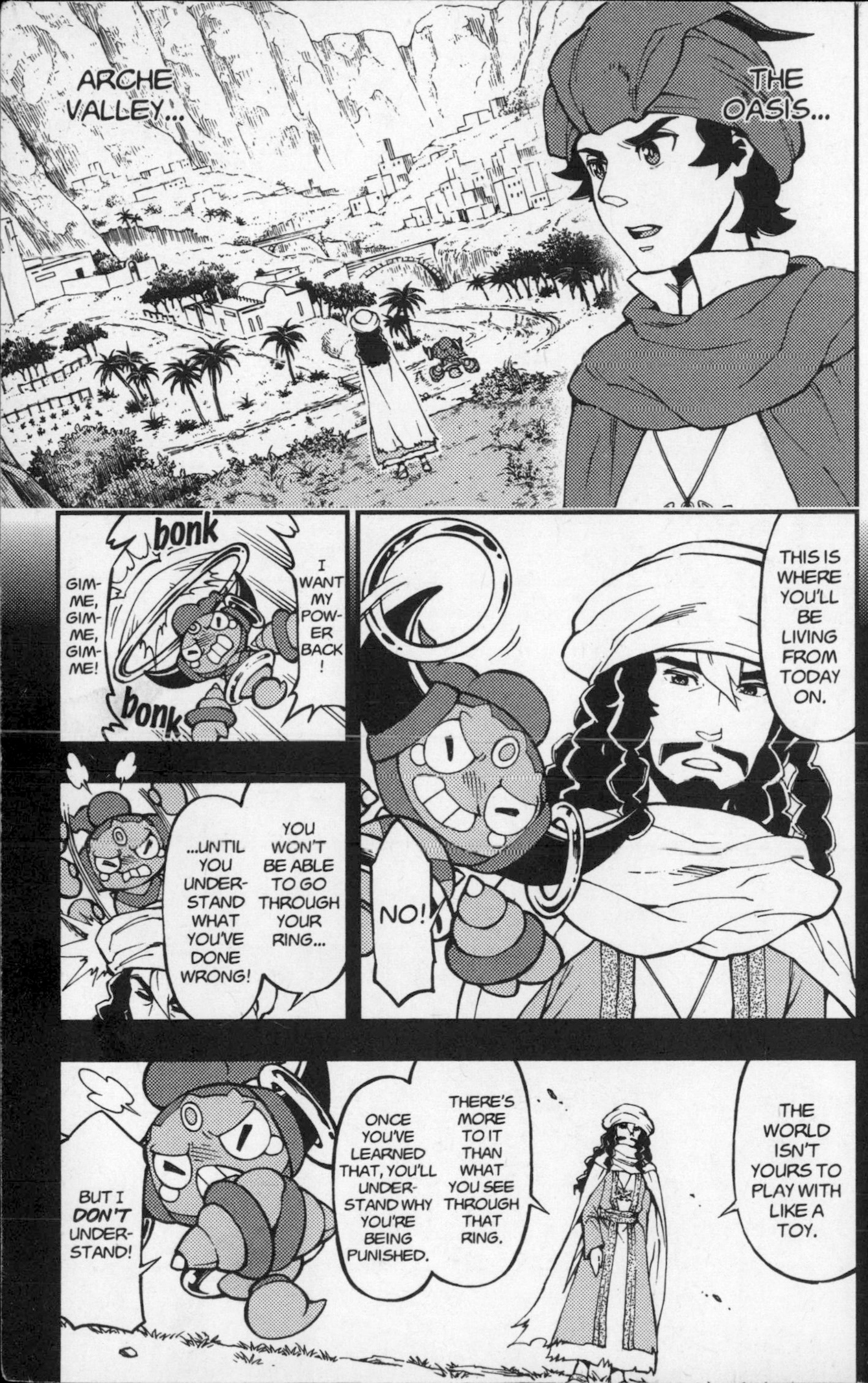
THE OASIS...
ARCHE VALLEY...
THIS IS WHERE YOU'LL BE LIVING FROM TODAY ON.
NO!
I WANT MY POWER BACK!
GIMME, GIMME, GIMME!
bonk
bonk
YOU WON'T BE ABLE TO GO THROUGH YOUR RING...
...UNTIL YOU UNDERSTAND WHAT YOU'VE DONE WRONG!
THE WORLD ISN'T YOURS TO PLAY WITH LIKE A TOY.
THERE'S MORE TO IT THAN WHAT YOU SEE THROUGH THAT RING.
ONCE YOU'VE LEARNED THAT, YOU'LL UNDERSTAND WHY YOU'RE BEING PUNISHED.
BUT I *DON'T* UNDERSTAND!

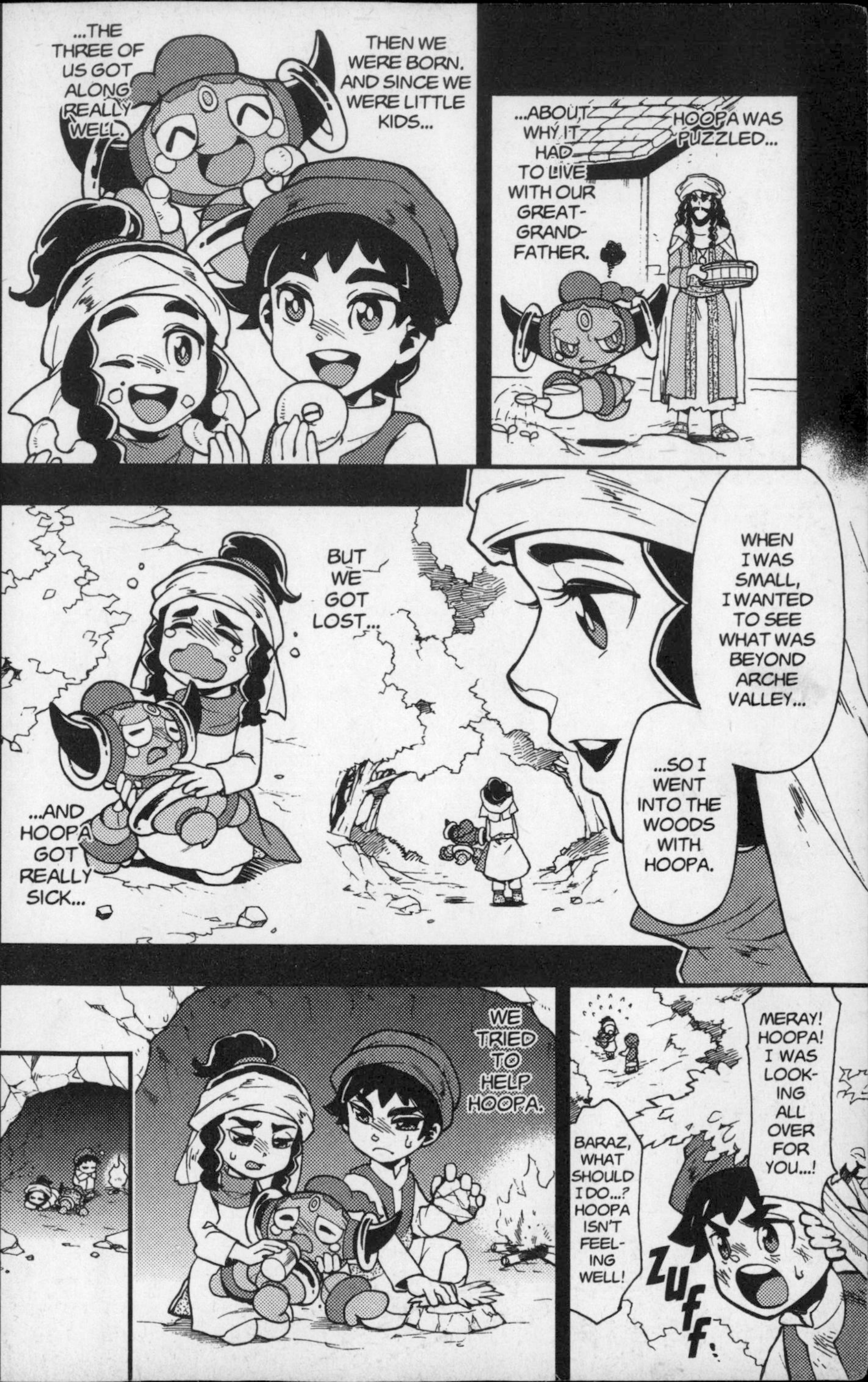
HOOPA WAS PUZZLED...
...ABOUT WHY IT HAD TO LIVE WITH OUR GREAT-GRANDFATHER.
THEN WE WERE BORN. AND SINCE WE WERE LITTLE KIDS...
...THE THREE OF US GOT ALONG REALLY WELL.
WHEN I WAS SMALL, I WANTED TO SEE WHAT WAS BEYOND ARCHE VALLEY...
...SO I WENT INTO THE WOODS WITH HOOPA.
BUT WE GOT LOST...
...AND HOOPA GOT REALLY SICK...
MERAY! HOOPA! I WAS LOOKING ALL OVER FOR YOU...!
ZUFF
BARAZ, WHAT SHOULD I DO...? HOOPA ISN'T FEELING WELL!
WE TRIED TO HELP HOOPA.

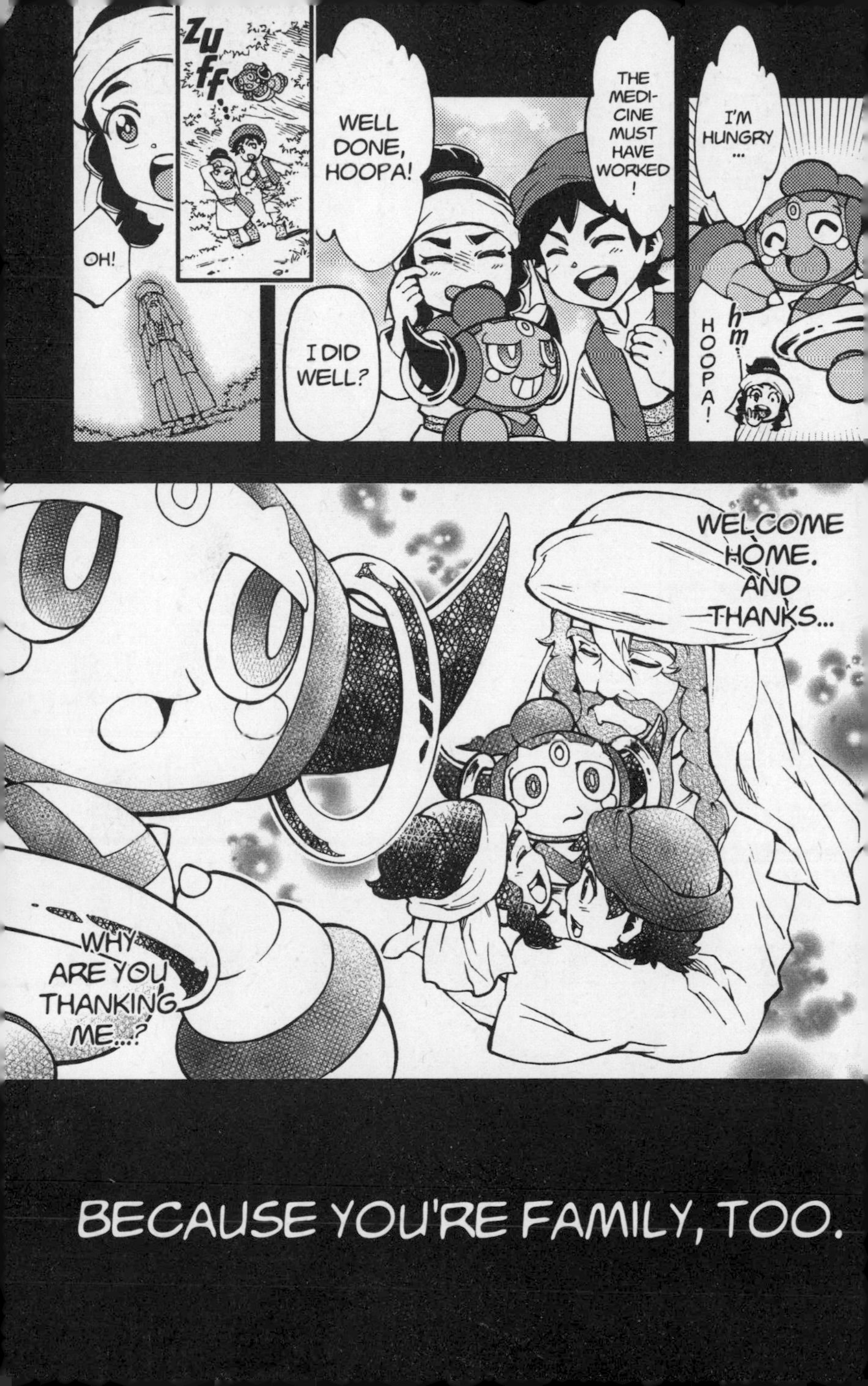
I'M HUNGRY...
hm
HOOPA!
THE MEDI-CINE MUST HAVE WORKED!
WELL DONE, HOOPA!
I DID WELL?
ZUFF
OH!
WELCOME HOME. AND THANKS...
WHY ARE YOU THANKING ME...?
BECAUSE YOU'RE FAMILY, TOO.

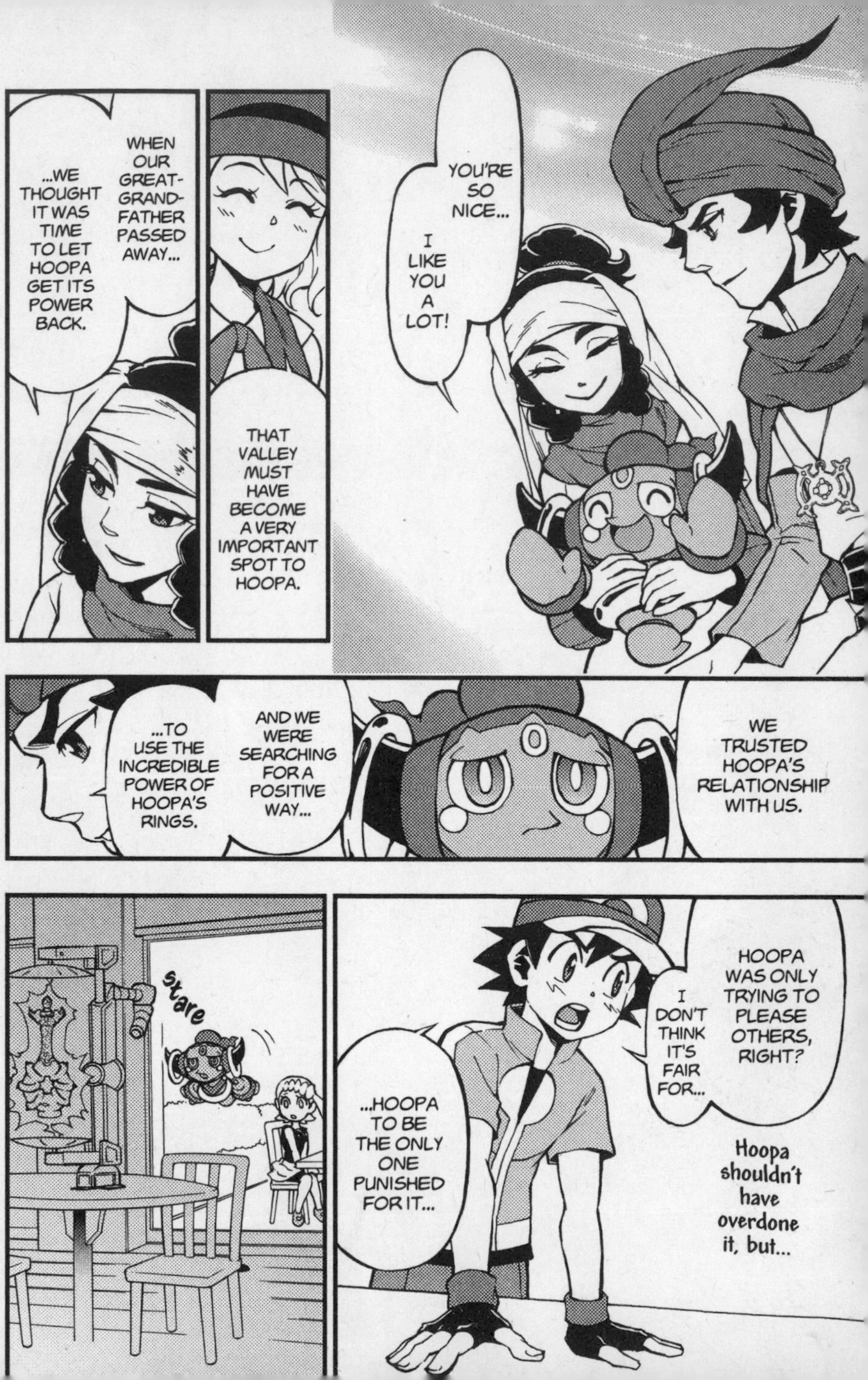
YOU'RE SO NICE...
I LIKE YOU A LOT!
THAT VALLEY MUST HAVE BECOME A VERY IMPORTANT SPOT TO HOOPA.
WHEN OUR GREAT-GRANDFATHER PASSED AWAY...
...WE THOUGHT IT WAS TIME TO LET HOOPA GET ITS POWER BACK.
WE TRUSTED HOOPA'S RELATIONSHIP WITH US.
AND WE WERE SEARCHING FOR A POSITIVE WAY...
...TO USE THE INCREDIBLE POWER OF HOOPA'S RINGS.
HOOPA WAS ONLY TRYING TO PLEASE OTHERS, RIGHT?
Hoopa shouldn't have overdone it, but...
I DON'T THINK IT'S FAIR FOR...
...HOOPA TO BE THE ONLY ONE PUNISHED FOR IT...
stare

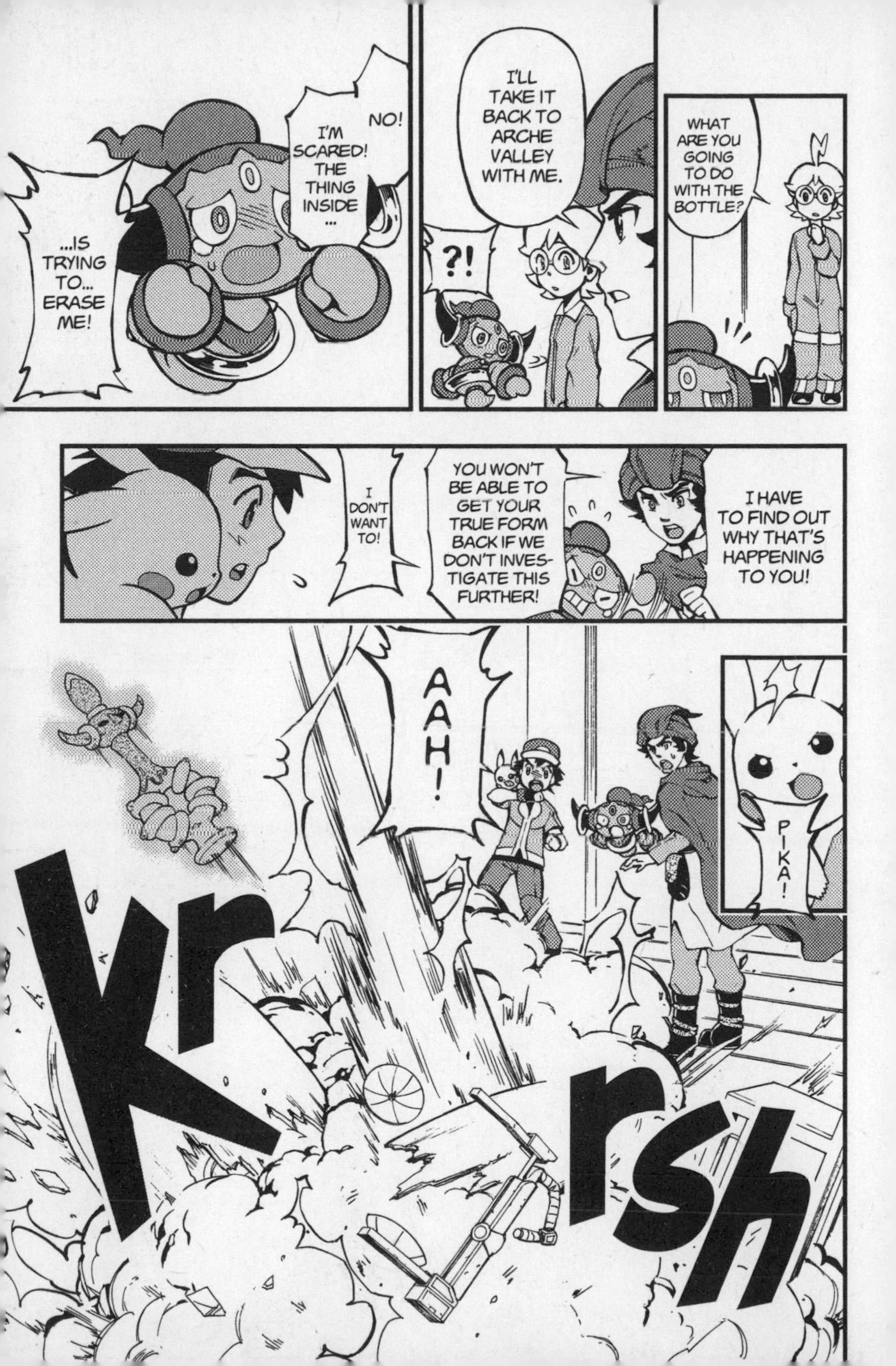
WHAT ARE YOU GOING TO DO WITH THE BOTTLE?
I'LL TAKE IT BACK TO ARCHE VALLEY WITH ME.
?!
NO!
I'M SCARED! THE THING INSIDE ...
...IS TRYING TO... ERASE ME!
I HAVE TO FIND OUT WHY THAT'S HAPPENING TO YOU!
YOU WON'T BE ABLE TO GET YOUR TRUE FORM BACK IF WE DON'T INVESTIGATE THIS FURTHER!
I DON'T WANT TO!
PIKA!
AAH!
Krrsh

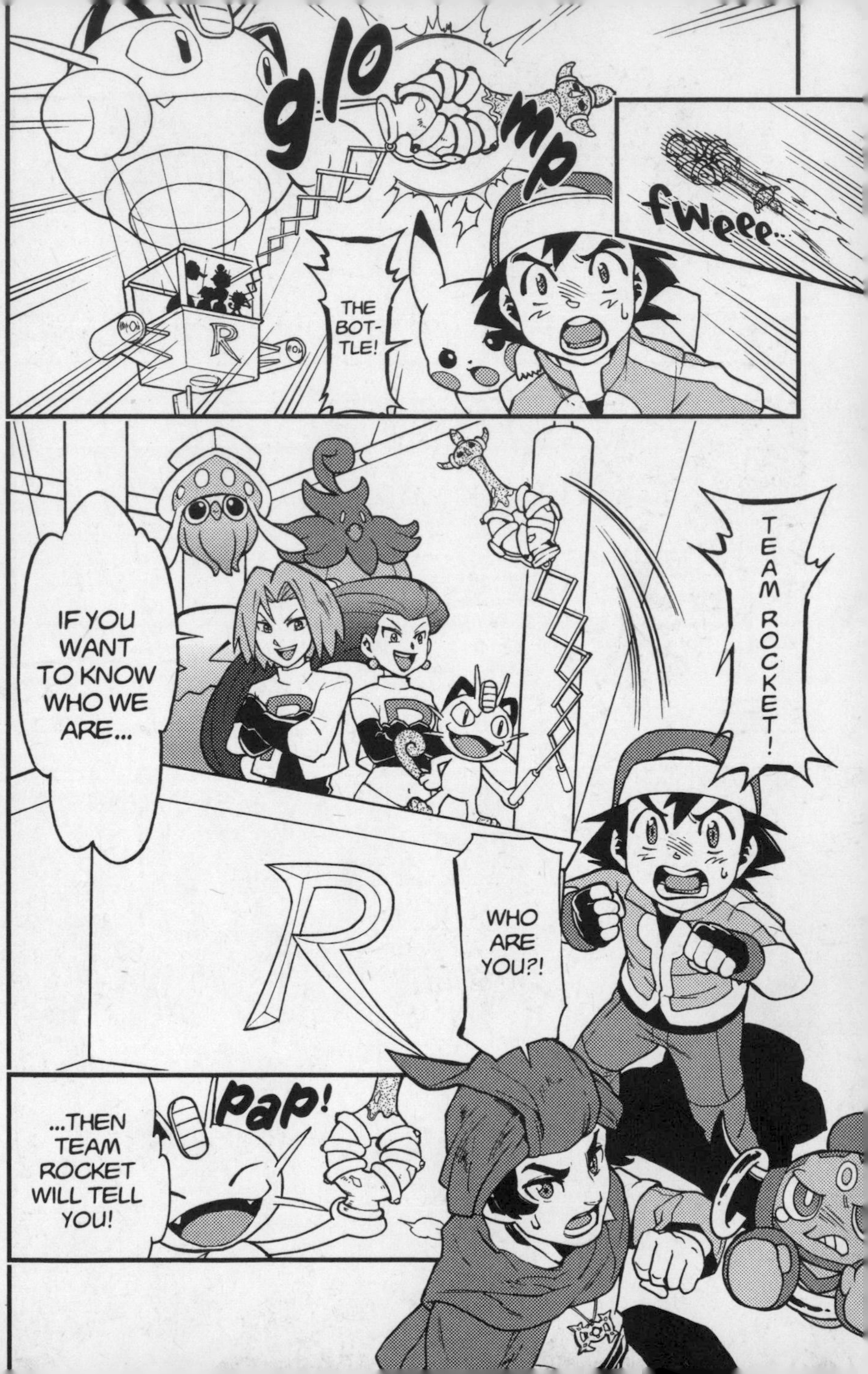
fweee...
glomp
THE BOT-TLE!
TEAM ROCKET!
WHO ARE YOU?!
IF YOU WANT TO KNOW WHO WE ARE...
pap!
...THEN TEAM ROCKET WILL TELL YOU!

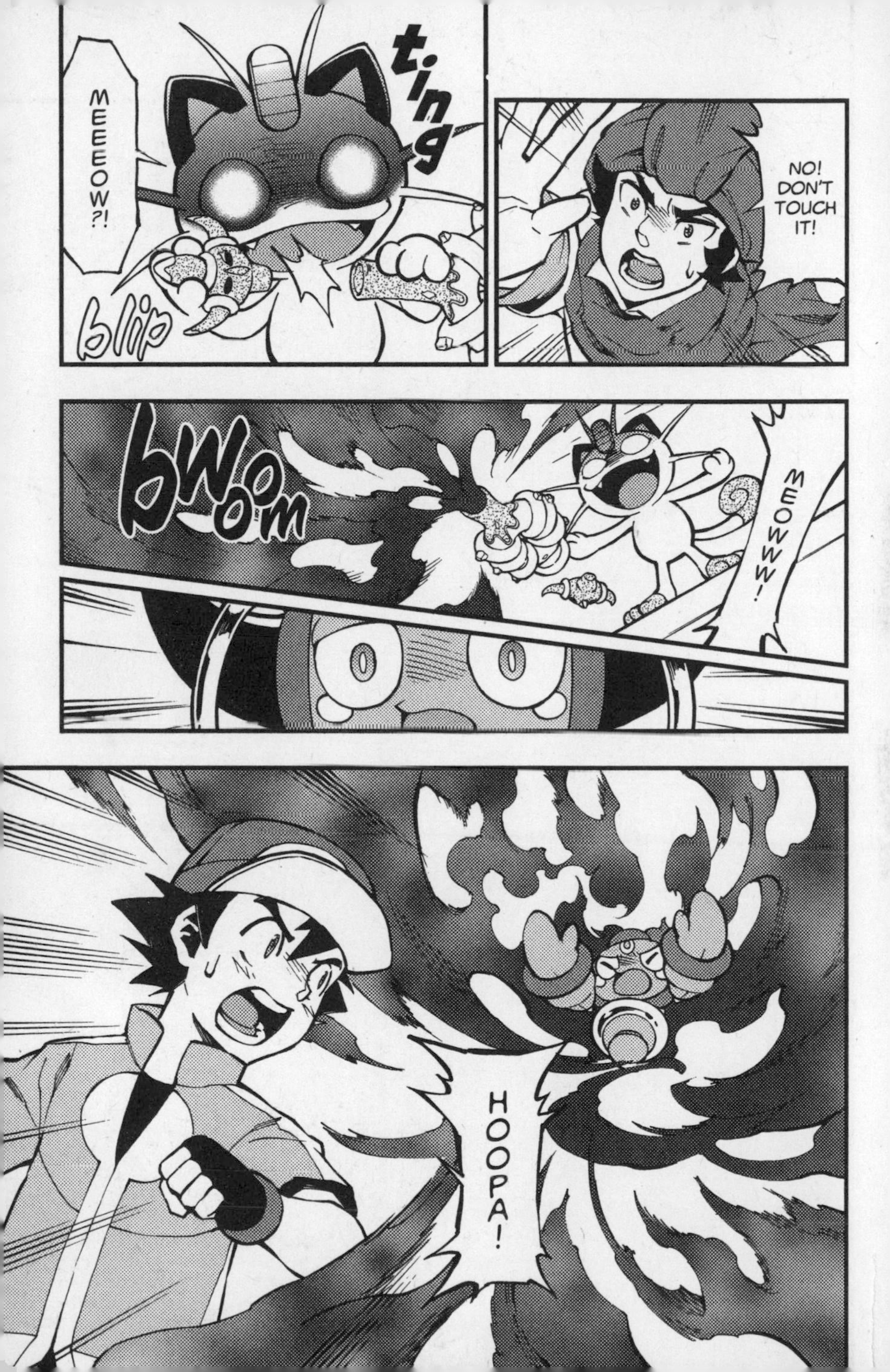
NO! DON'T TOUCH IT!
ting
MEEEEOW?!
blip
bwoom
MEOWWW!
HOOPA!

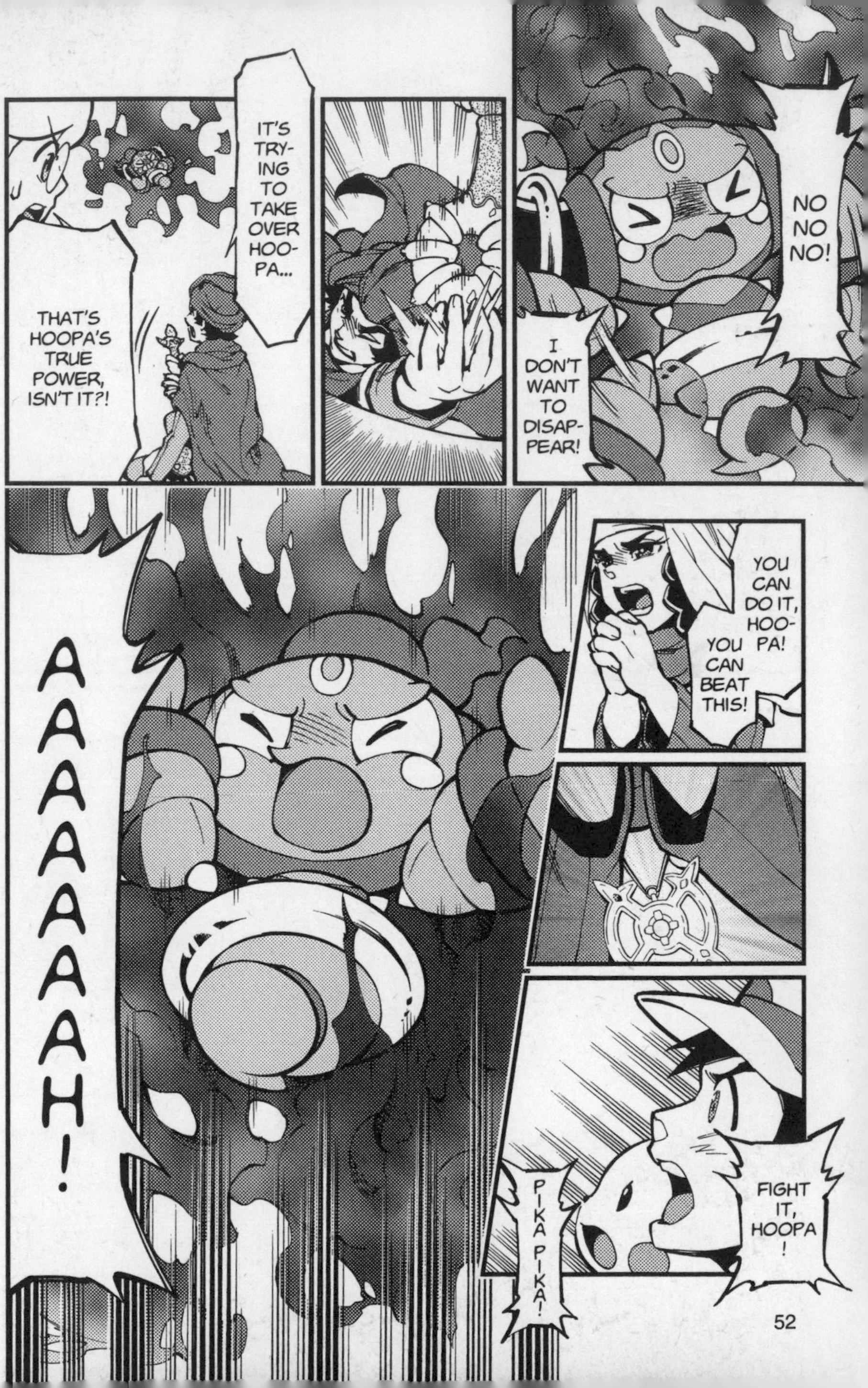

NO NO NO!
I DON'T WANT TO DISAPPEAR!
IT'S TRYING TO TAKE OVER HOOPA...
THAT'S HOOPA'S TRUE POWER, ISN'T IT?!
YOU CAN DO IT, HOOPA!
YOU CAN BEAT THIS!
FIGHT IT, HOOPA!
PIKA PIKA!
AAAAAAAH!

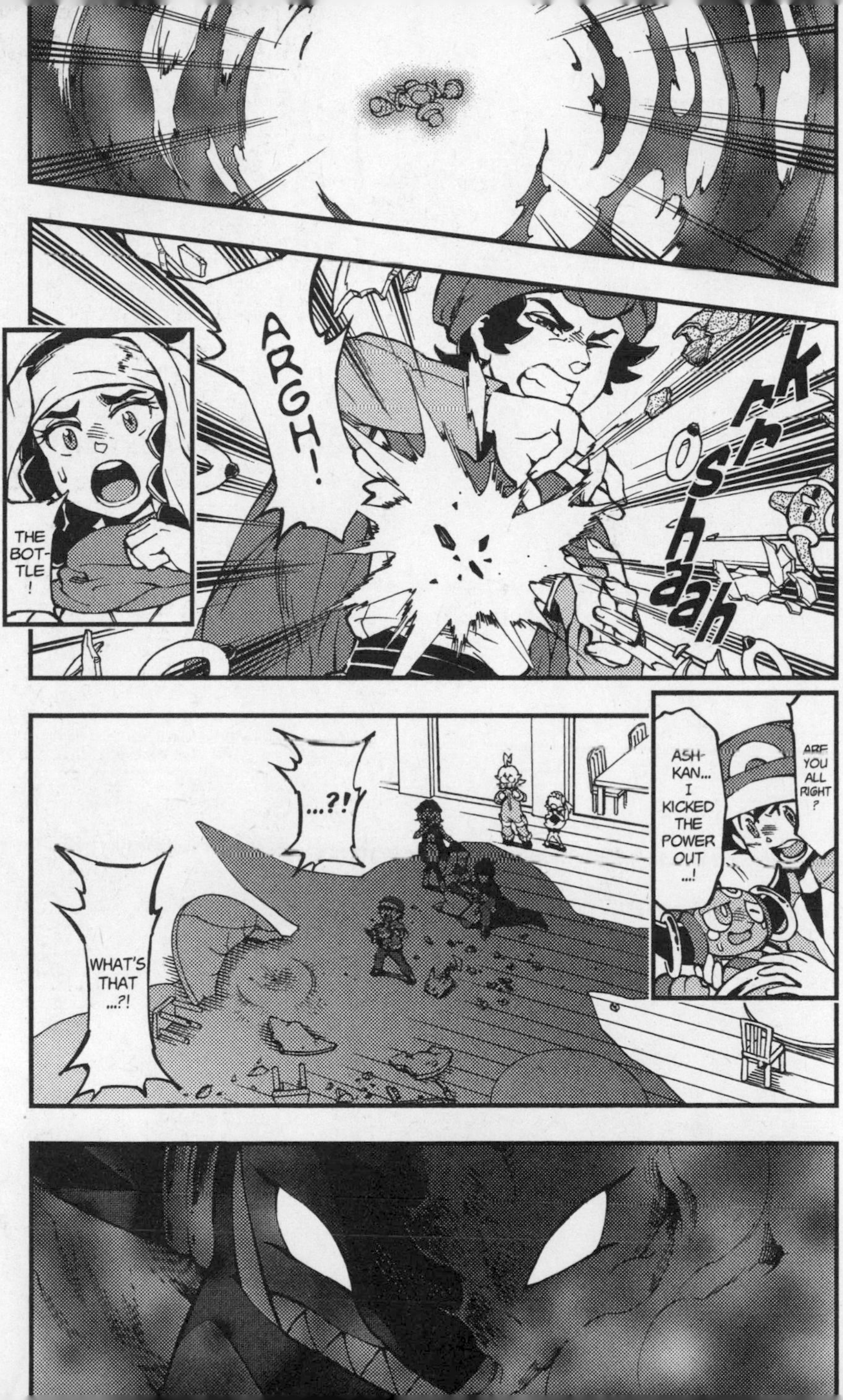
krrshaah
ARGH!
THE BOTTLE!
ARE YOU ALL RIGHT?
ASH-KAN... I KICKED THE POWER OUT...!
...?!
WHAT'S THAT...?!

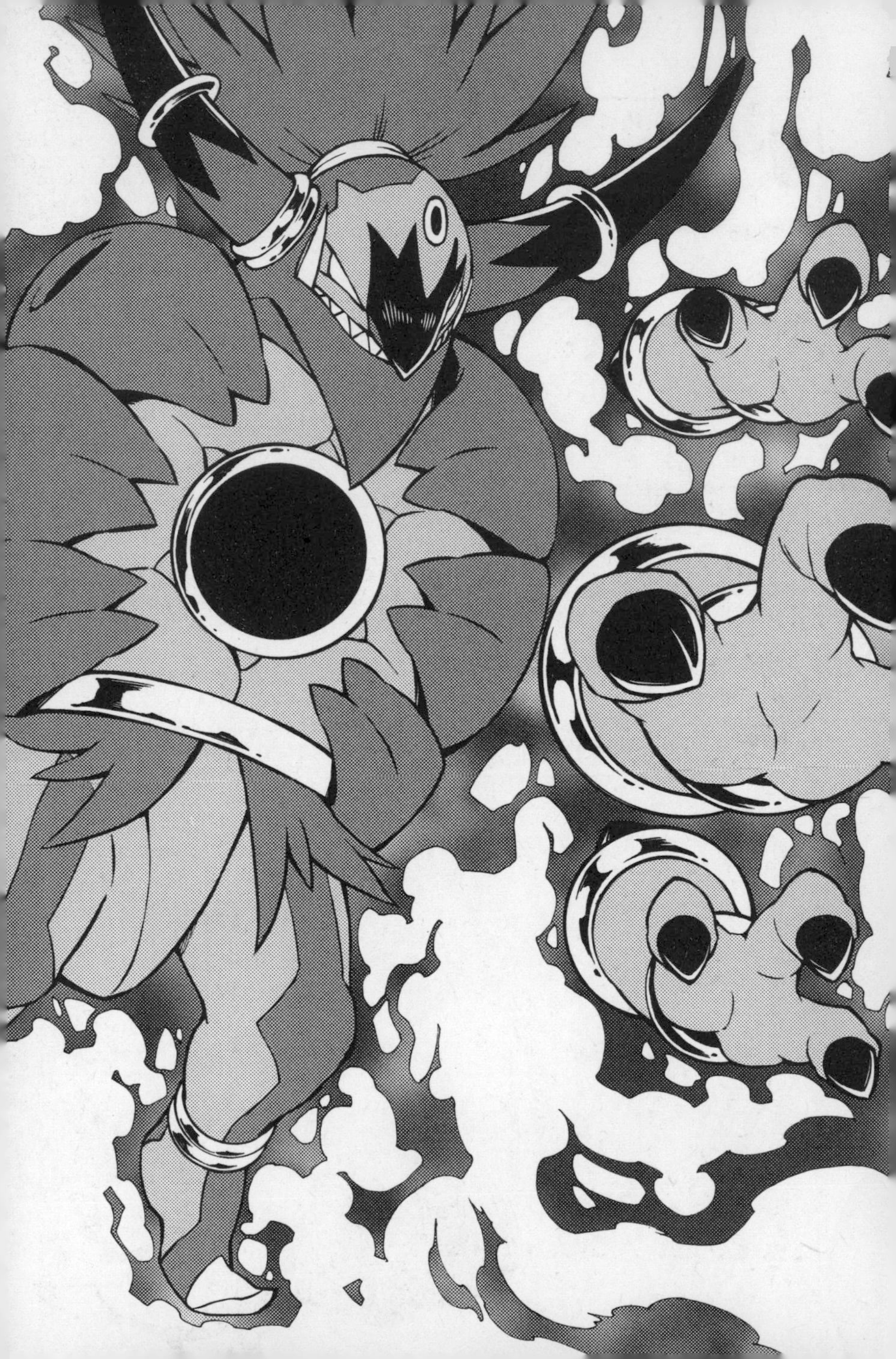

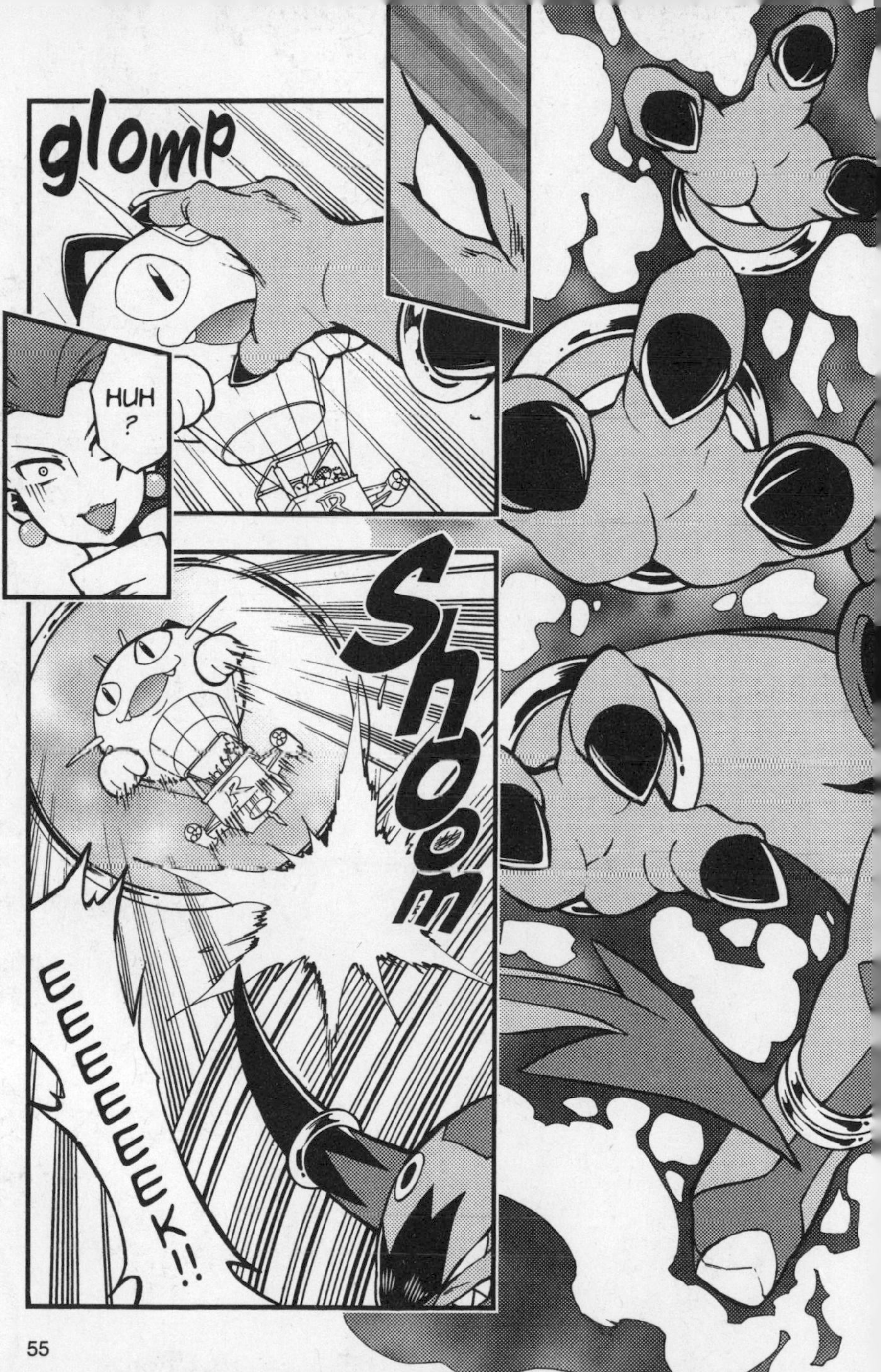
glomp
HUH ?
SHOOOM
EEEEEEK!!

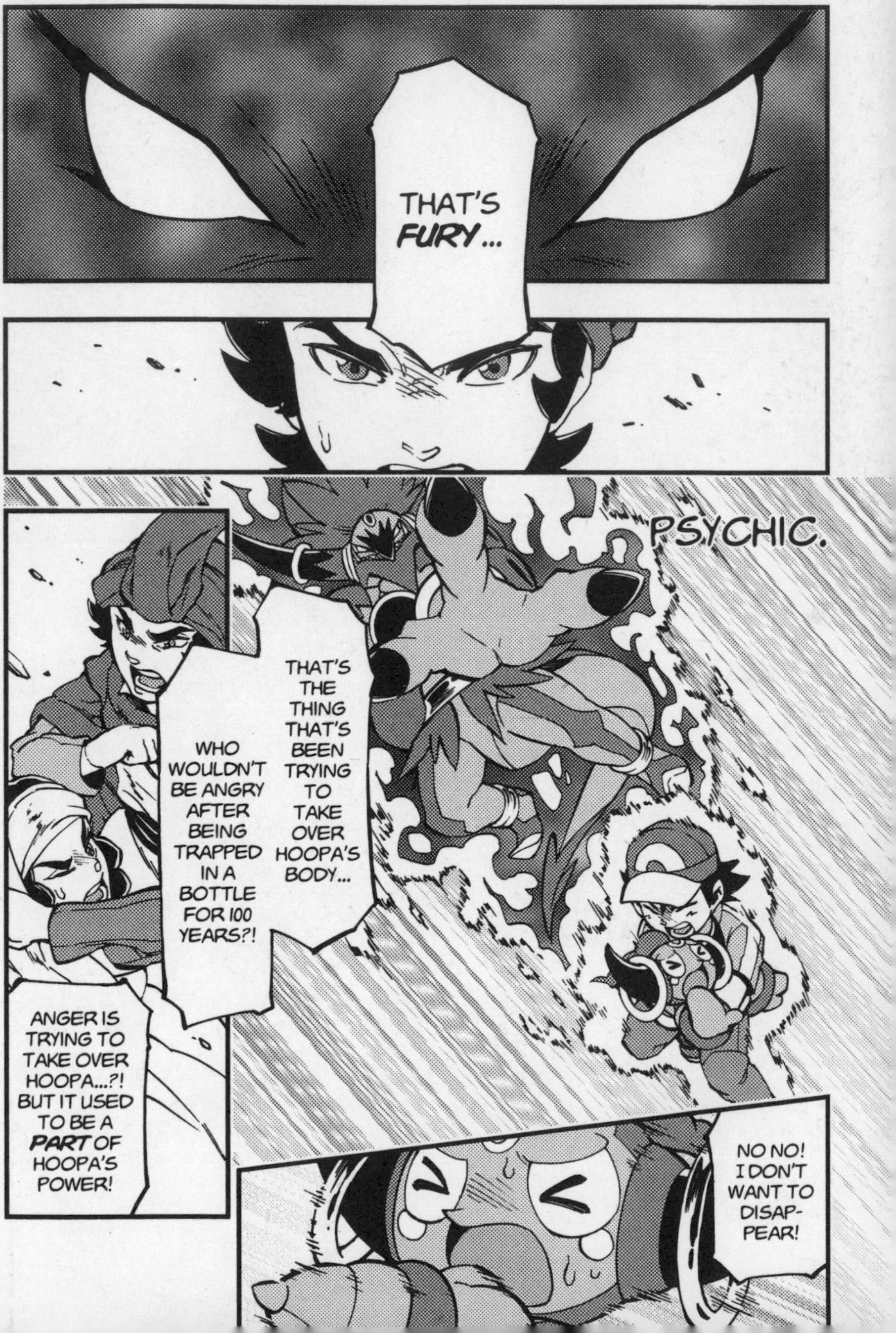
THAT'S **FURY**...
PSYCHIC.
THAT'S THE THING THAT'S BEEN TRYING TO TAKE OVER HOOPA'S BODY...
WHO WOULDN'T BE ANGRY AFTER BEING TRAPPED IN A BOTTLE FOR 100 YEARS?!
ANGER IS TRYING TO TAKE OVER HOOPA...?! BUT IT USED TO BE A **PART** OF HOOPA'S POWER!
NO NO! I DON'T WANT TO DISAP-PEAR!

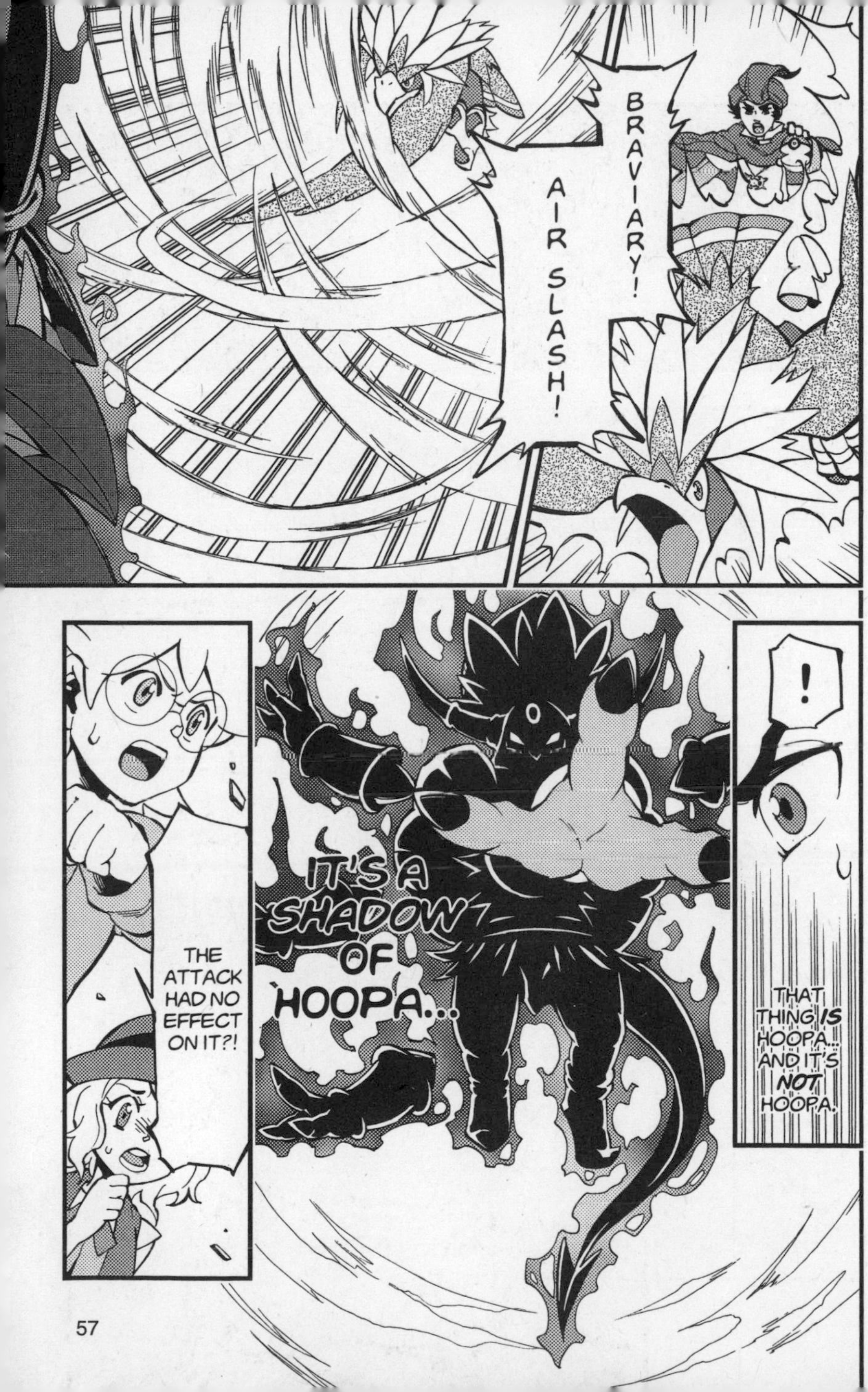
BRAVIARY!
AIR SLASH!
!
THAT THING *IS* HOOPA... AND IT'S *NOT* HOOPA.
IT'S A SHADOW OF HOOPA...
THE ATTACK HAD NO EFFECT ON IT?!

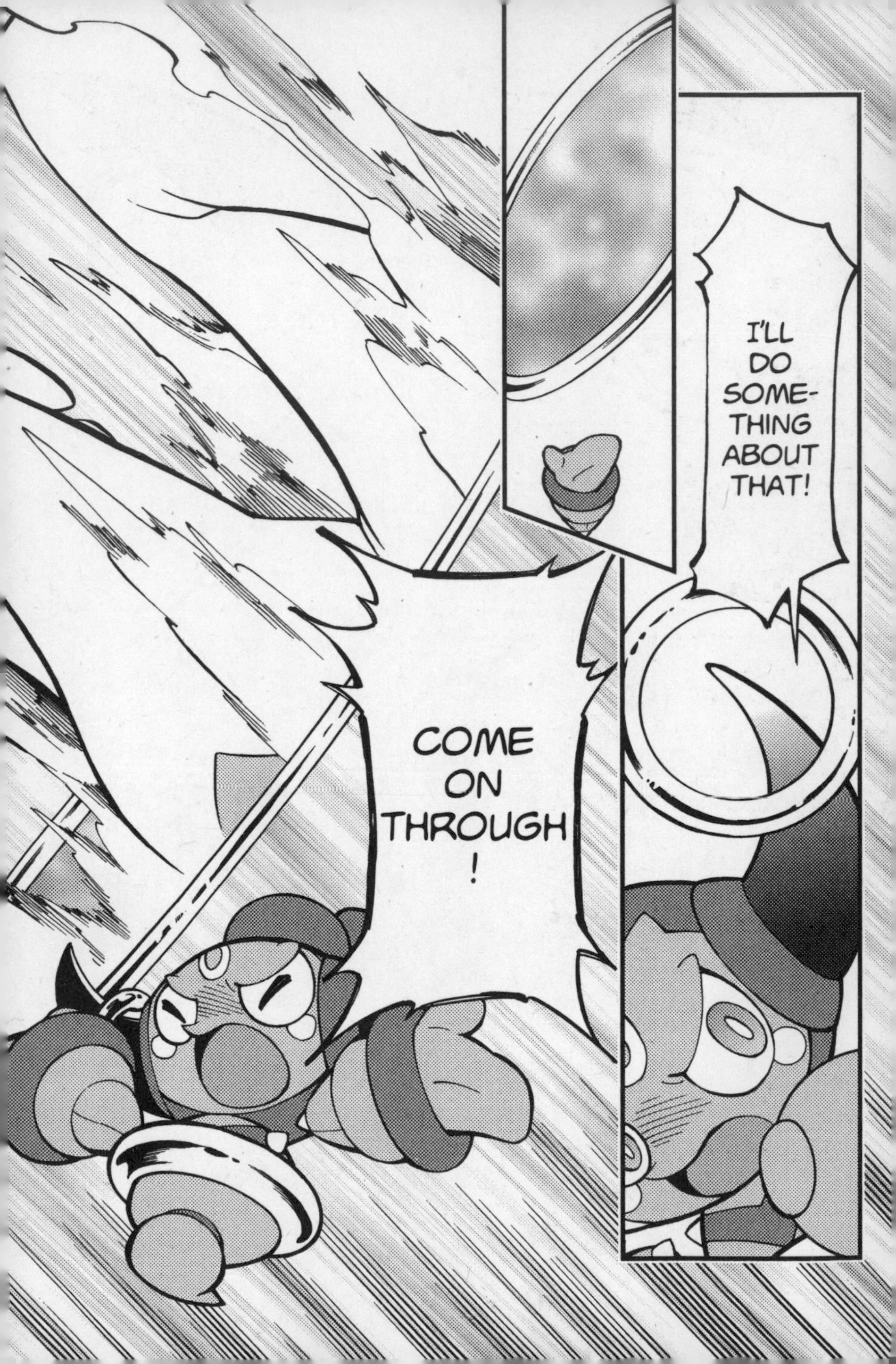
I'LL DO SOME-THING ABOUT THAT!
COME ON THROUGH!

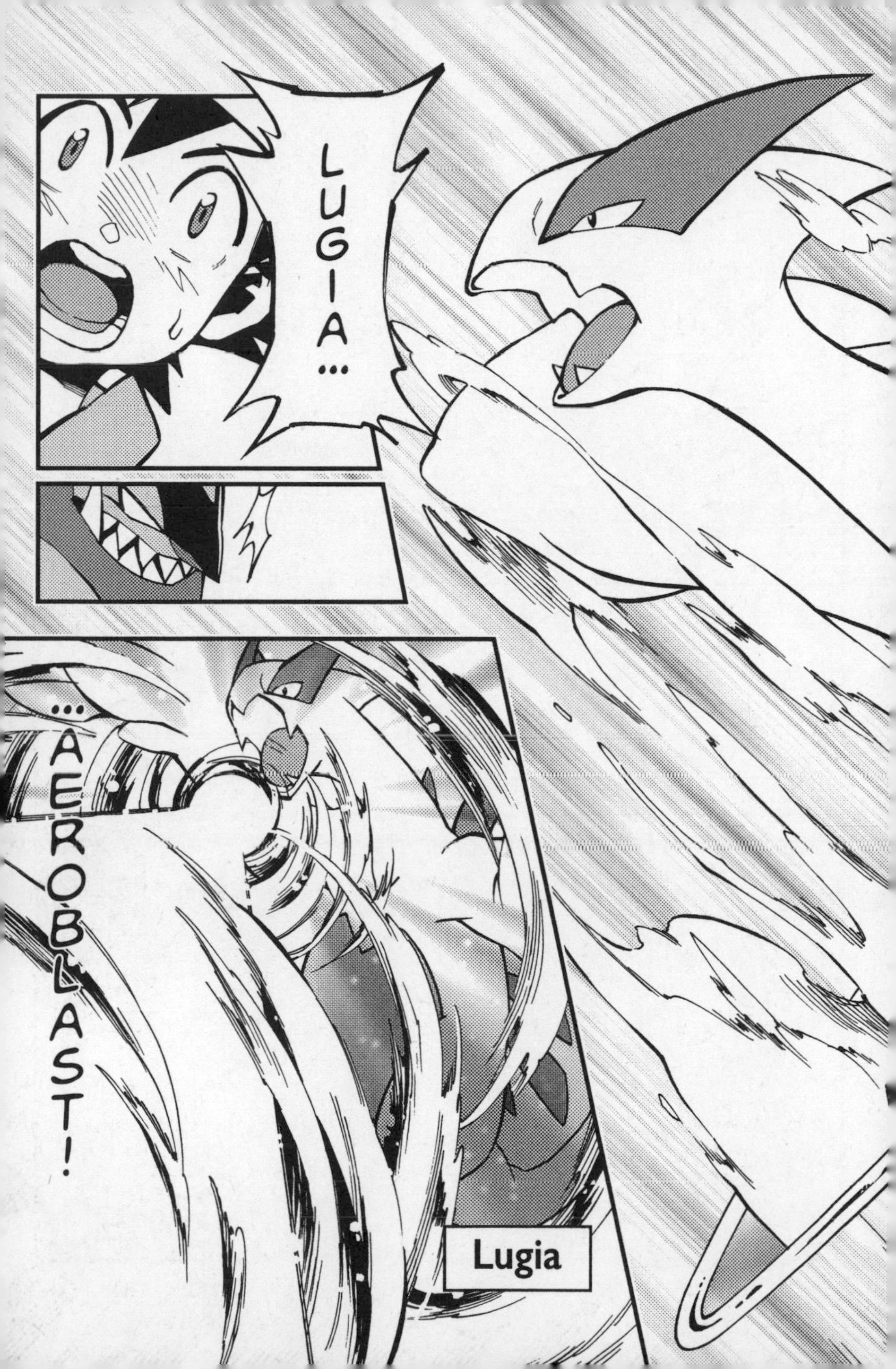
LUGIA...
...AEROBLAST!
Lugia

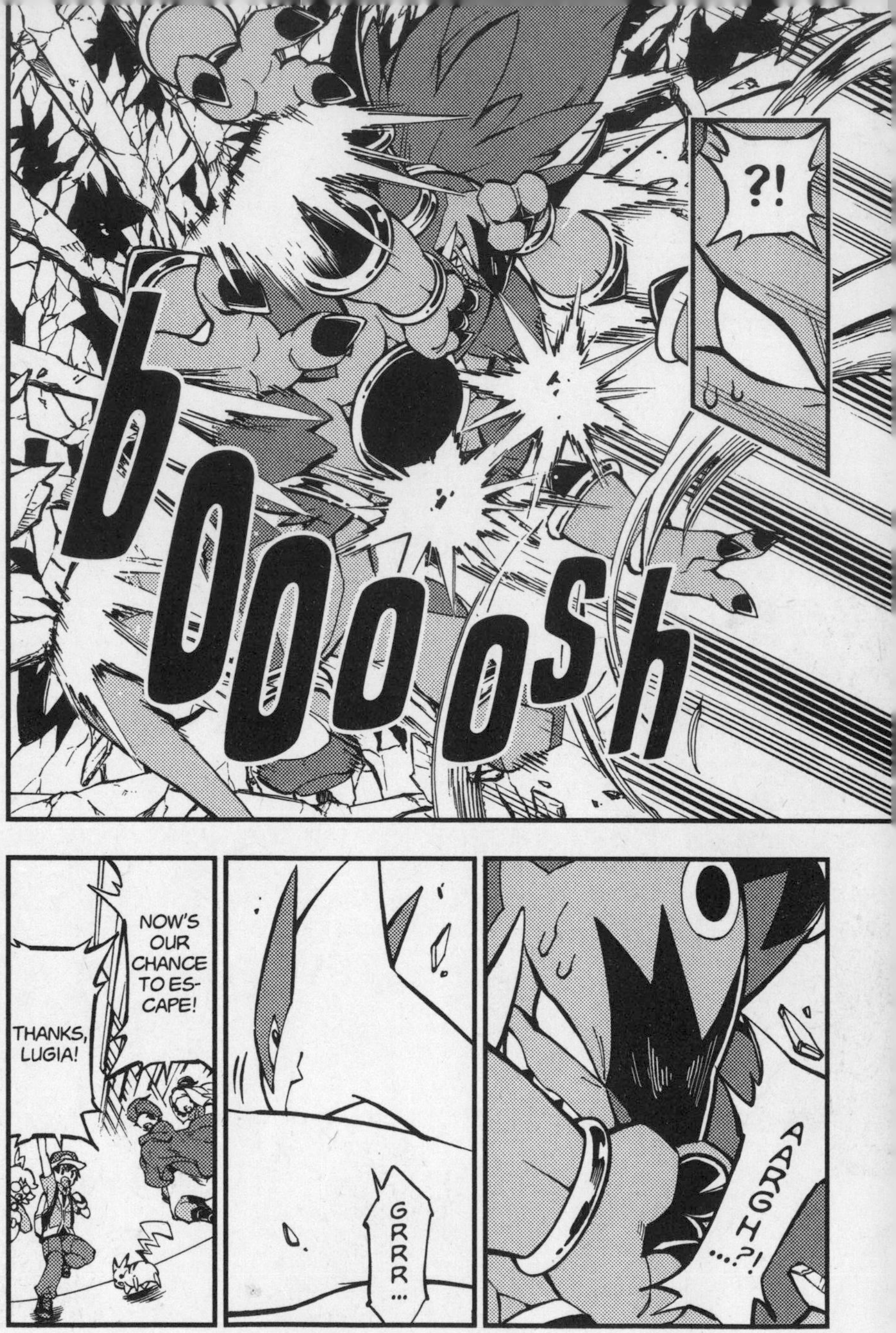
?!
boooosh
AARGH...?!
GRRR...
NOW'S OUR CHANCE TO ES-CAPE!
THANKS, LUGIA!

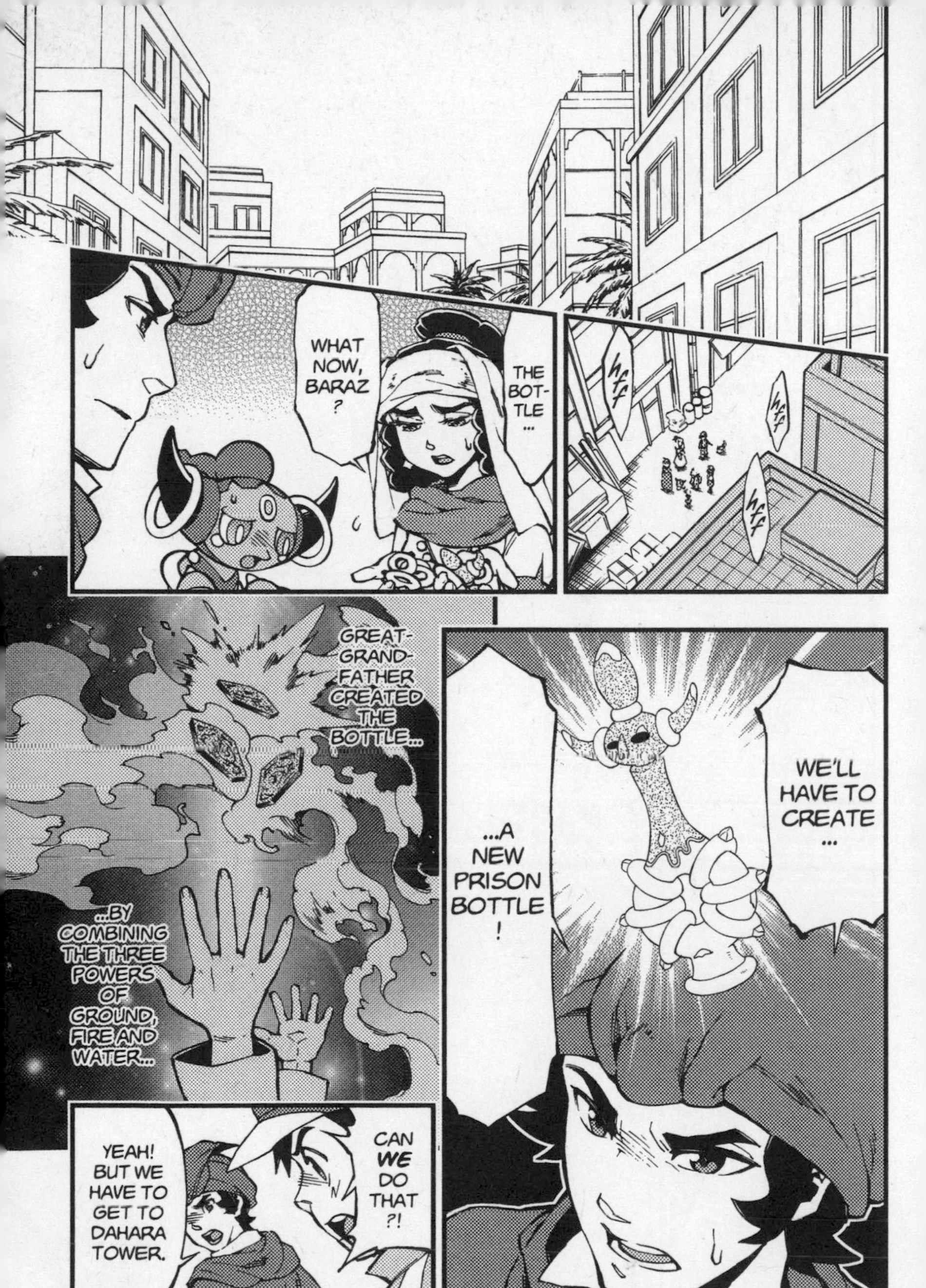

hff
hff
hff
THE BOTTLE...
WHAT NOW, BARAZ?
WE'LL HAVE TO CREATE...
...A NEW PRISON BOTTLE!
GREAT-GRANDFATHER CREATED THE BOTTLE...
...BY COMBINING THE THREE POWERS OF GROUND, FIRE AND WATER...
CAN *WE* DO THAT?!
YEAH! BUT WE HAVE TO GET TO DAHARA TOWER.

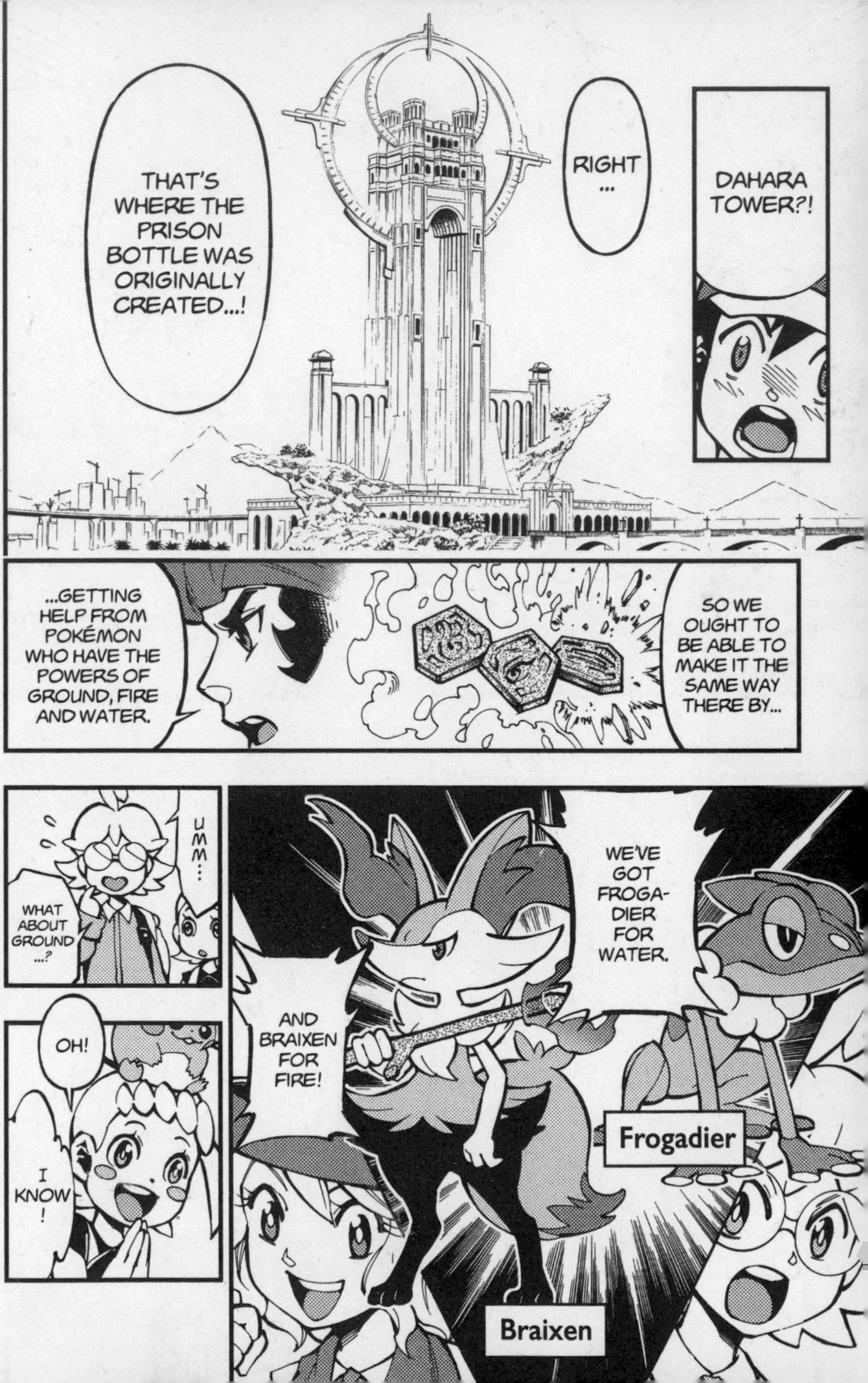
DAHARA TOWER?!
RIGHT ...
THAT'S WHERE THE PRISON BOTTLE WAS ORIGINALLY CREATED...!
SO WE OUGHT TO BE ABLE TO MAKE IT THE SAME WAY THERE BY...
...GETTING HELP FROM POKÉMON WHO HAVE THE POWERS OF GROUND, FIRE AND WATER.
WE'VE GOT FROGA-DIER FOR WATER.
Frogadier
AND BRAIXEN FOR FIRE!
Braixen
UMM...
WHAT ABOUT GROUND ...?
OH!
I KNOW!

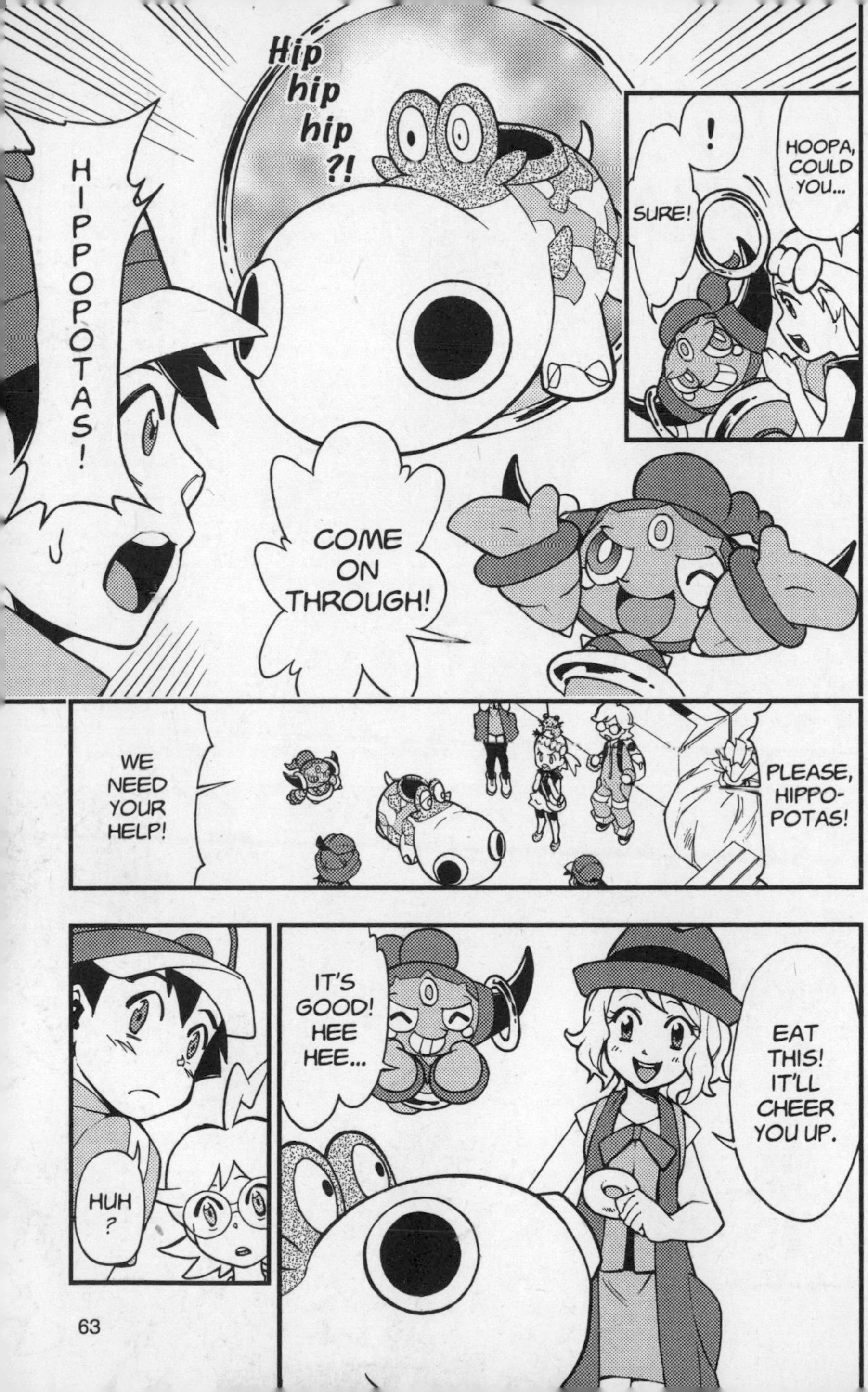
HOOPA, COULD YOU...
!
SURE!
Hip hip hip ?!
HIPPOPOTAS!
COME ON THROUGH!
PLEASE, HIPPO-POTAS!
WE NEED YOUR HELP!
EAT THIS! IT'LL CHEER YOU UP.
IT'S GOOD! HEE HEE...
HUH?

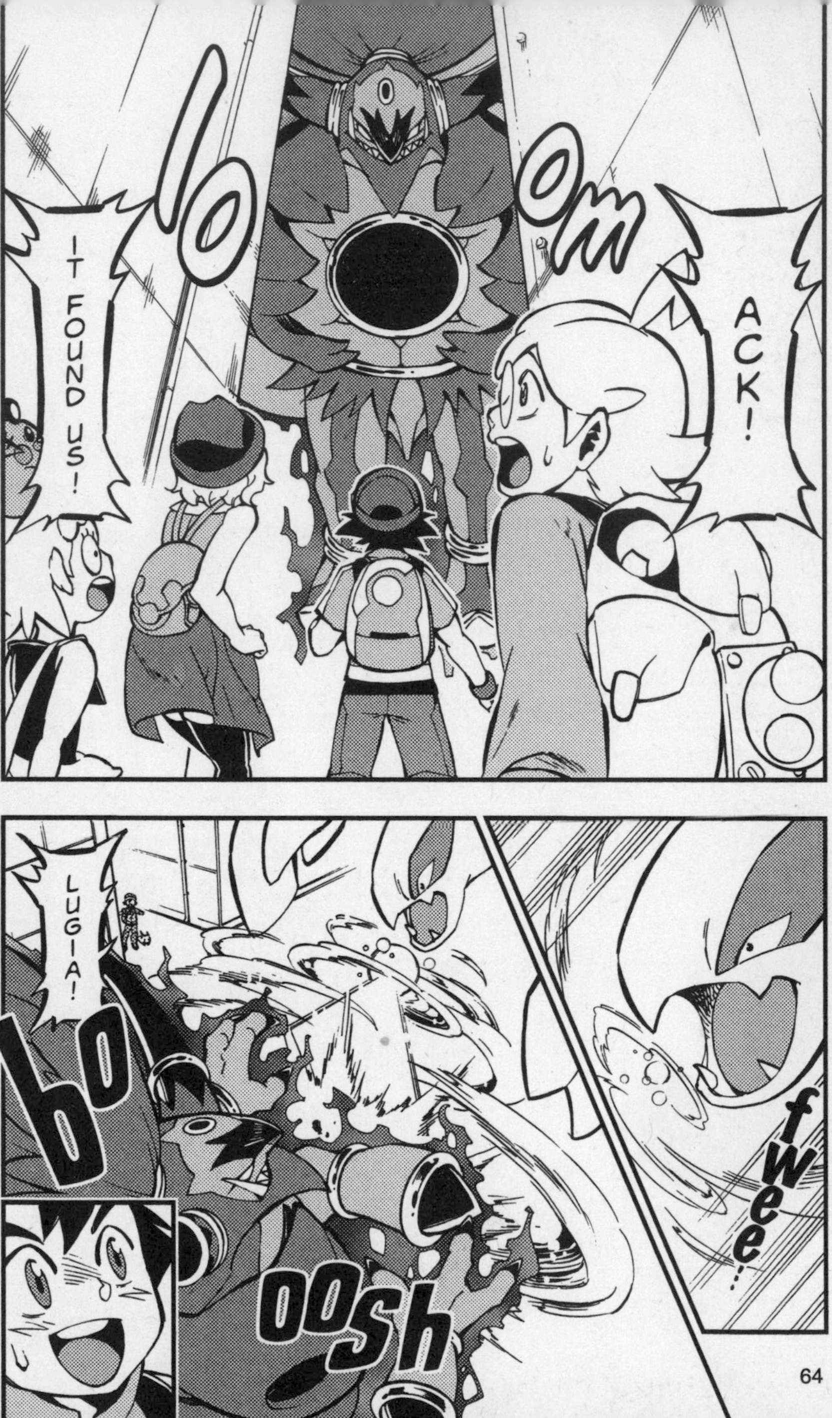
ACK!
IT FOUND US!
loom
fweee!
LUGIA!
booosh

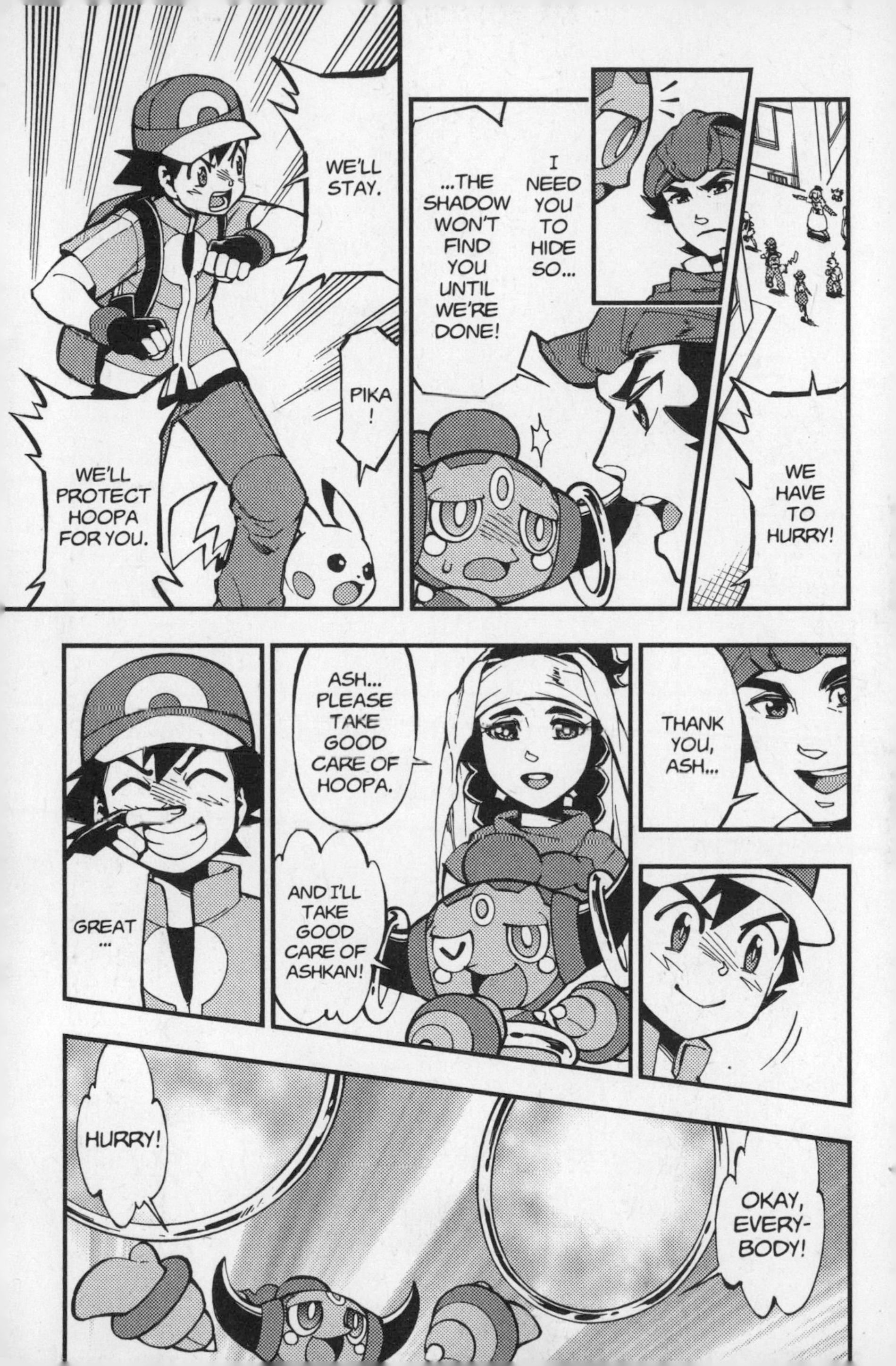
WE HAVE TO HURRY!
I NEED YOU TO HIDE SO...
...THE SHADOW WON'T FIND YOU UNTIL WE'RE DONE!
WE'LL STAY.
WE'LL PROTECT HOOPA FOR YOU.
PIKA!
THANK YOU, ASH...
ASH... PLEASE TAKE GOOD CARE OF HOOPA.
AND I'LL TAKE GOOD CARE OF ASHKAN!
GREAT...
OKAY, EVERY-BODY!
HURRY!

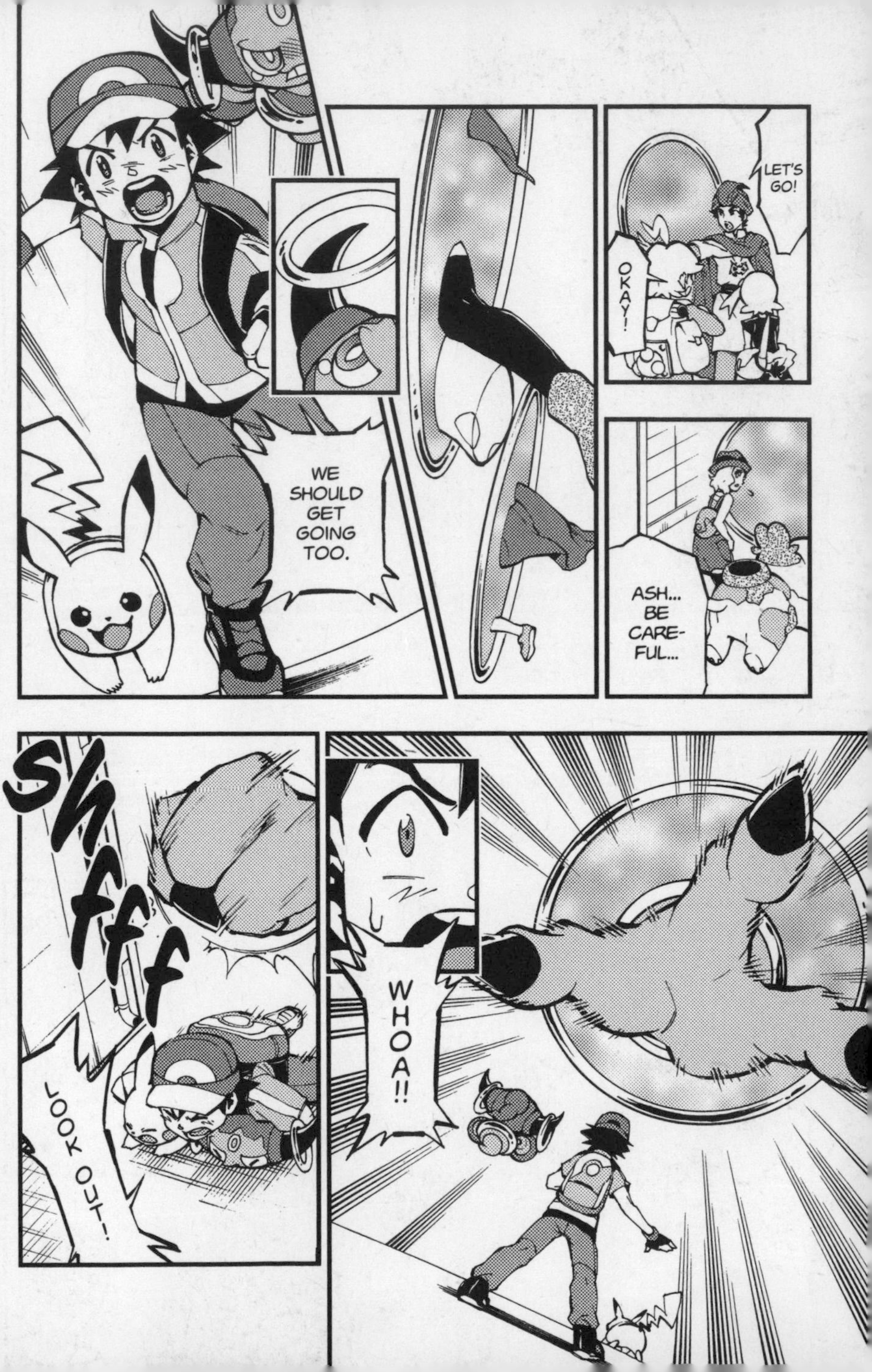
LET'S GO!
OKAY!
ASH... BE CARE-FUL...
WE SHOULD GET GOING TOO.
WHOA!!
SHFFF
LOOK OUT!

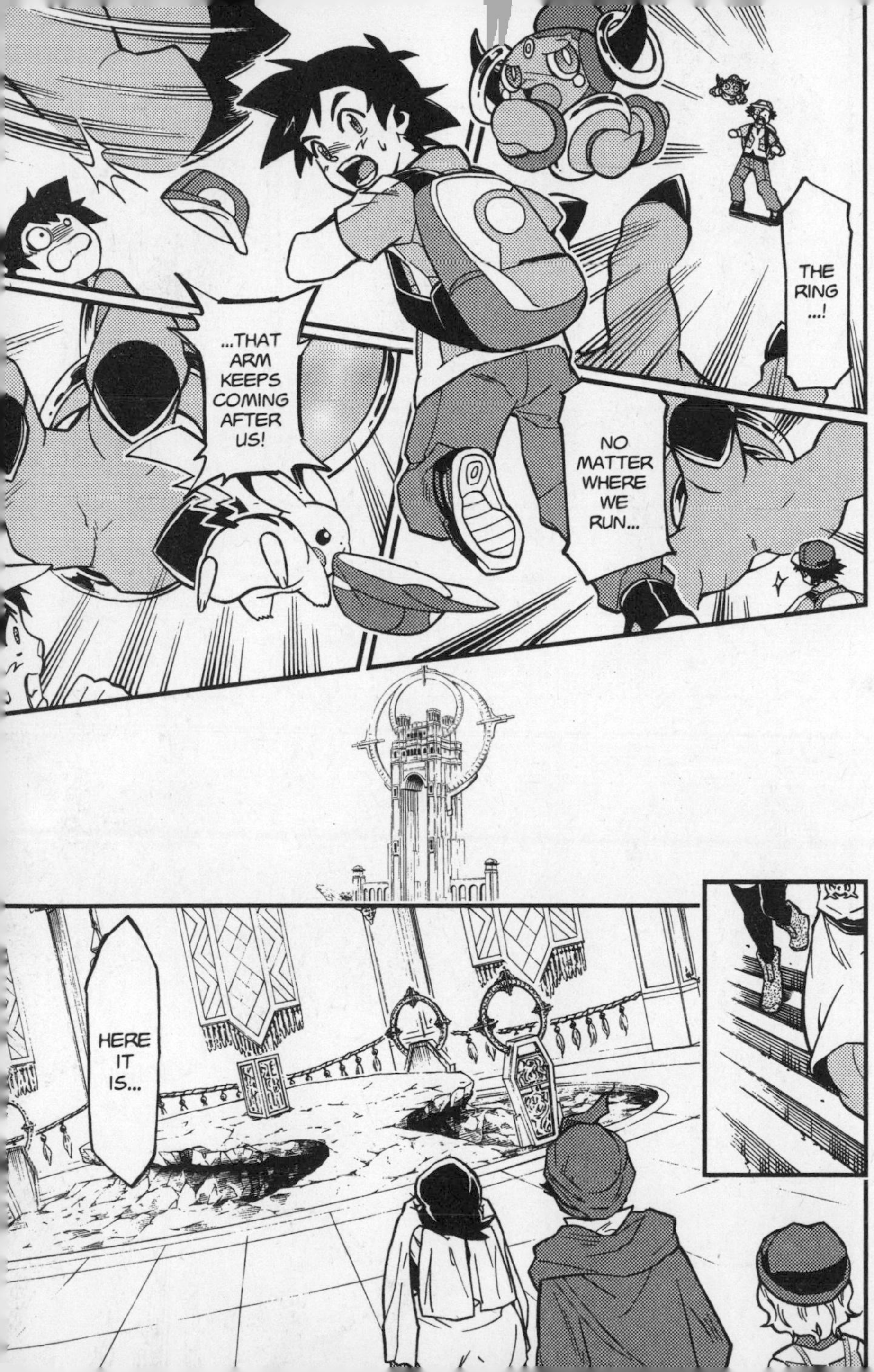
THE RING ...!
NO MATTER WHERE WE RUN...
...THAT ARM KEEPS COMING AFTER US!
HERE IT IS...

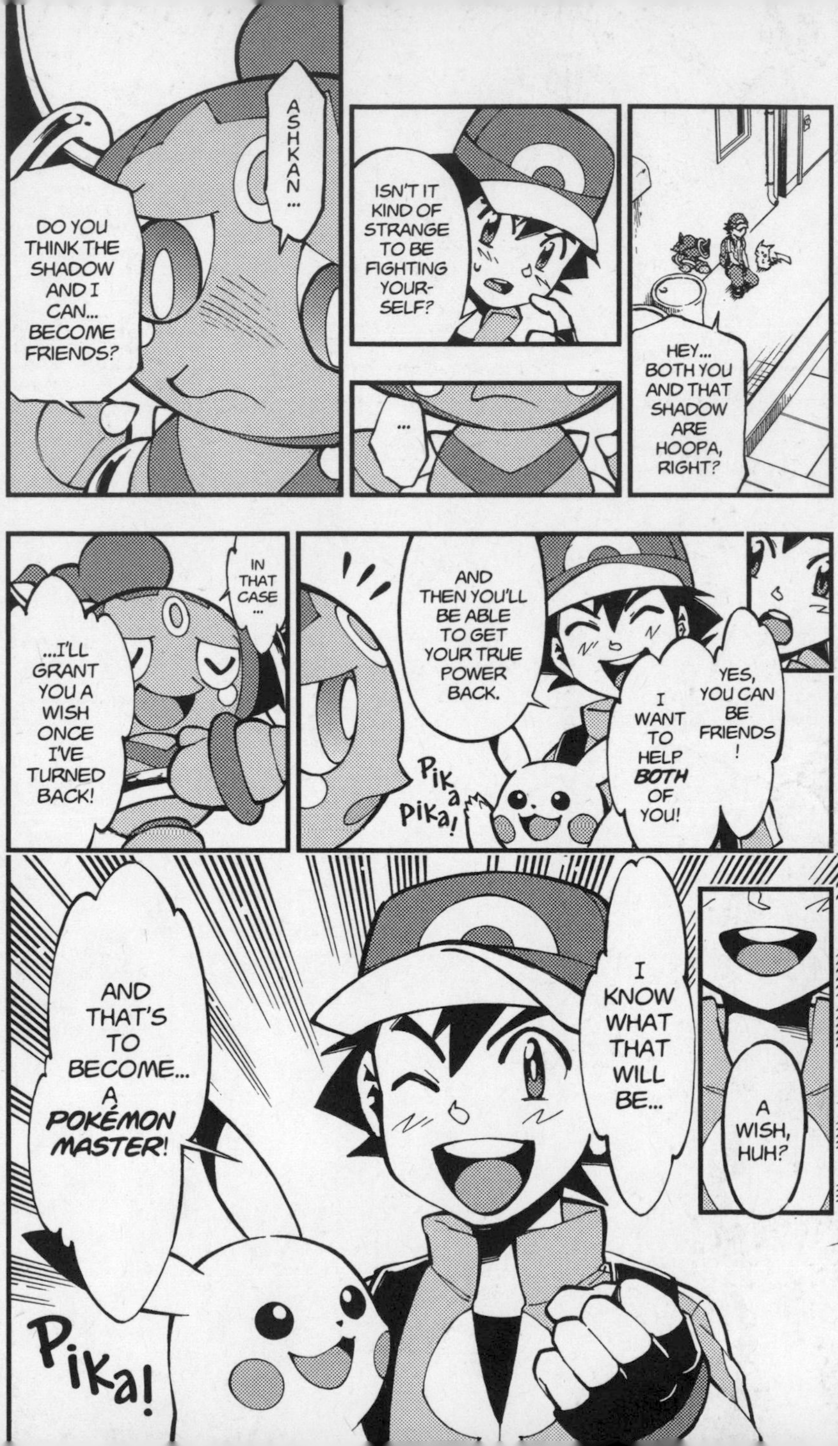
HEY... BOTH YOU AND THAT SHADOW ARE HOOPA, RIGHT?
ISN'T IT KIND OF STRANGE TO BE FIGHTING YOUR-SELF?
...
ASHKAN...
DO YOU THINK THE SHADOW AND I CAN... BECOME FRIENDS?
YES, YOU CAN BE FRIENDS!
I WANT TO HELP **BOTH** OF YOU!
AND THEN YOU'LL BE ABLE TO GET YOUR TRUE POWER BACK.
Pika pika!
IN THAT CASE...
...I'LL GRANT YOU A WISH ONCE I'VE TURNED BACK!
A WISH, HUH?
I KNOW WHAT THAT WILL BE...
AND THAT'S TO BECOME... A ***POKÉMON MASTER***!
Pika!

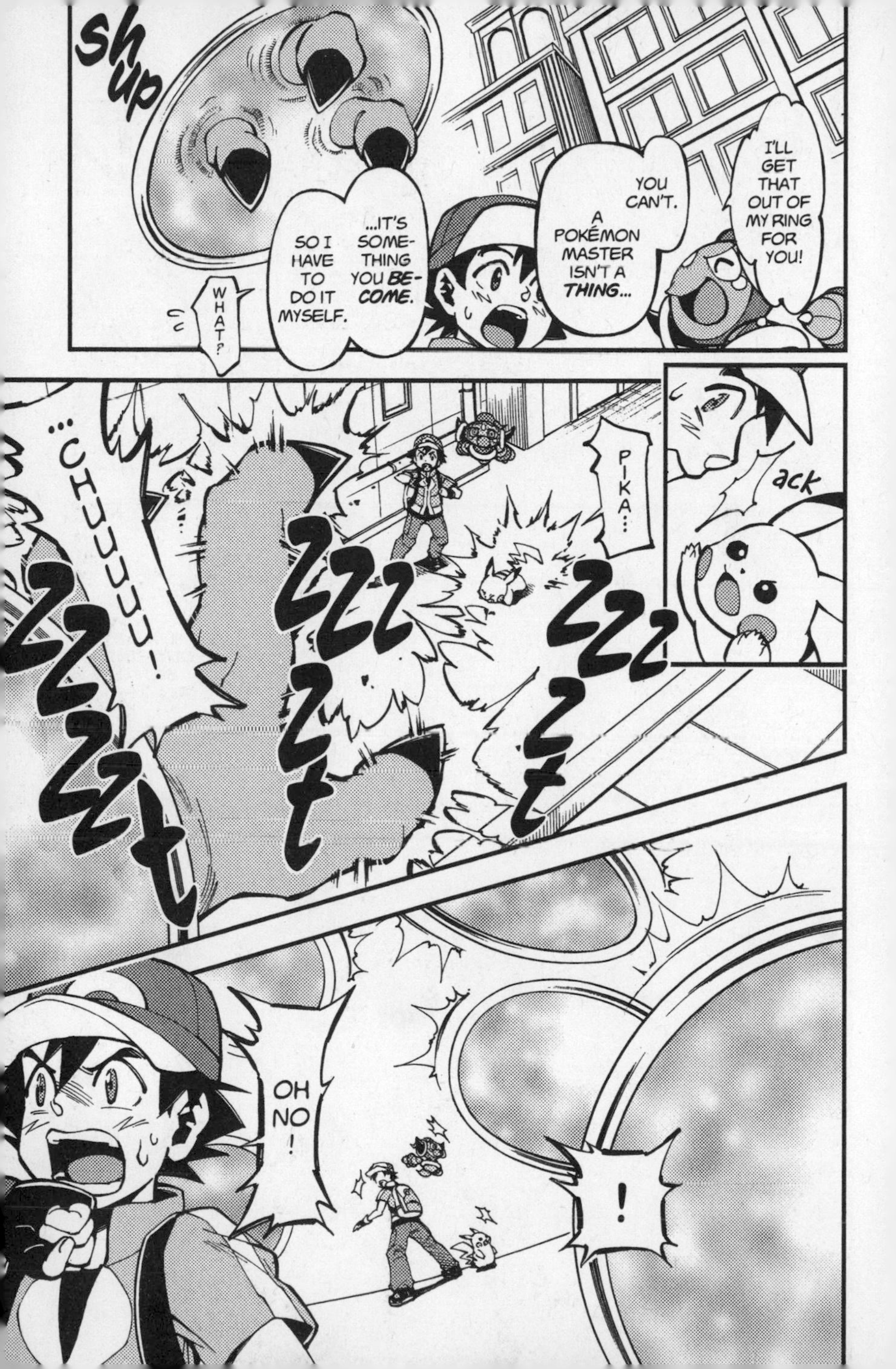
I'LL GET THAT OUT OF MY RING FOR YOU!
YOU CAN'T. A POKÉMON MASTER ISN'T A THING...
...IT'S SOME-THING YOU BE-COME.
SO I HAVE TO DO IT MYSELF.
WHAT?
shup
ack
PIKA...
ZZZZt
...CHUUUUU!
ZZZZt
ZZZZt
!
OH NO!

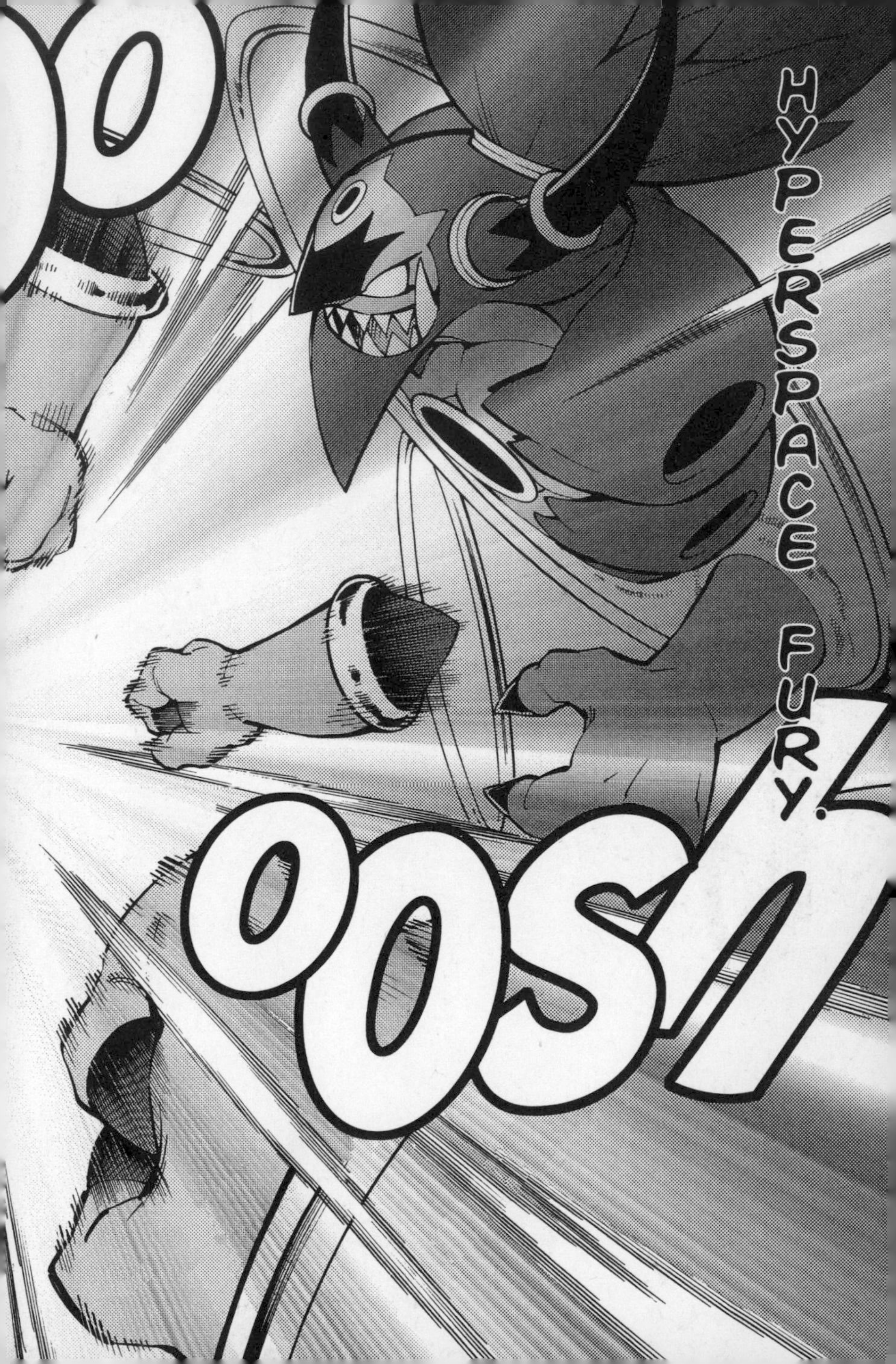
HYPERSPACE FURY!
OOSH

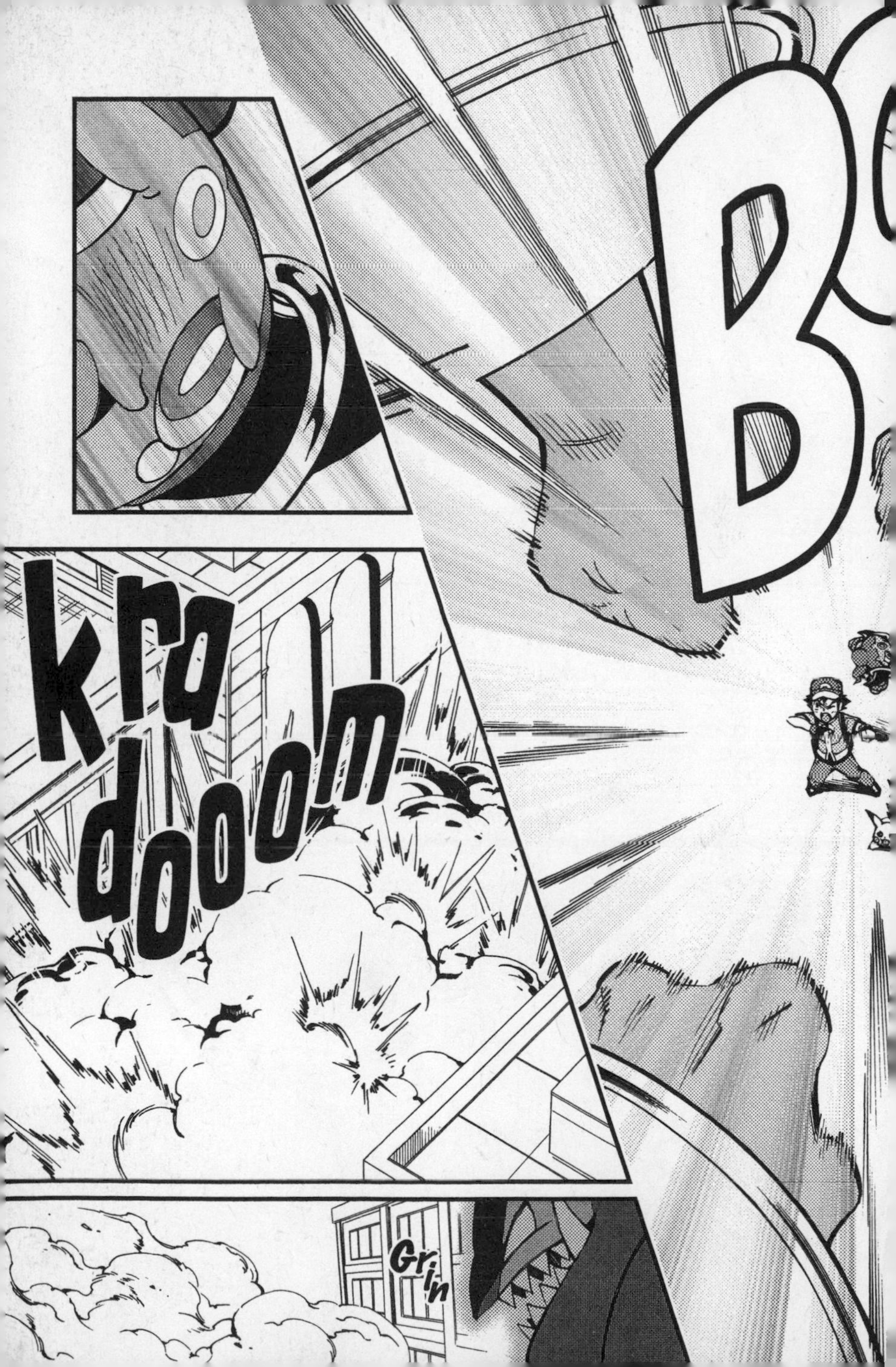
BO
kra dooooom
Grin

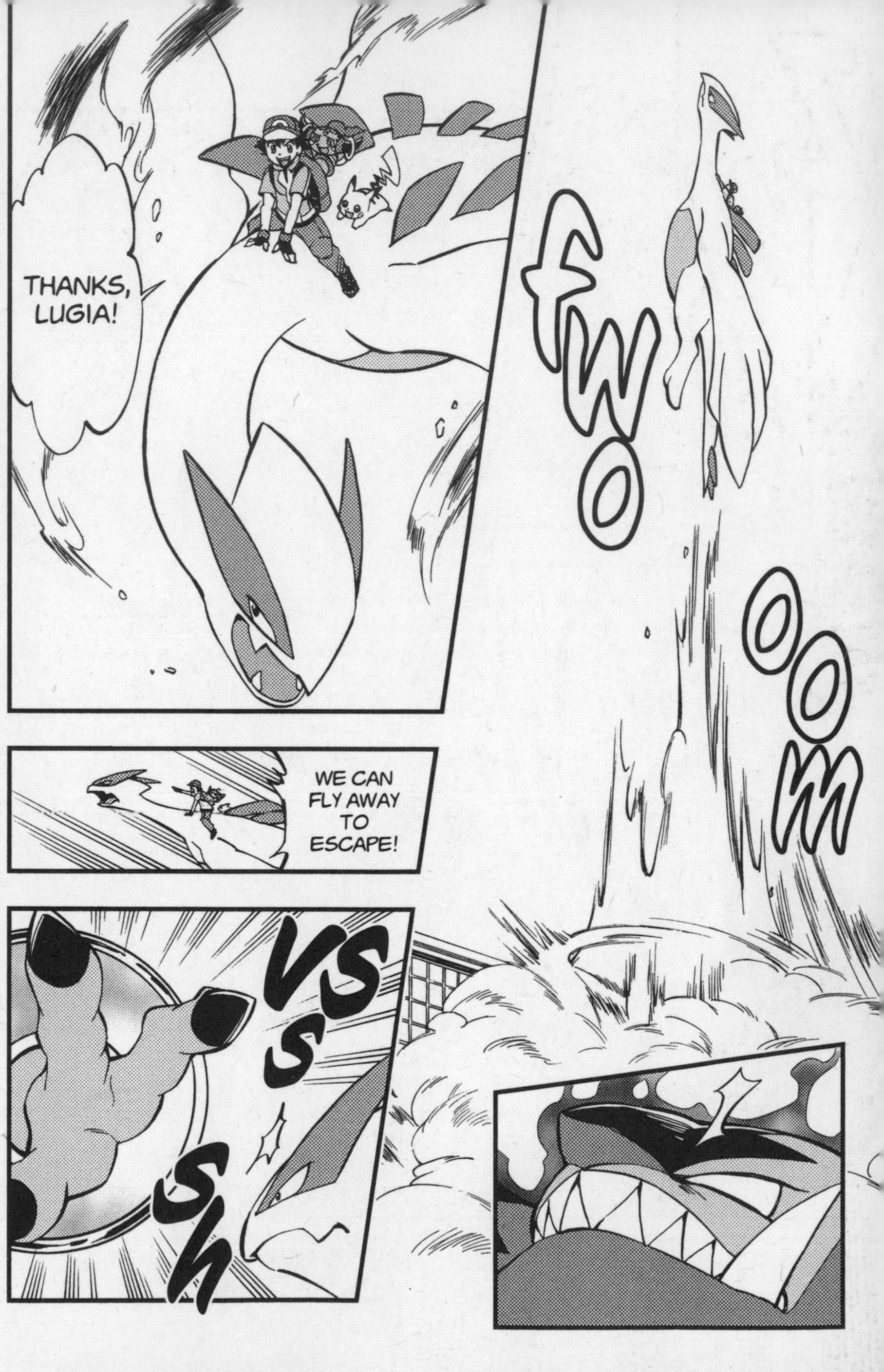
FWOOOM
THANKS, LUGIA!
WE CAN FLY AWAY TO ESCAPE!
VSSSH

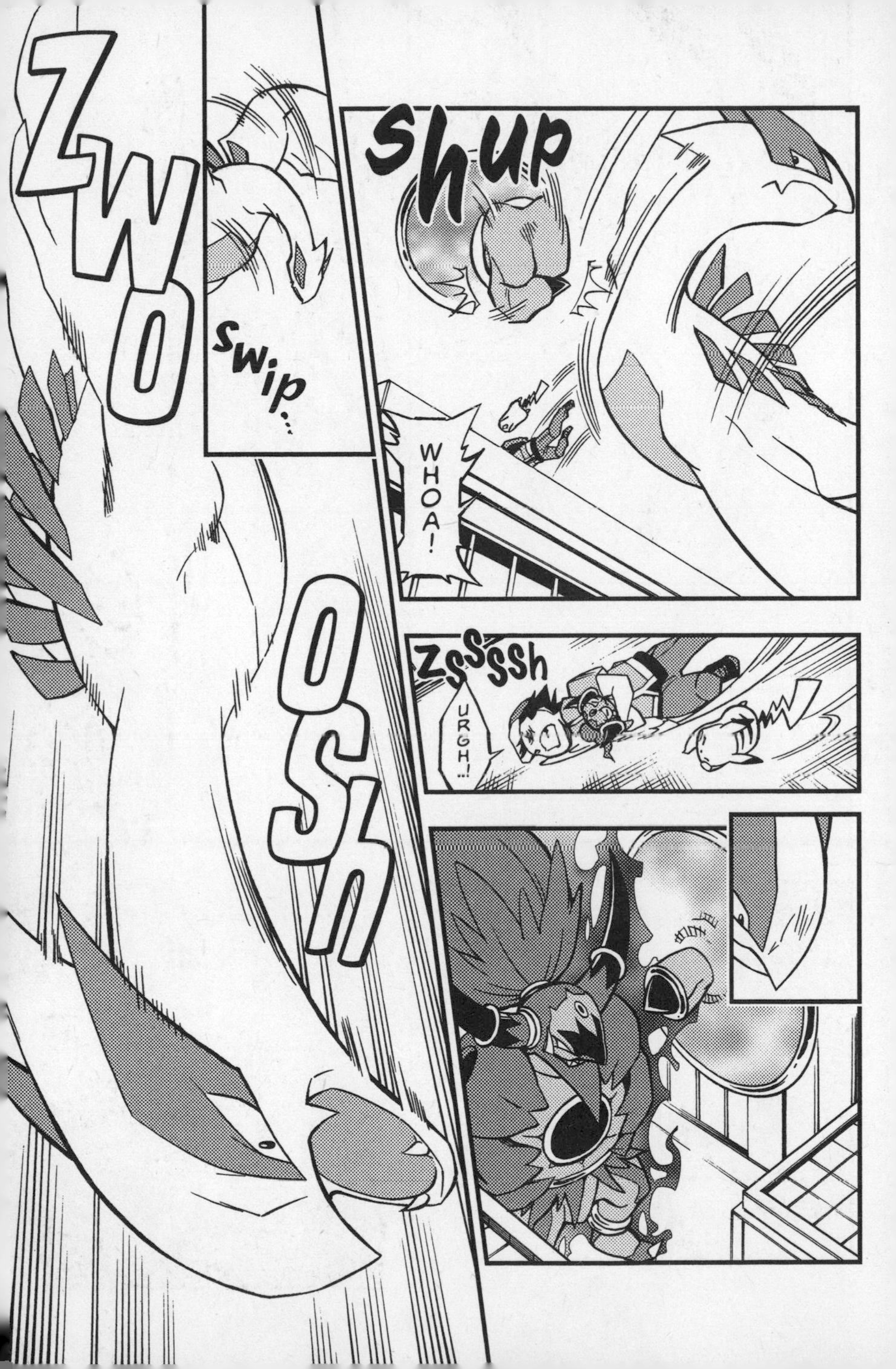
SHUP
WHOA!
ZSSSSH
URGH..!
SWIP...
ZWOOSH

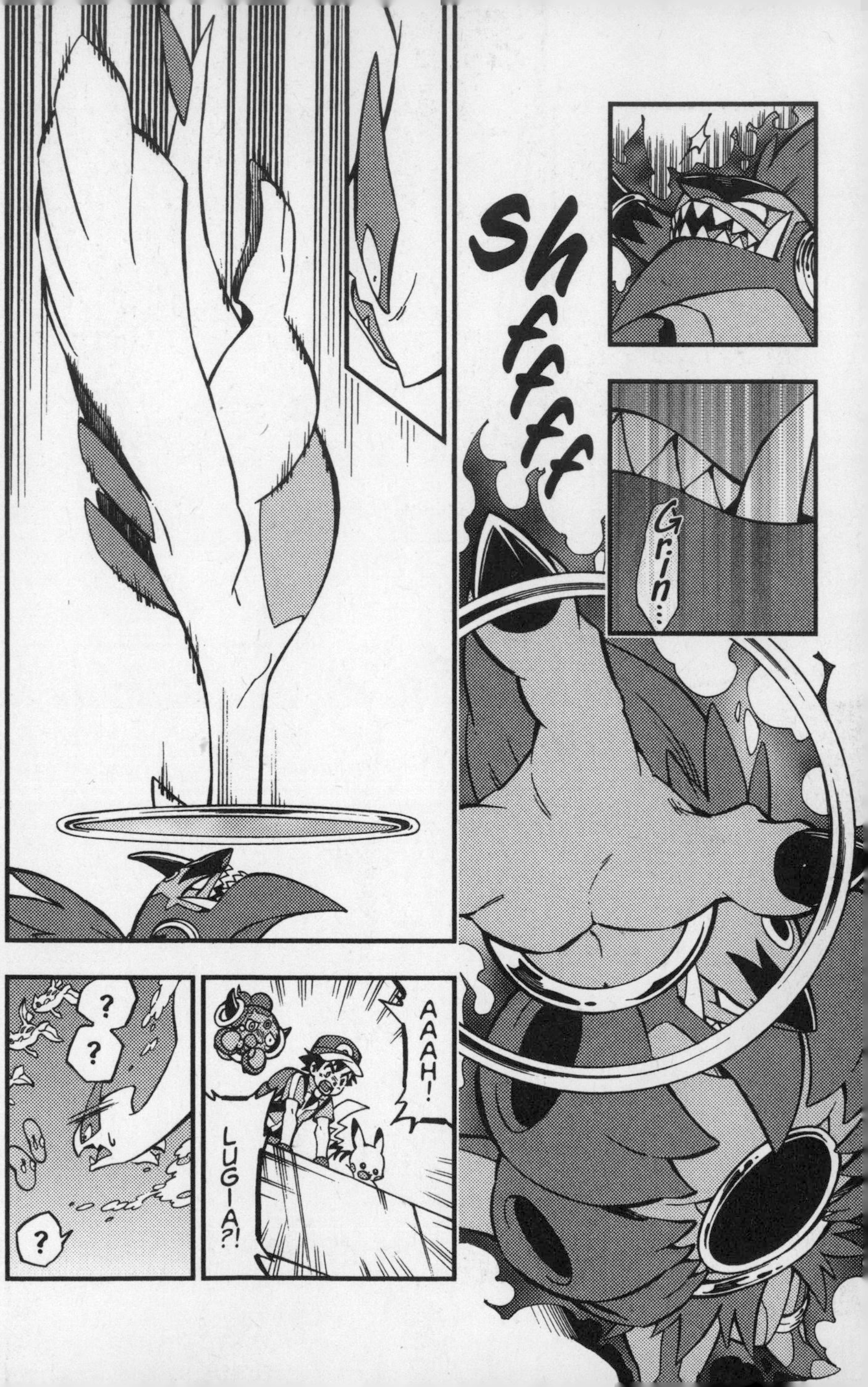

Shffff
Grin...
AAAH!
LUGIA?!
?
?
?

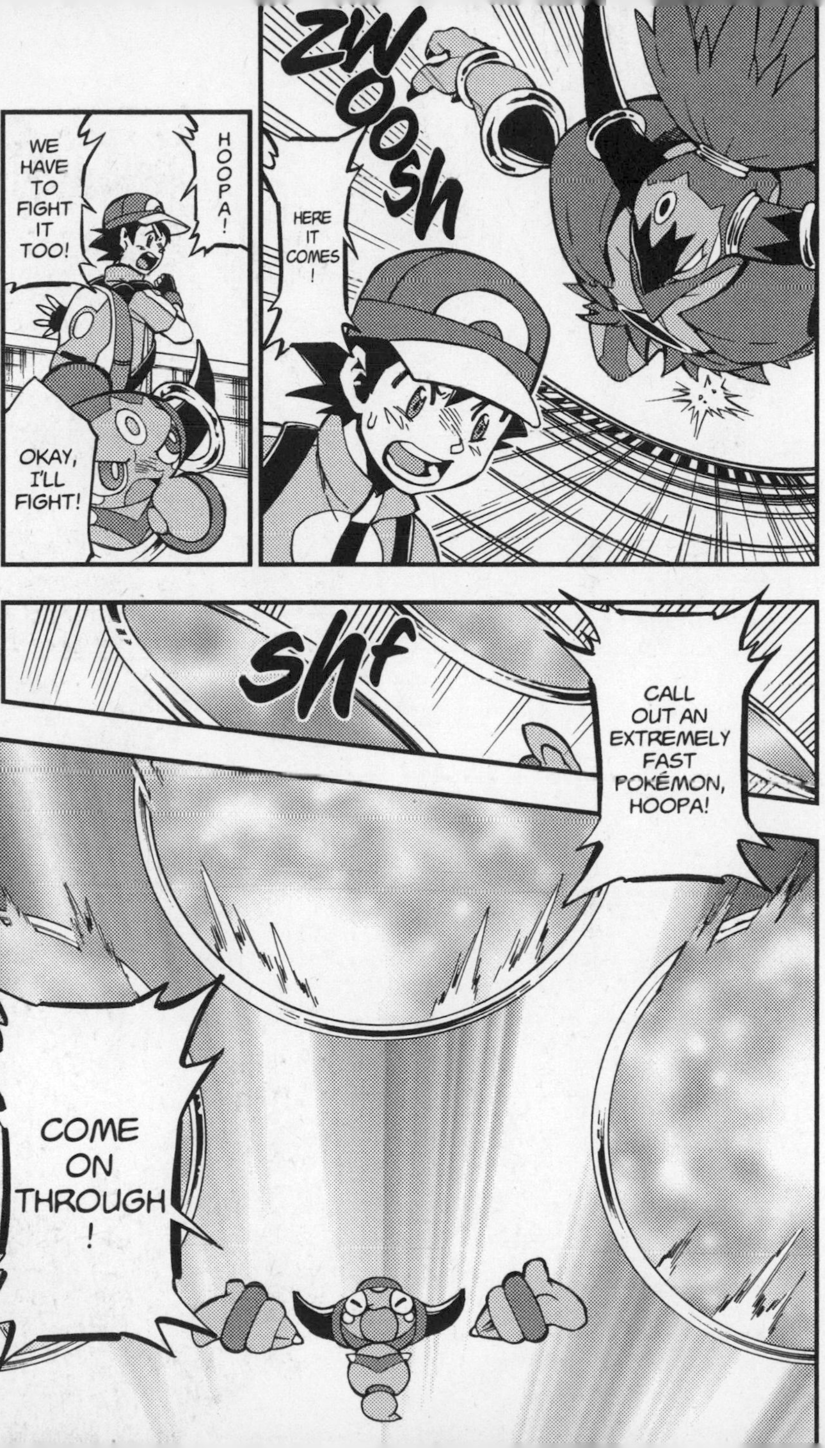
ZWOOSH
HERE IT COMES!
HOOPA!
WE HAVE TO FIGHT IT TOO!
OKAY, I'LL FIGHT!
SHF
CALL OUT AN EXTREMELY FAST POKÉMON, HOOPA!
COME ON THROUGH!

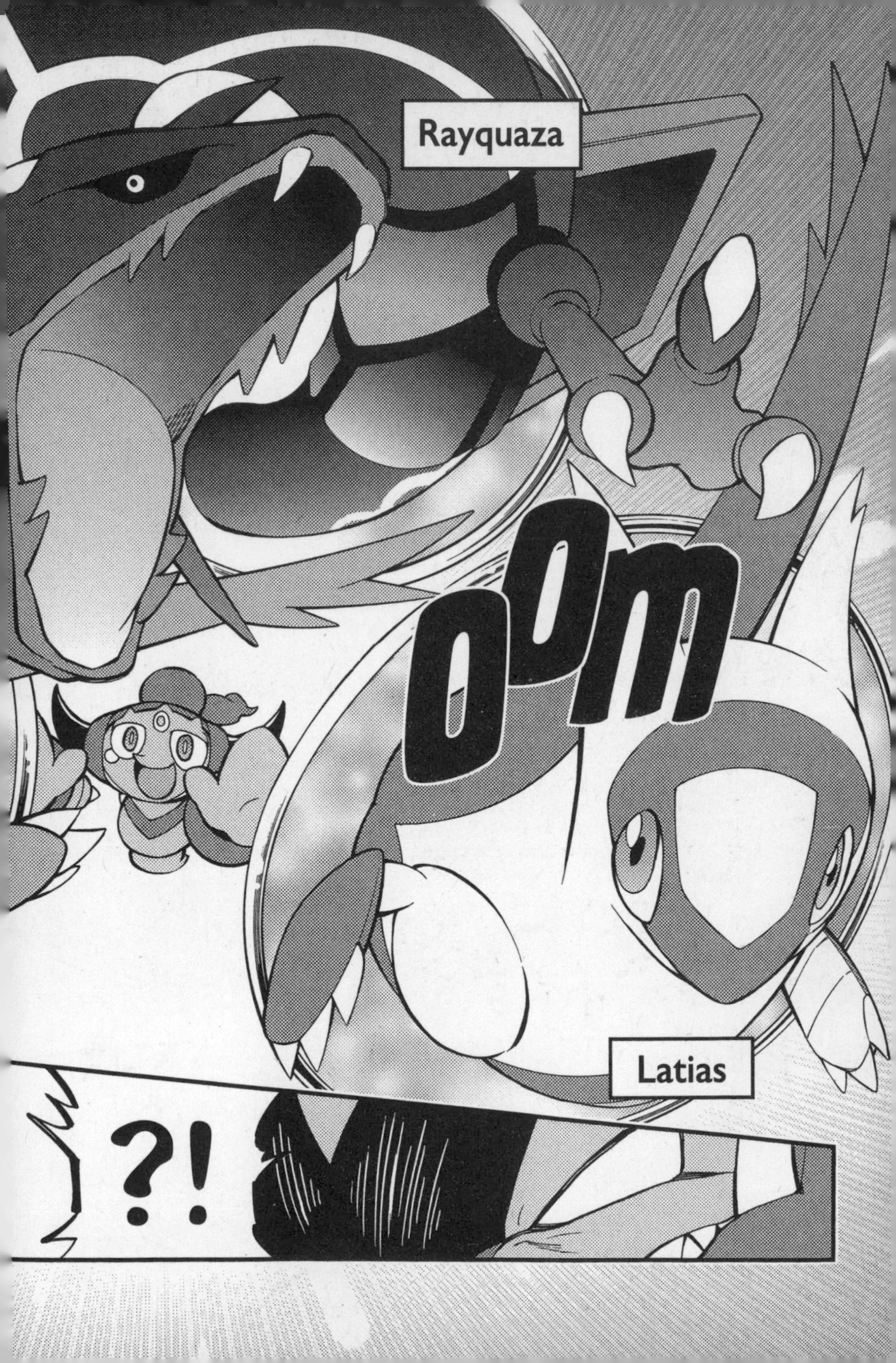
Rayquaza
OOM
Latias
?!

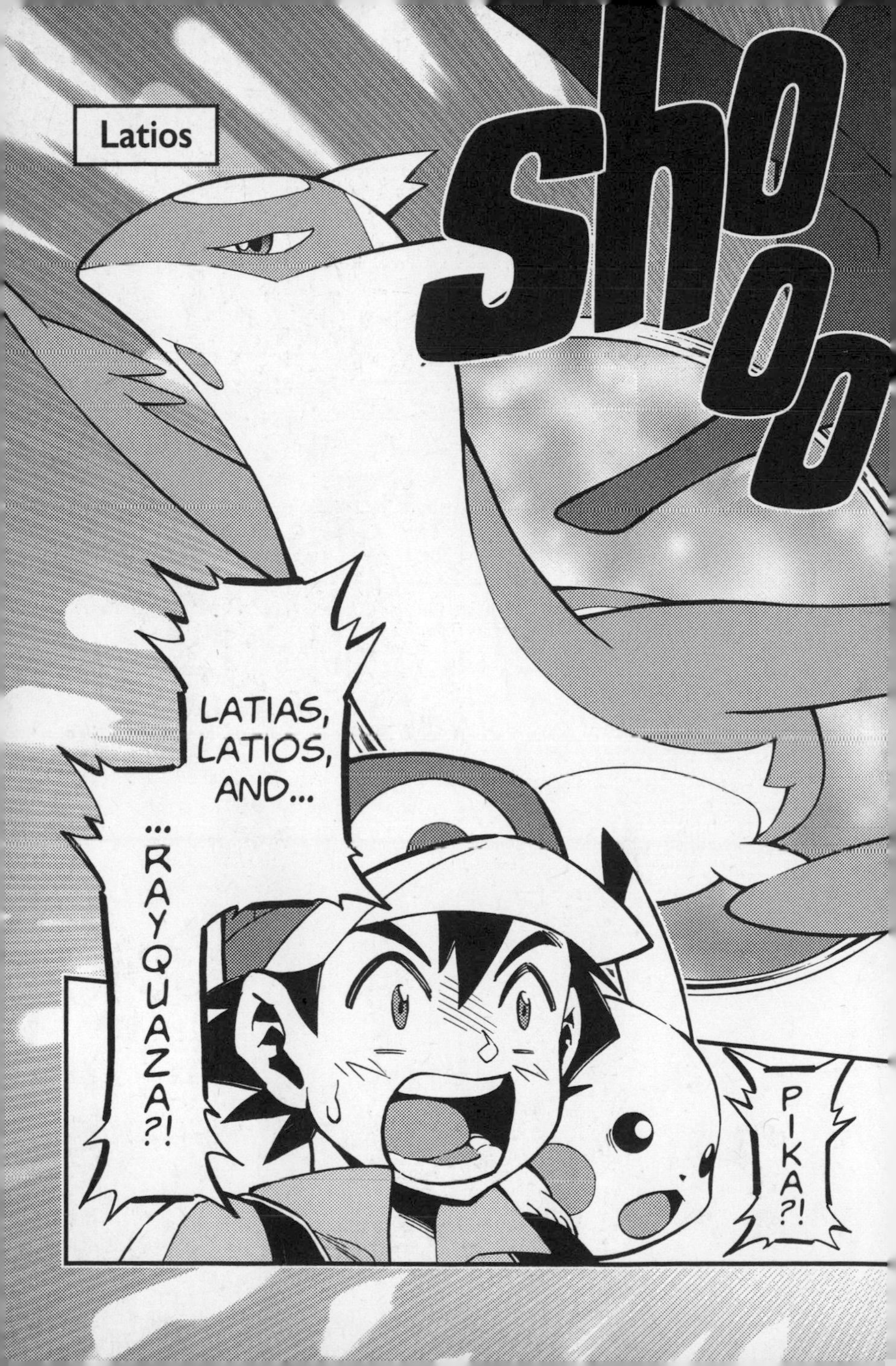

Latios
SHOOOO
LATIAS, LATIOS, AND...
...RAYQUAZA?!
PIKA?!

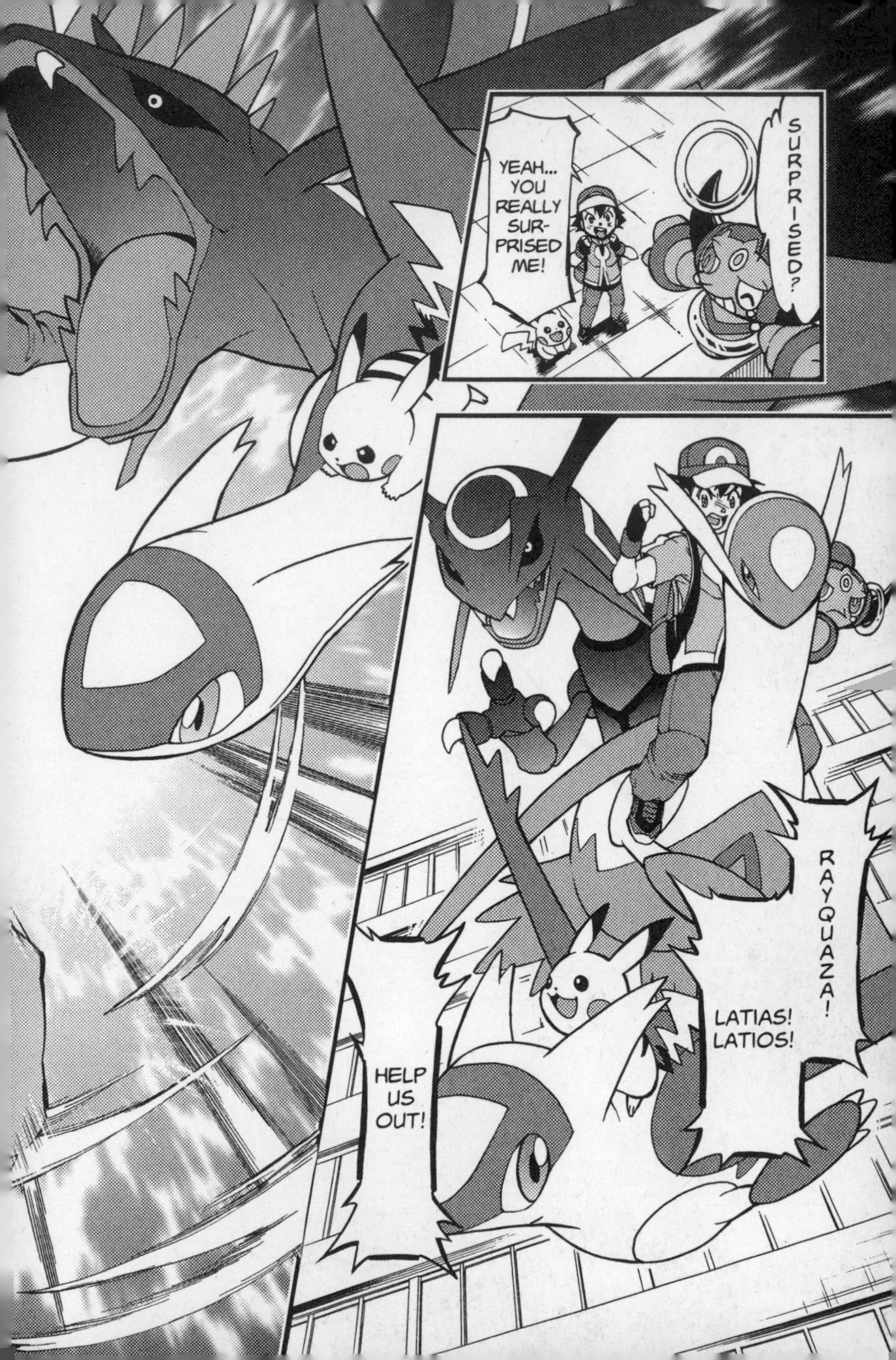
SURPRISED?
YEAH... YOU REALLY SUR-PRISED ME!
RAYQUAZA!
LATIAS! LATIOS!
HELP US OUT!

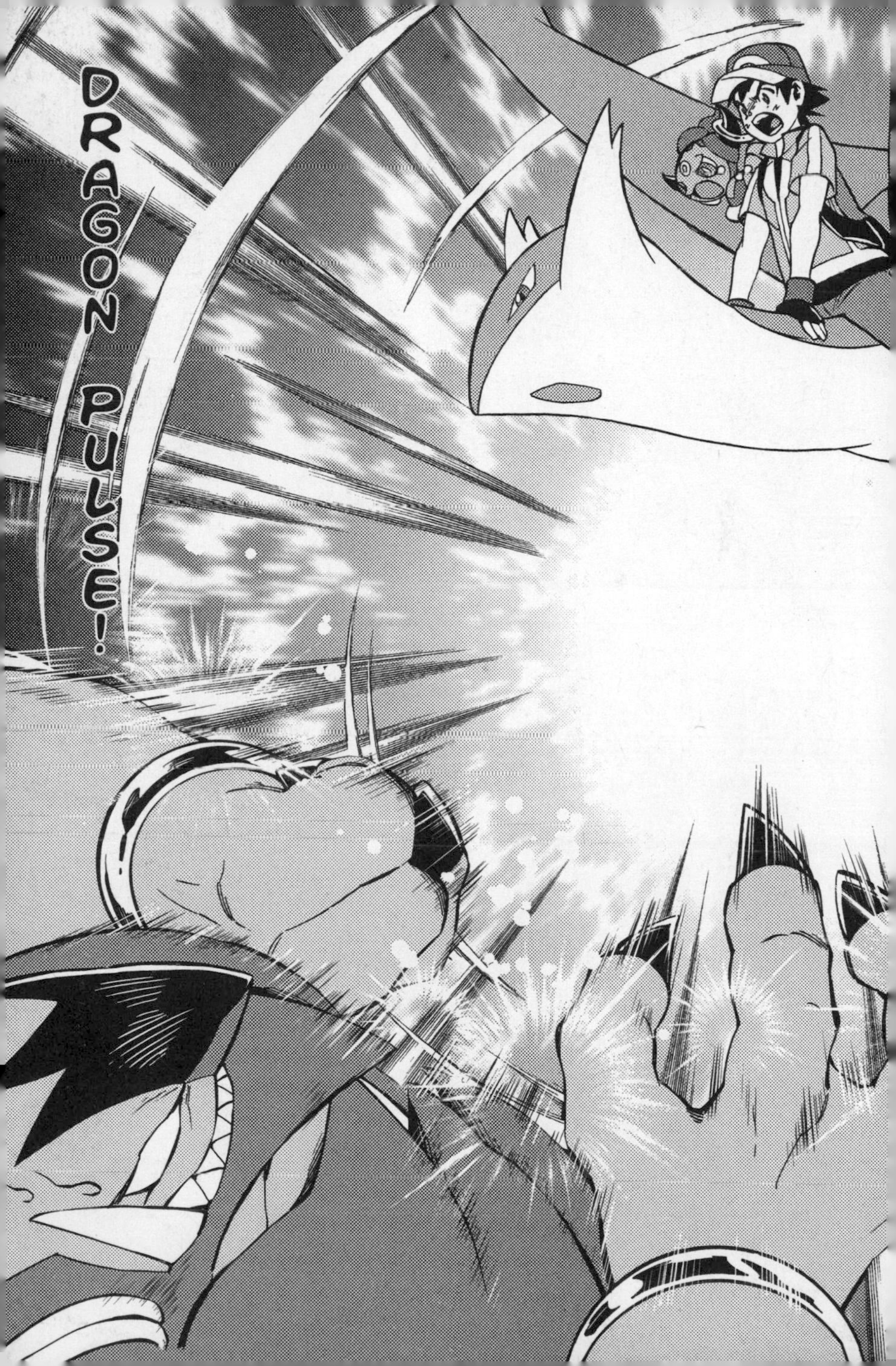
DRAGON PULSE!

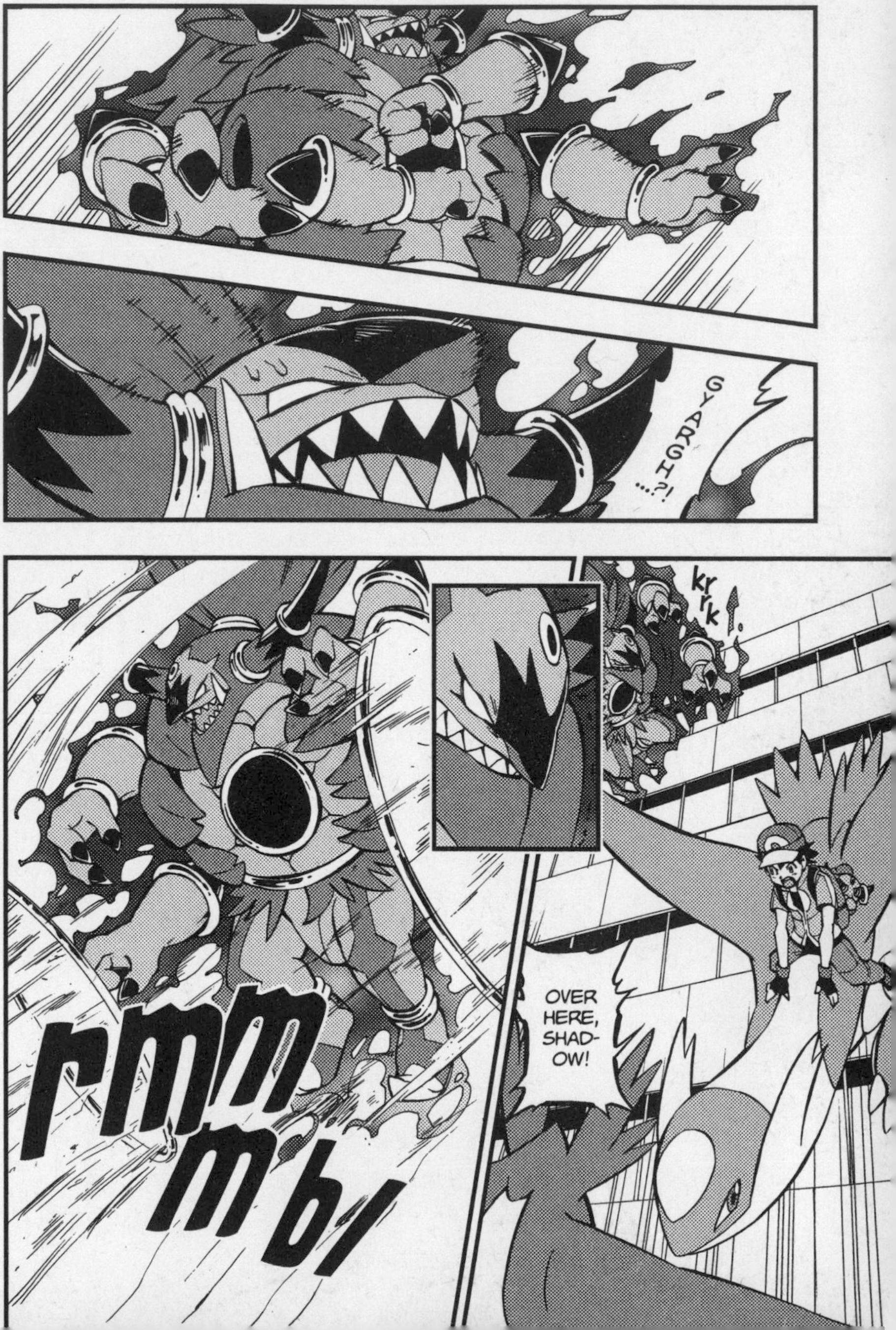
GYARGH...?!
krrk!
OVER HERE, SHADOW!
rmmmb!

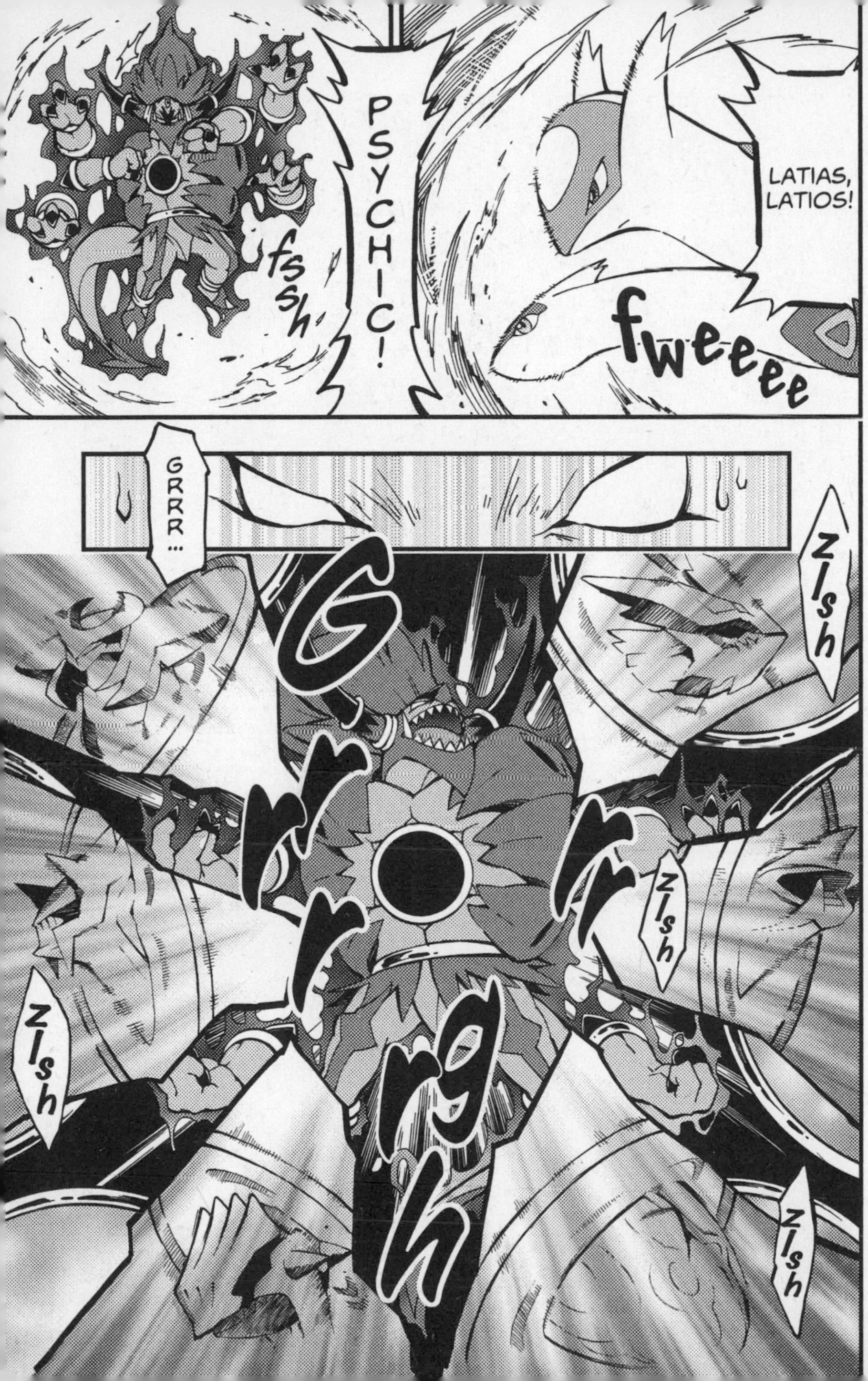
LATIAS, LATIOS!
fweeeee
PSYCHIC!
fssh
GRRR...
ZIsh
Grrrgh
ZIsh
ZIsh
ZIsh

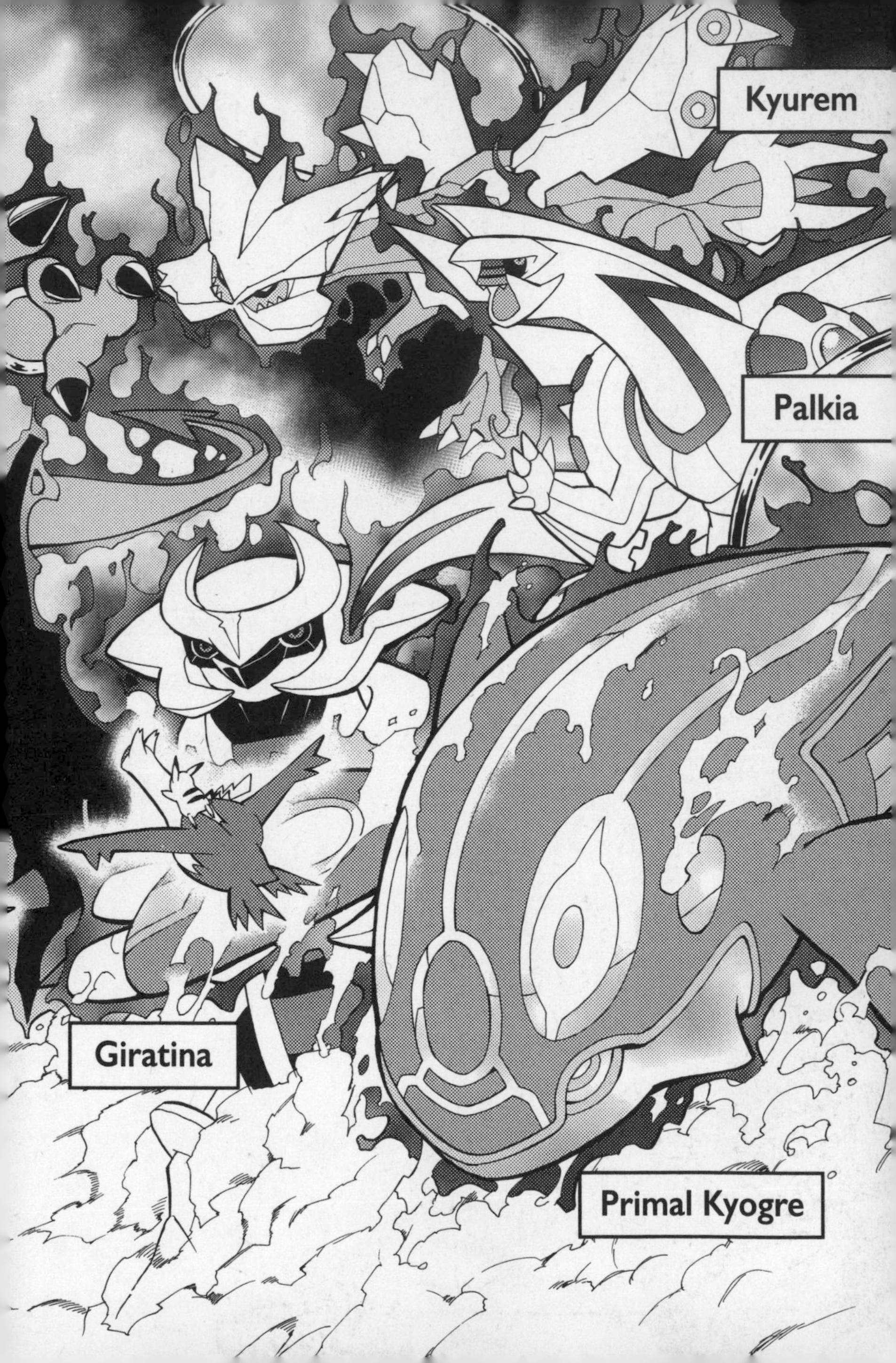
Kyurem
Palkia
Giratina
Primal Kyogre

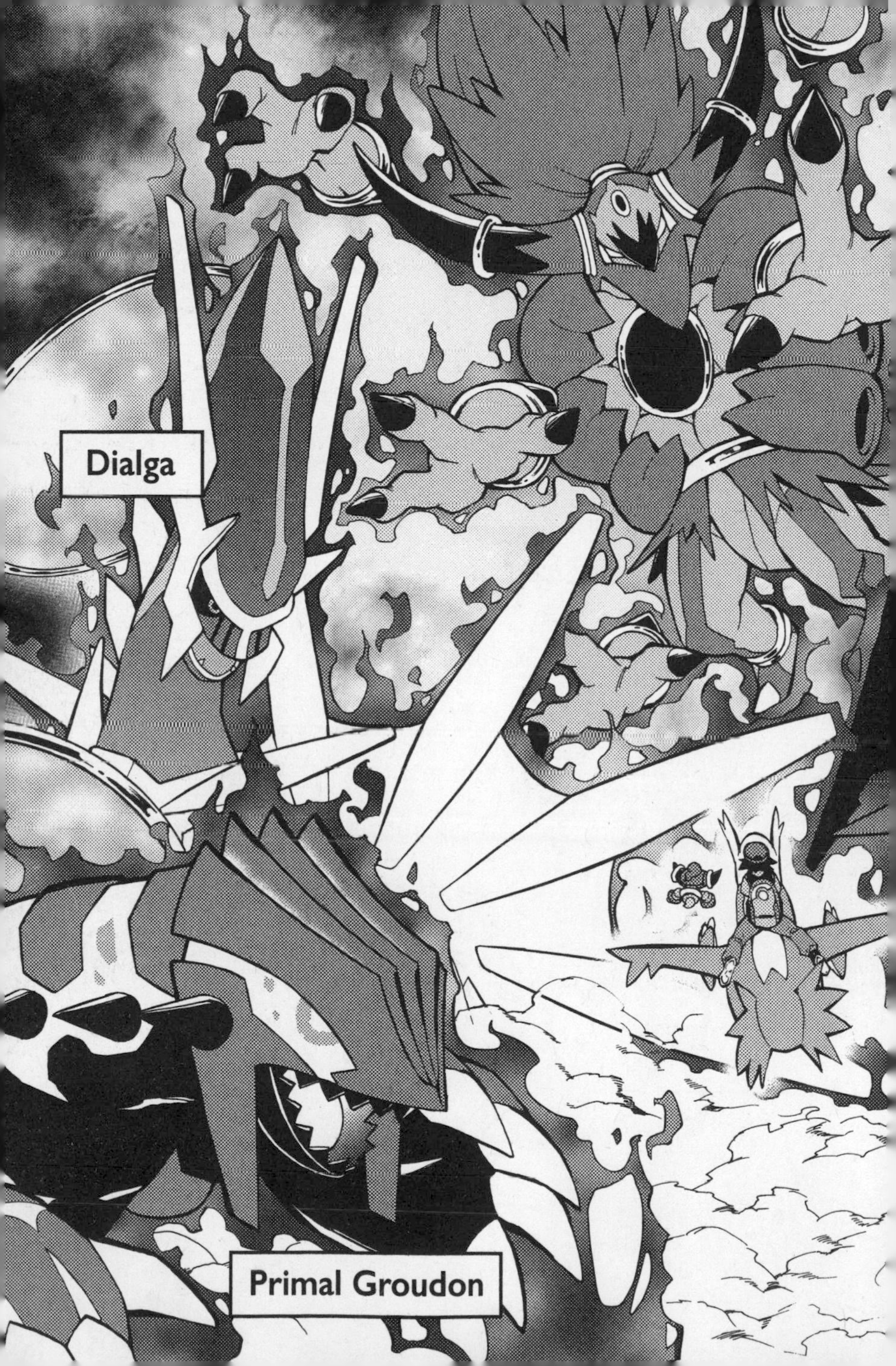
Dialga
Primal Groudon

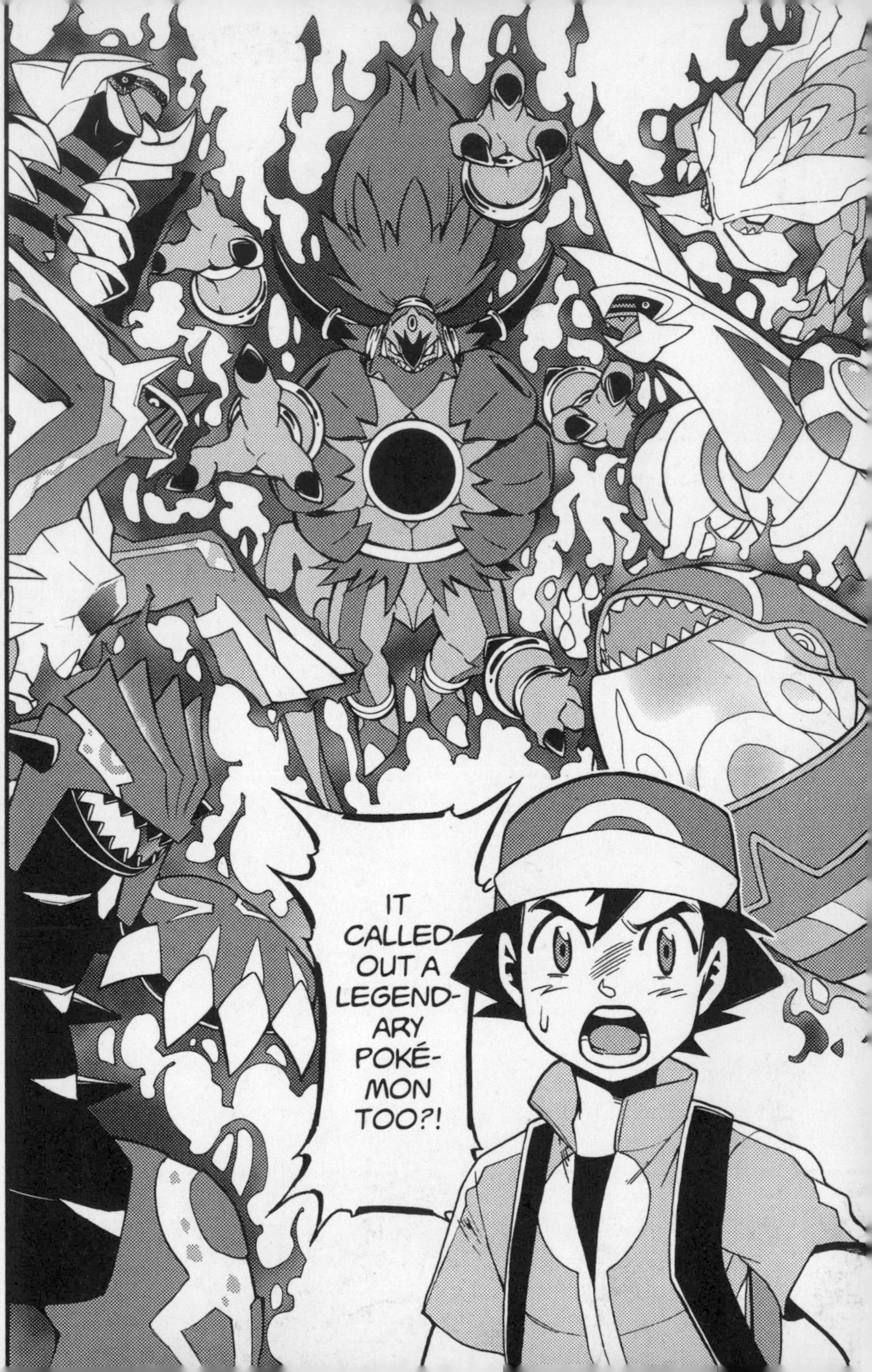
IT CALLED OUT A LEGEND-ARY POKÉ-MON TOO?!

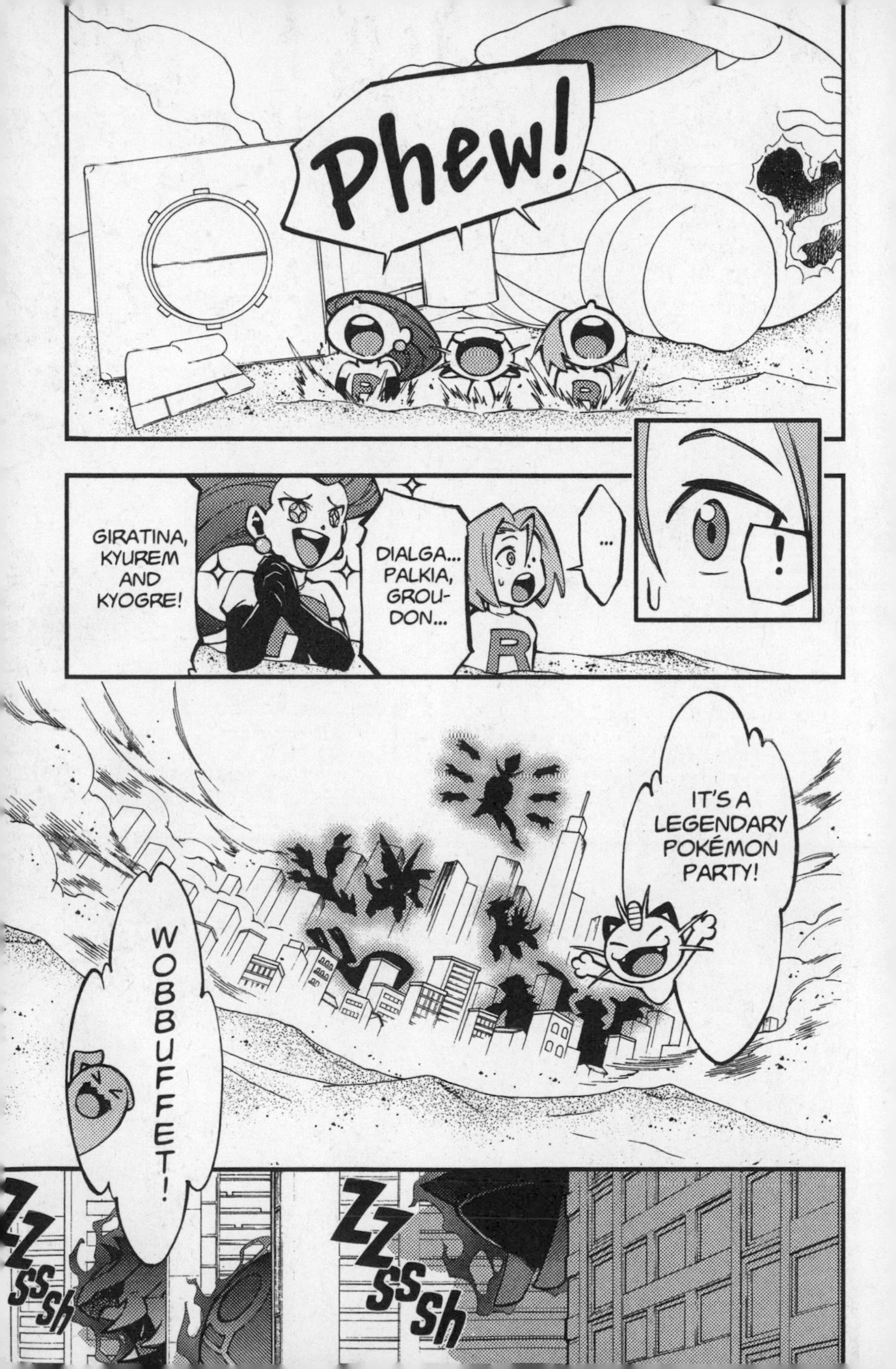
Phew!
!
...
DIALGA... PALKIA, GROU-DON...
GIRATINA, KYUREM AND KYOGRE!
IT'S A LEGENDARY POKÉMON PARTY!
WOBBUFFET!
ZZSSSh
ZZSSSh

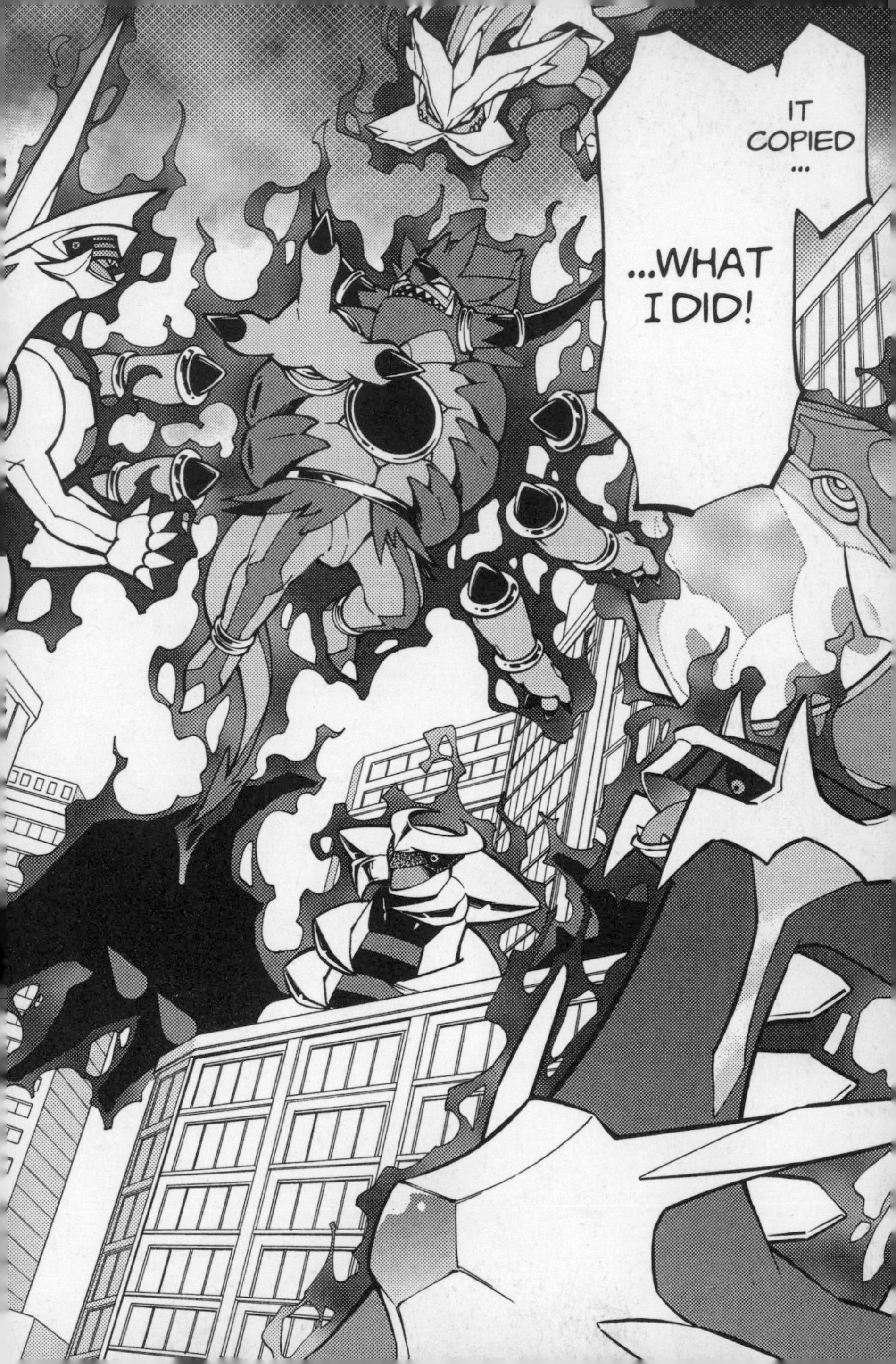
IT COPIED ...
...WHAT I DID!

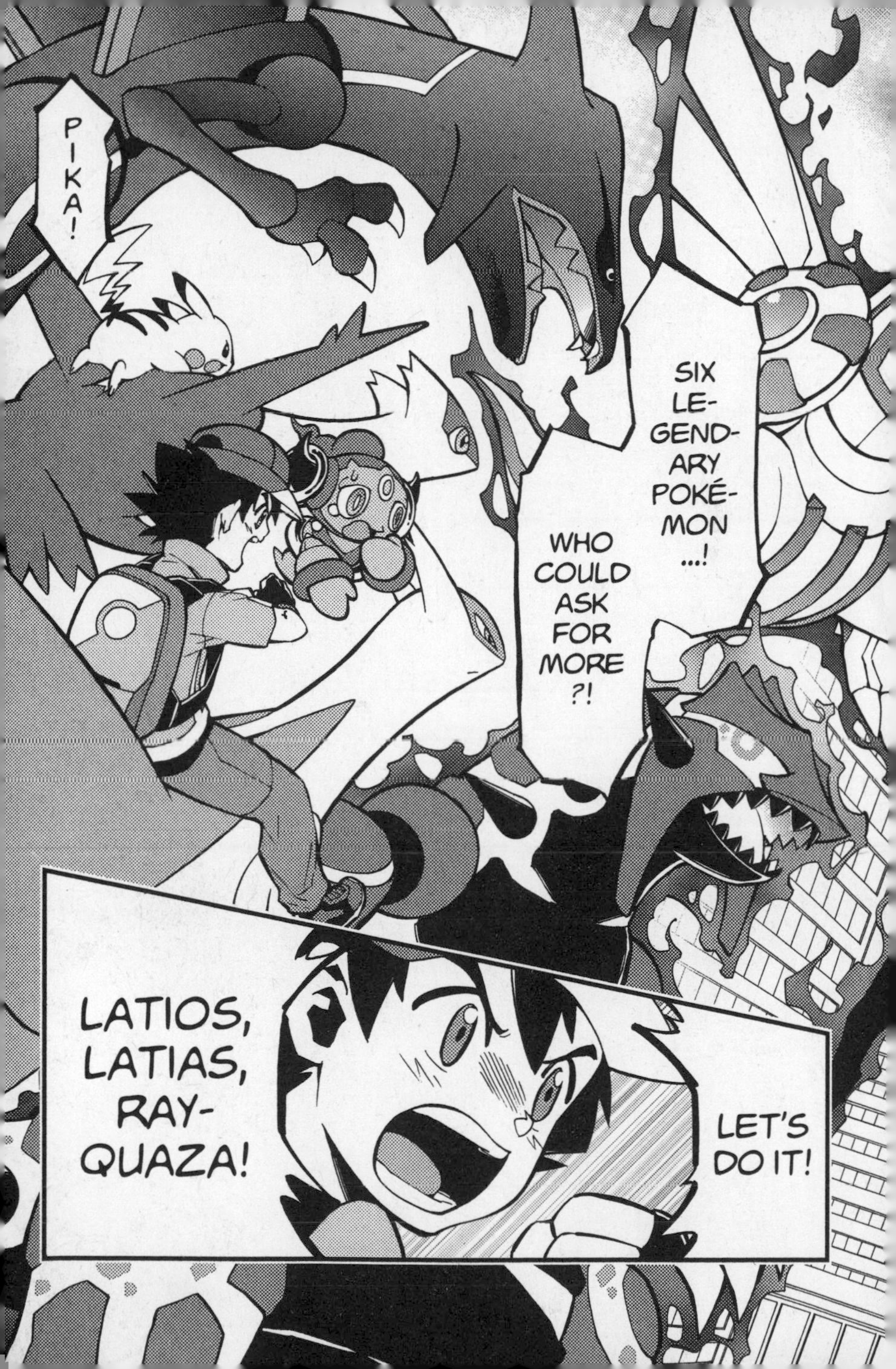
SIX LE- GEND- ARY POKÉ- MON ...!
WHO COULD ASK FOR MORE ?!
PIKA!
LATIOS, LATIAS, RAY- QUAZA!
LET'S DO IT!

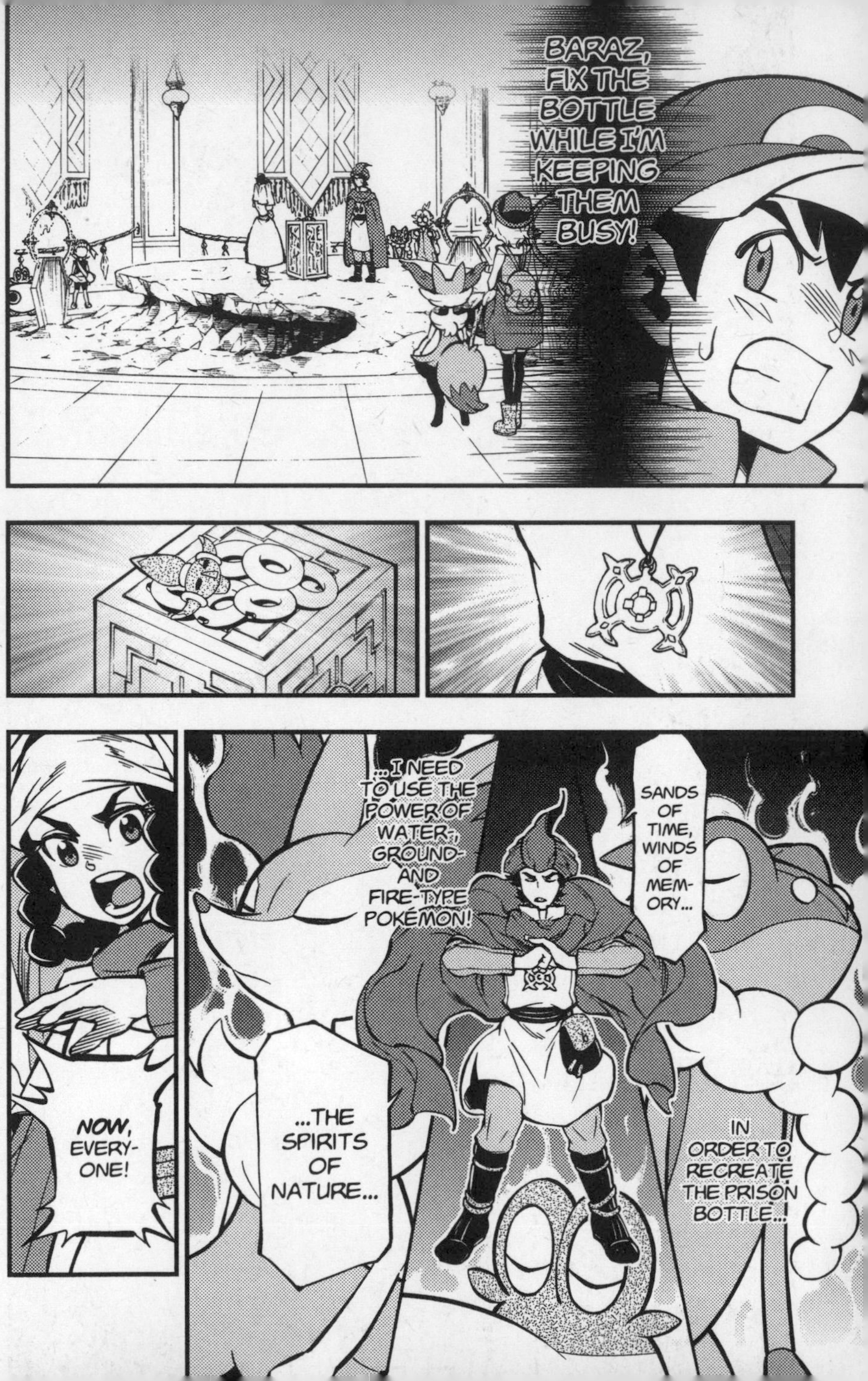
BARAZ, FIX THE BOTTLE WHILE I'M KEEPING THEM BUSY!
SANDS OF TIME, WINDS OF MEM-ORY...
...I NEED TO USE THE POWER OF WATER-, GROUND- AND FIRE-TYPE POKÉMON!
IN ORDER TO RECREATE THE PRISON BOTTLE...
...THE SPIRITS OF NATURE...
NOW, EVERY-ONE!

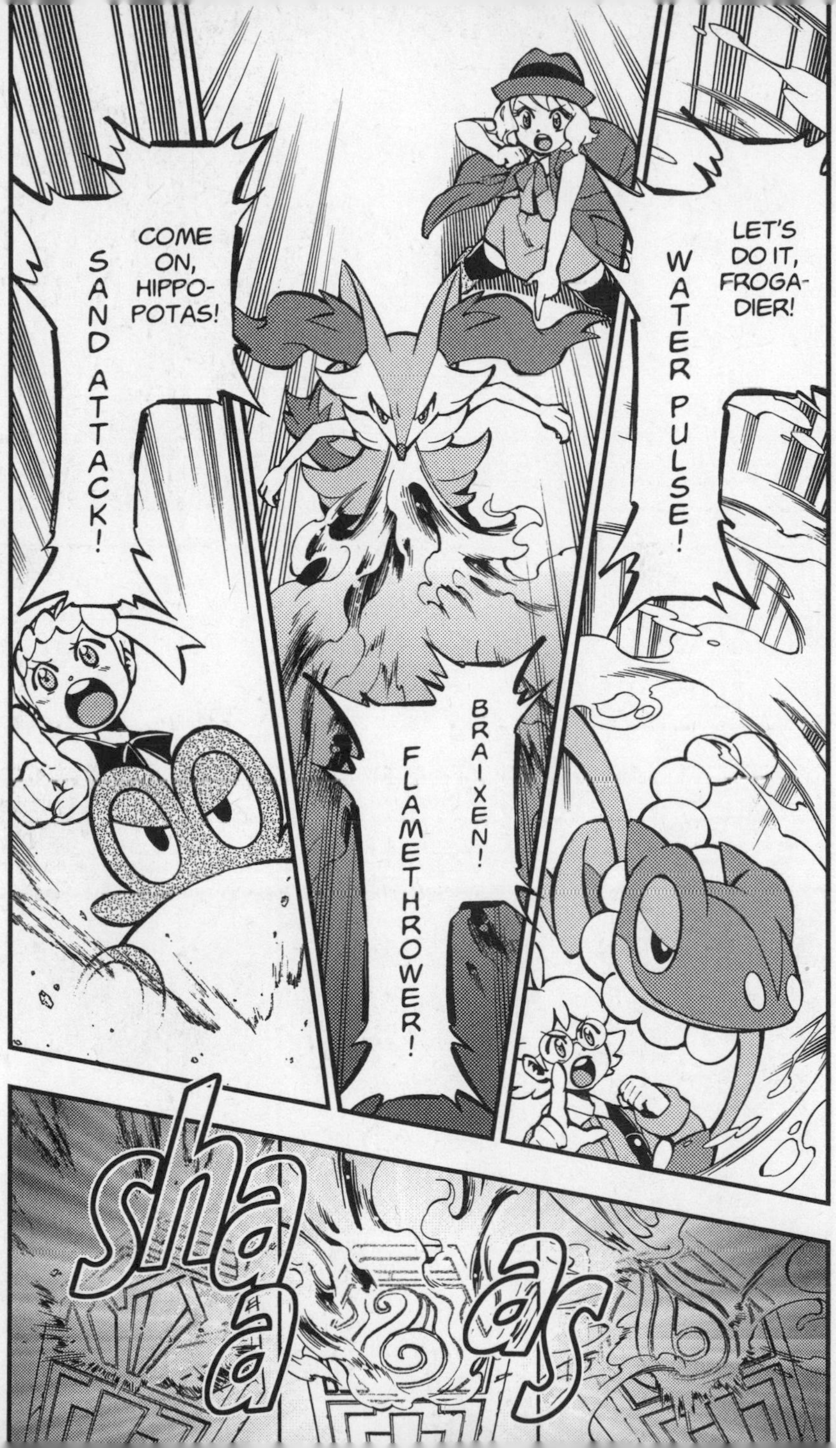
LET'S DO IT, FROGADIER!
WATER PULSE!
BRAIXEN!
FLAMETHROWER!
COME ON, HIPPOPOTAS!
SAND ATTACK!
shaaaas

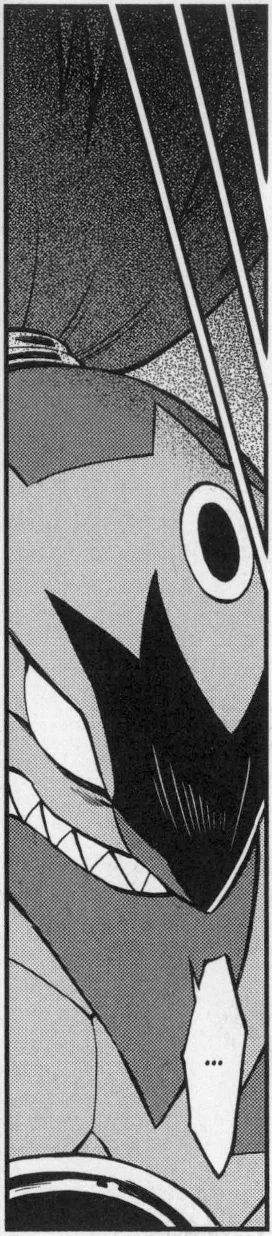
...

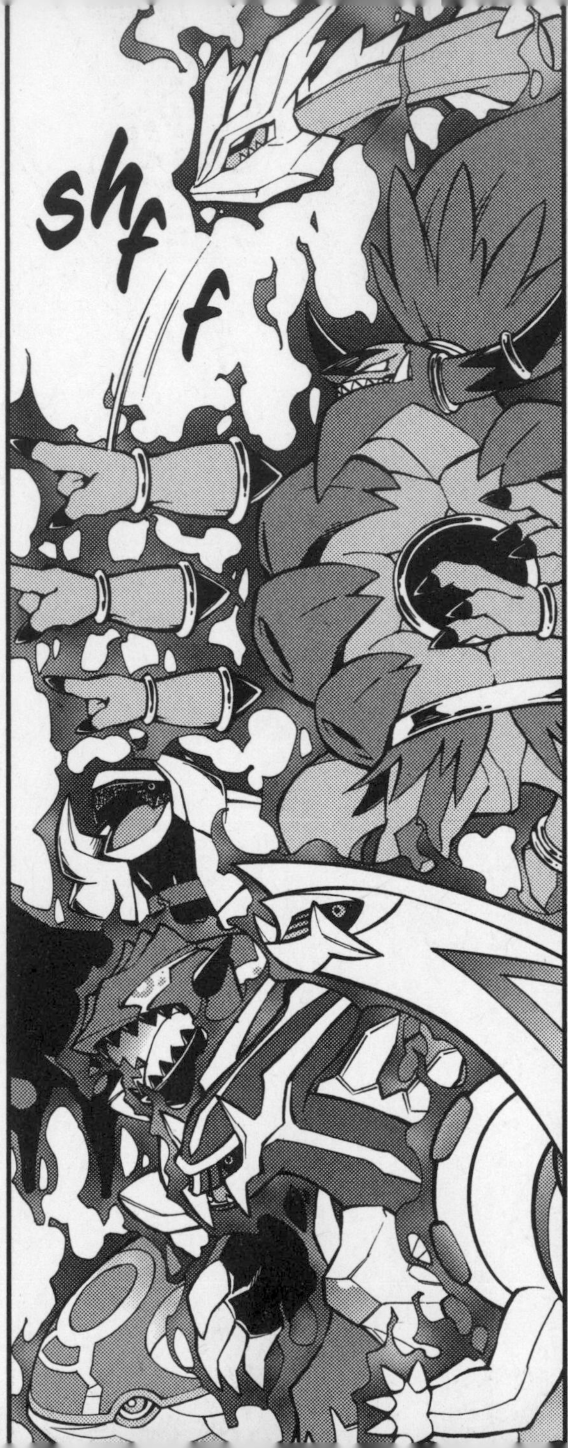
shf f

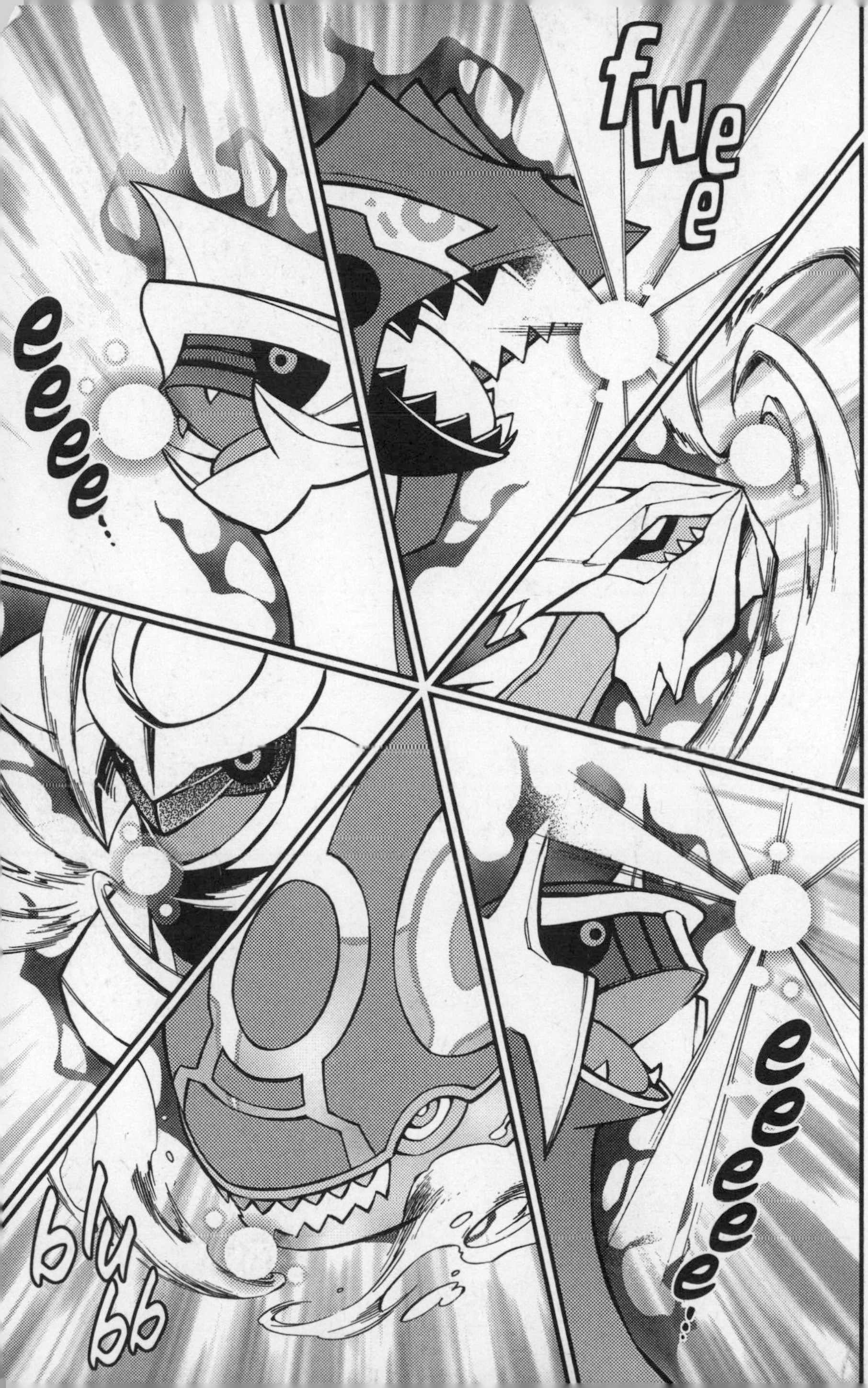
fweee
eeee...
eeeee...
blubb

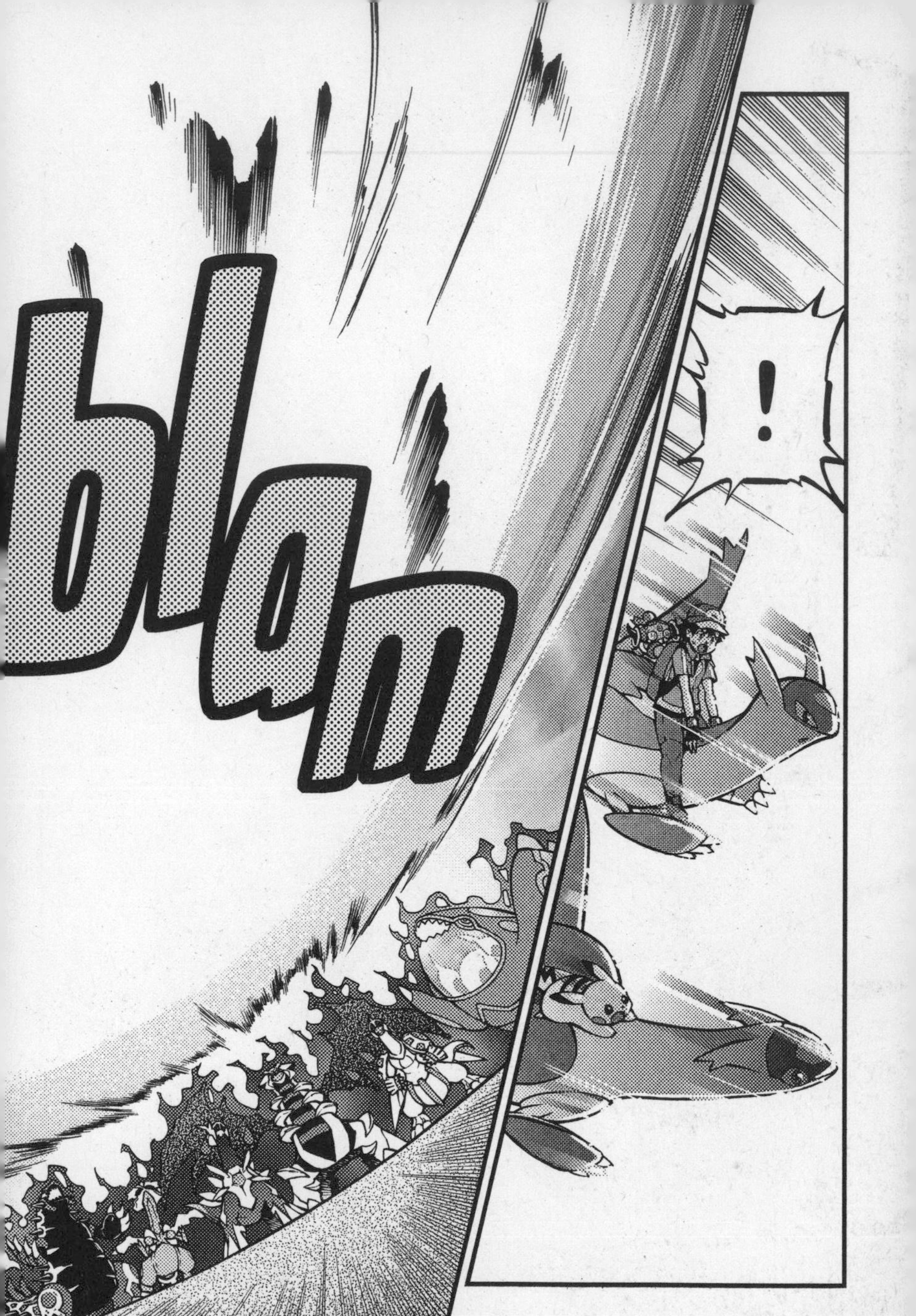
!
blam

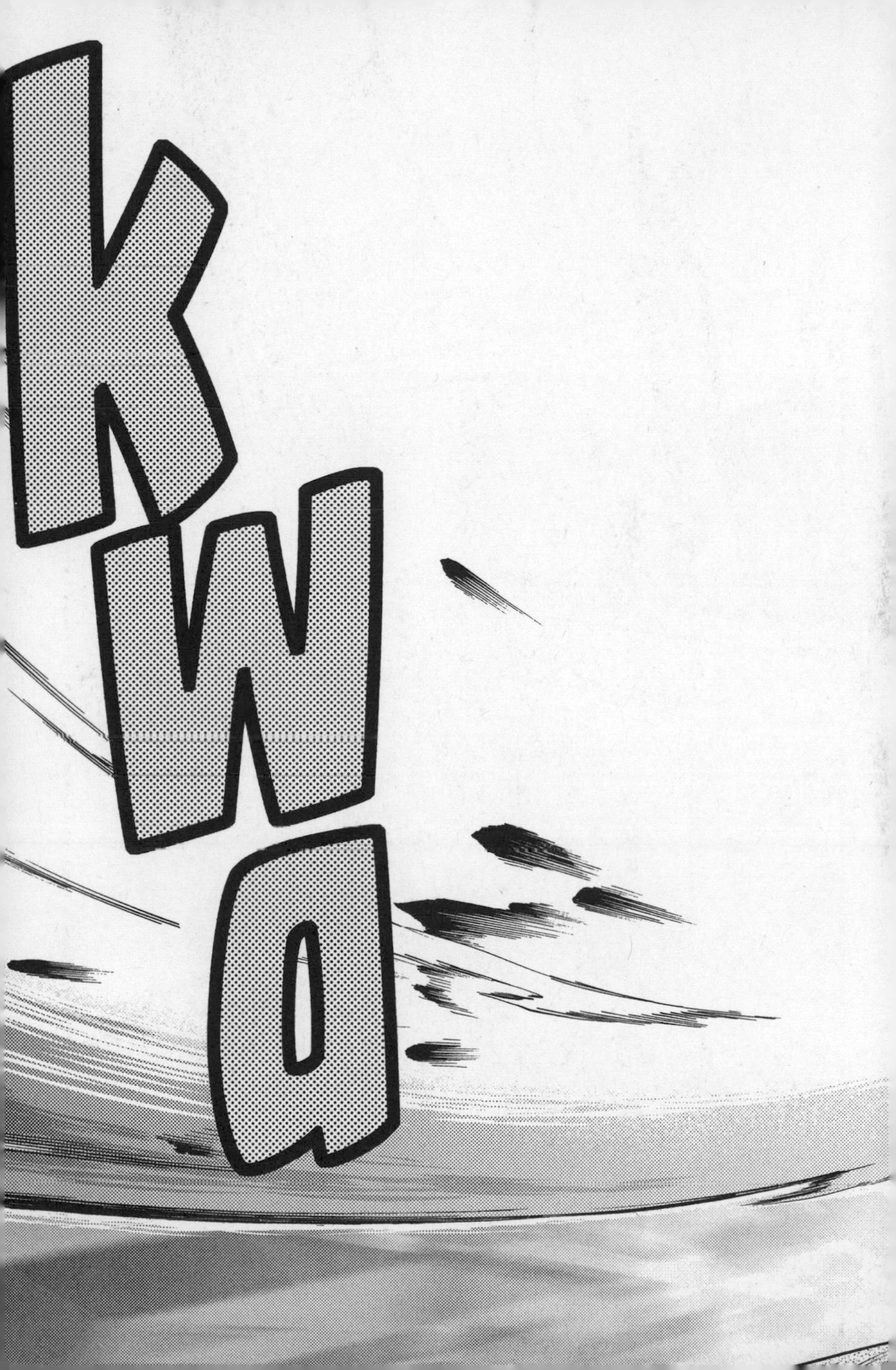
KWA

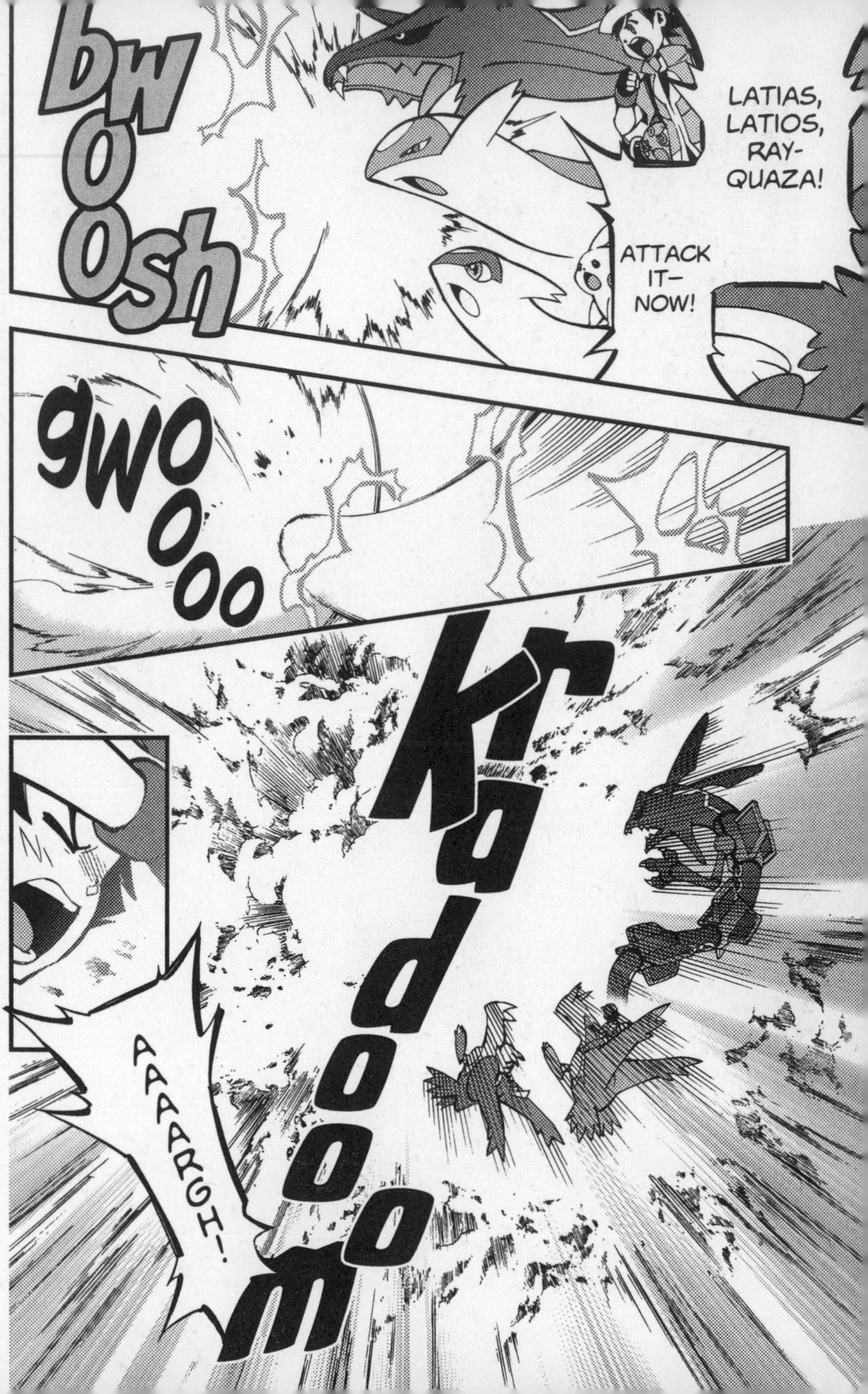
LATIAS, LATIOS, RAY-QUAZA!
ATTACK IT—NOW!
bwOOOsh
gwOOOO
kradoooom
AAAARGH!

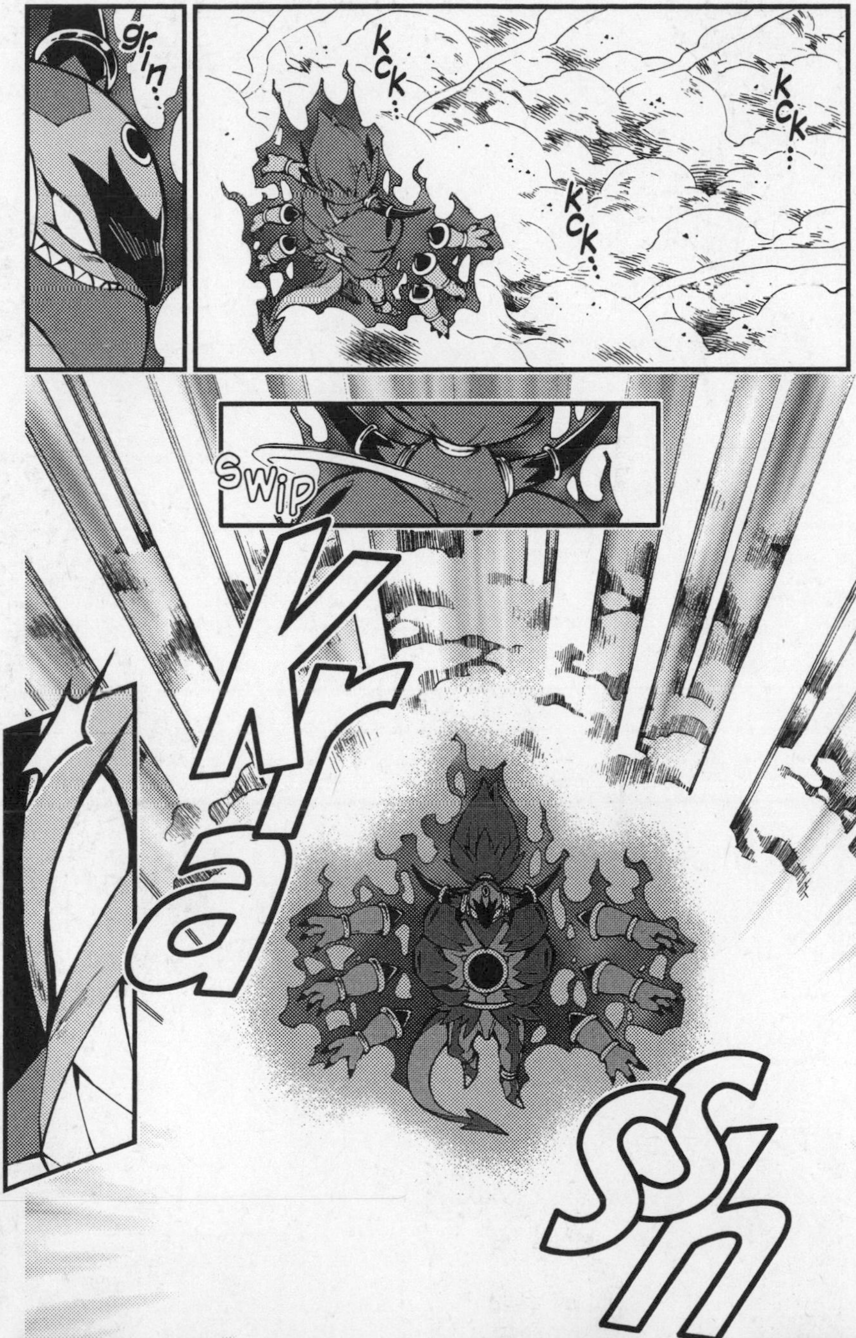

kck...
kck...
kck...
grin...
swip
Kra
ssh

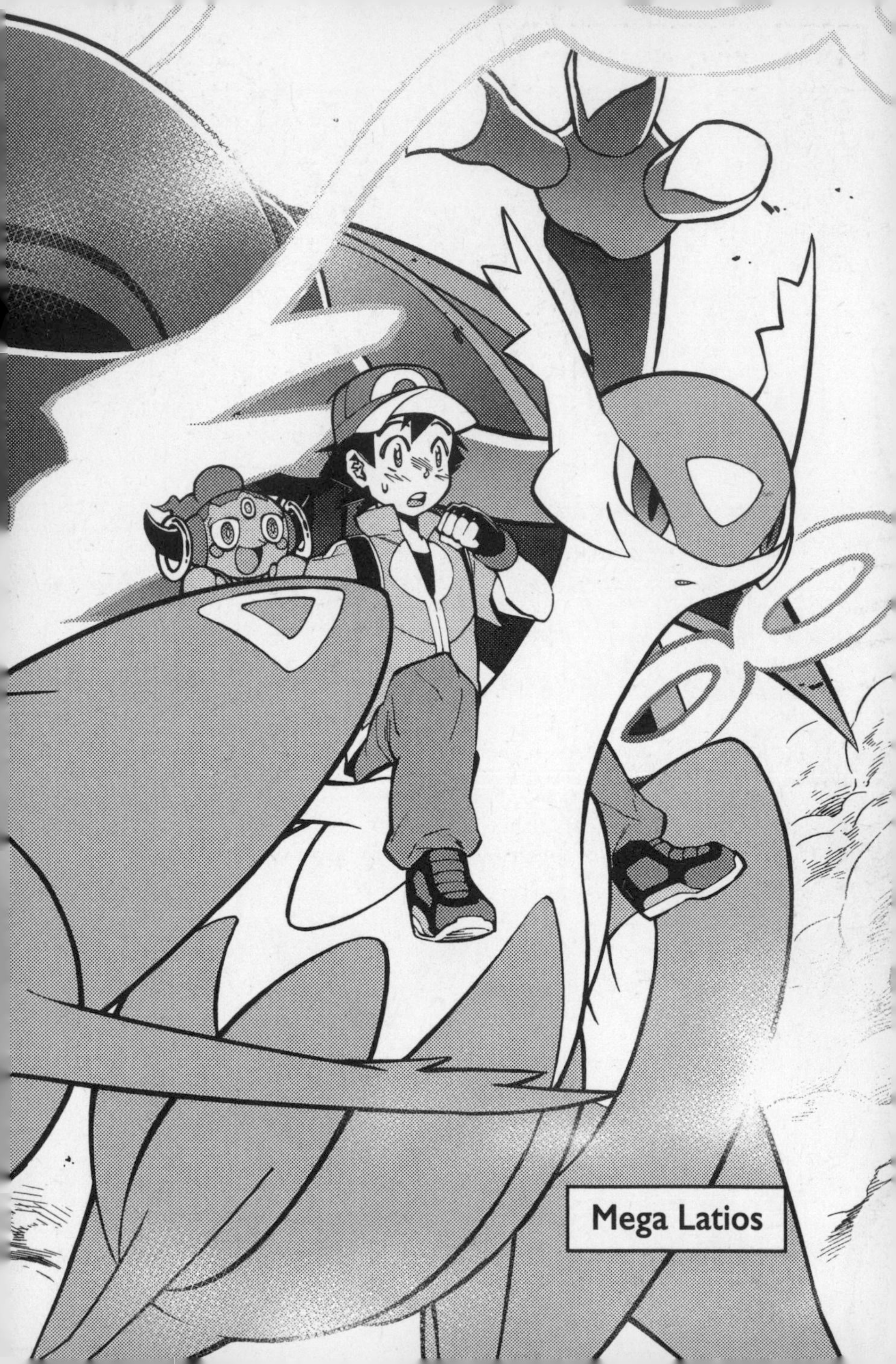
Mega Latios

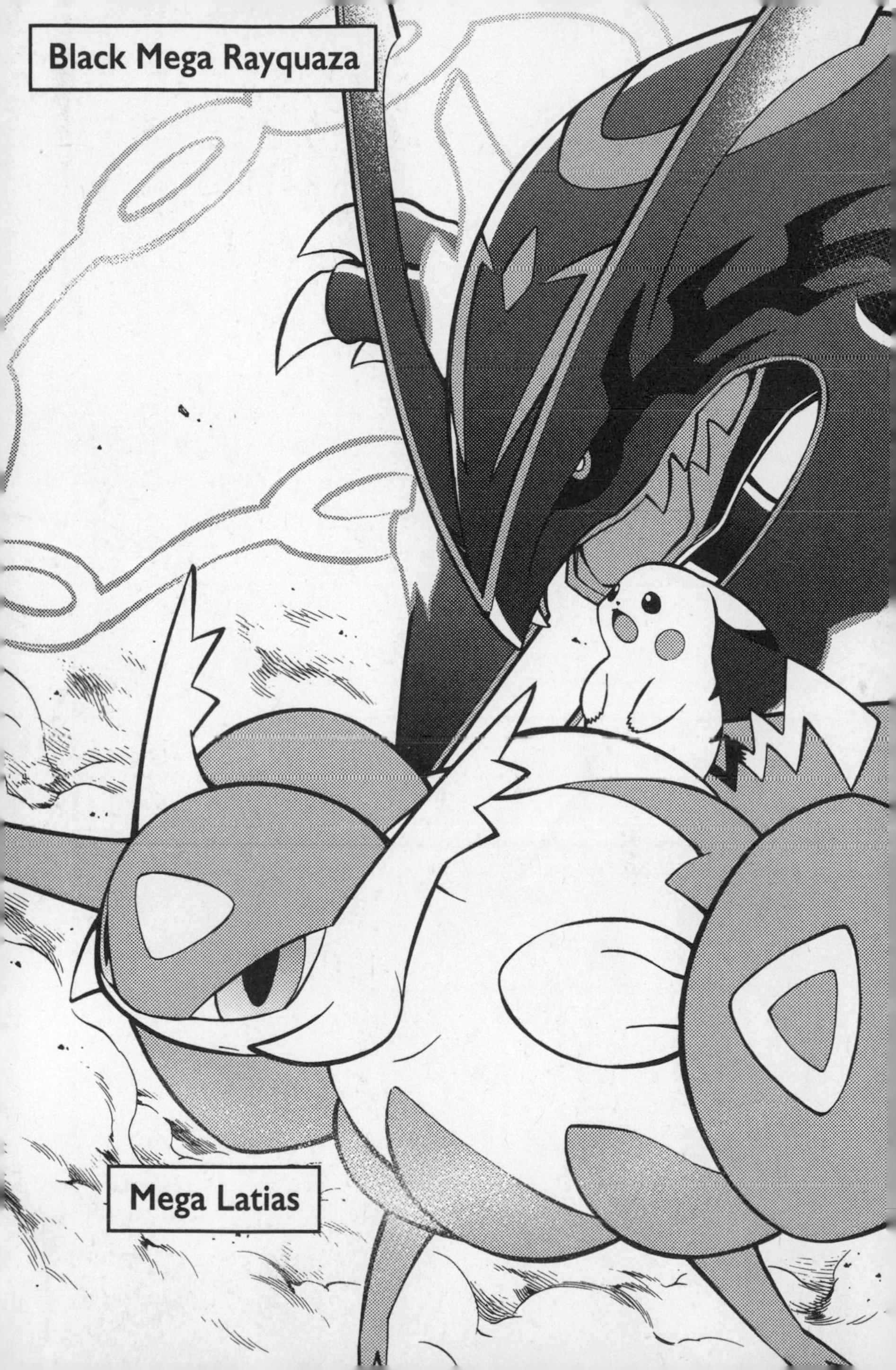
Black Mega Rayquaza
Mega Latias

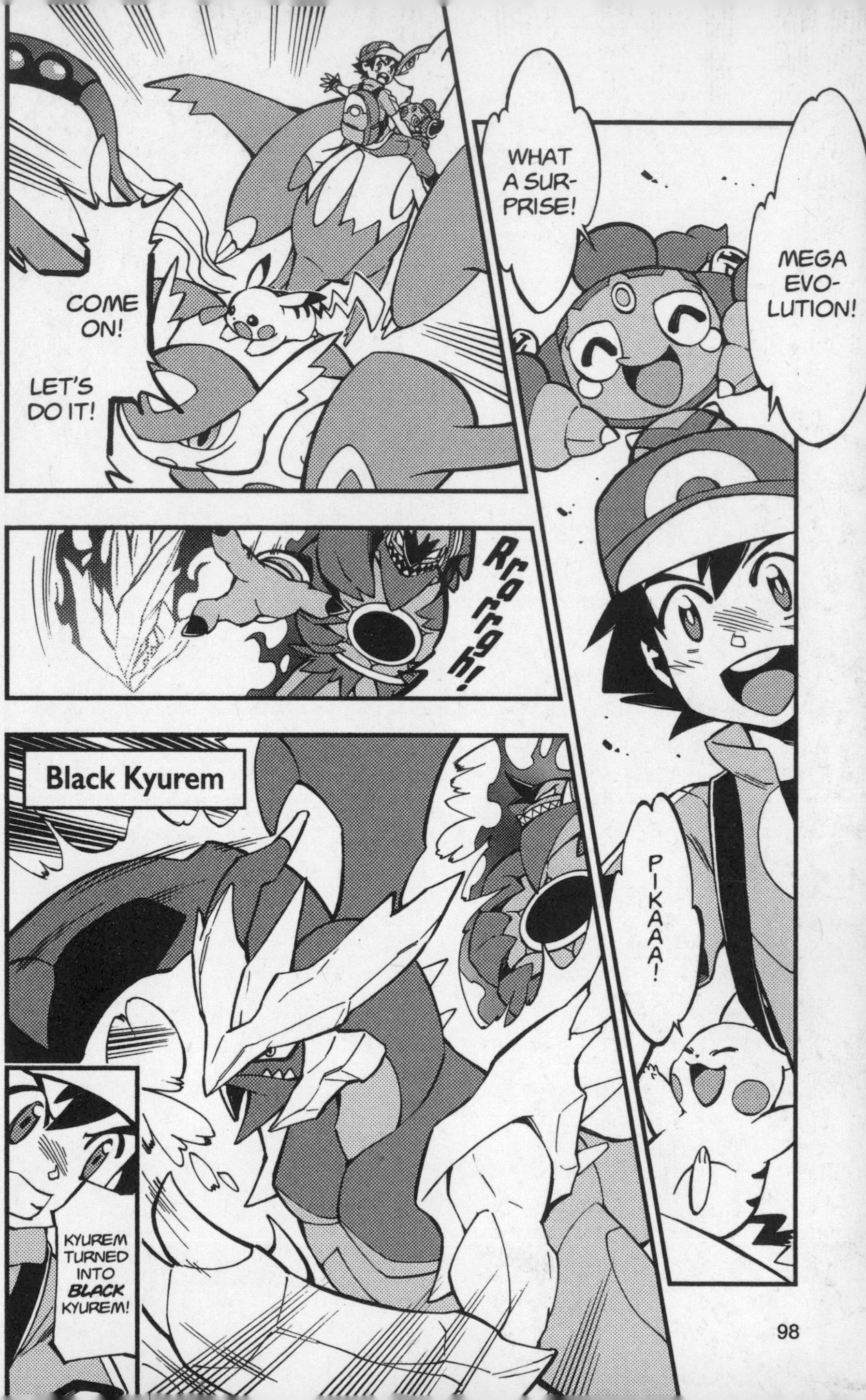
MEGA EVO-LUTION!
WHAT A SUR-PRISE!
PIKAAA!
COME ON!
LET'S DO IT!
Rrrorrgh!
Black Kyurem
KYUREM TURNED INTO BLACK KYUREM!

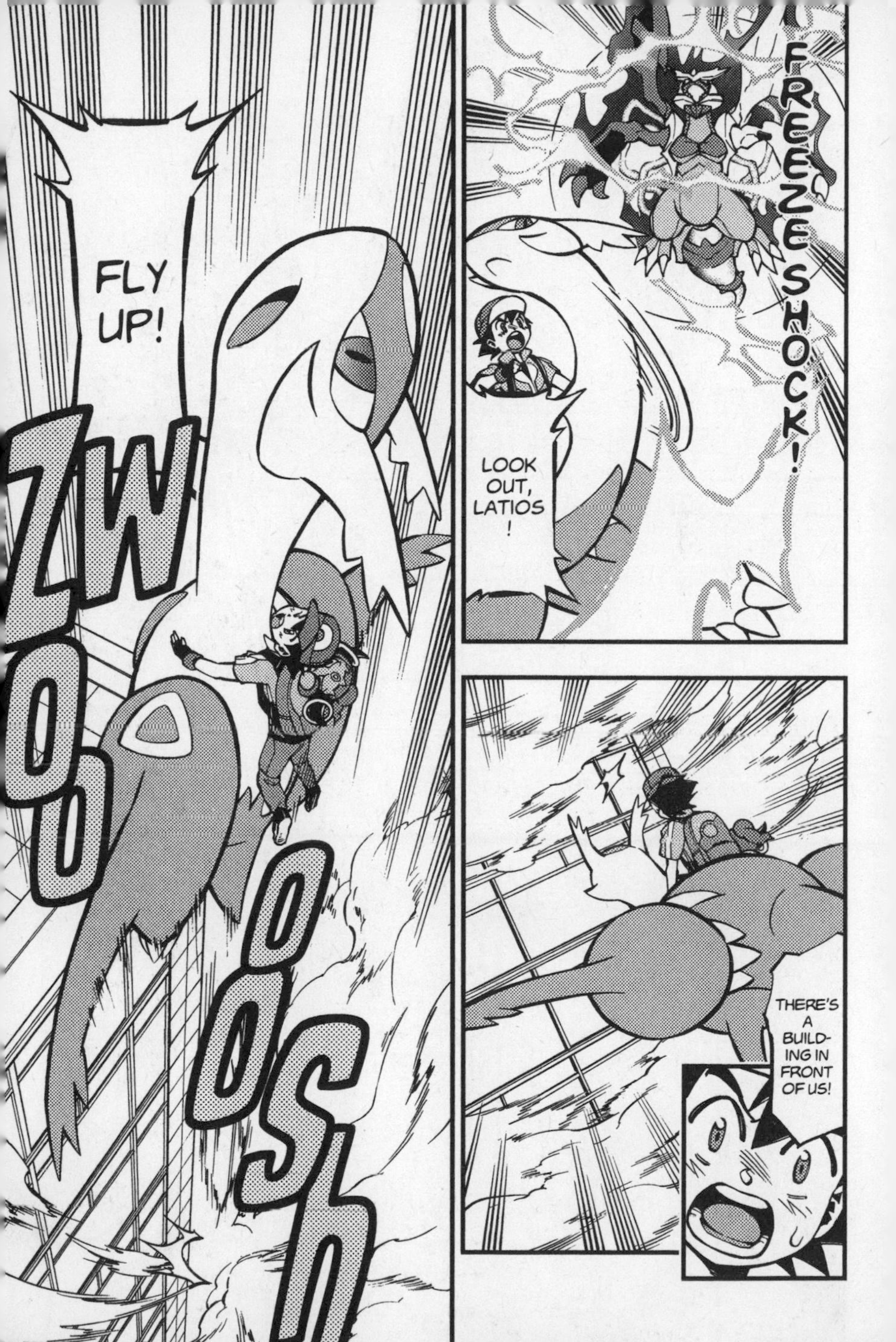
FREEZE SHOCK!
LOOK OUT, LATIOS!
THERE'S A BUILDING IN FRONT OF US!
FLY UP!
ZWOOOOSH

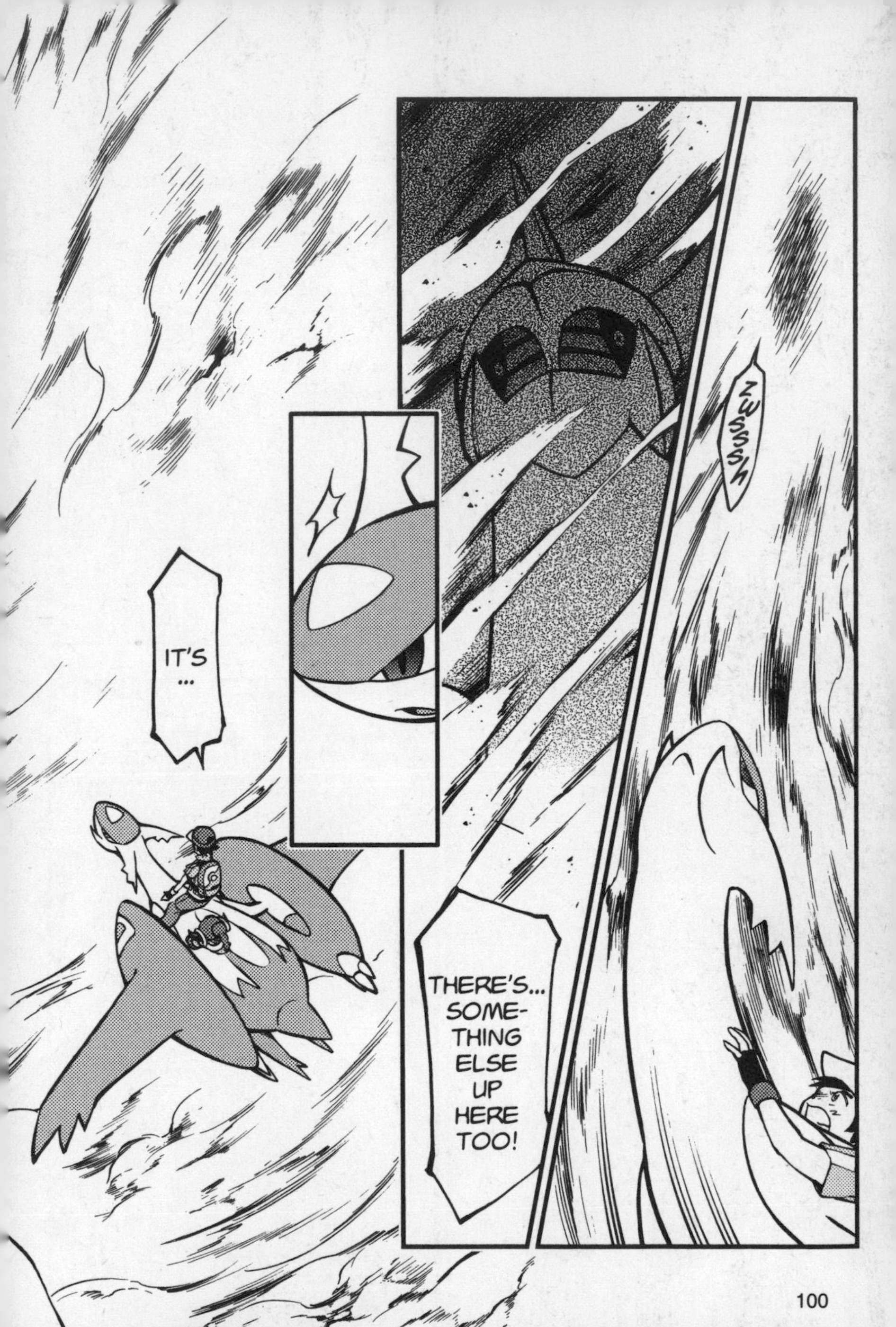
ZWSSSH
THERE'S... SOME-THING ELSE UP HERE TOO!
IT'S ...

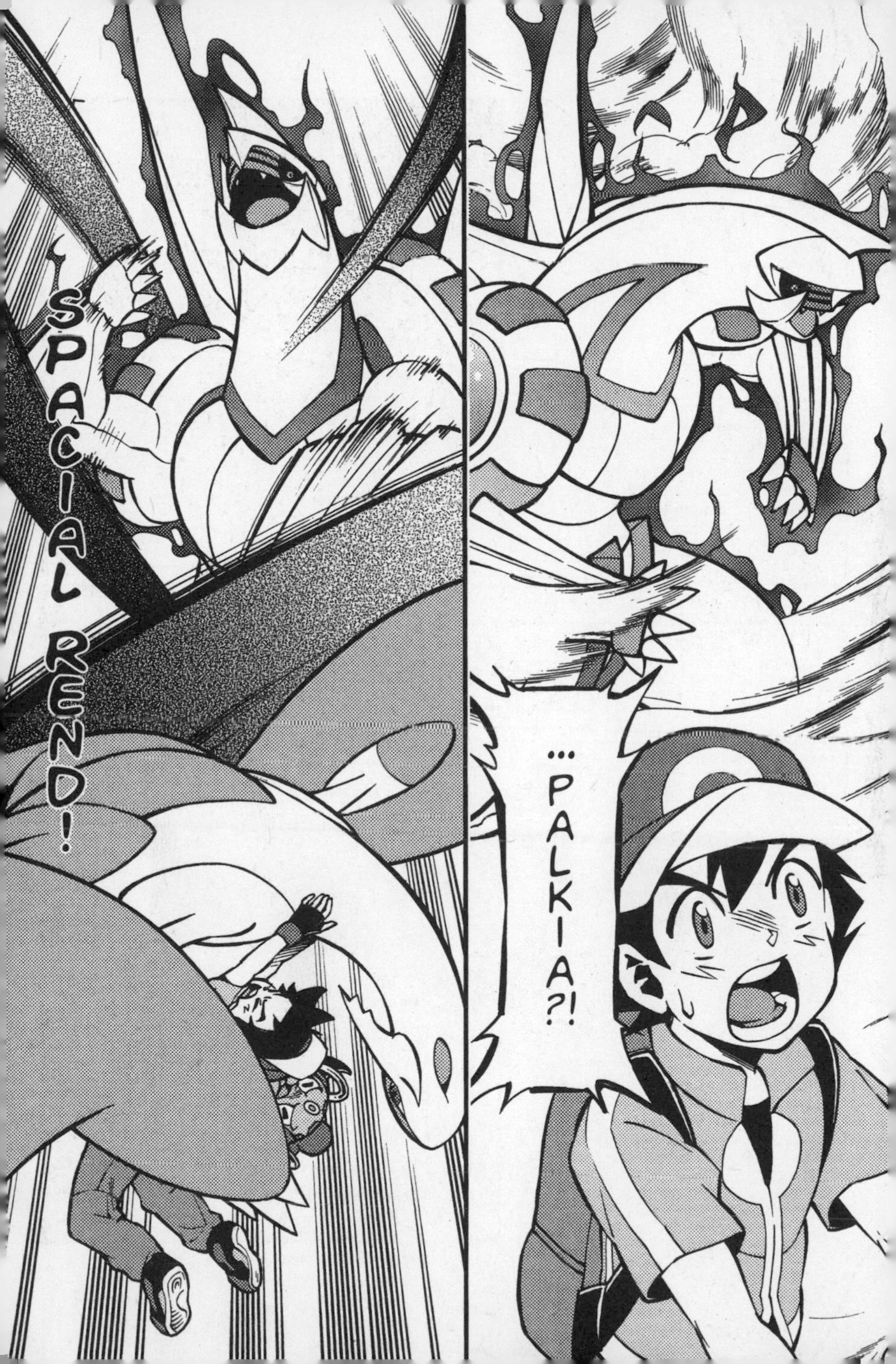
...PALKIA?!
SPACIAL REND!

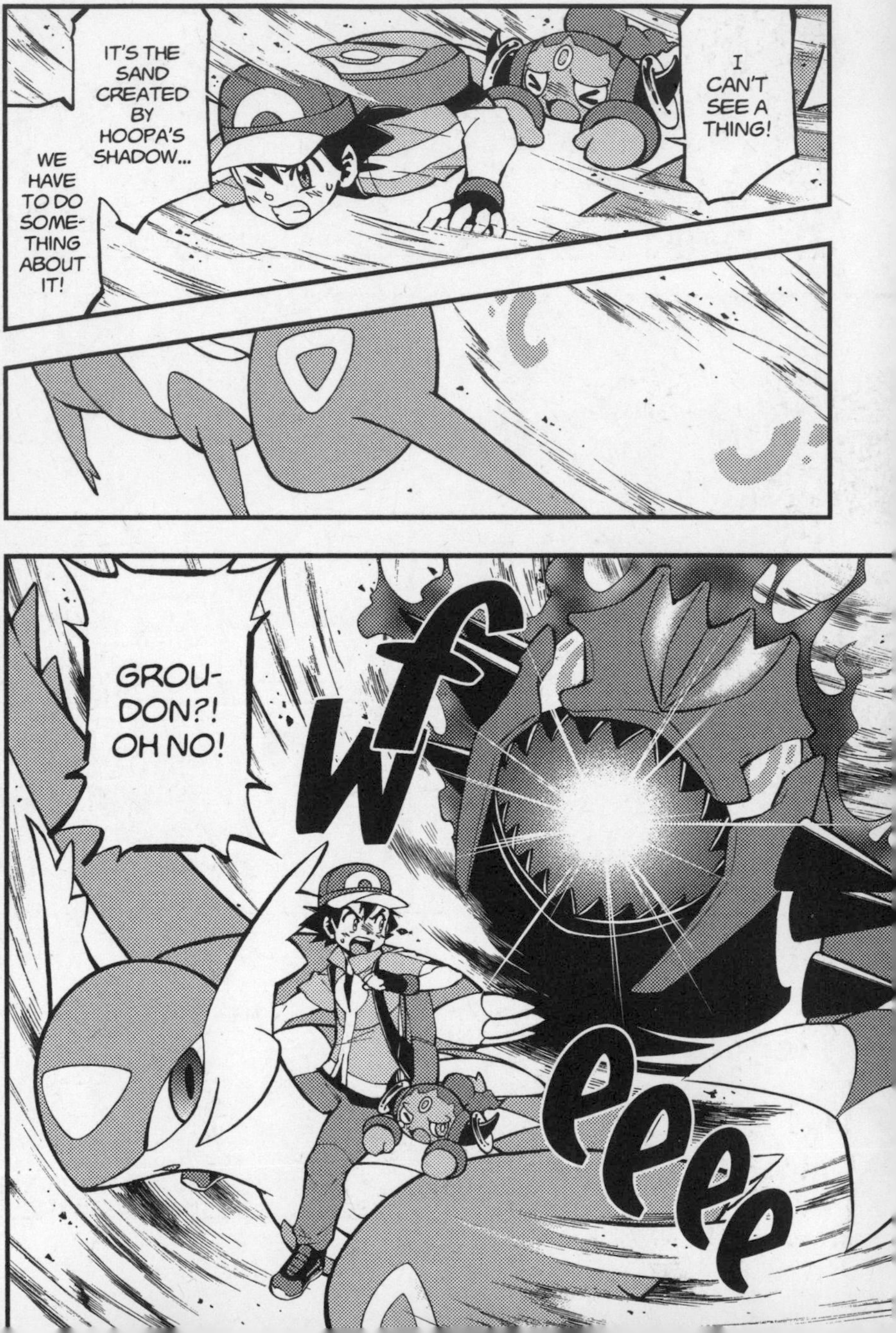
I CAN'T SEE A THING!
IT'S THE SAND CREATED BY HOOPA'S SHADOW...
WE HAVE TO DO SOME-THING ABOUT IT!
wf
GROU-DON?! OH NO!
eeee

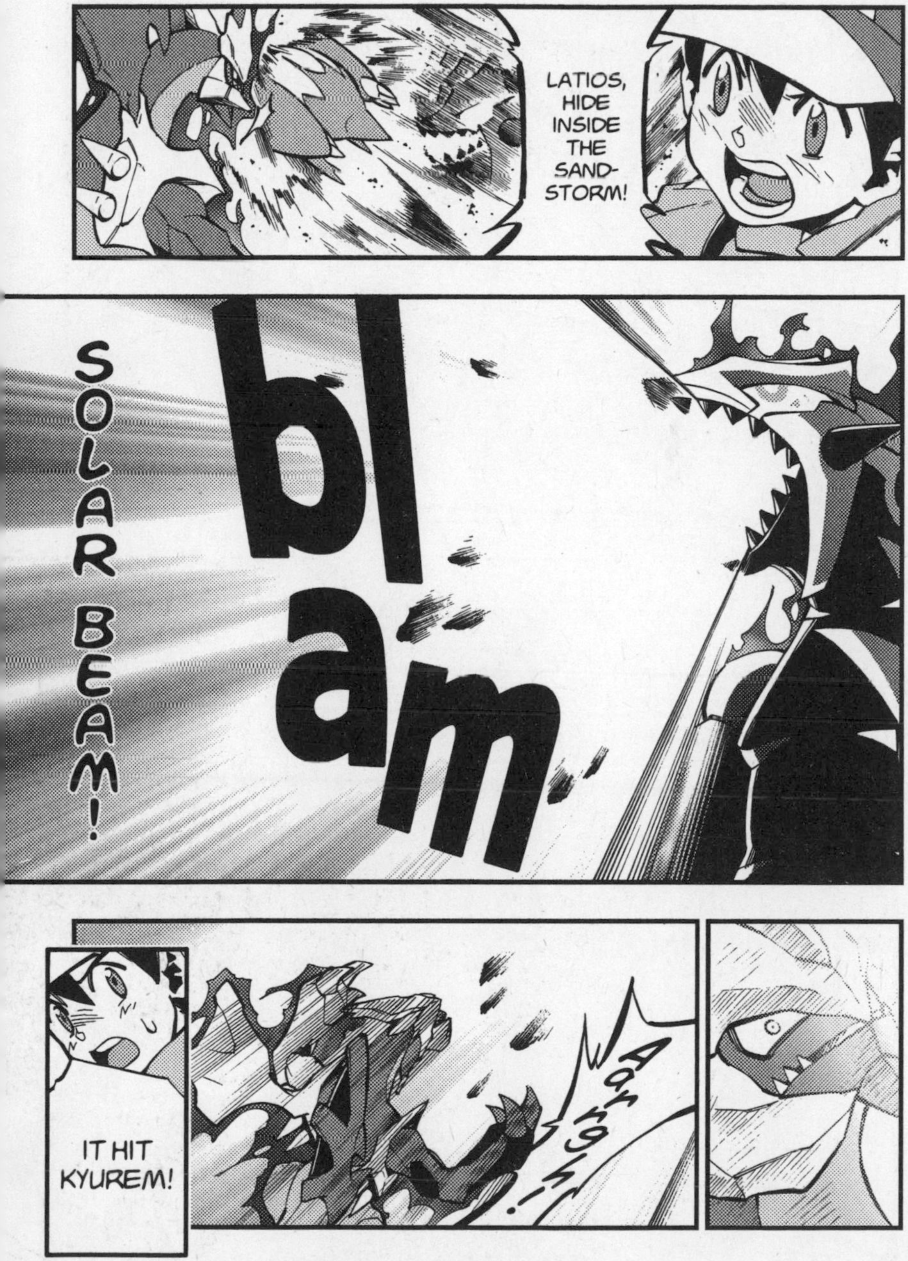
LATIOS, HIDE INSIDE THE SAND-STORM!
blam
SOLAR BEAM!
Aarrgh!!
IT HIT KYUREM!

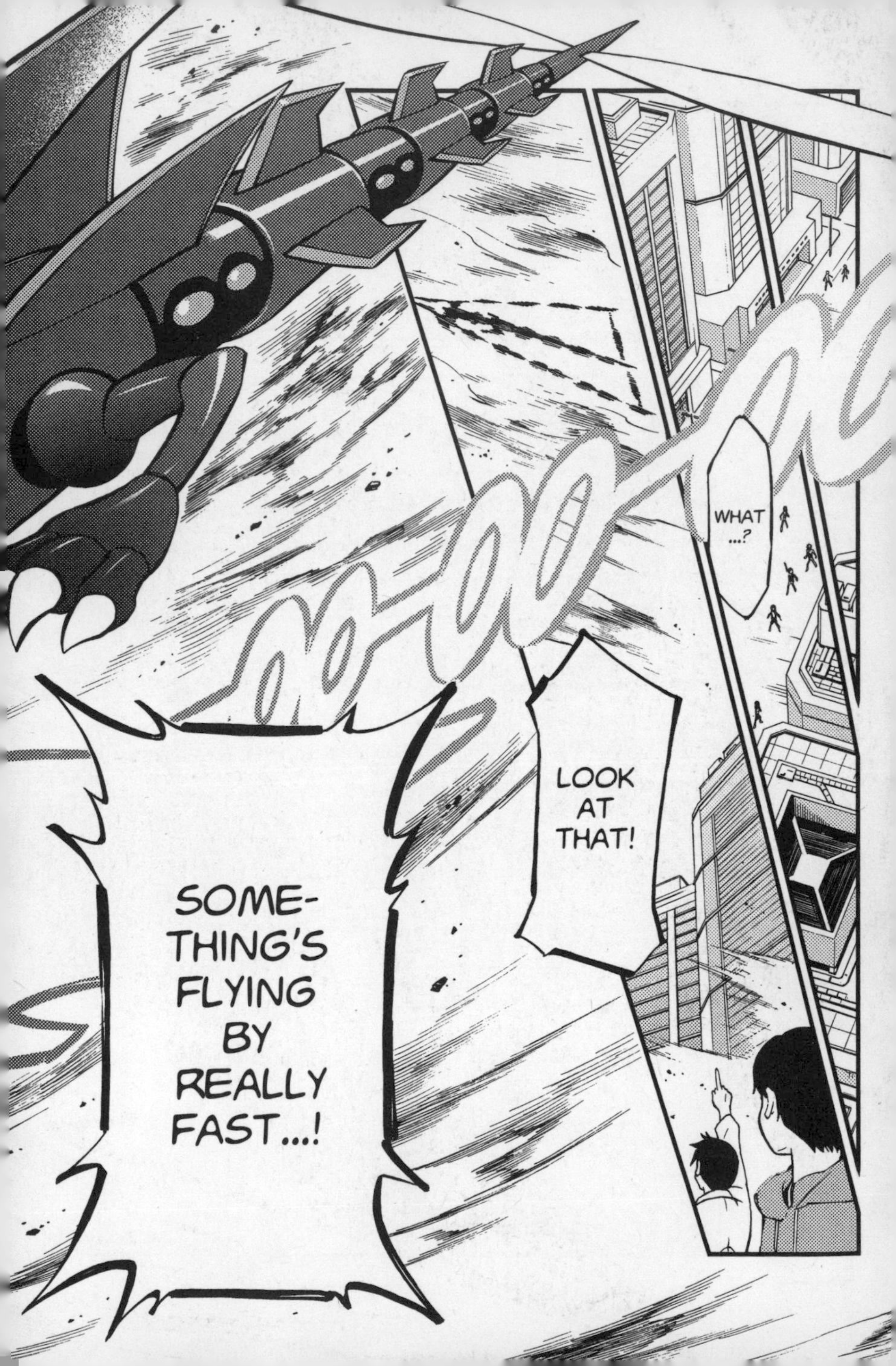
WHAT ...?
LOOK AT THAT!
SOME-THING'S FLYING BY REALLY FAST...!

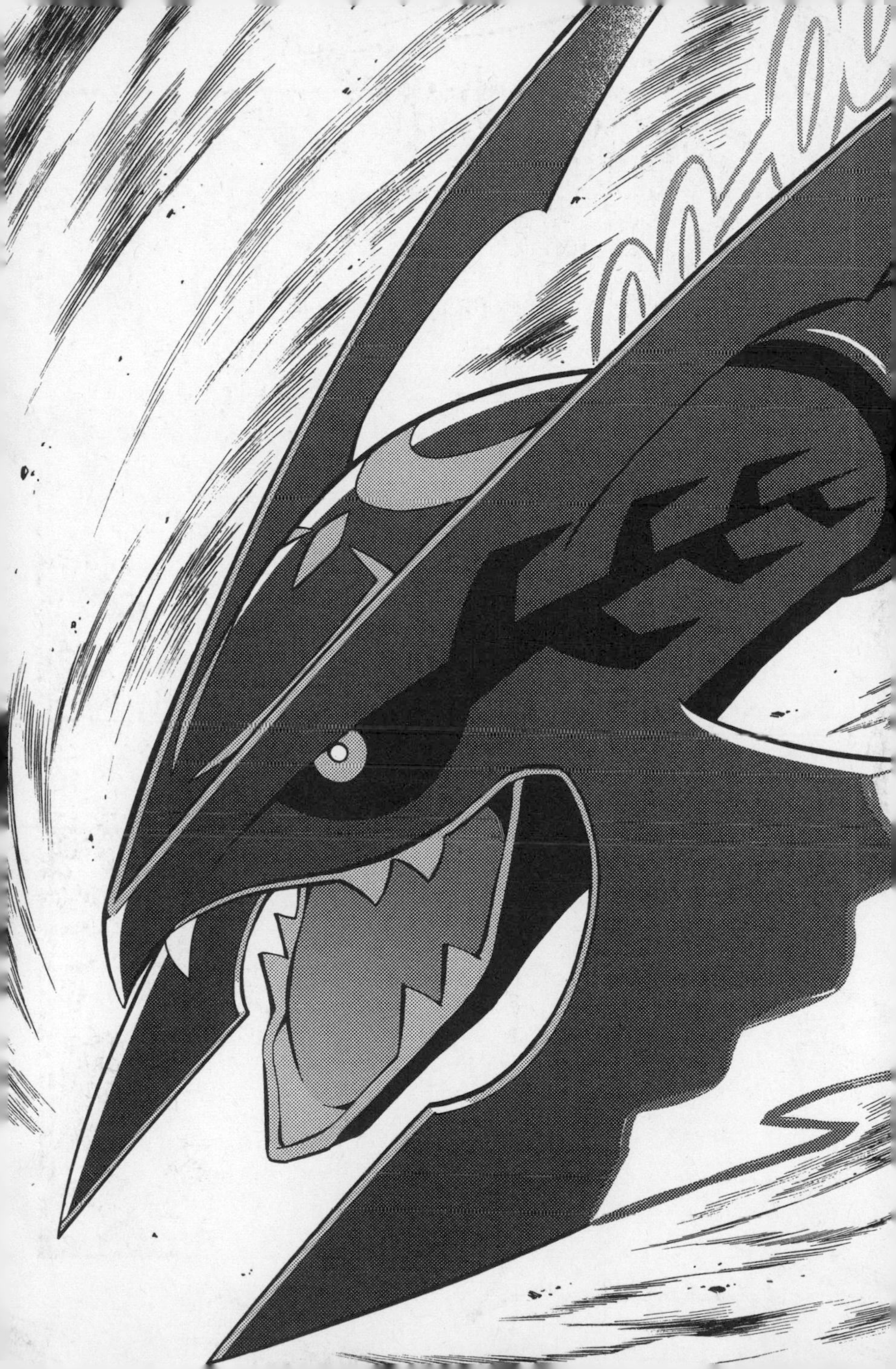

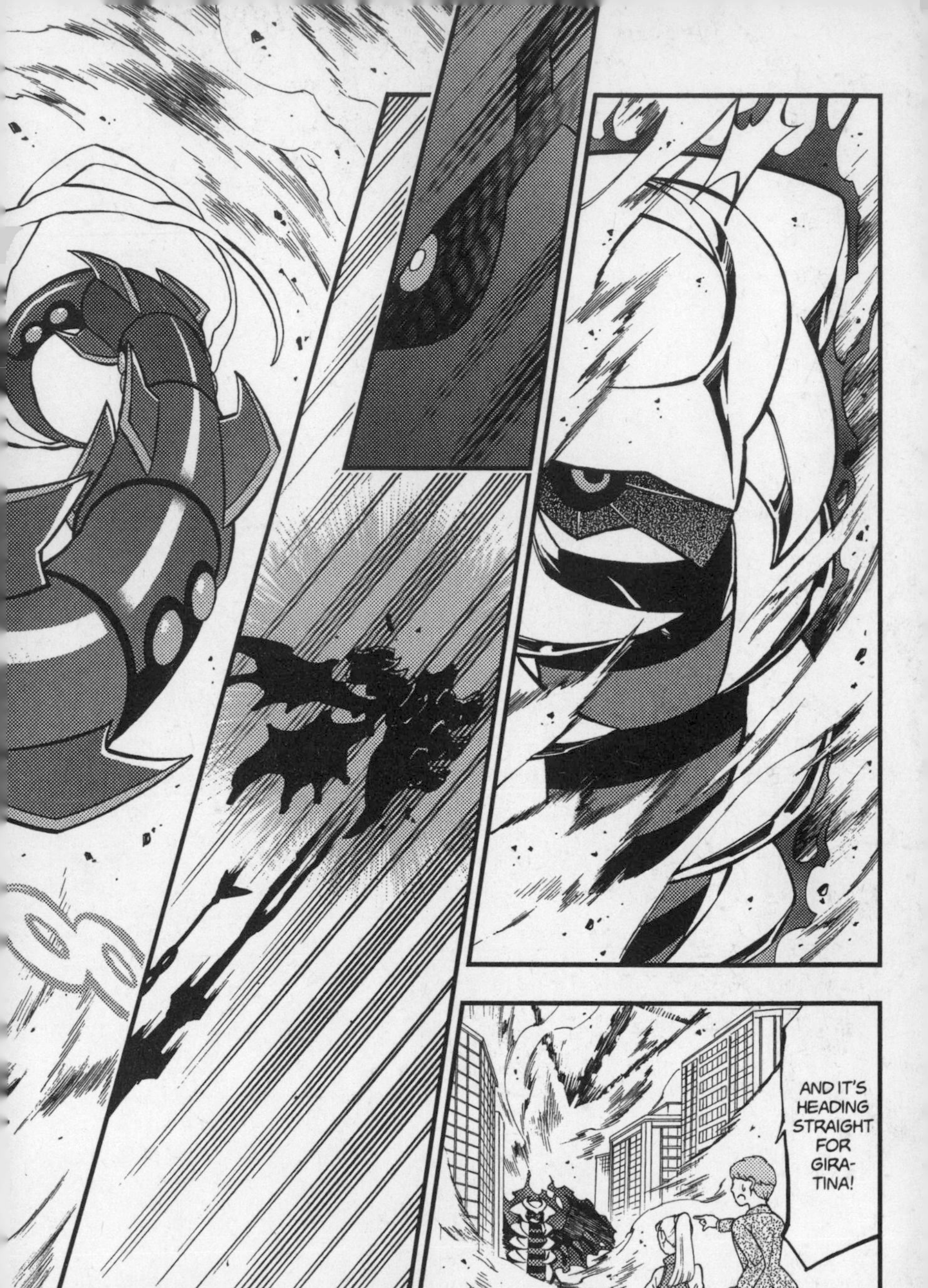
AND IT'S HEADING STRAIGHT FOR GIRA-TINA!

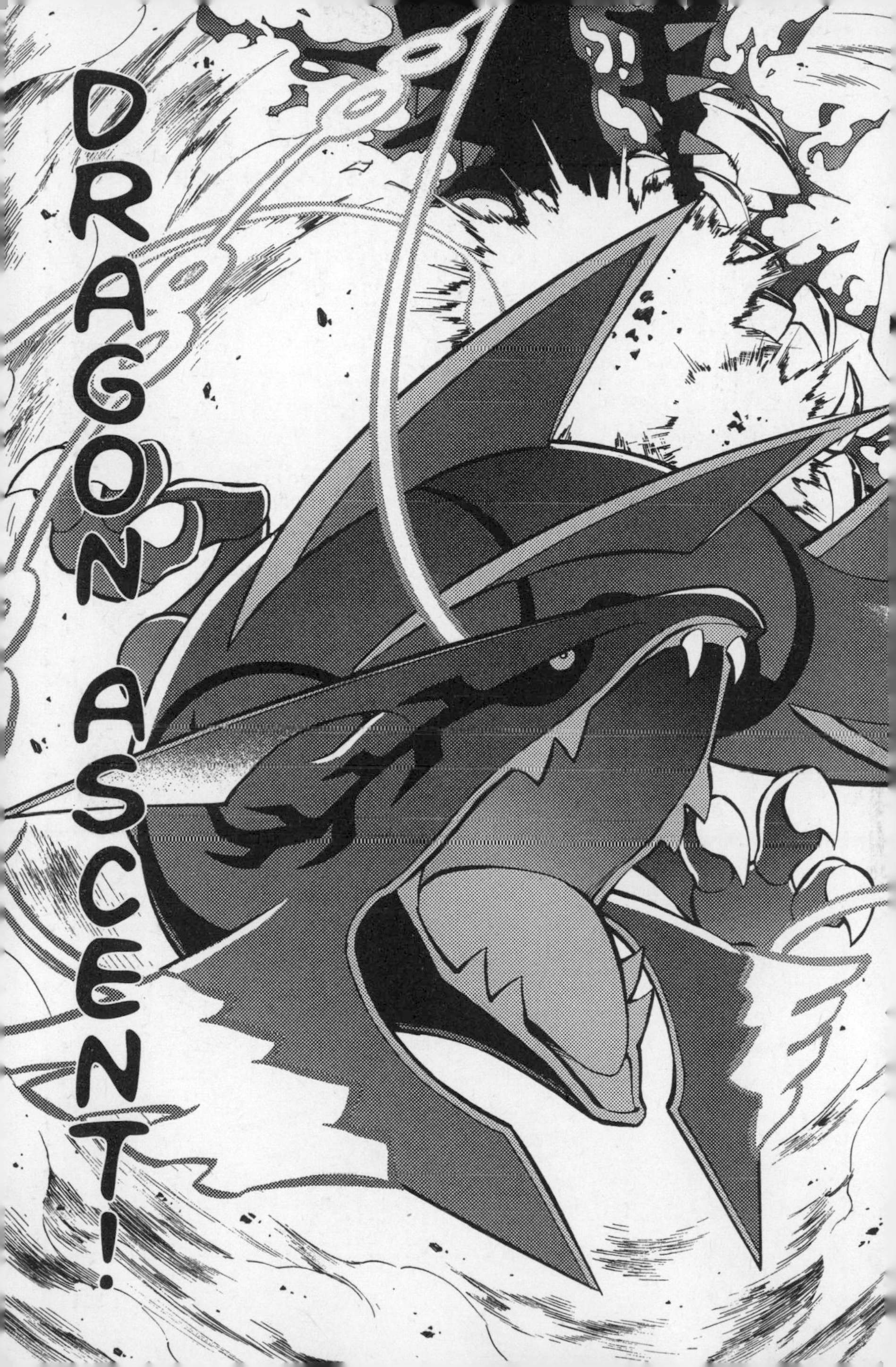
DRAGON ASCENT!

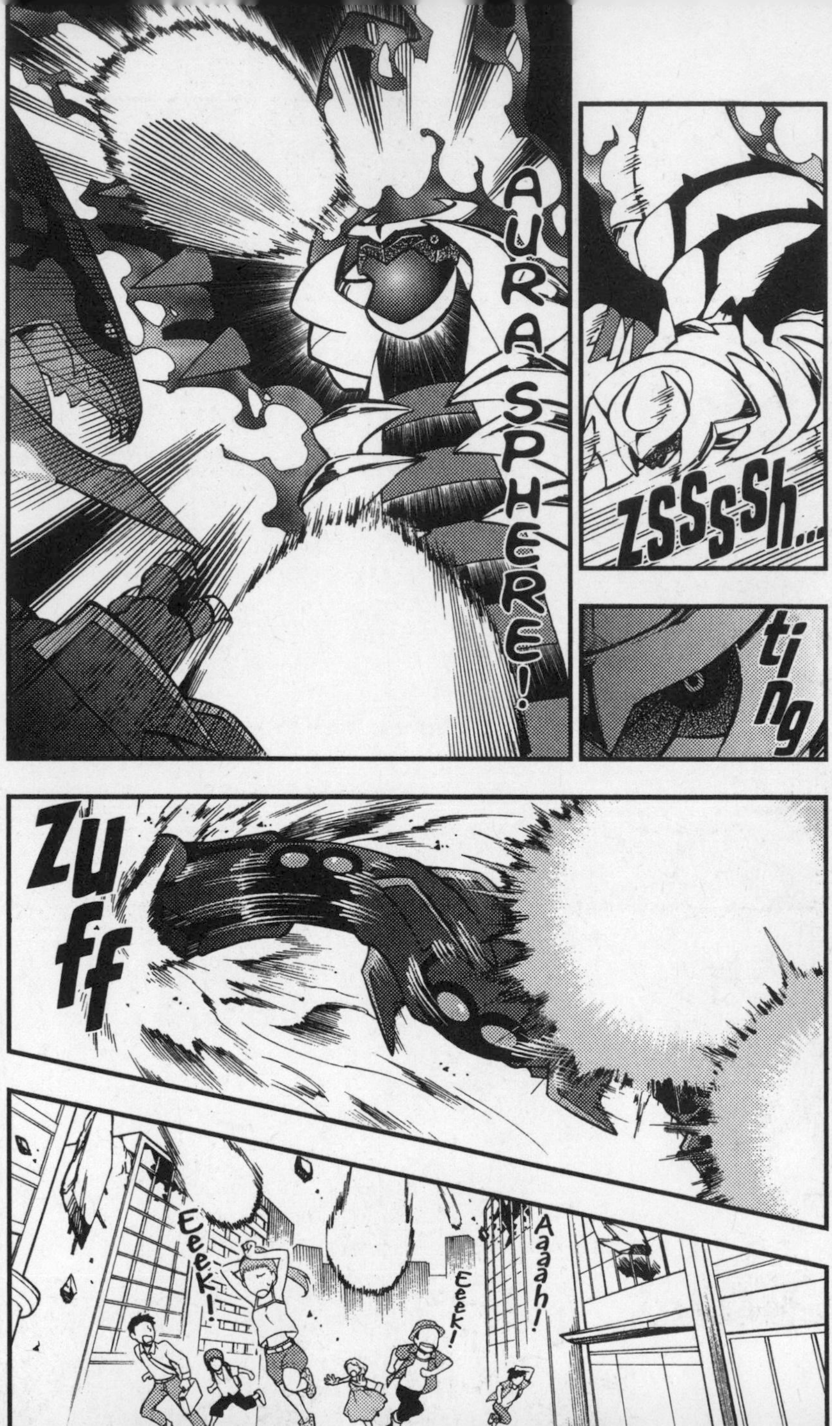
ZSSSSh...
ting
AURA SPHERE!
Zuff
Aaaah!
Eeeek!
Eeeek!

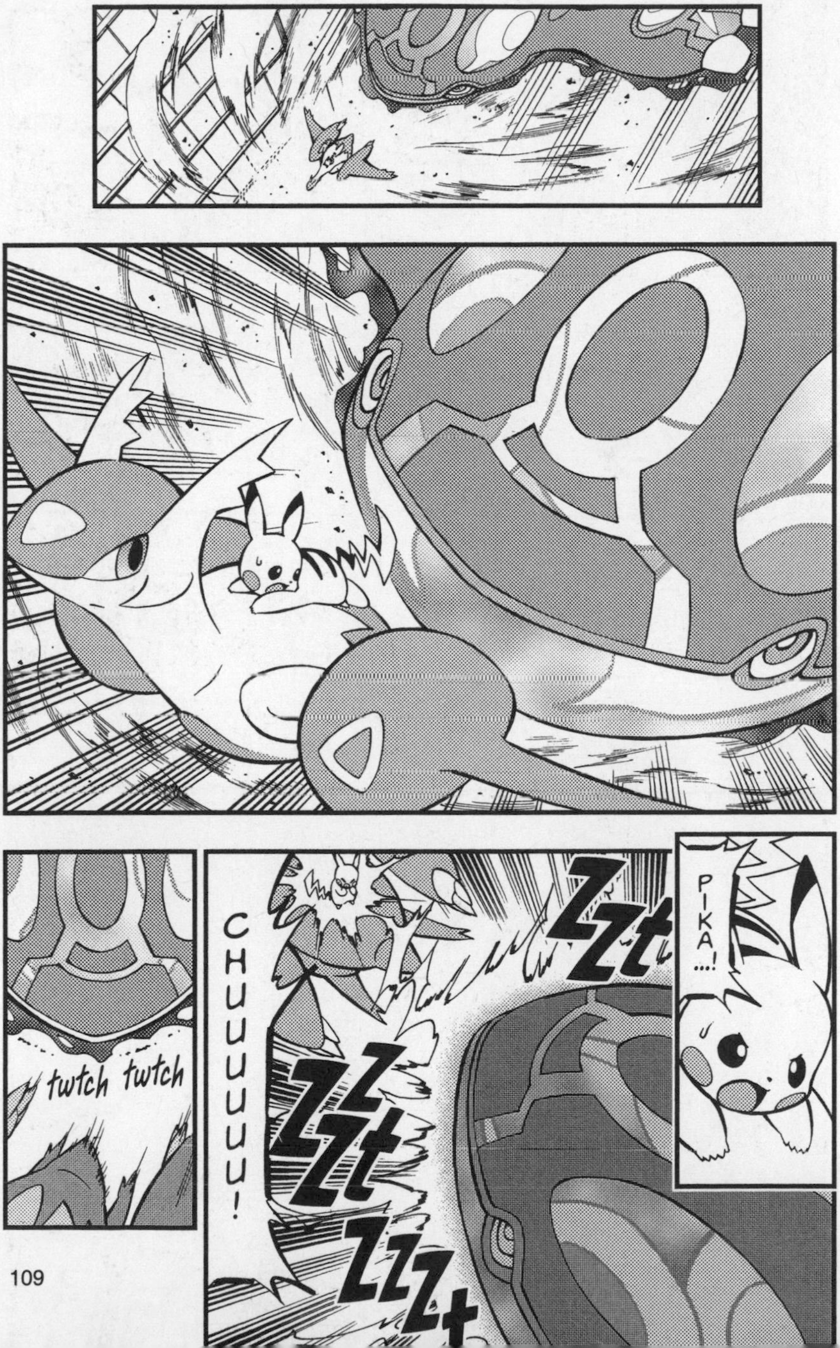

PIKA...!
ZZt
CHUUUUUUU!
ZZZt
ZZZt
twitch twitch

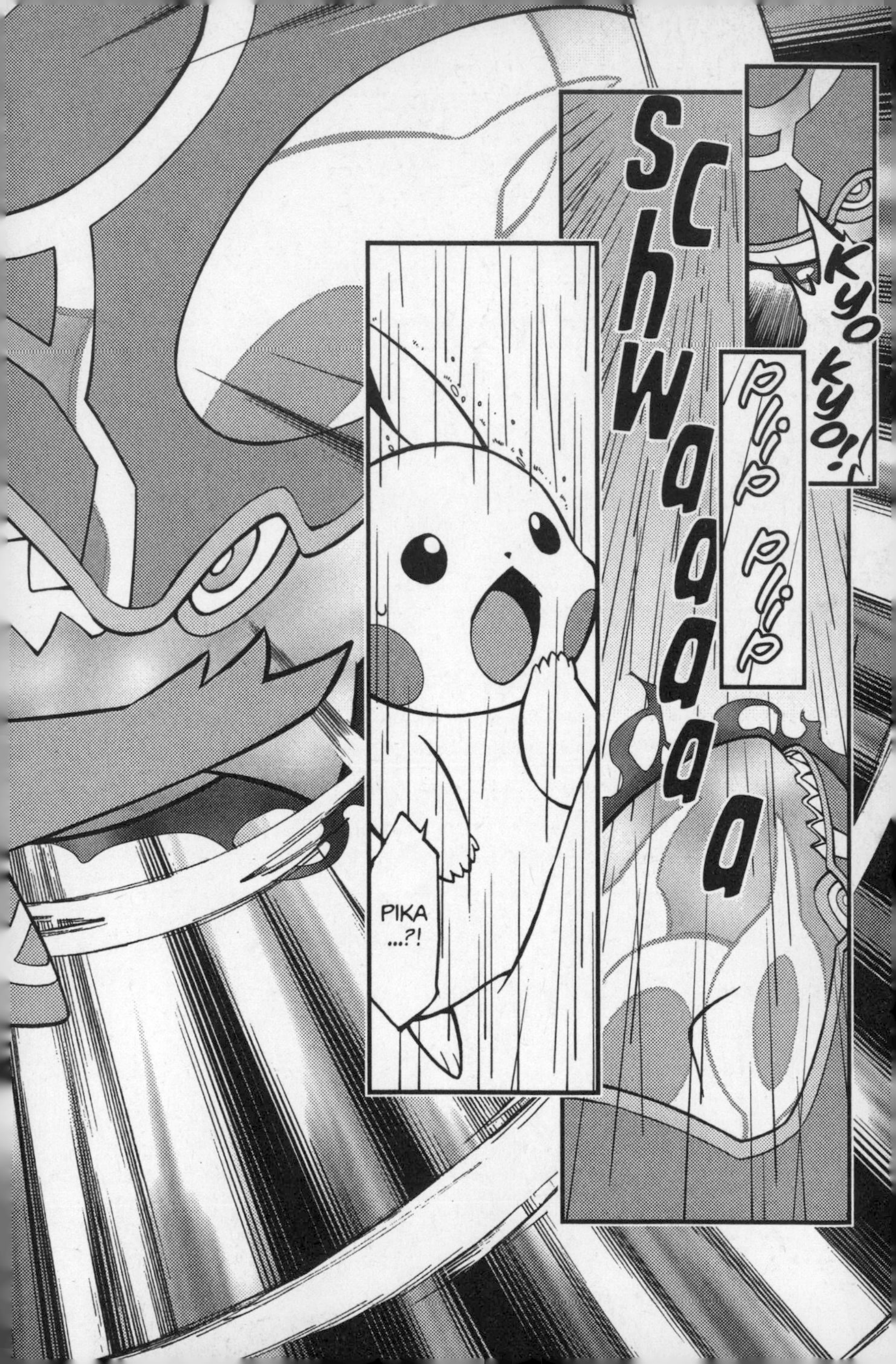
KYO KYO KYO!!
plip plip
SCHWAAAAAA
PIKA ...?!

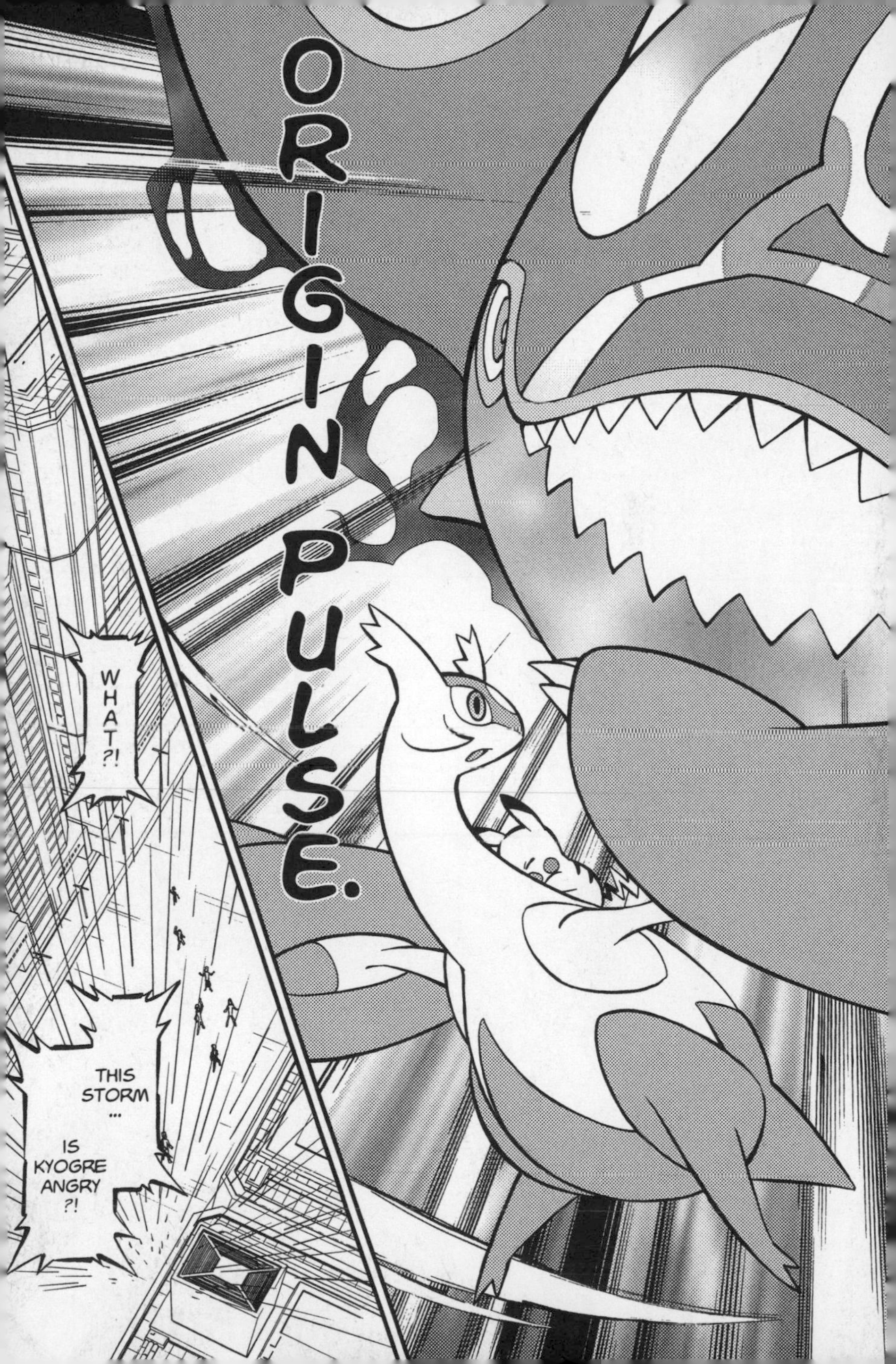
ORIGIN PULSE.
WHAT?!
THIS STORM ... IS KYOGRE ANGRY?!

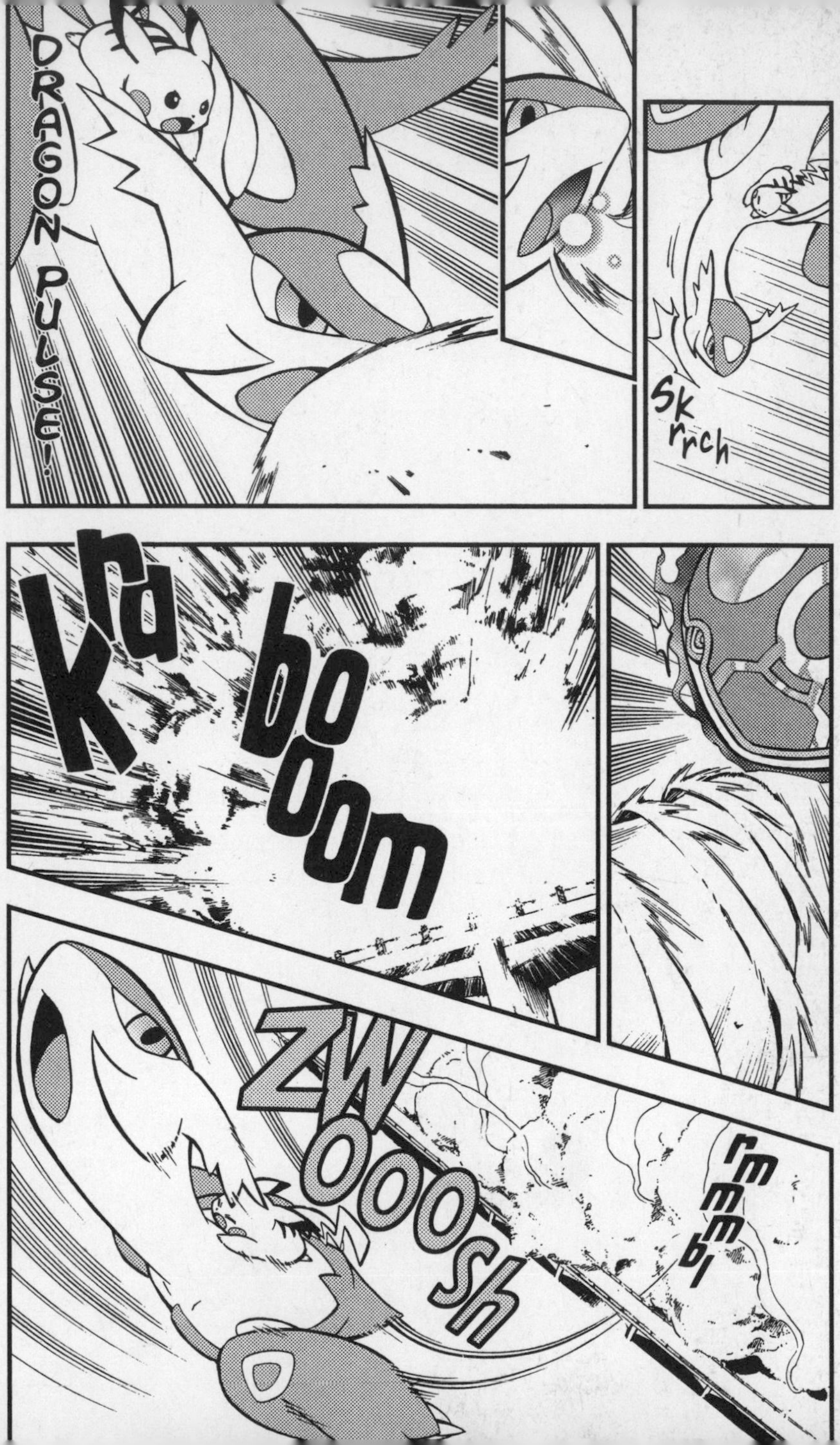
Skrrch
DRAGON PULSE!
krabooom
ZWOOOOSh
rmmmbl

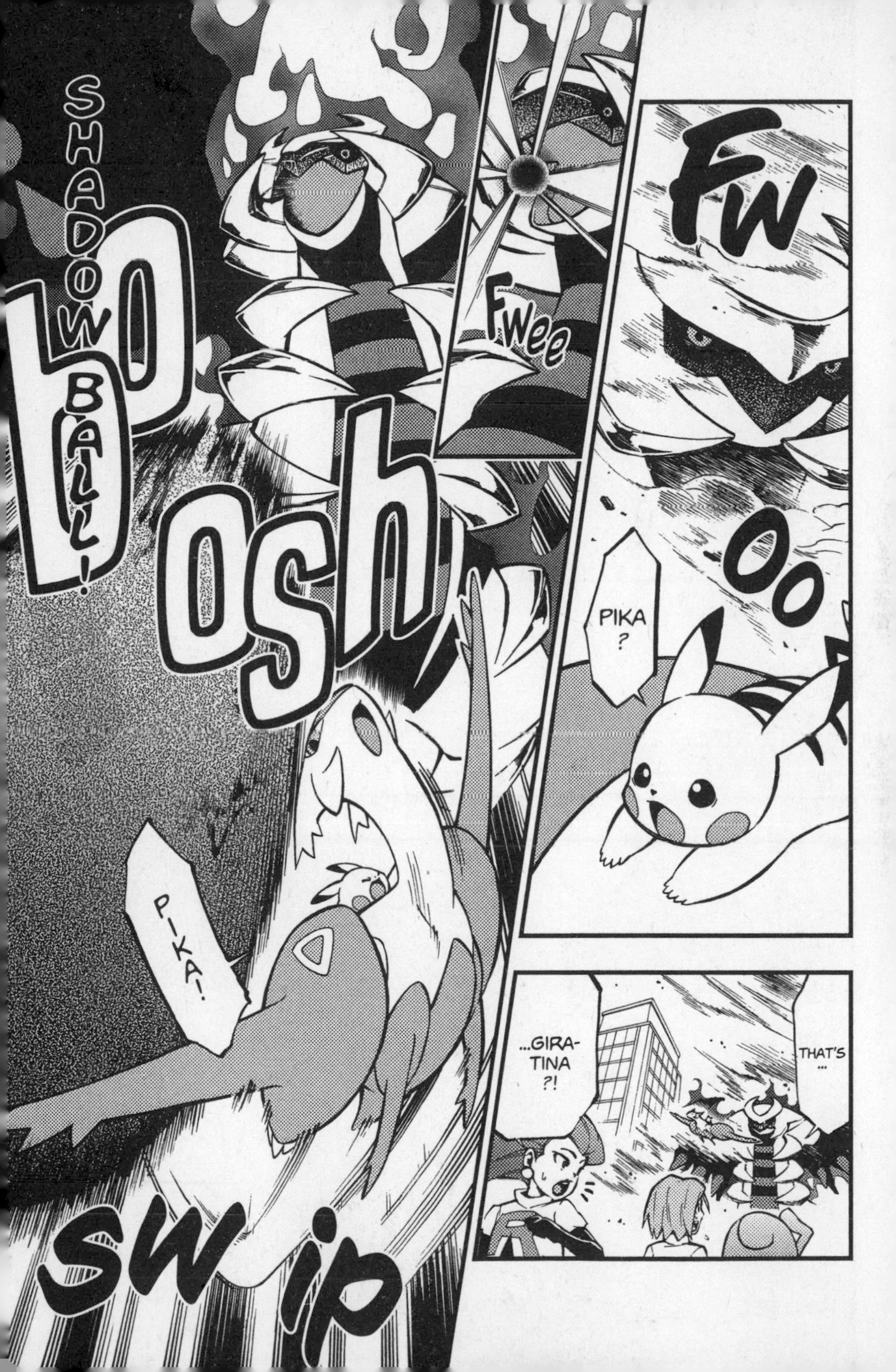
Fw
oo
PIKA?
Fwee
SHADOW BALL!
Wo
osh
PIKA!
Sw
ip
THAT'S...
...GIRATINA?!

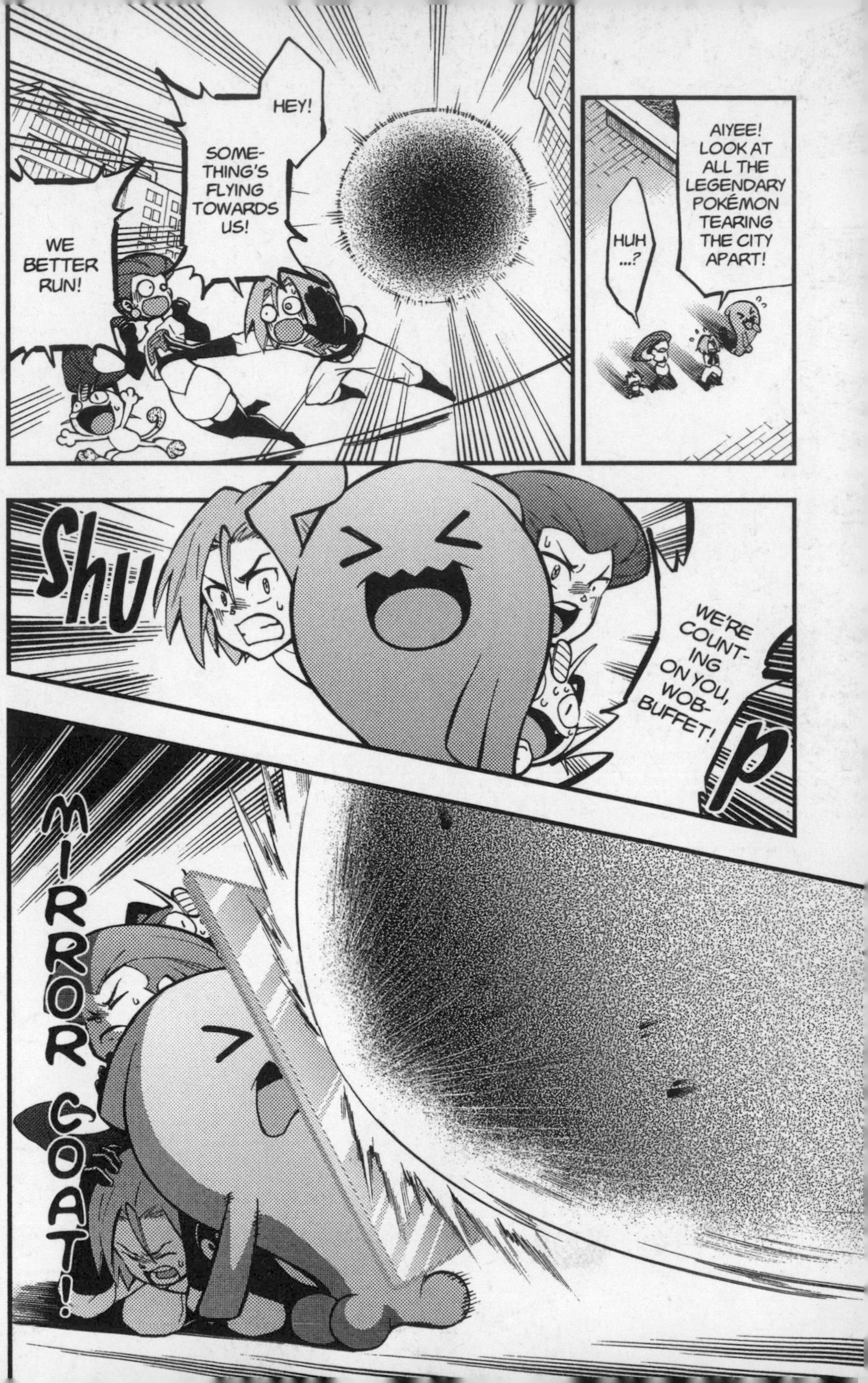

AIYEE! LOOK AT ALL THE LEGENDARY POKÉMON TEARING THE CITY APART!
HUH ...?
HEY!
SOME-THING'S FLYING TOWARDS US!
WE BETTER RUN!
WE'RE COUNT-ING ON YOU, WOB-BUFFET!
Shu
p
MIRROR COAT!

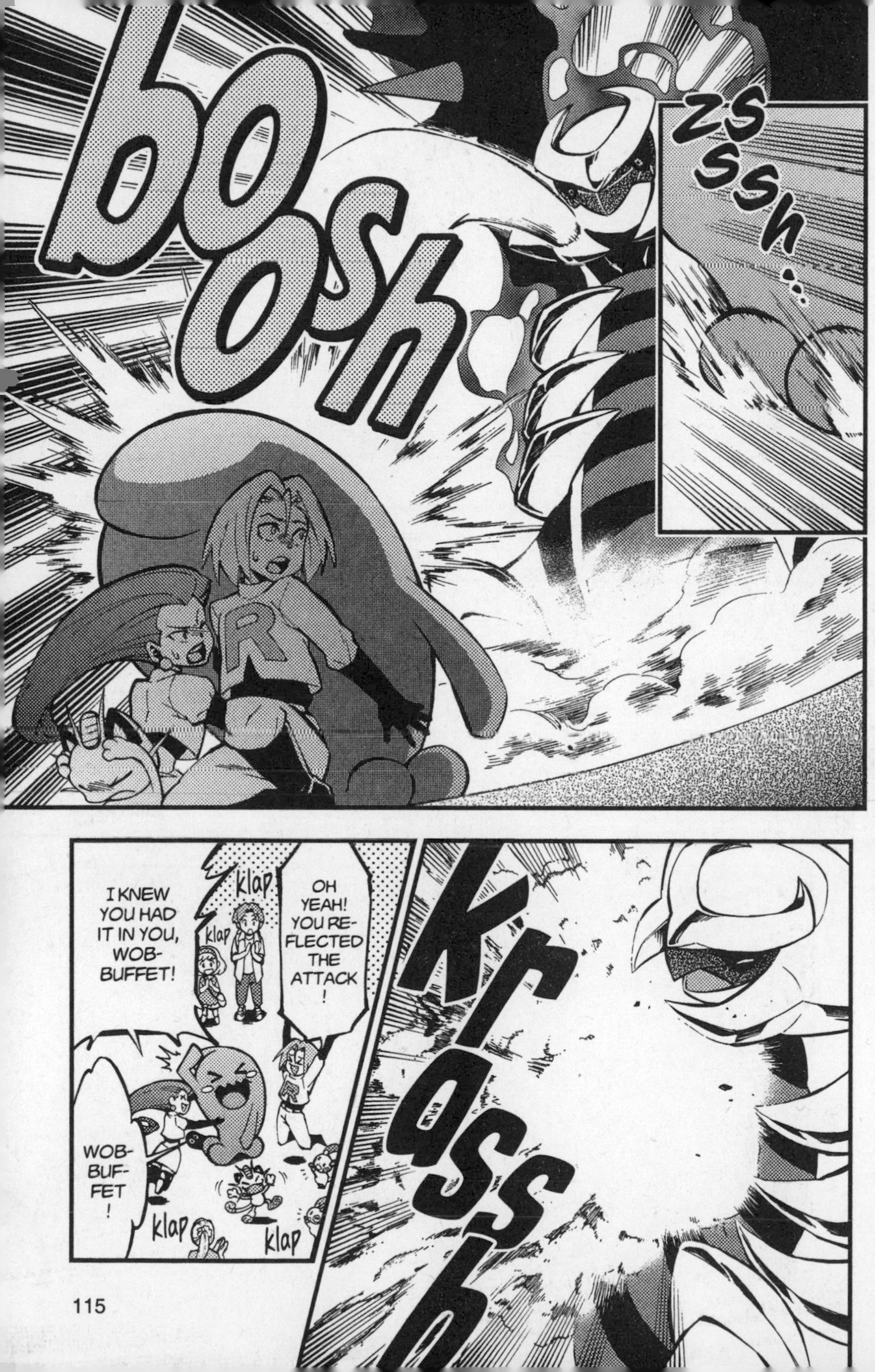
zsssh...
boosh
krassh
OH YEAH! YOU RE-FLECTED THE ATTACK!
klap
I KNEW YOU HAD IT IN YOU, WOB-BUFFET!
klap
WOB-BUF-FET!
klap
klap

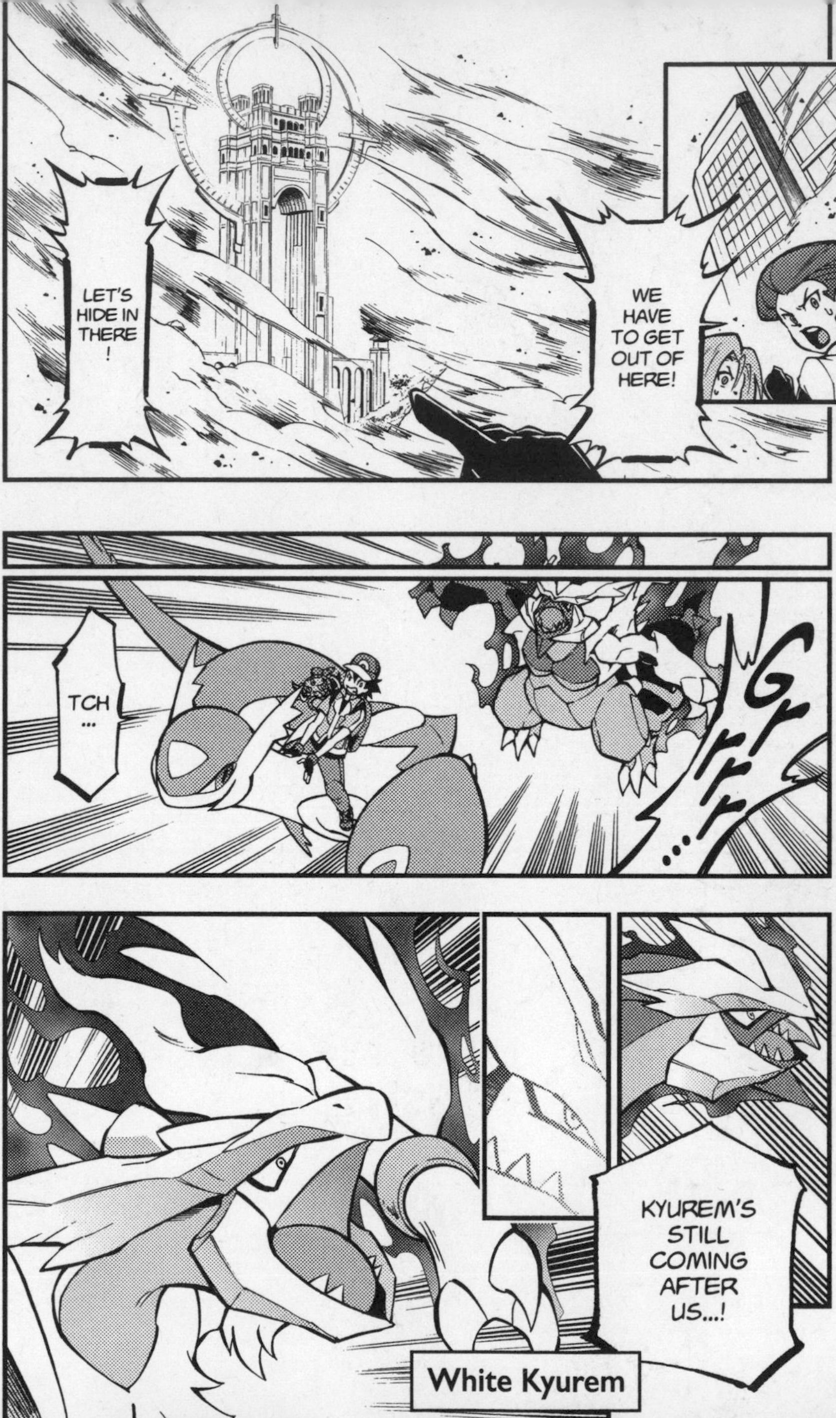
WE HAVE TO GET OUT OF HERE!
LET'S HIDE IN THERE!
Grrrr...
TCH...
KYUREM'S STILL COMING AFTER US...!
White Kyurem

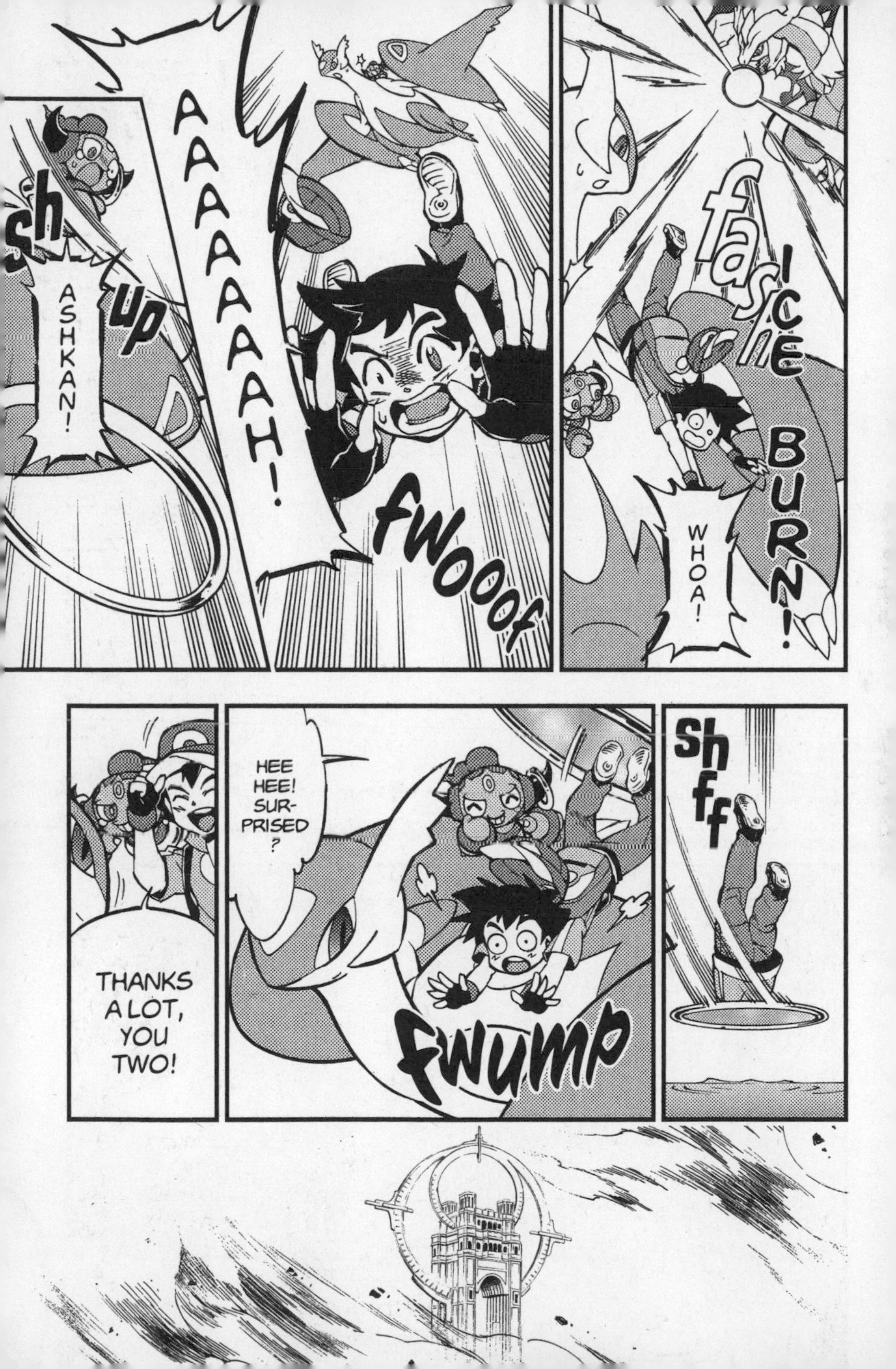

fasche
ICE BURN!
WHOA!
AAAAAAAH!
fwooof
Sh
up
ASHKAN!
Shff
HEE HEE! SUR-PRISED?
fwump
THANKS A LOT, YOU TWO!

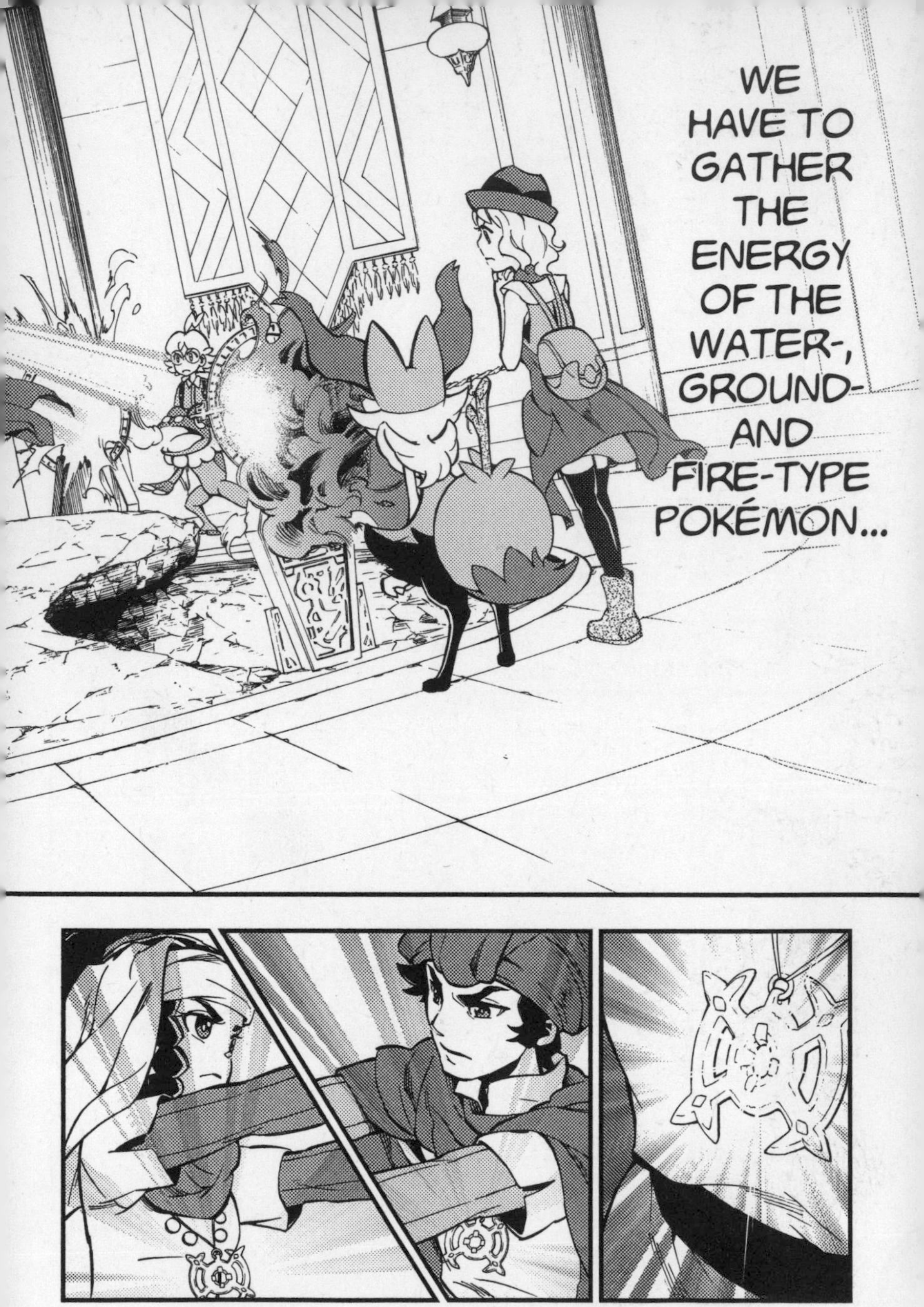
WE HAVE TO GATHER THE ENERGY OF THE WATER-, GROUND- AND FIRE-TYPE POKÉMON...

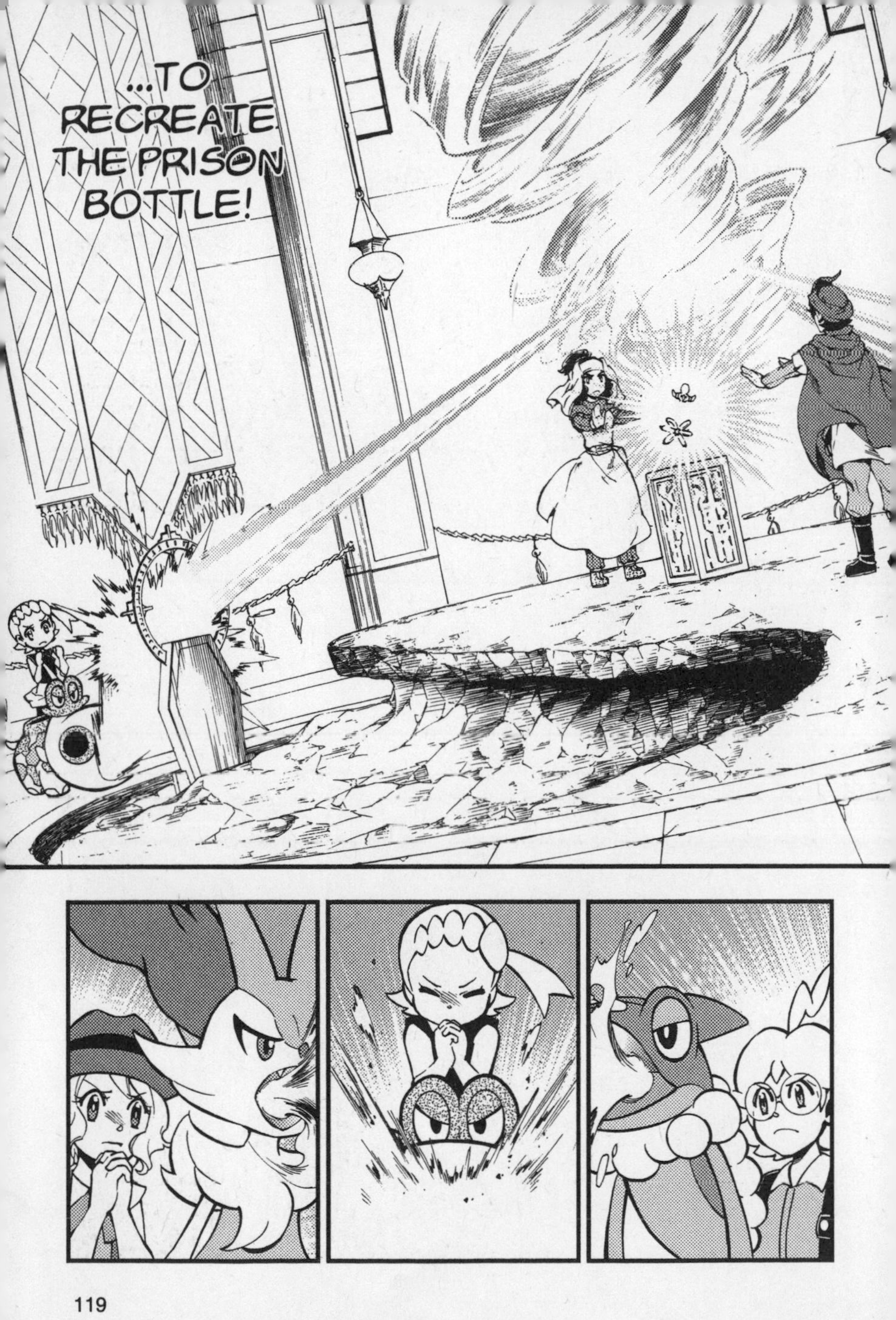
...TO RECREATE THE PRISON BOTTLE!

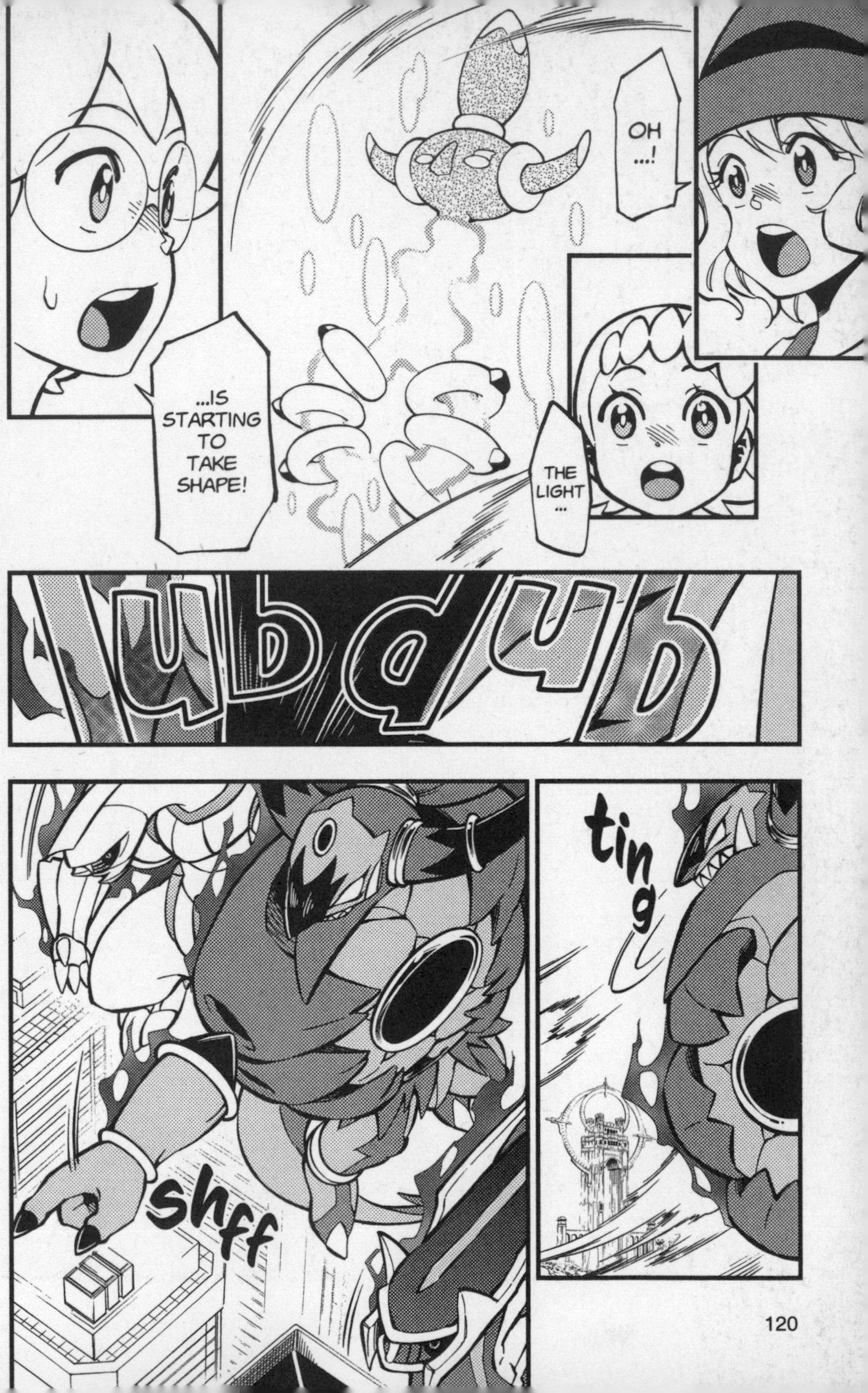
OH ...!
THE LIGHT ...
...IS STARTING TO TAKE SHAPE!
ubdub
ting
shff

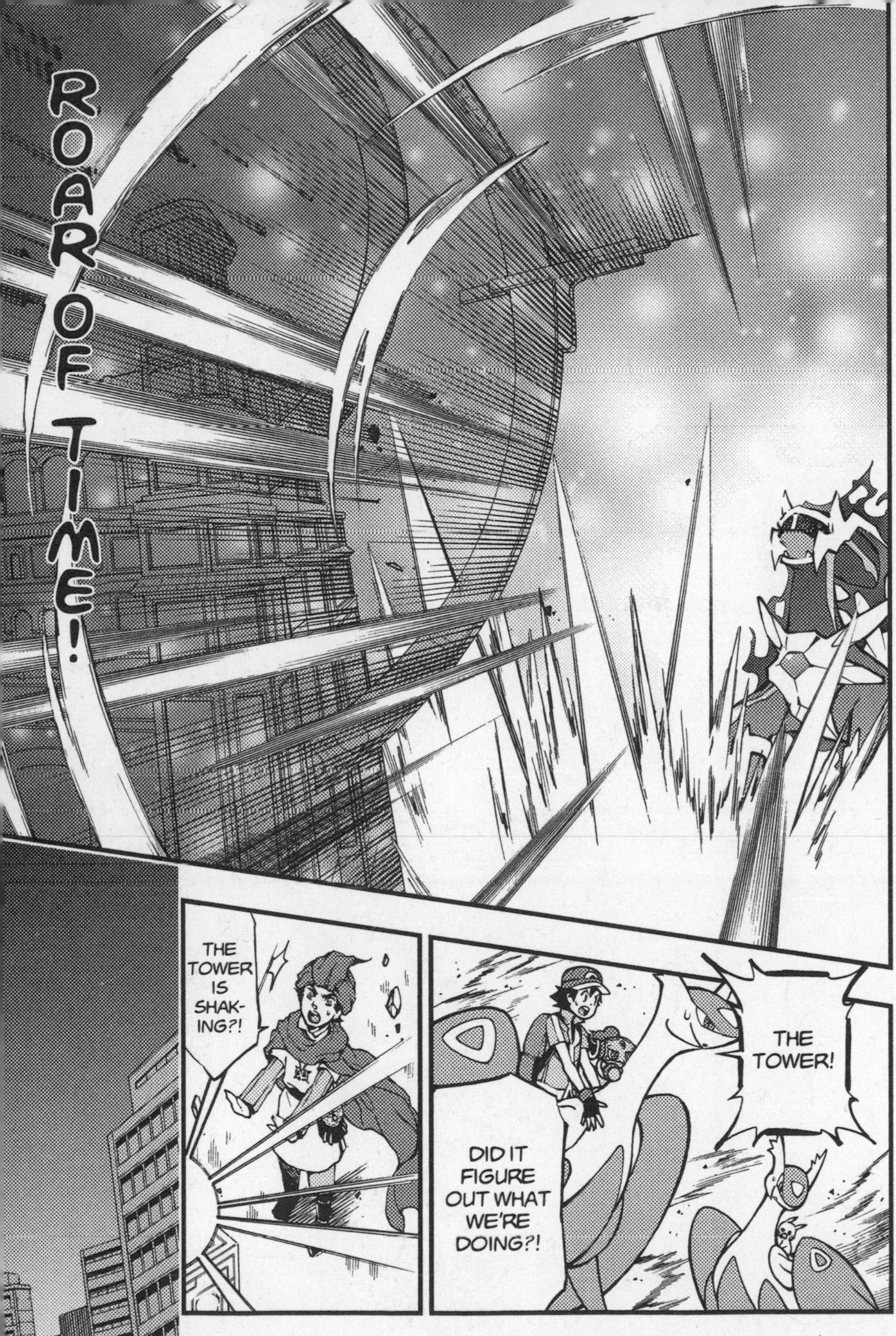
ROAR OF TIME!
THE TOWER!
DID IT FIGURE OUT WHAT WE'RE DOING?!
THE TOWER IS SHAK-ING?!

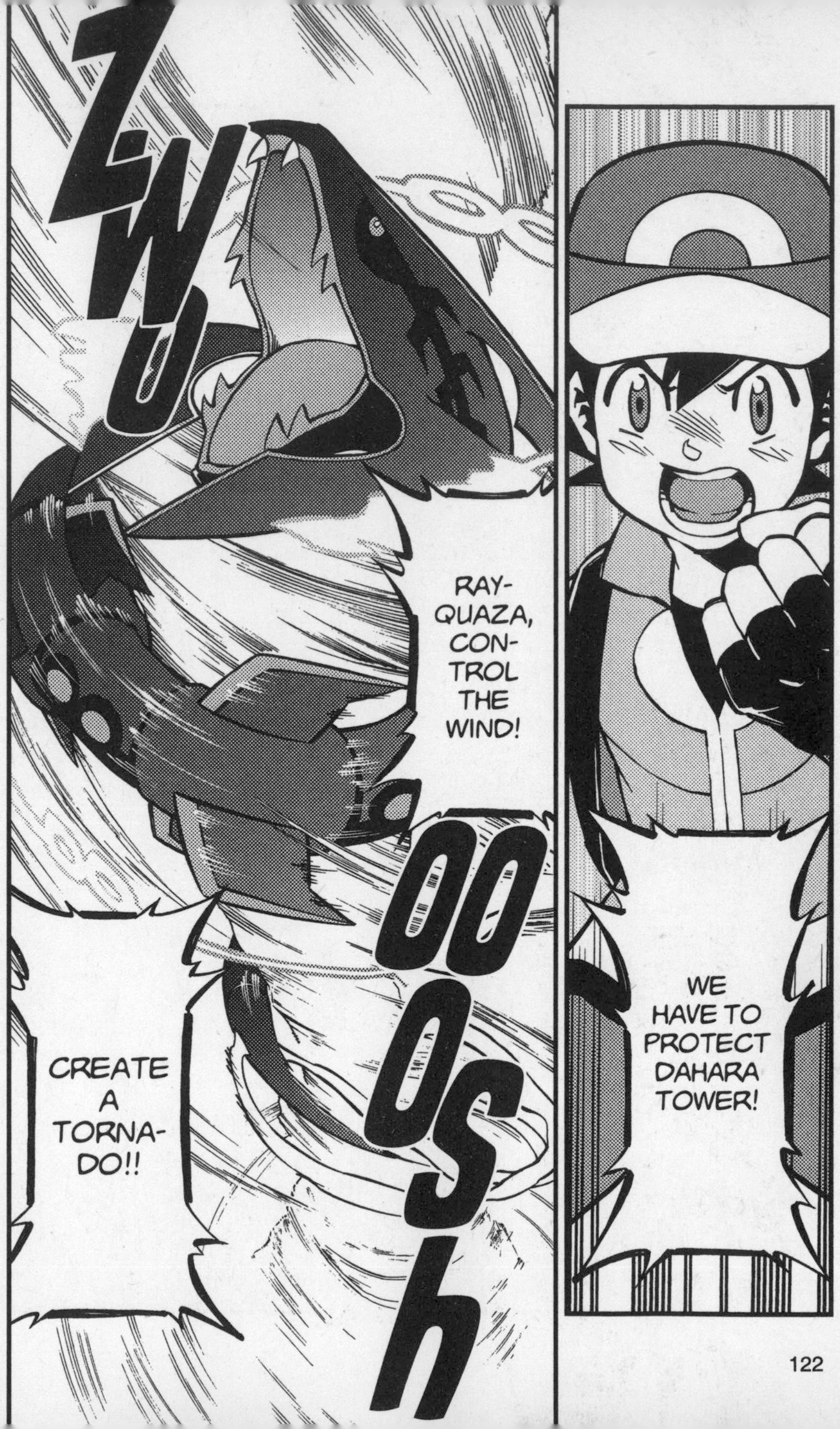
WE HAVE TO PROTECT DAHARA TOWER!
RAY-QUAZA, CONTROL THE WIND!
CREATE A TORNADO!!

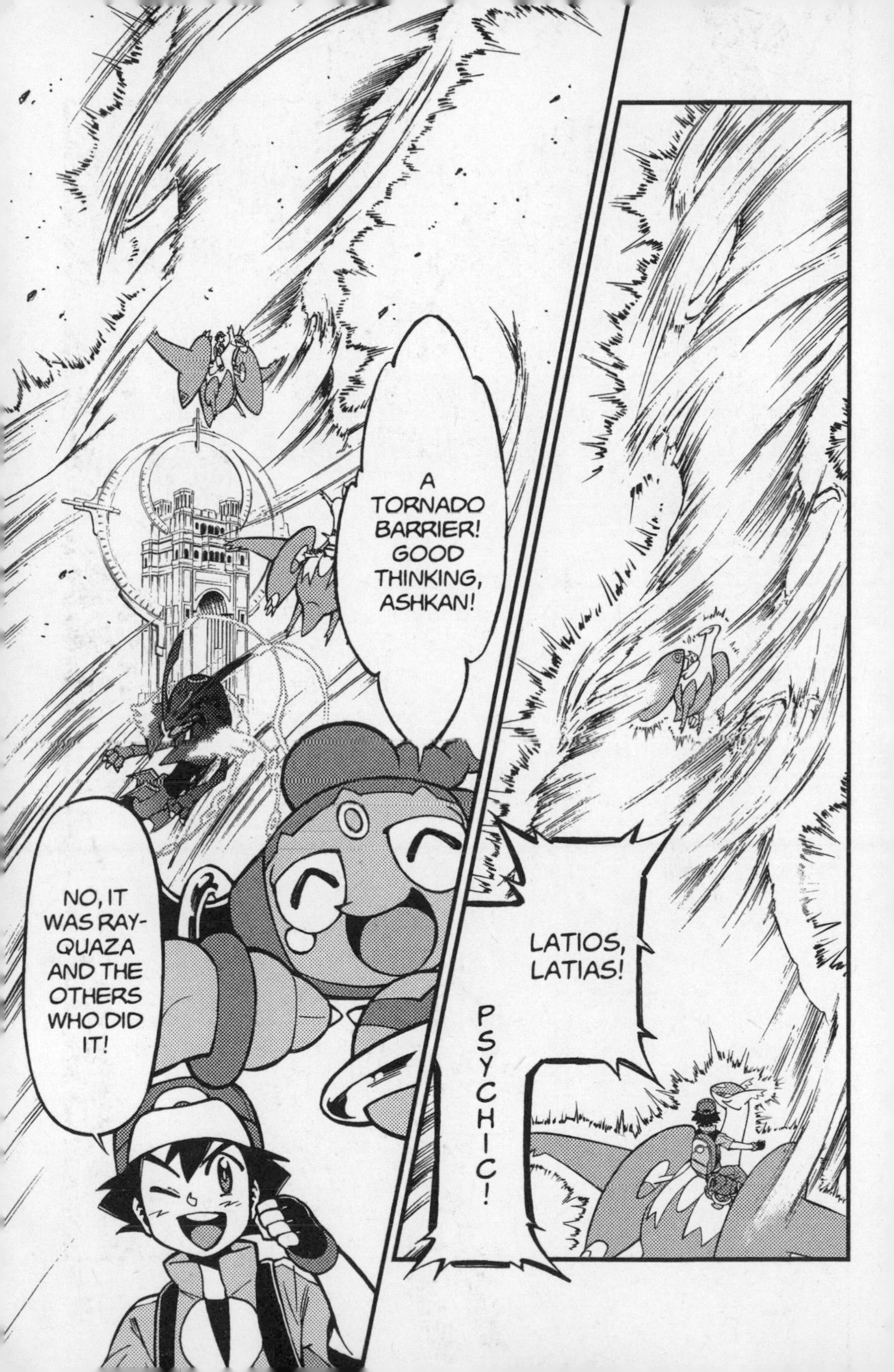
LATIOS, LATIAS!
PSYCHIC!
A TORNADO BARRIER! GOOD THINKING, ASHKAN!
NO, IT WAS RAY-QUAZA AND THE OTHERS WHO DID IT!

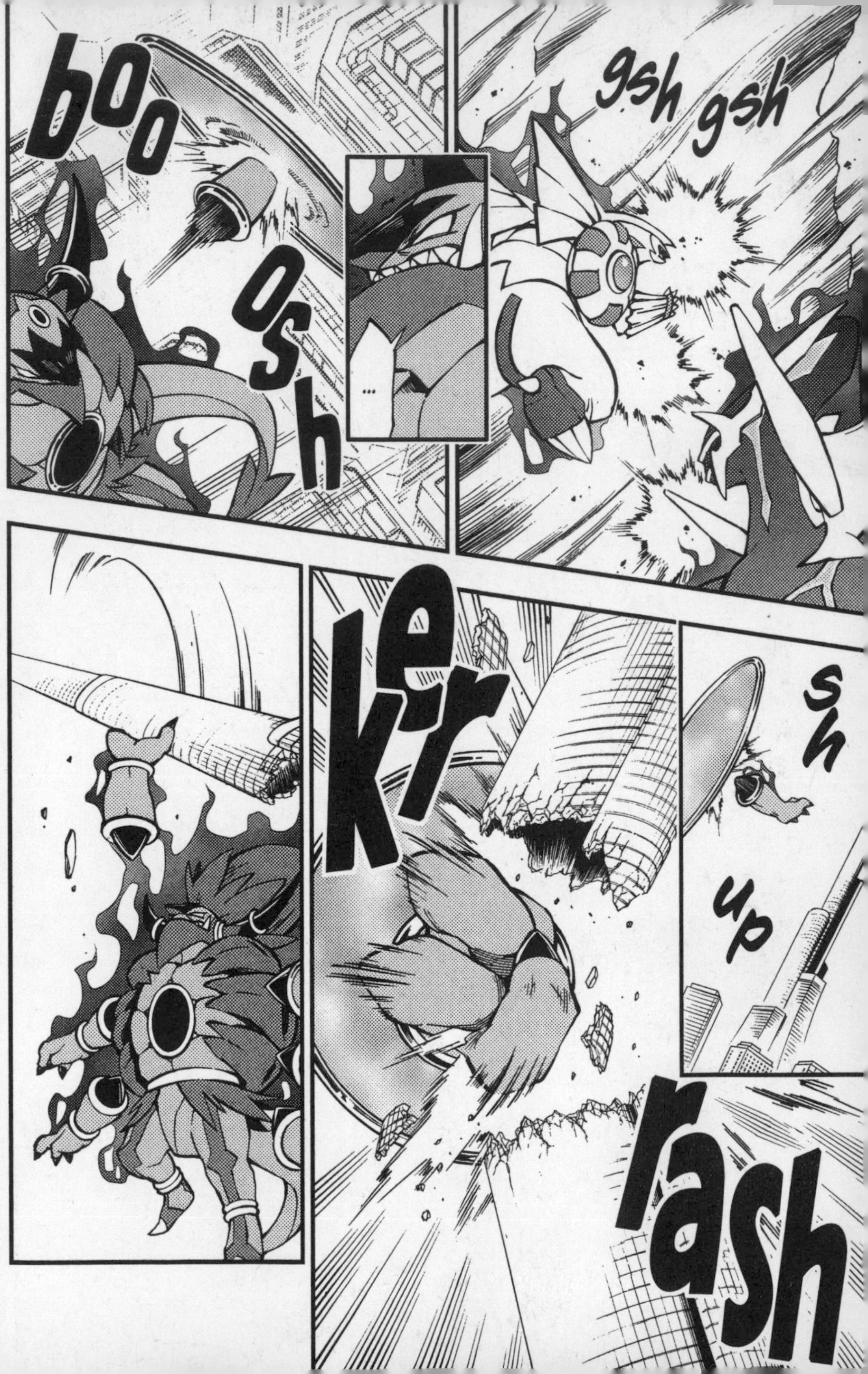
gsh gsh
...
booosh
shup
kerrash

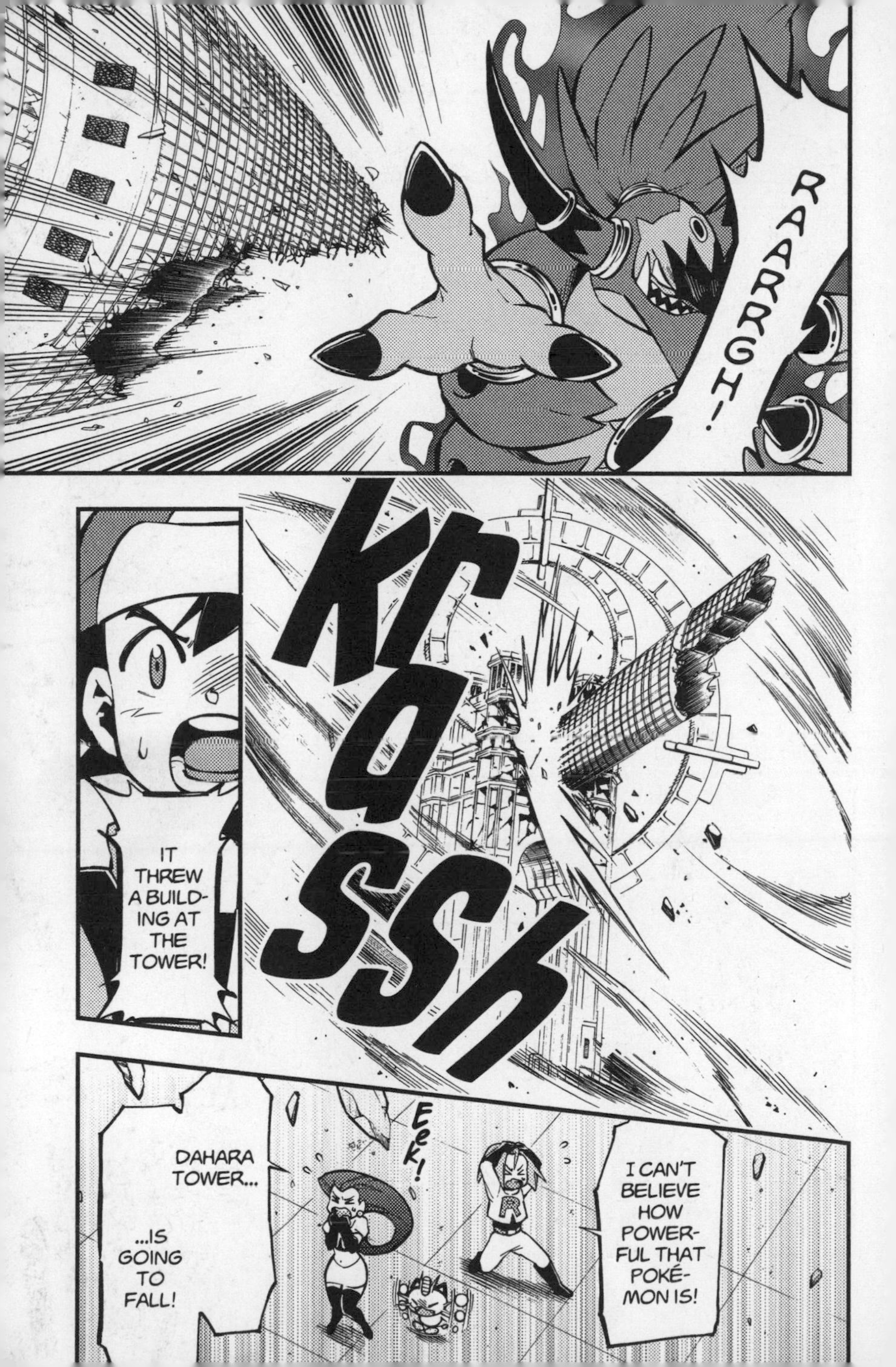
RAARRGH!
KRASSH
IT THREW A BUILDING AT THE TOWER!
I CAN'T BELIEVE HOW POWERFUL THAT POKÉMON IS!
Eek!
DAHARA TOWER...
...IS GOING TO FALL!

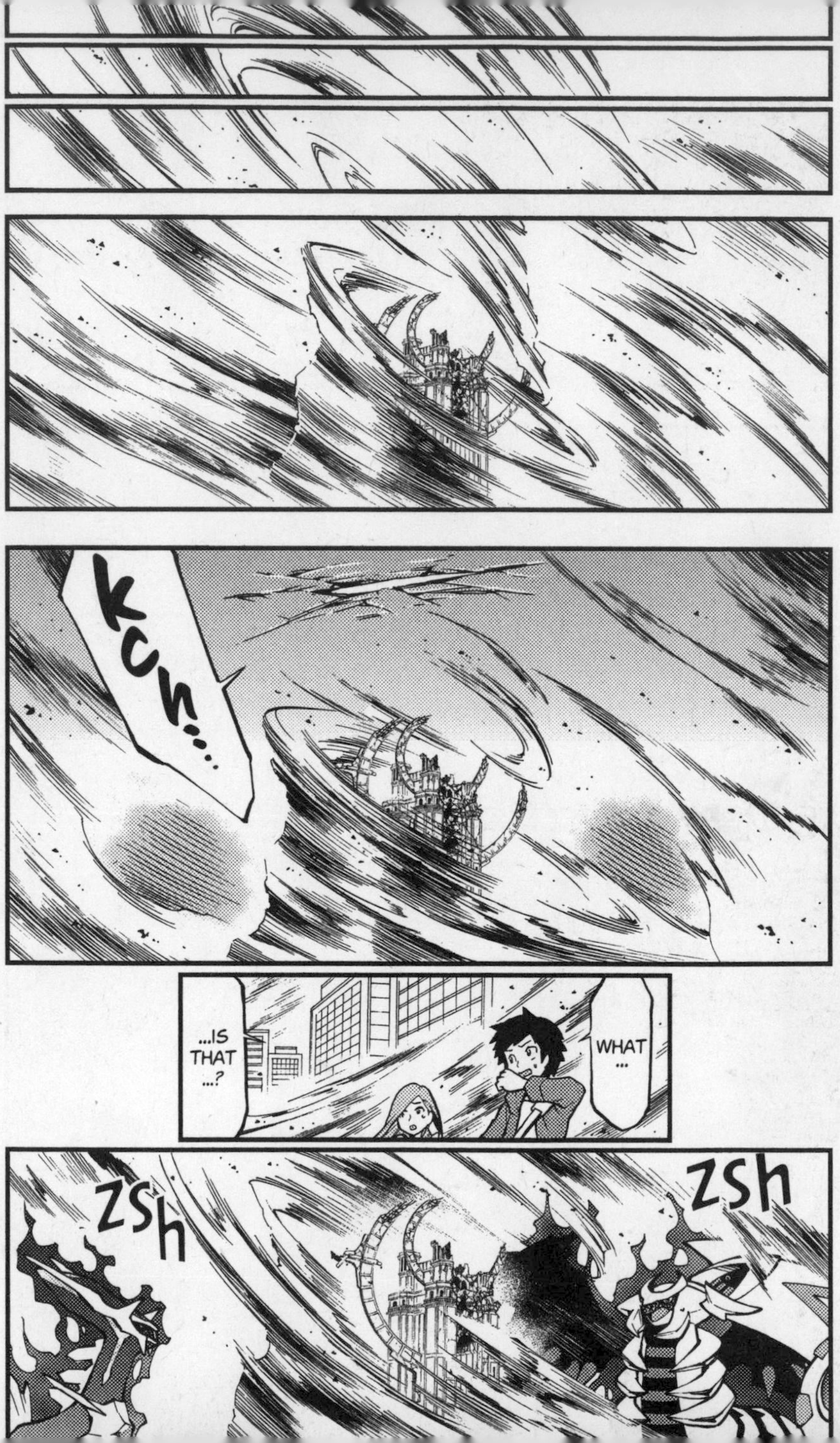
KUN...
WHAT...
...IS THAT ...?
ZSh
ZSh

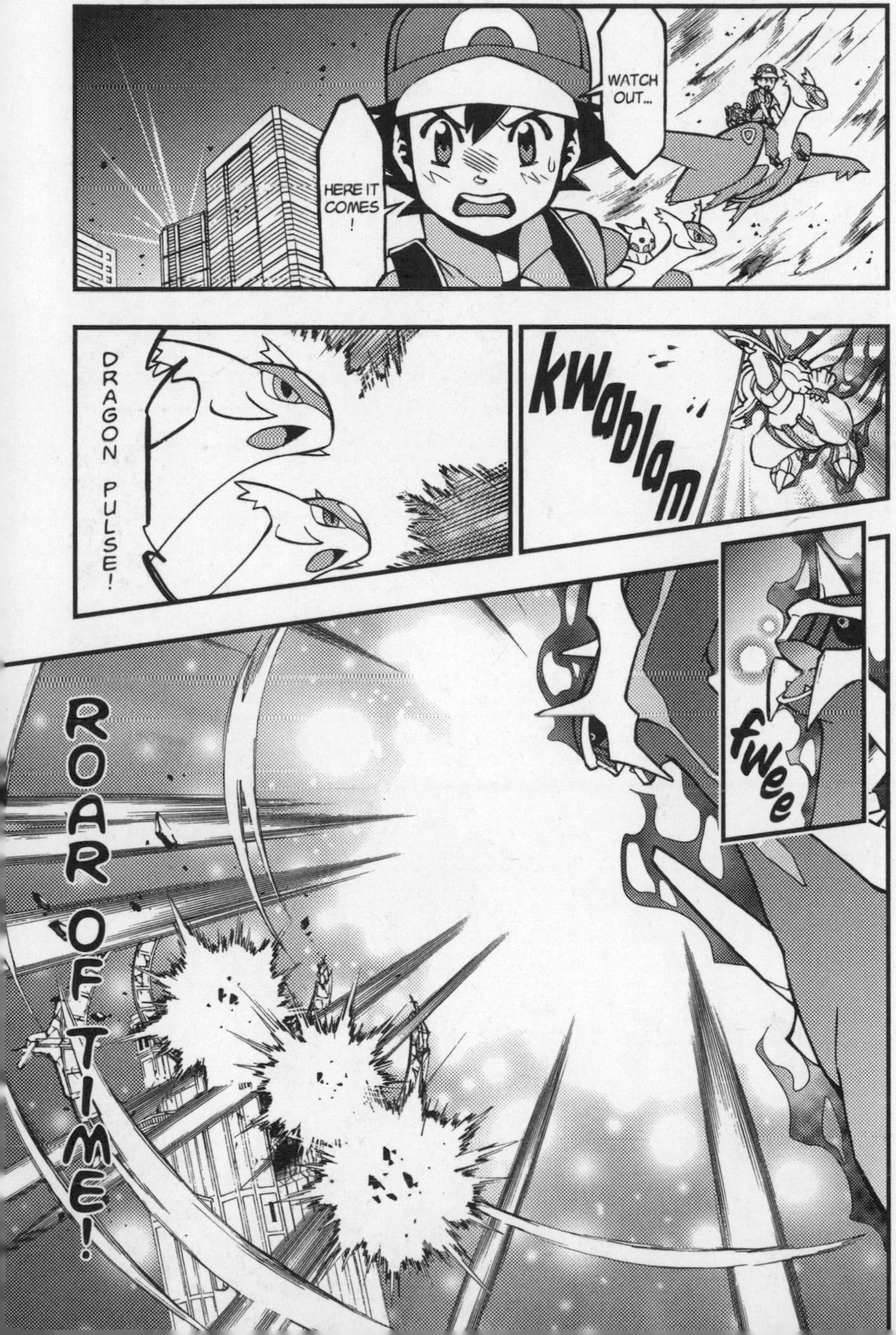
WATCH OUT...
HERE IT COMES!
kwablam
DRAGON PULSE!
fweee
ROAR OF TIME!

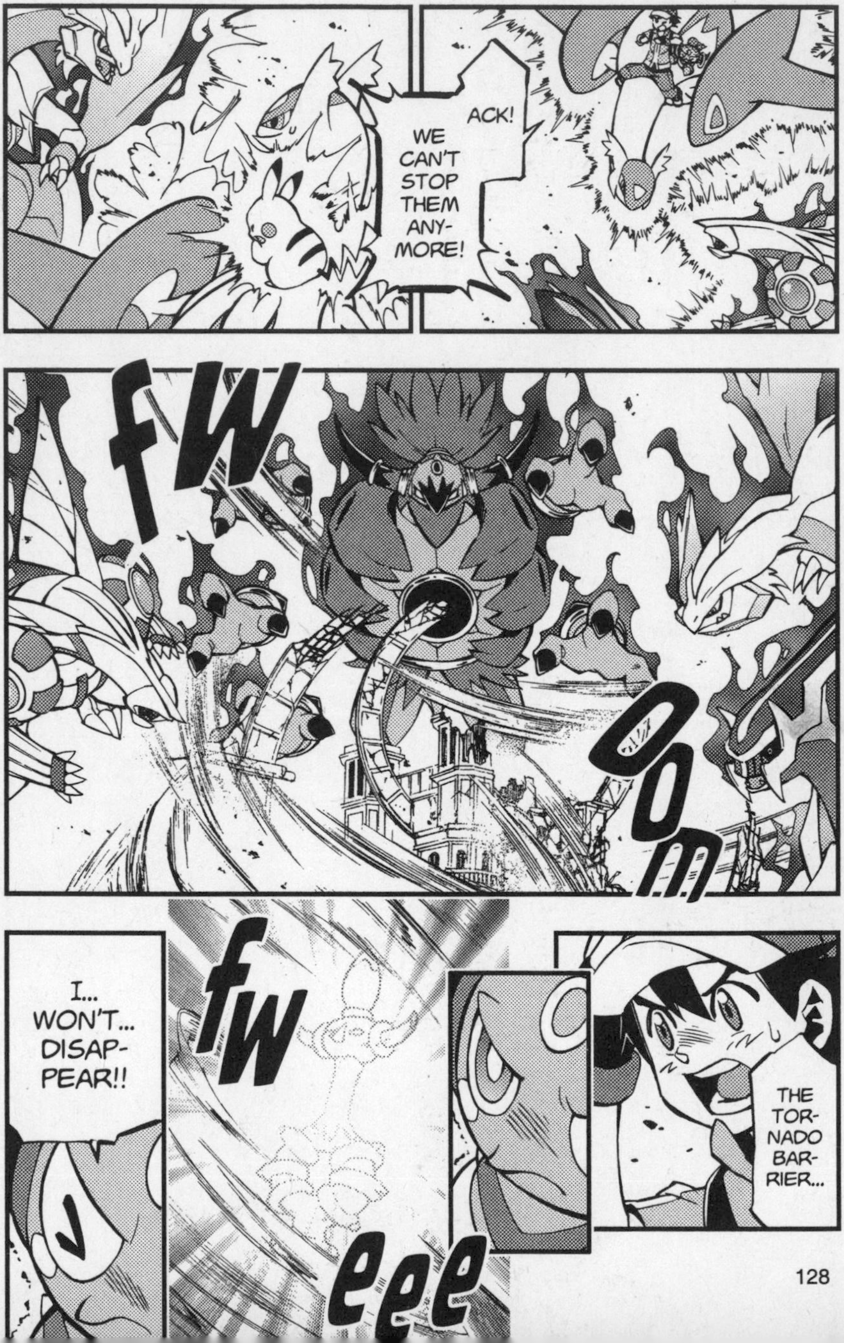
ACK!
WE CAN'T STOP THEM ANYMORE!
FWOOM
THE TORNADO BARRIER...
FWEEE
I... WON'T... DISAPPEAR!!

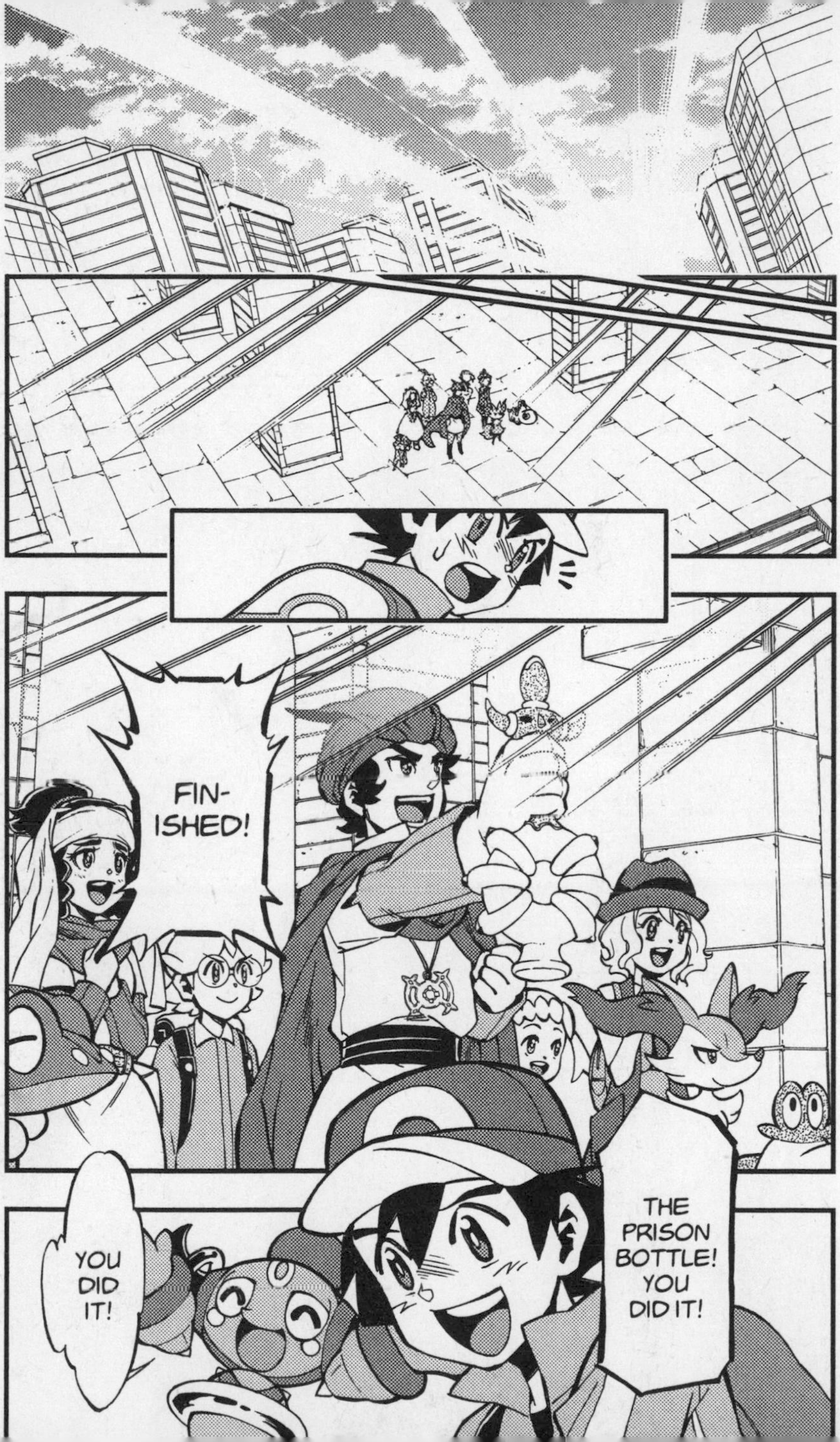
FIN-
ISHED!
THE PRISON BOTTLE! YOU DID IT!
YOU DID IT!

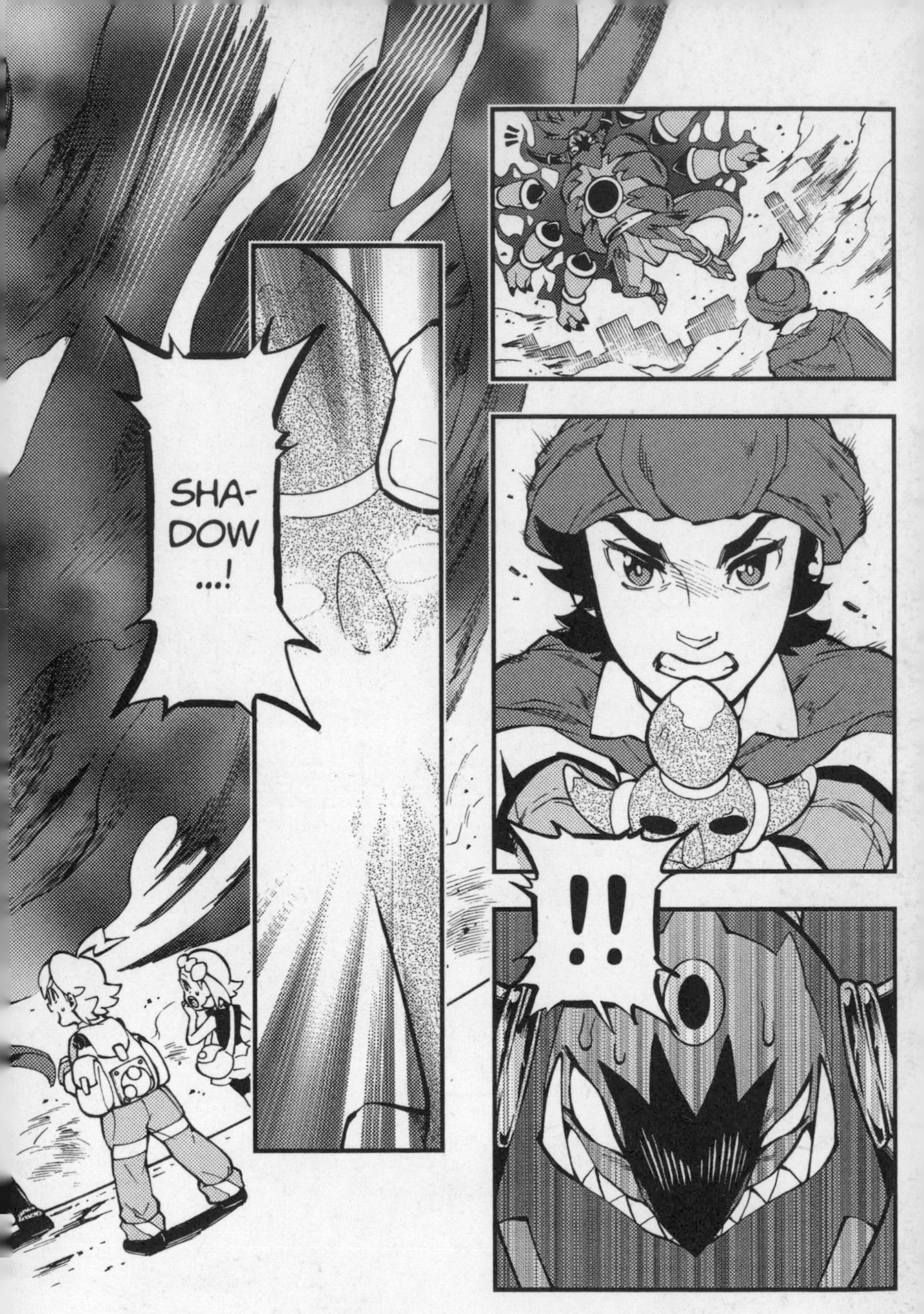
!!
SHA-
DOW
...!

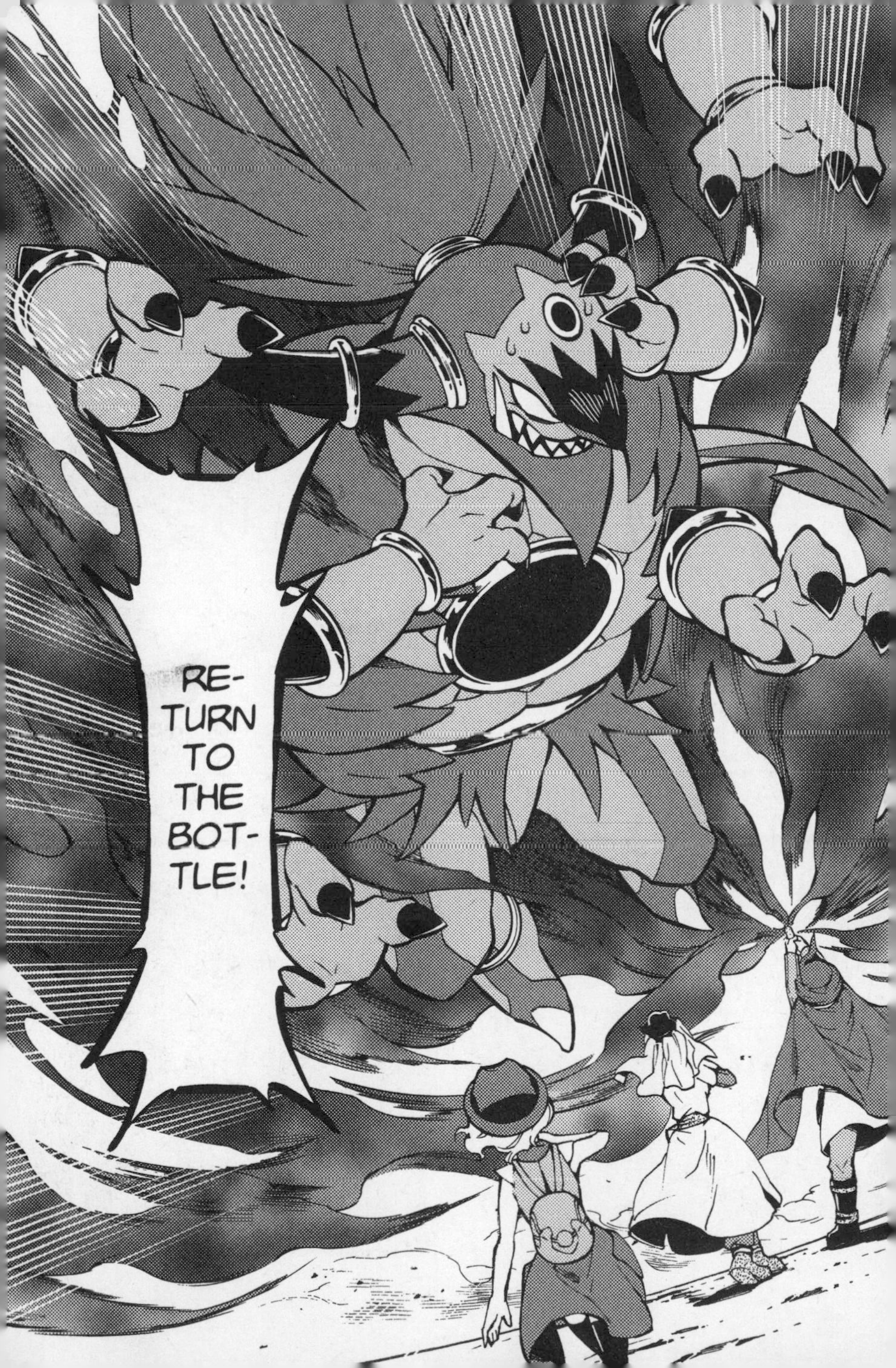
RE-TURN TO THE BOT-TLE!

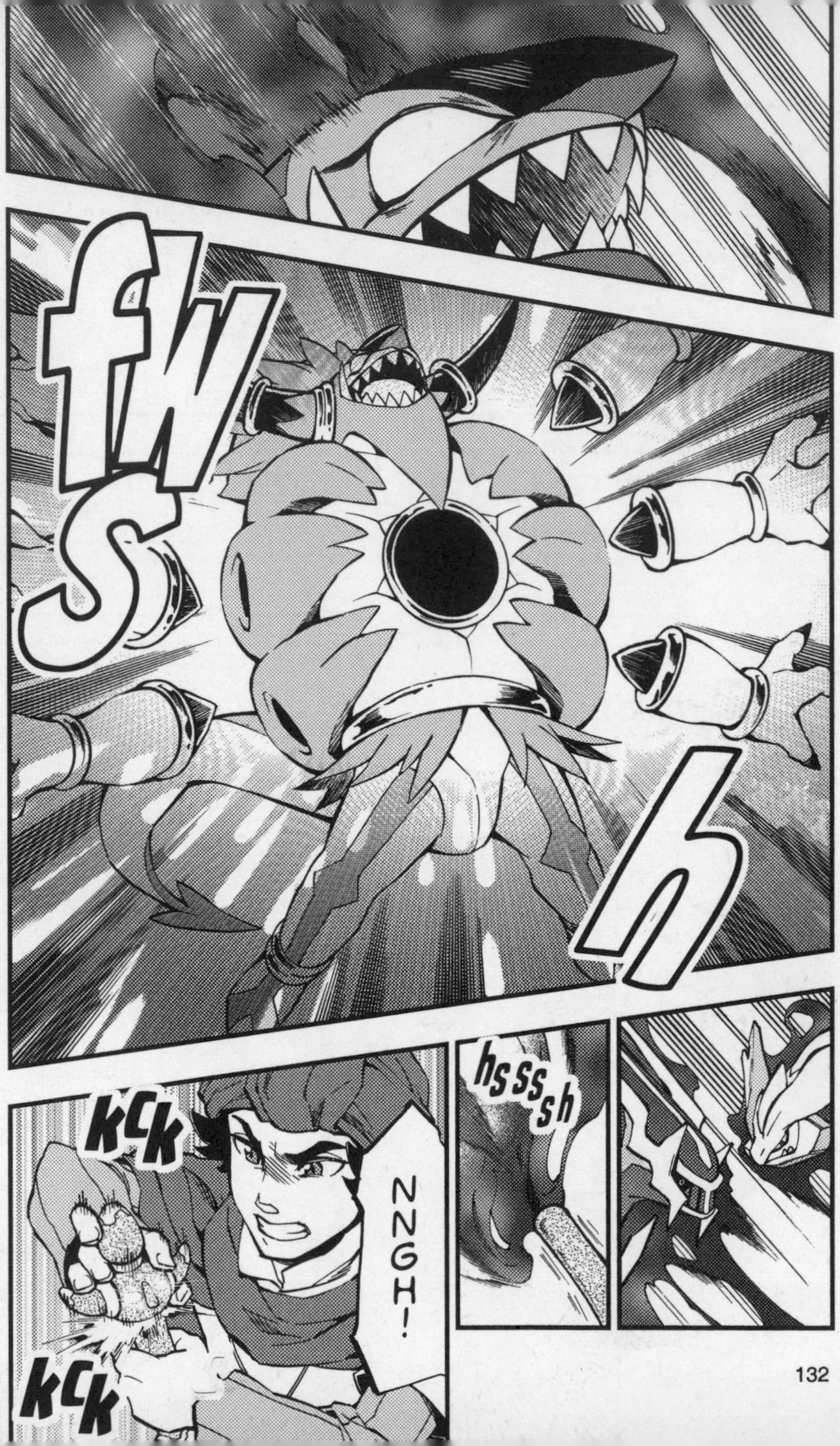
fwsh
hssssh
kck
NNGH!
kck

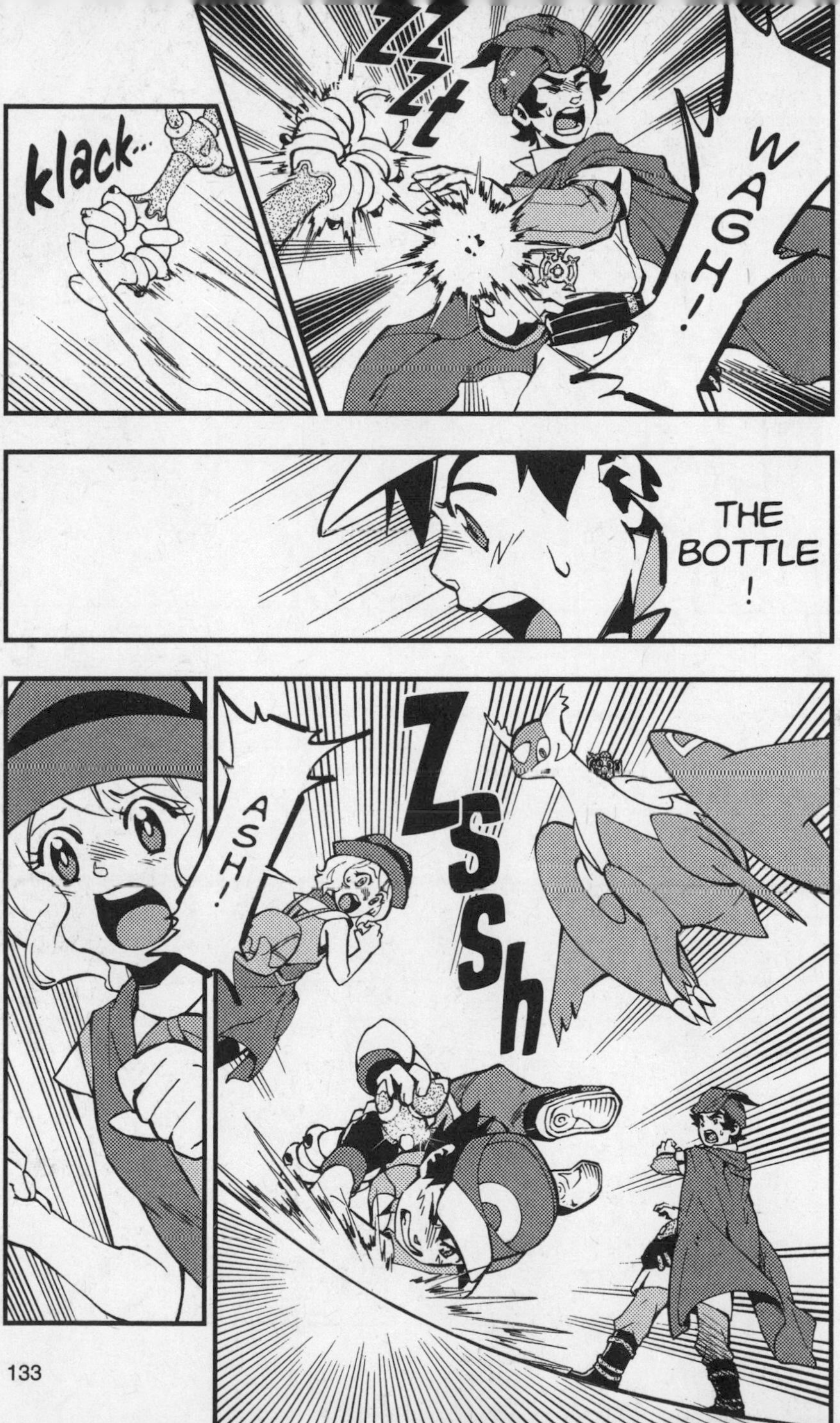
ZZZt
WAGH!
klack...
THE BOTTLE!
ZSSh
ASH!

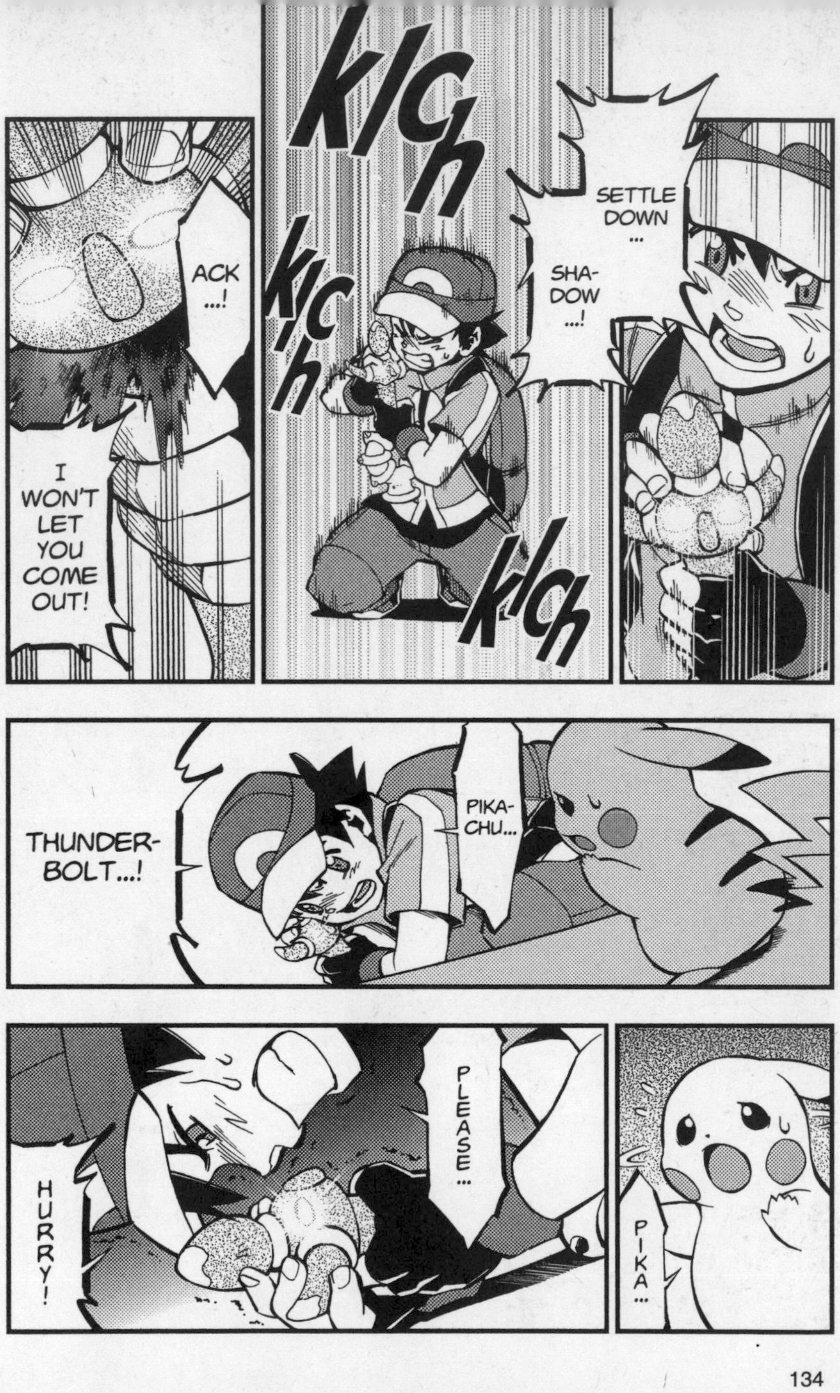

SETTLE DOWN ...
SHADOW ...!
KLCH
KLCH
KLCH
ACK ...!
I WON'T LET YOU COME OUT!
PIKA-CHU...
THUNDER-BOLT...!
PIKA...
PLEASE...
HURRY!

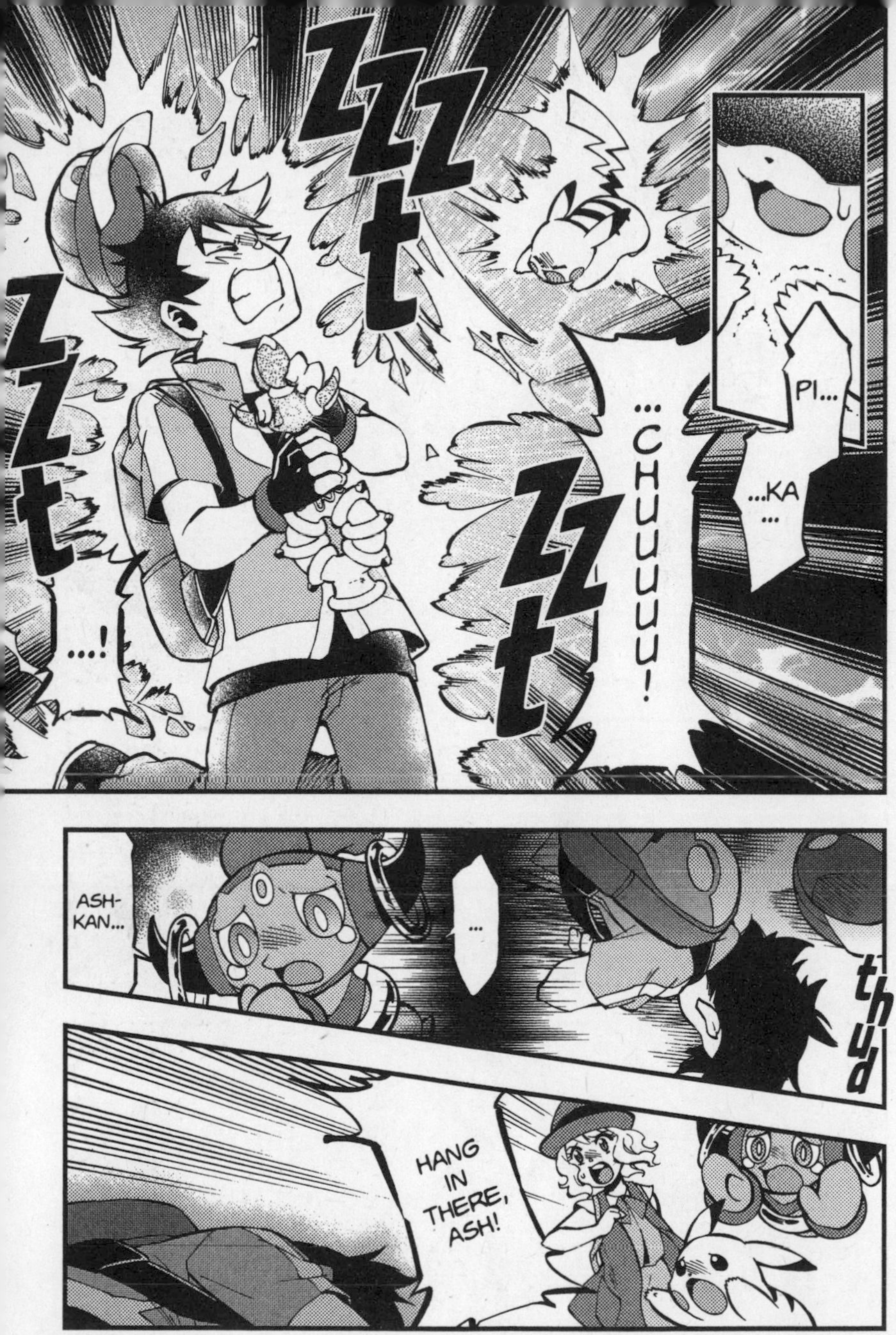
PI...
...KA ...
ZZZT
...CHUUUUUU!
ZZT
ZZT
...!
thud
...
ASH-KAN...
HANG IN THERE, ASH!

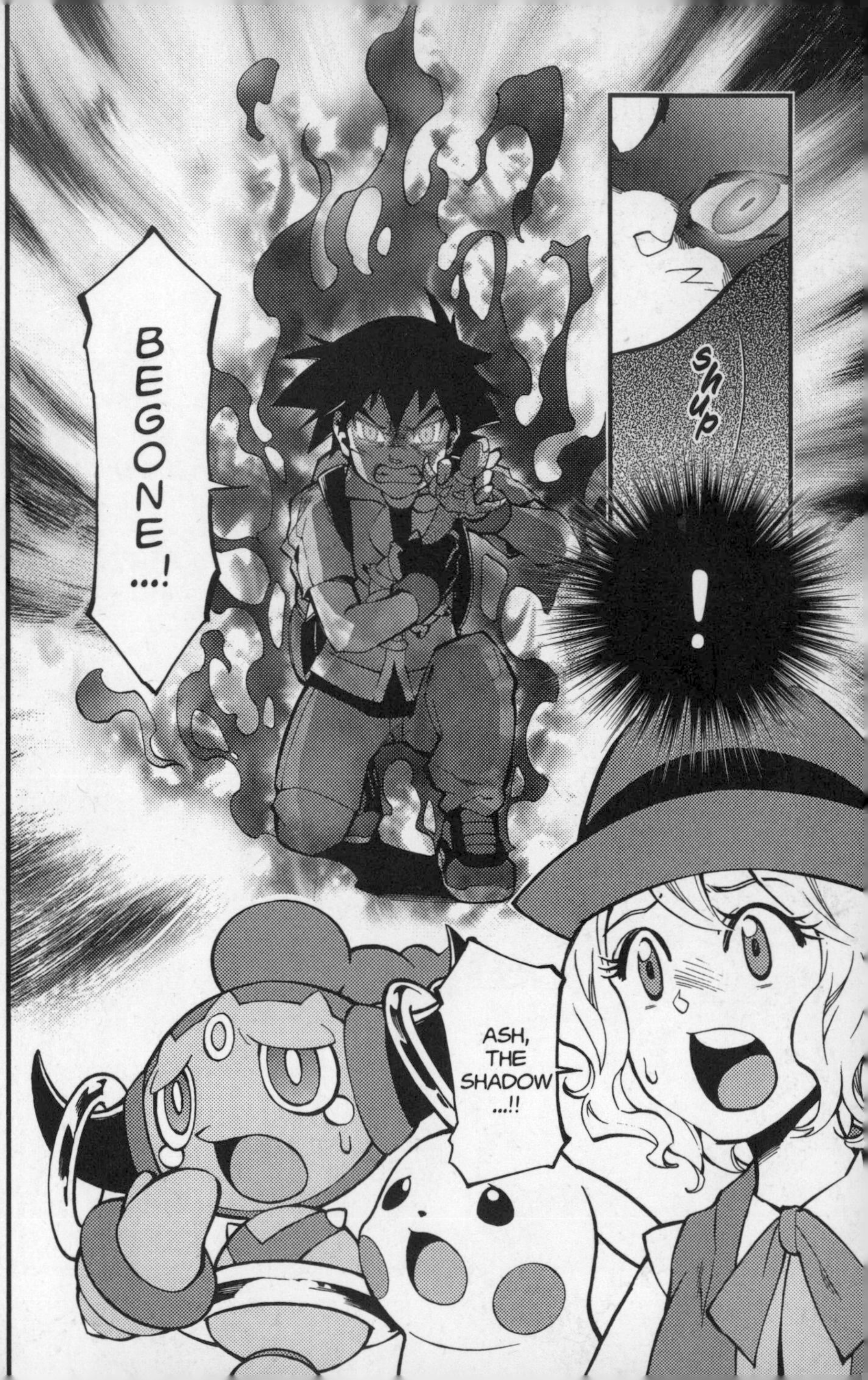
shup
BEGONE...!
!
ASH, THE SHADOW...!!

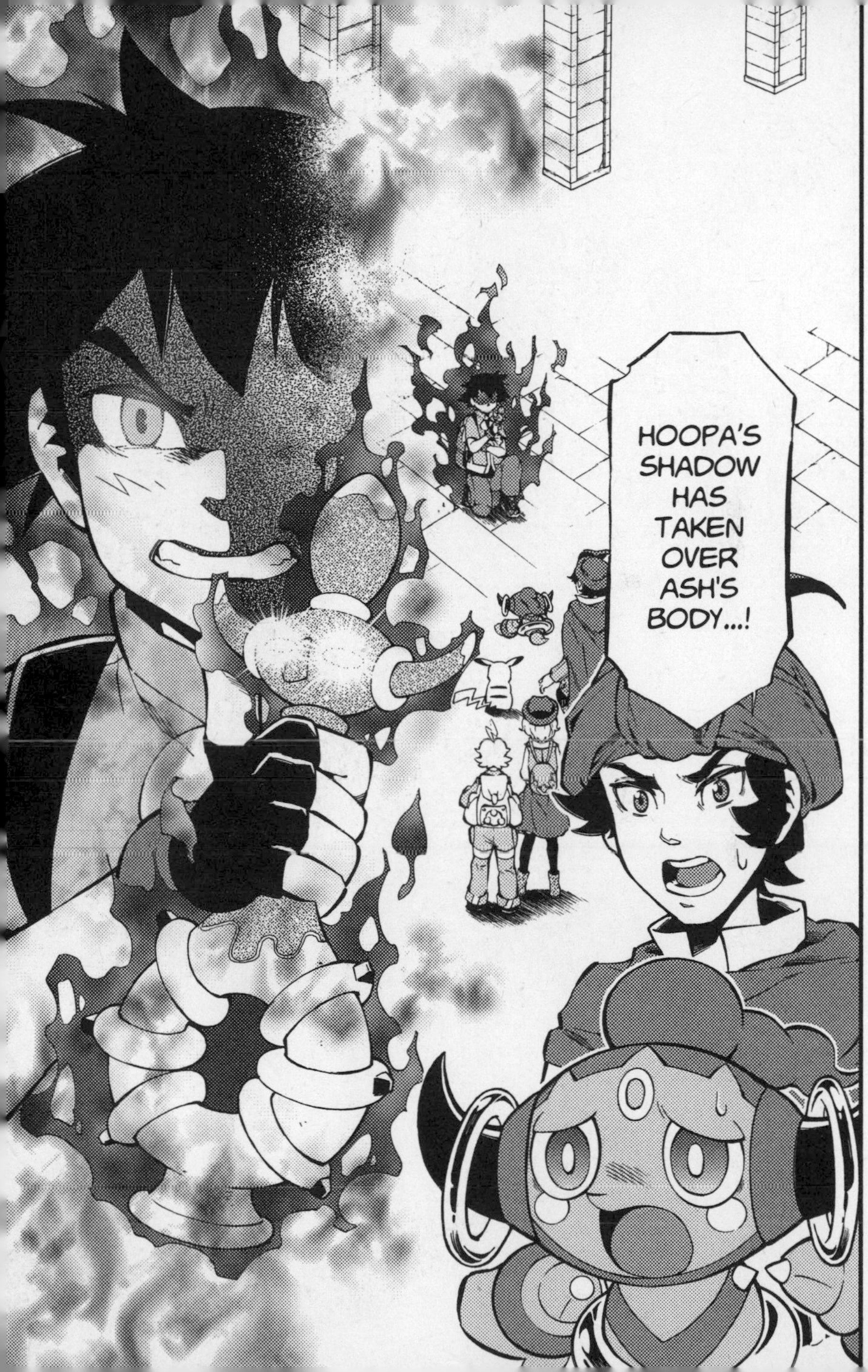
HOOPA'S SHADOW HAS TAKEN OVER ASH'S BODY...!

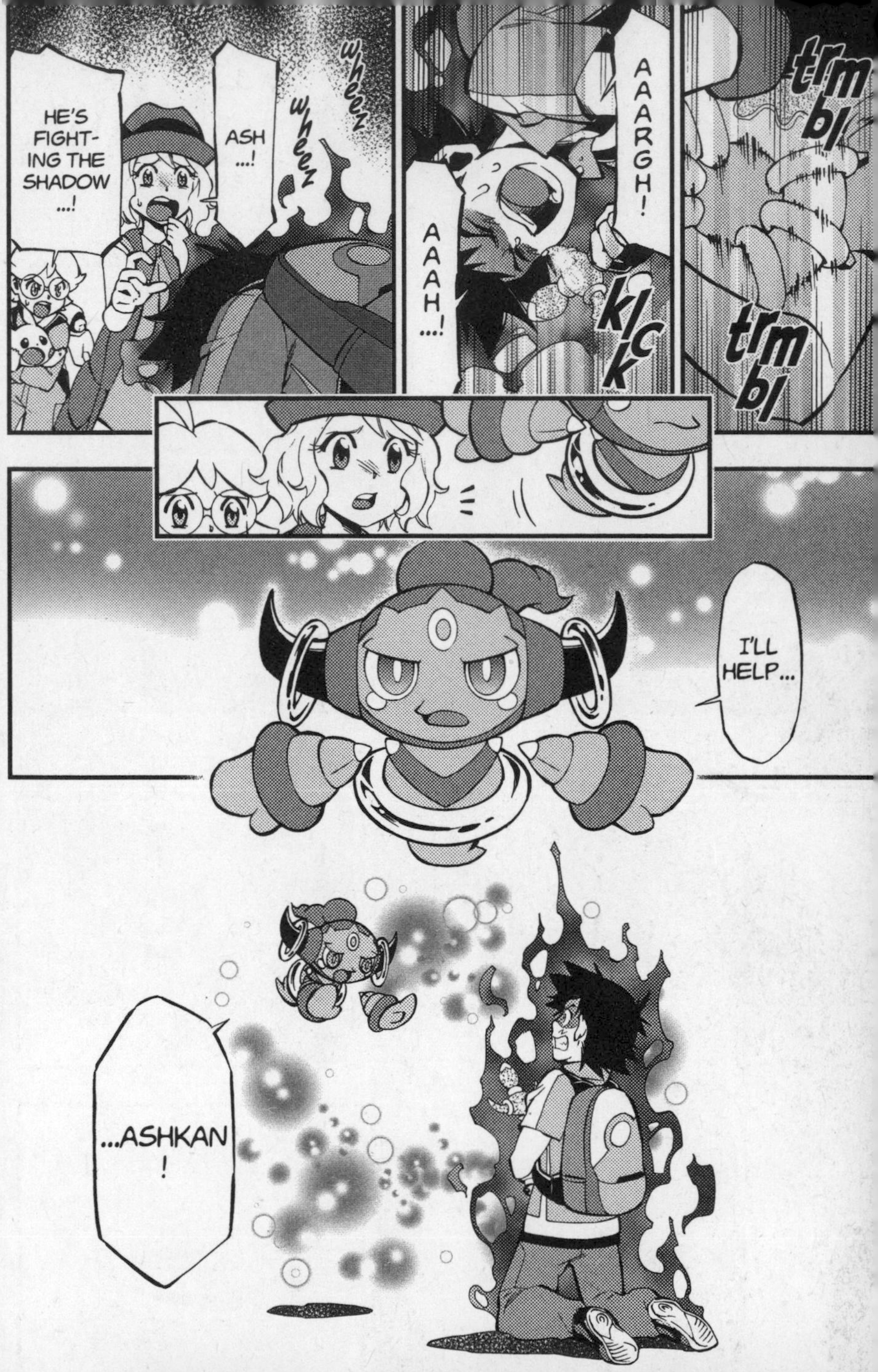
trm bl
trm bl
AAAARGH!
AAAAH ...!
klck
wheez
wheez
ASH ...!
HE'S FIGHTING THE SHADOW ...!
I'LL HELP...
...ASHKAN!

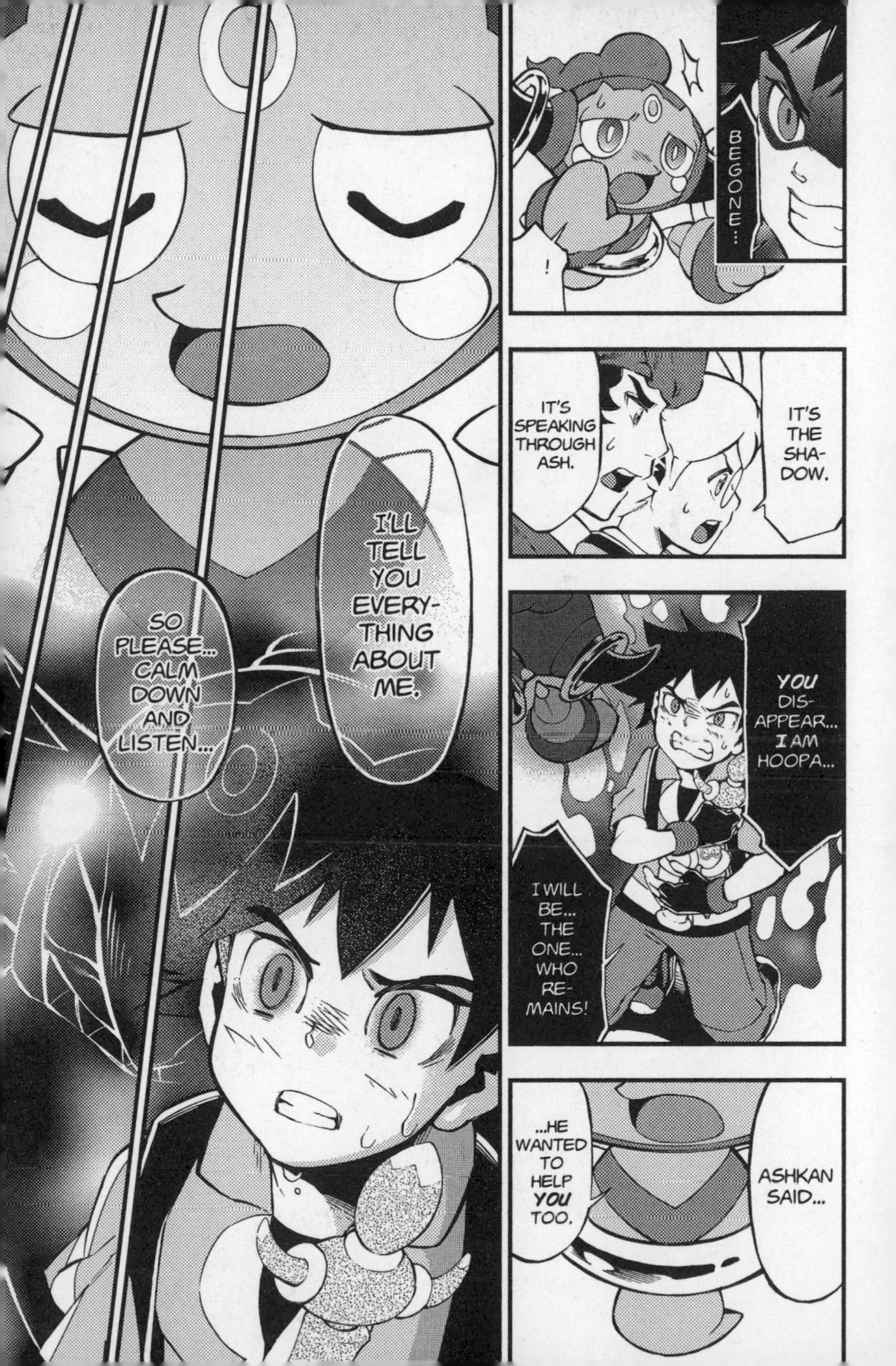
BEGONE...
!
IT'S THE SHA-DOW.
IT'S SPEAKING THROUGH ASH.
YOU DIS-APPEAR... I AM HOOPA...
I WILL BE... THE ONE... WHO RE-MAINS!
ASHKAN SAID...
...HE WANTED TO HELP YOU TOO.
I'LL TELL YOU EVERY-THING ABOUT ME.
SO PLEASE... CALM DOWN AND LISTEN...

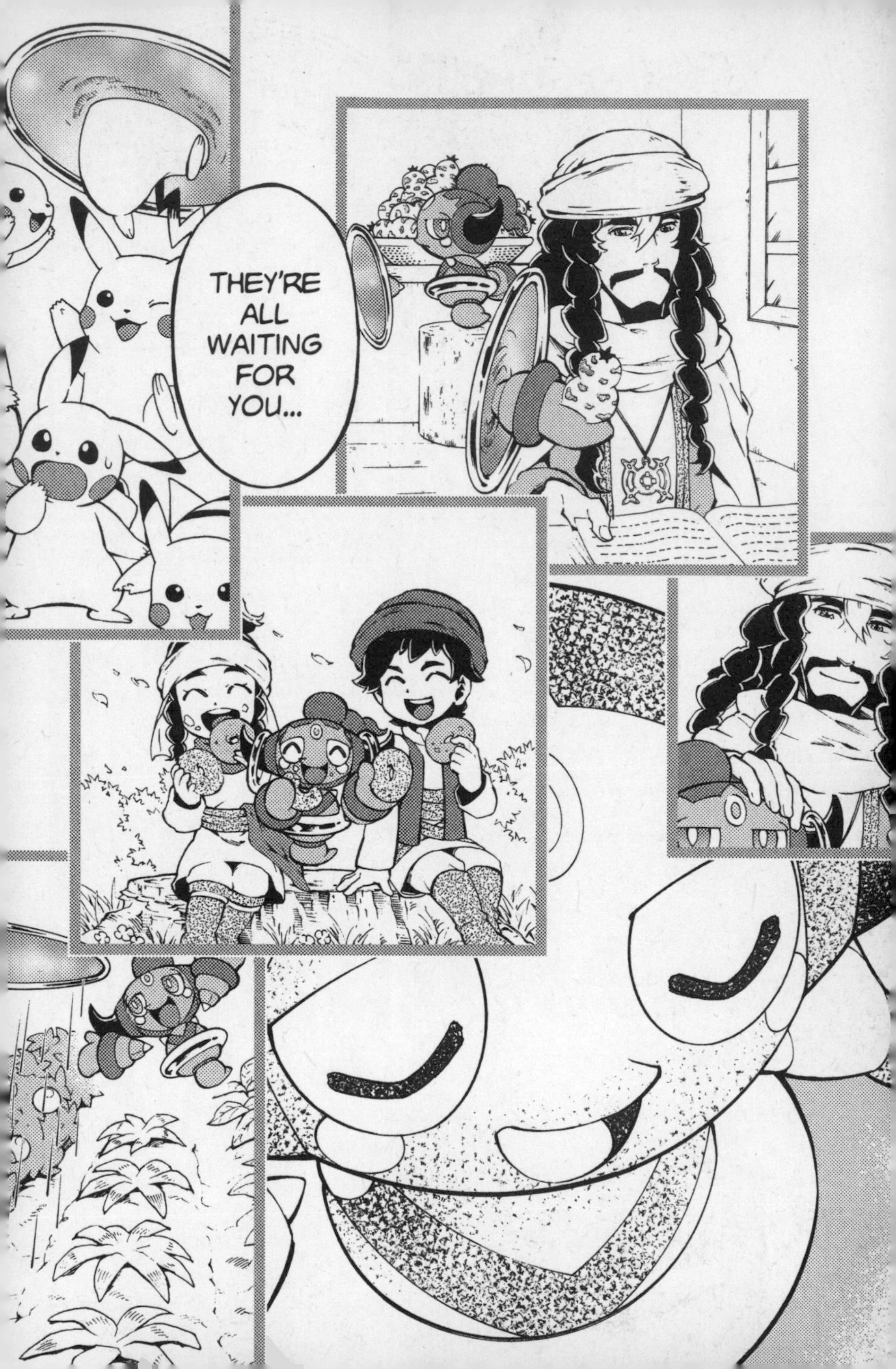
THEY'RE ALL WAITING FOR YOU...

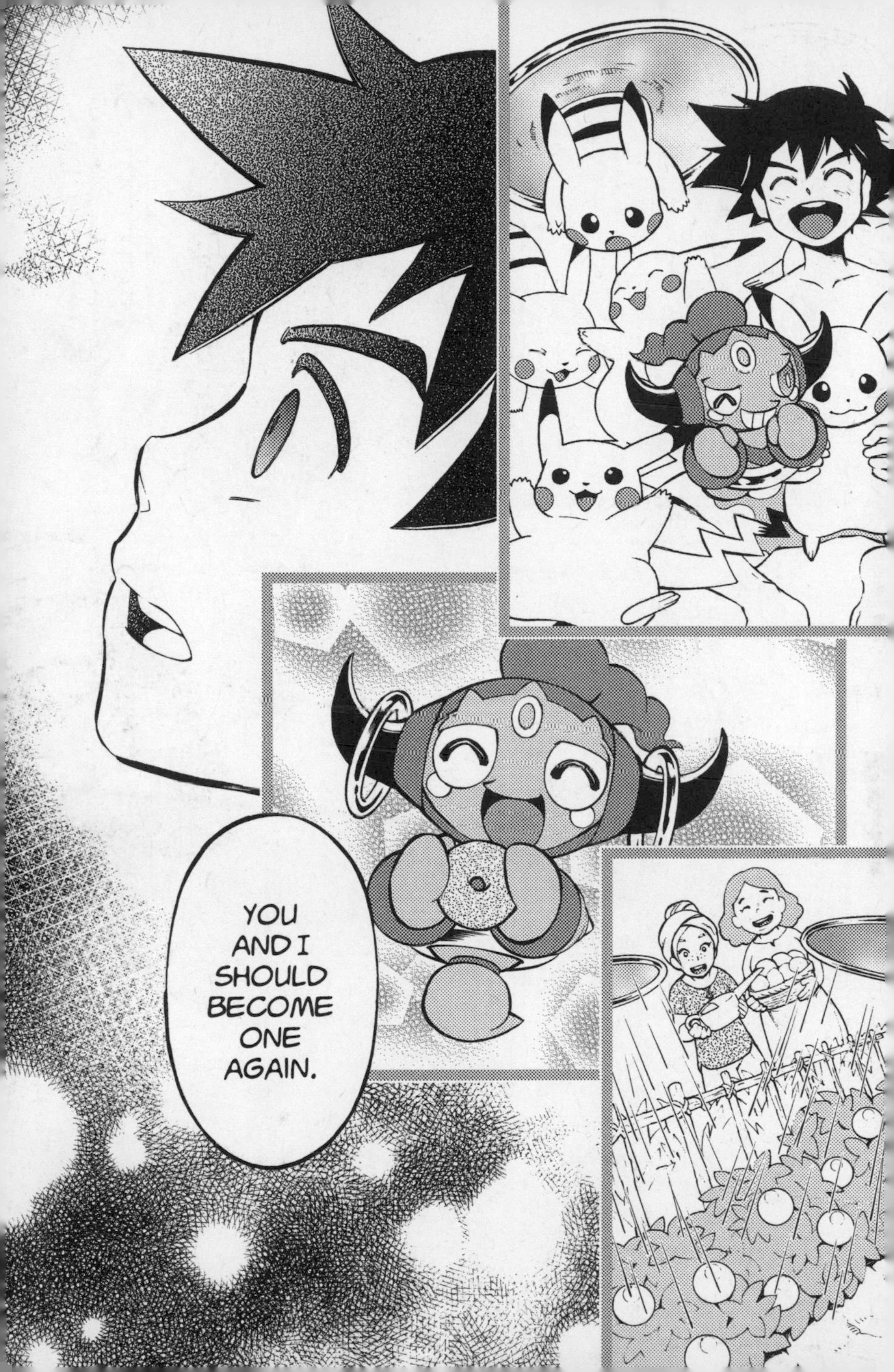
YOU AND I SHOULD BECOME ONE AGAIN.

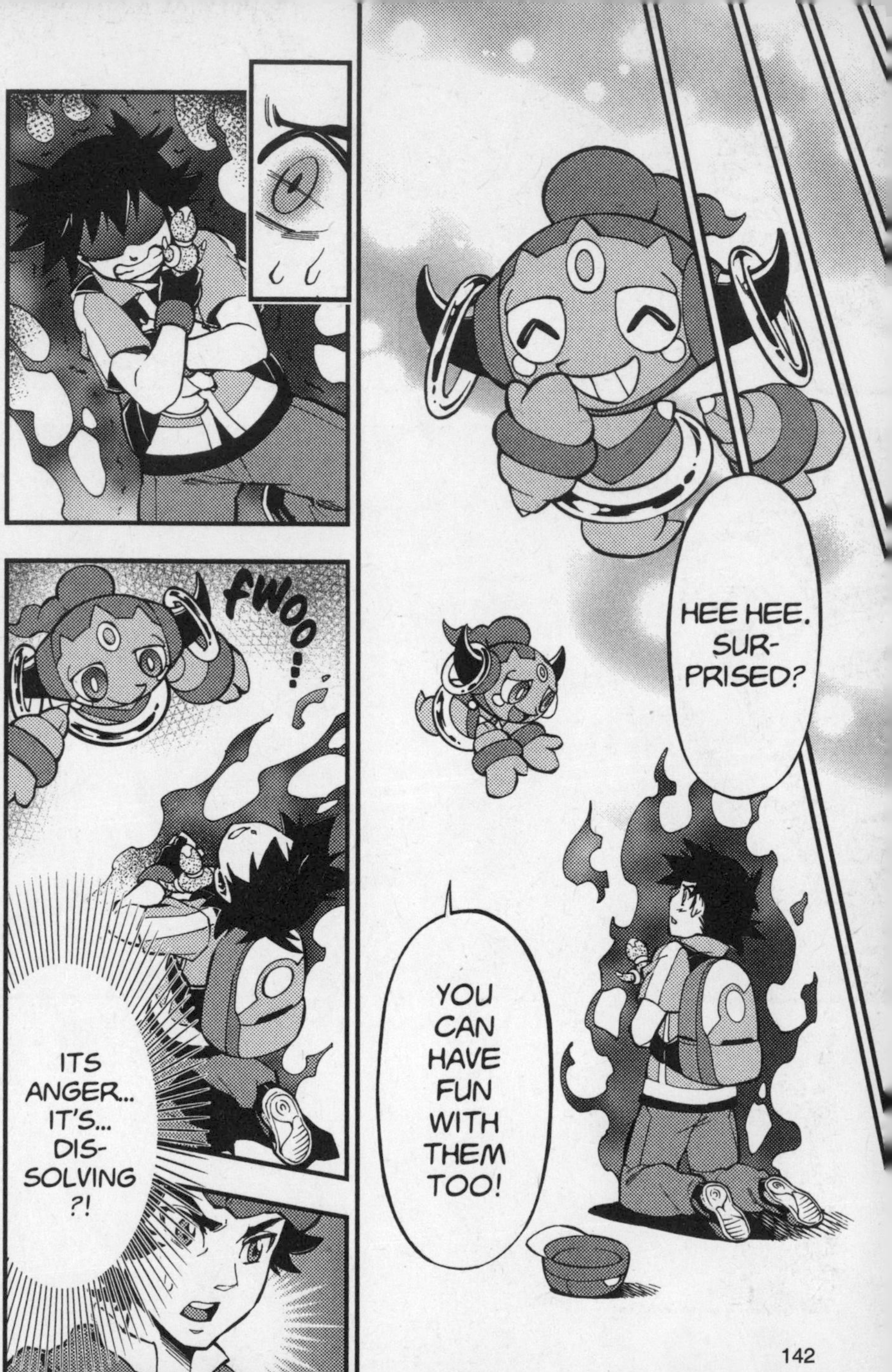
HEE HEE. SUR-PRISED?
YOU CAN HAVE FUN WITH THEM TOO!
FWOO...!
ITS ANGER... IT'S... DIS-SOLVING?!

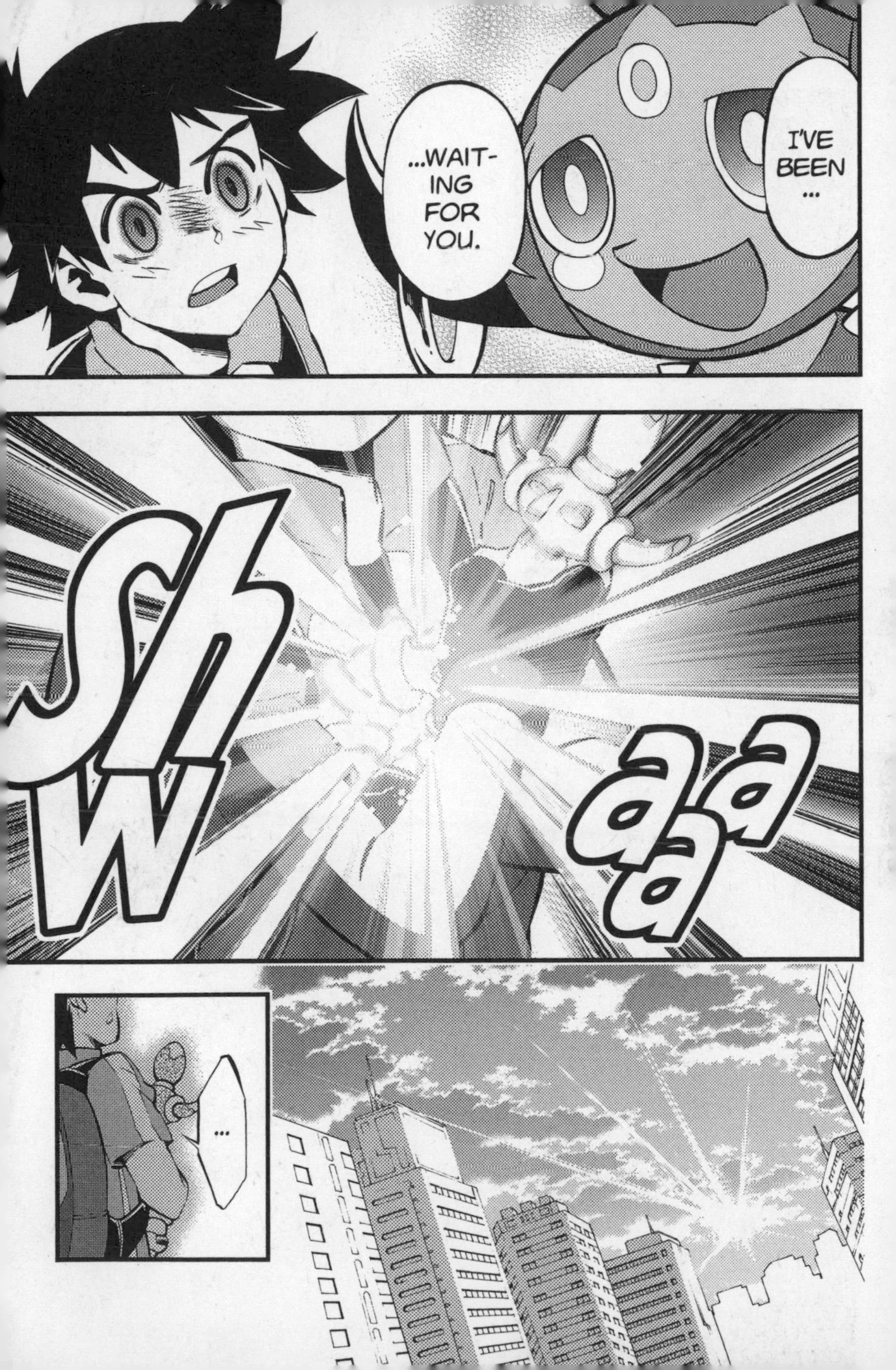
I'VE BEEN ...
...WAIT-ING FOR YOU.
Shwaaaa
...

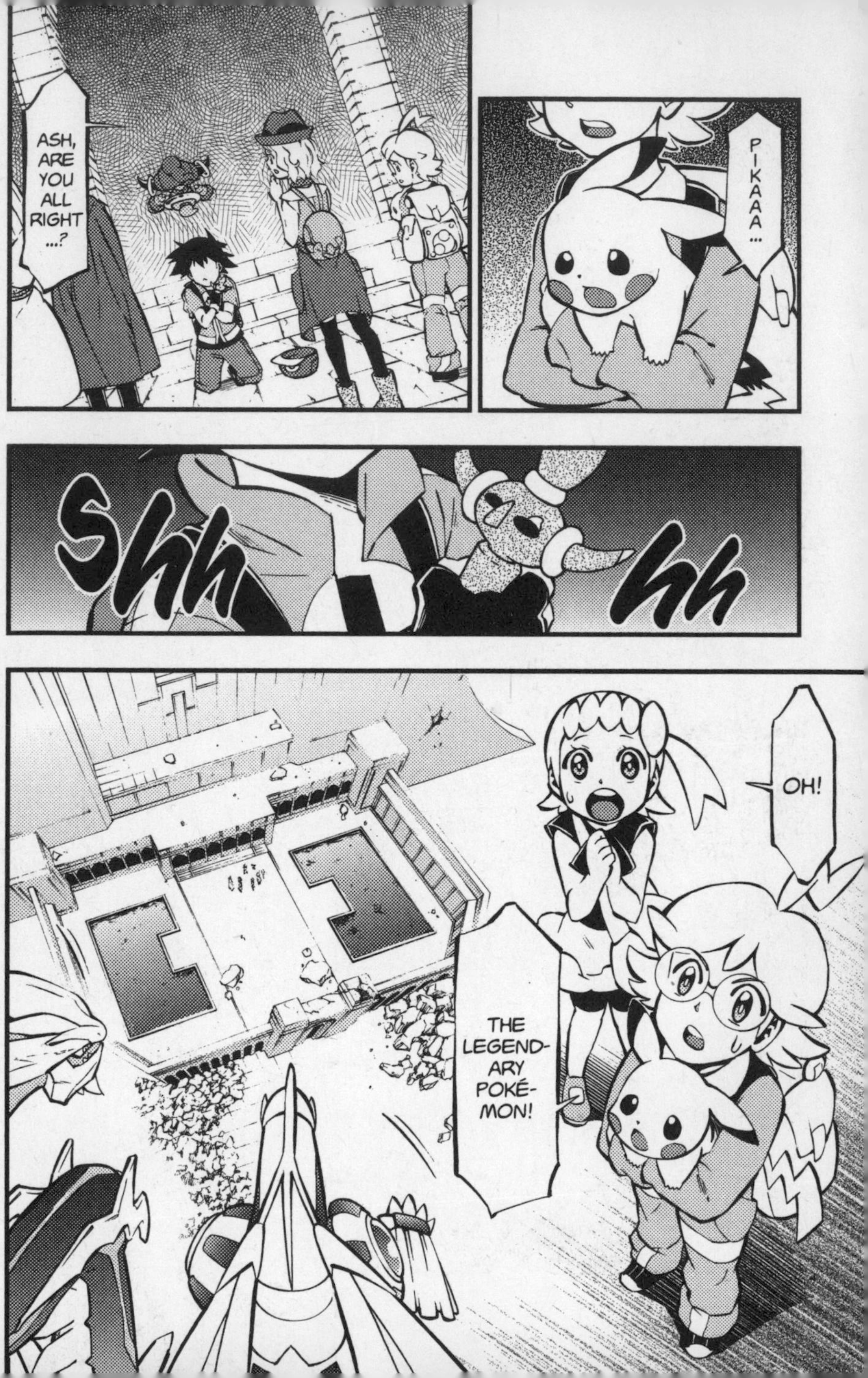
PIKAAA...
ASH, ARE YOU ALL RIGHT ...?
Shhhh
OH!
THE LEGENDARY POKÉMON!

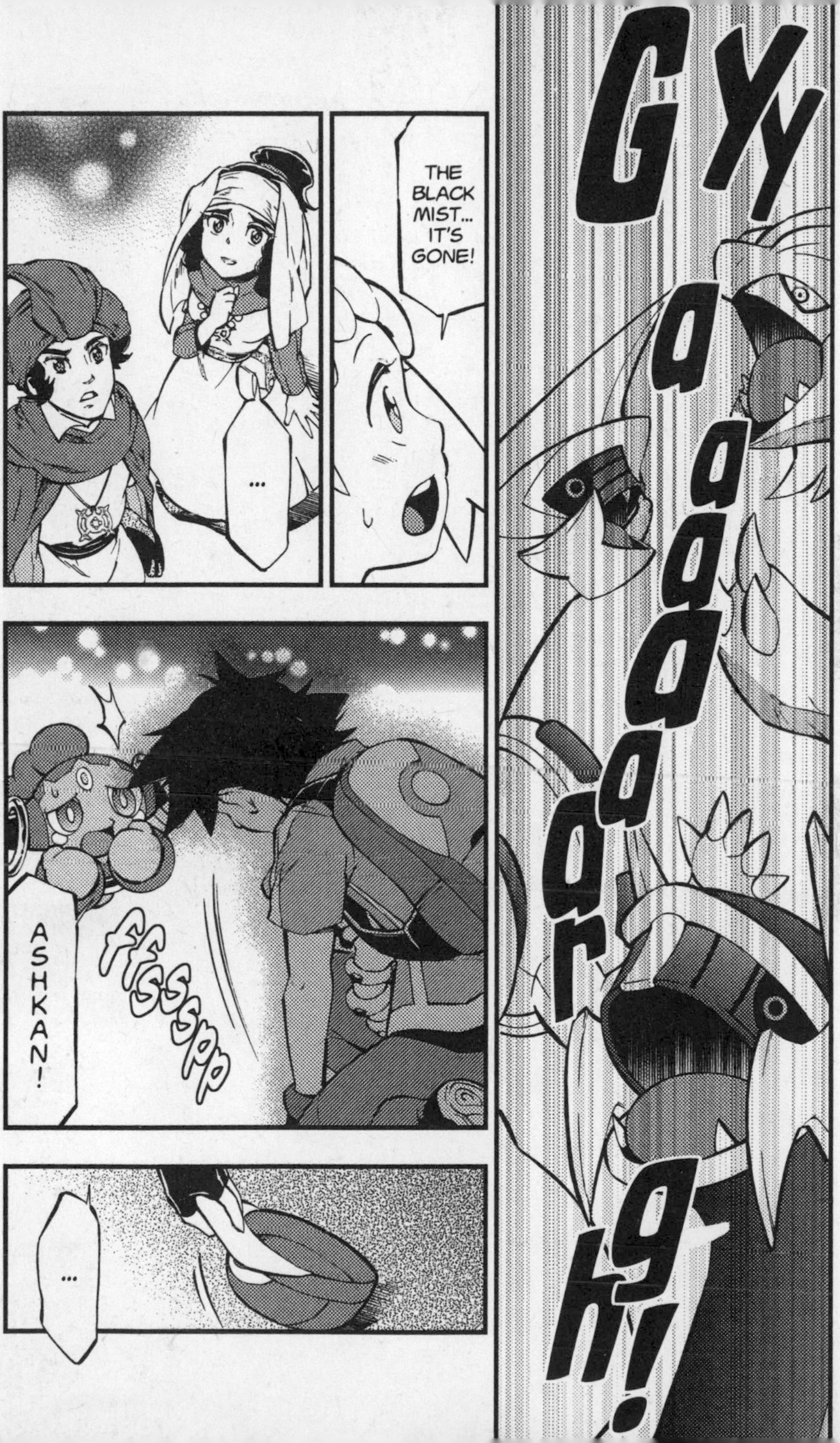
GYYaaaaaaargh!
THE BLACK MIST... IT'S GONE!
...
ASHKAN!
ffssspp
...

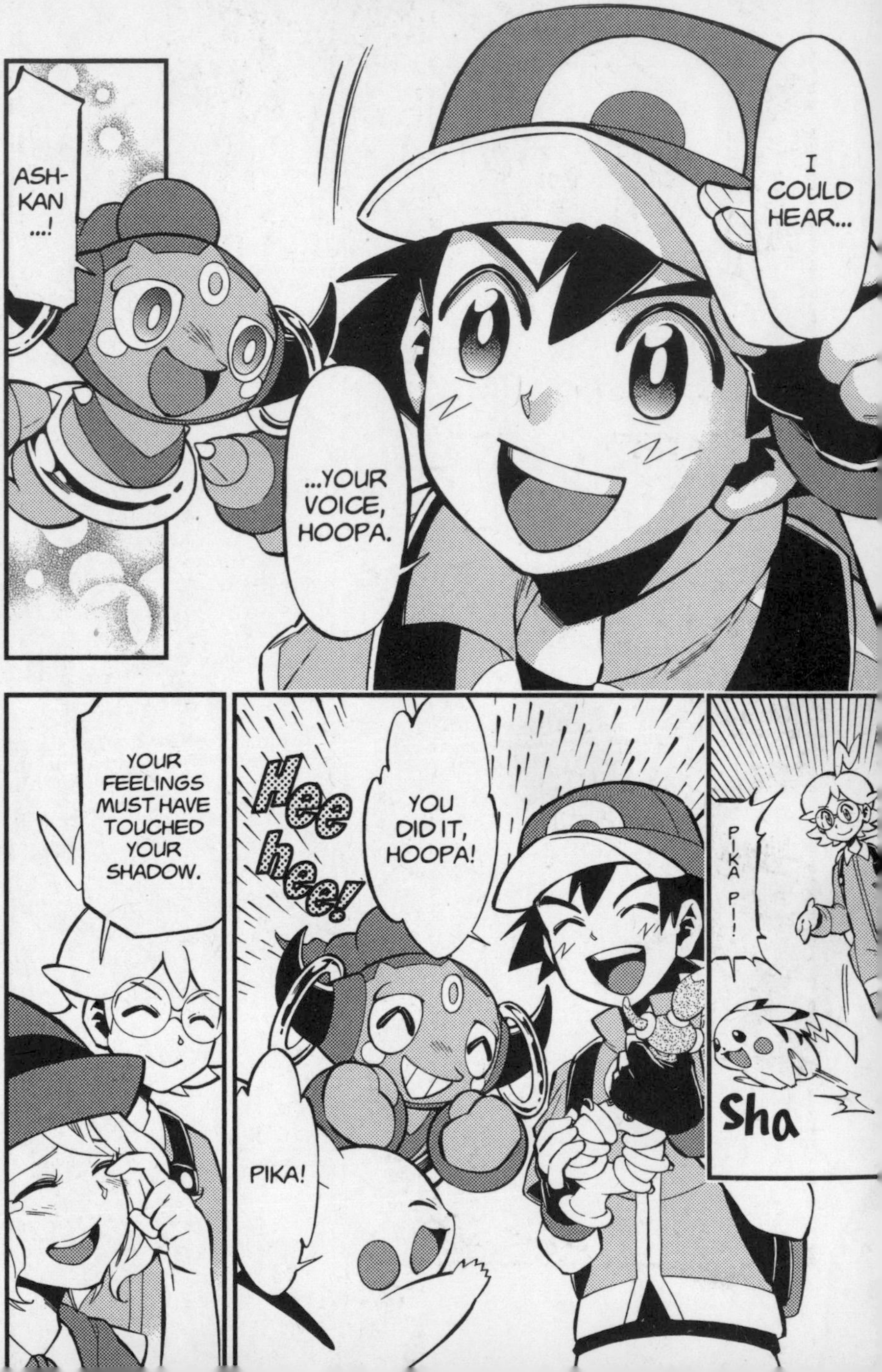
I COULD HEAR...
...YOUR VOICE, HOOPA.
ASH-KAN ...!
PIKA PI!!
Sha
YOU DID IT, HOOPA!
Hee hee!
PIKA!
YOUR FEELINGS MUST HAVE TOUCHED YOUR SHADOW.

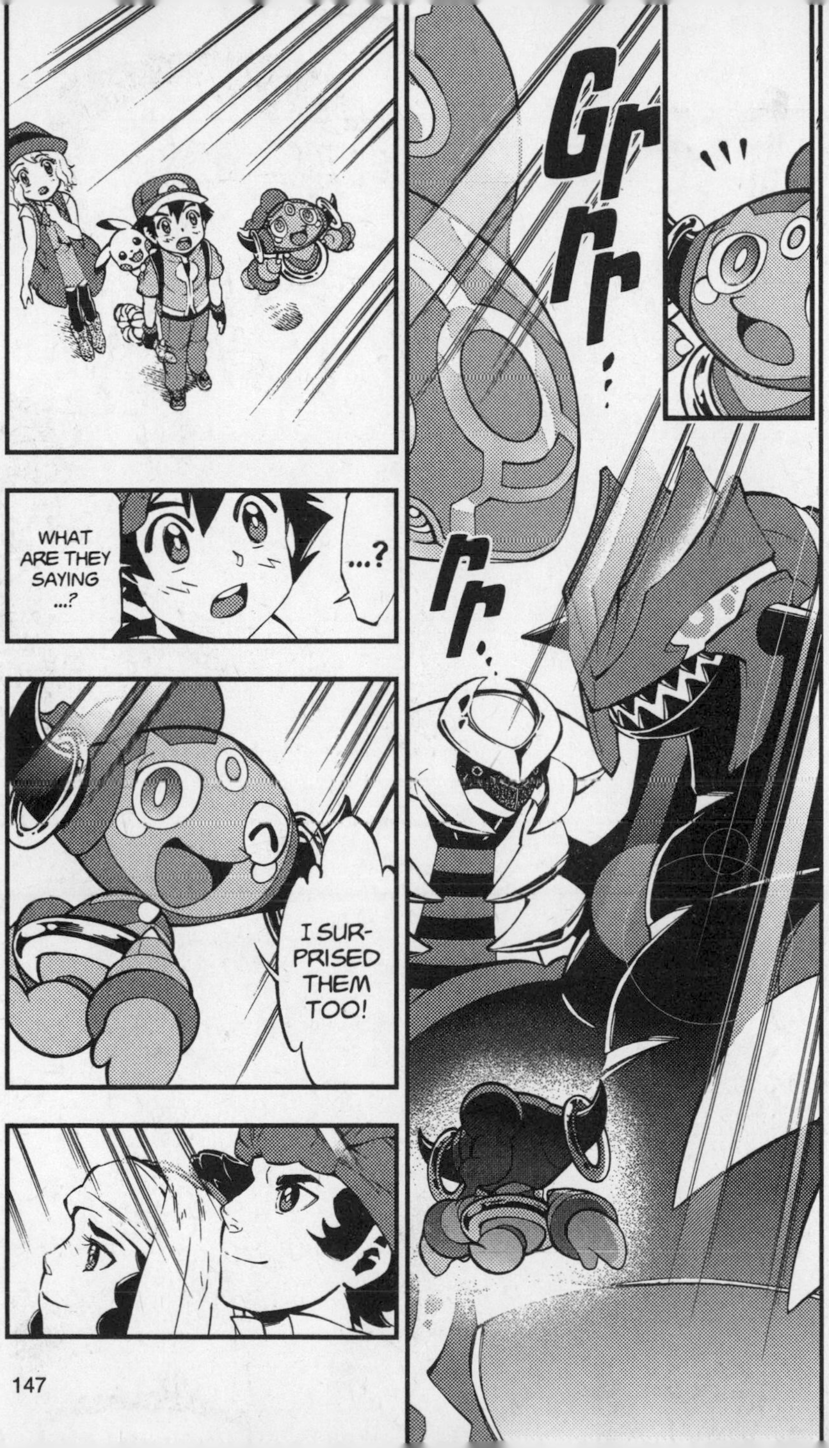
Grrr...
rr...
WHAT ARE THEY SAYING ...?
...?
I SUR-PRISED THEM TOO!

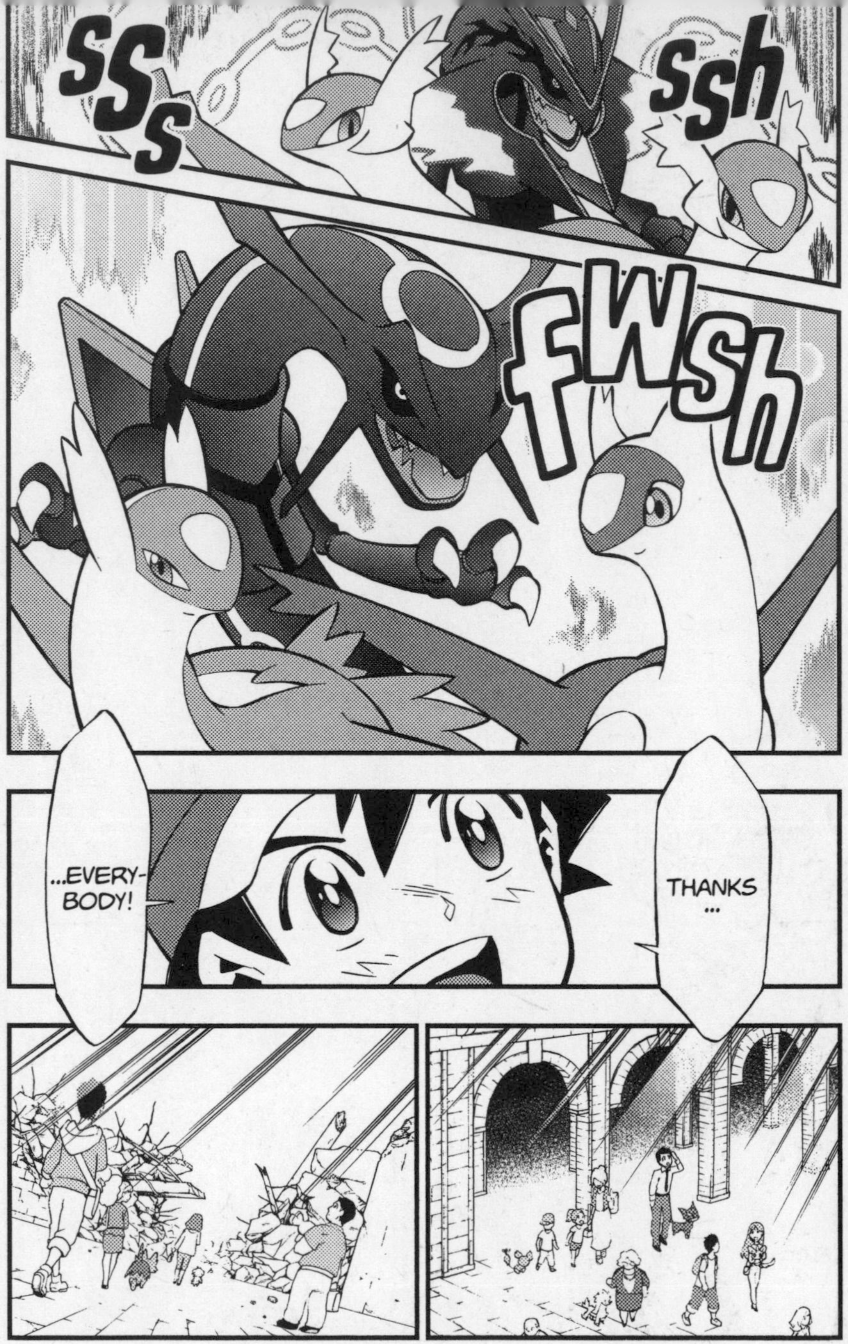
SSH
SSS
FWSH
THANKS...
...EVERYBODY!

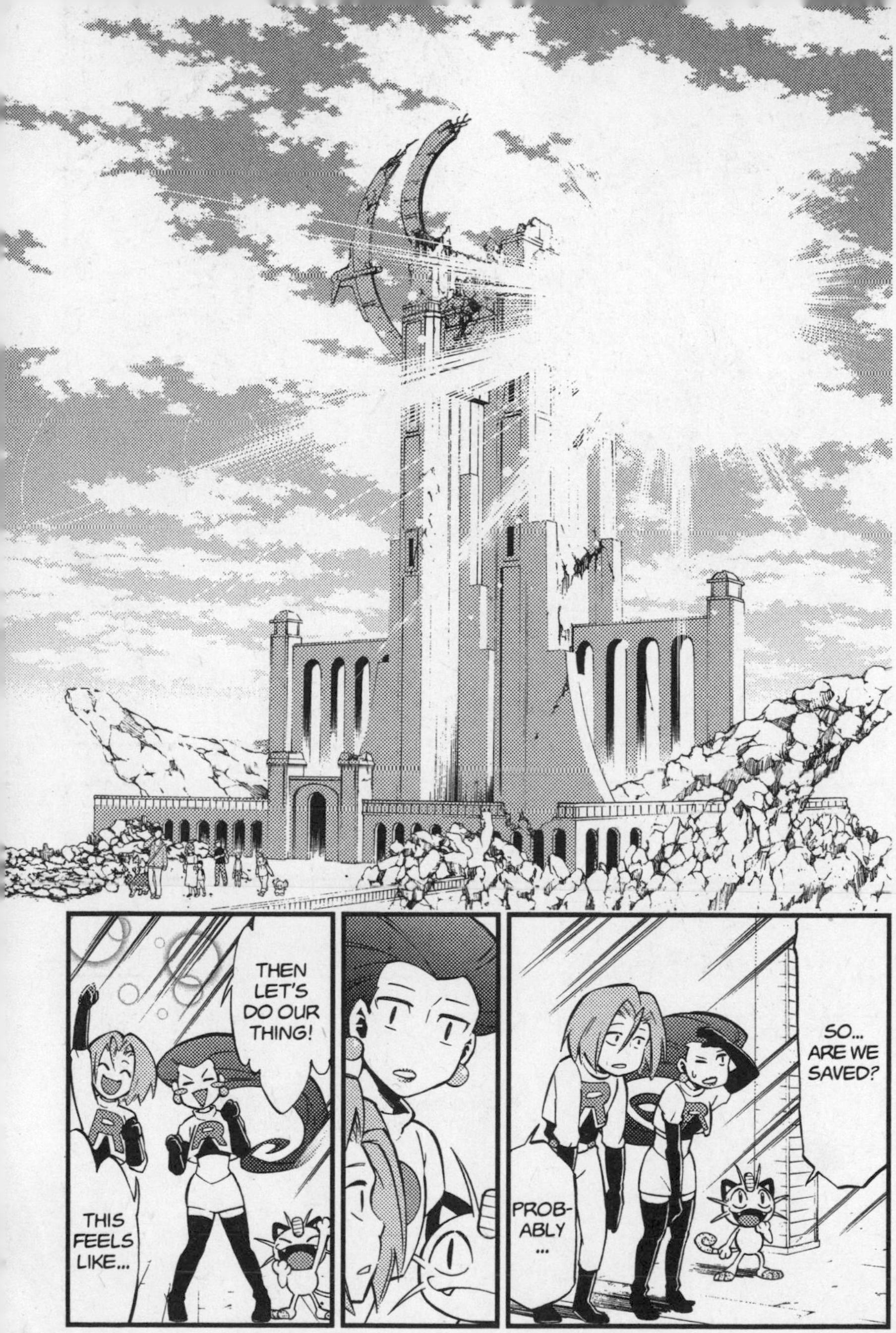
SO... ARE WE SAVED?
PROB-ABLY ...
THEN LET'S DO OUR THING!
THIS FEELS LIKE...

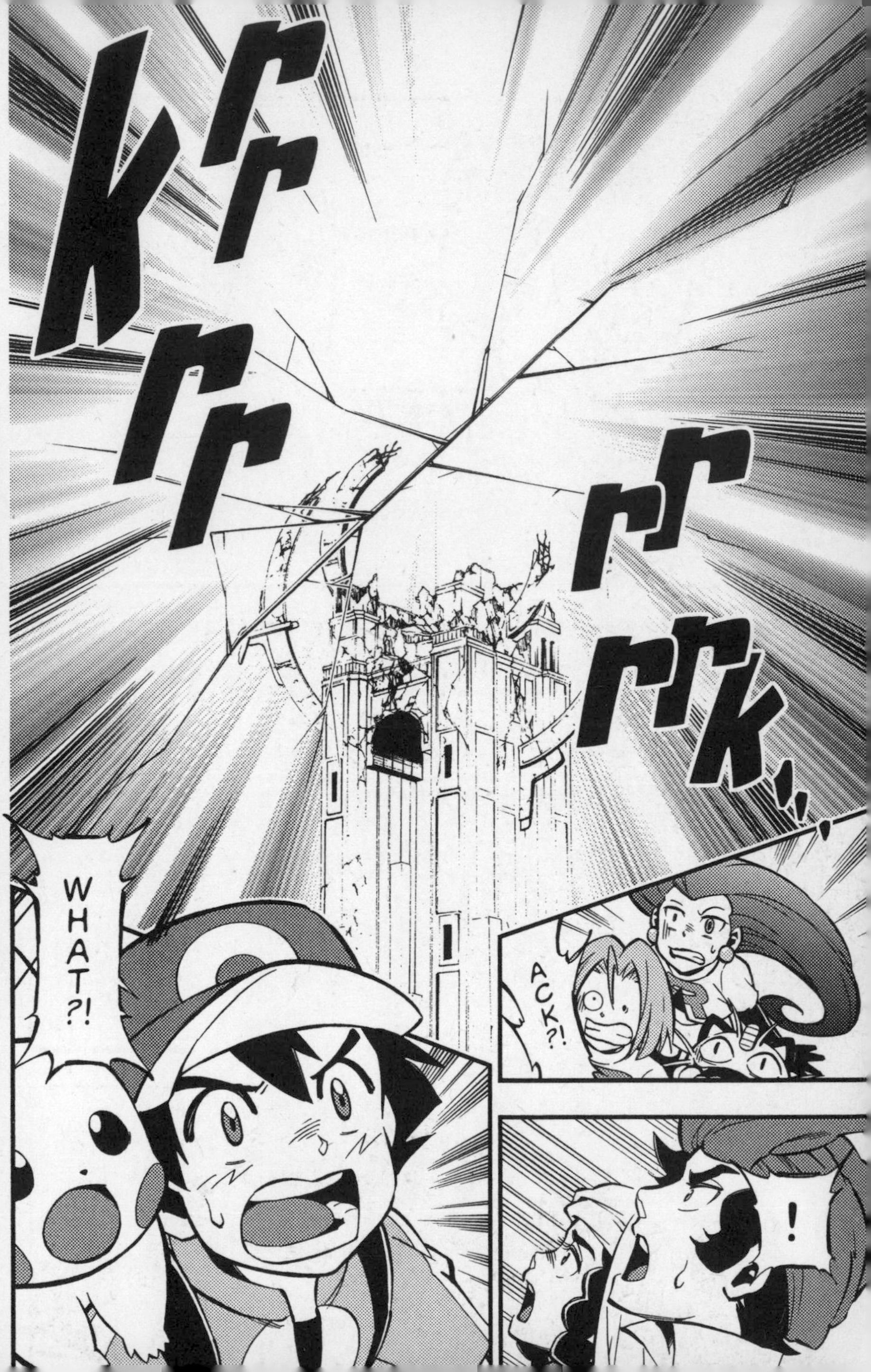
krrrr
rrrrk...
ACK?!
!
WHAT?!

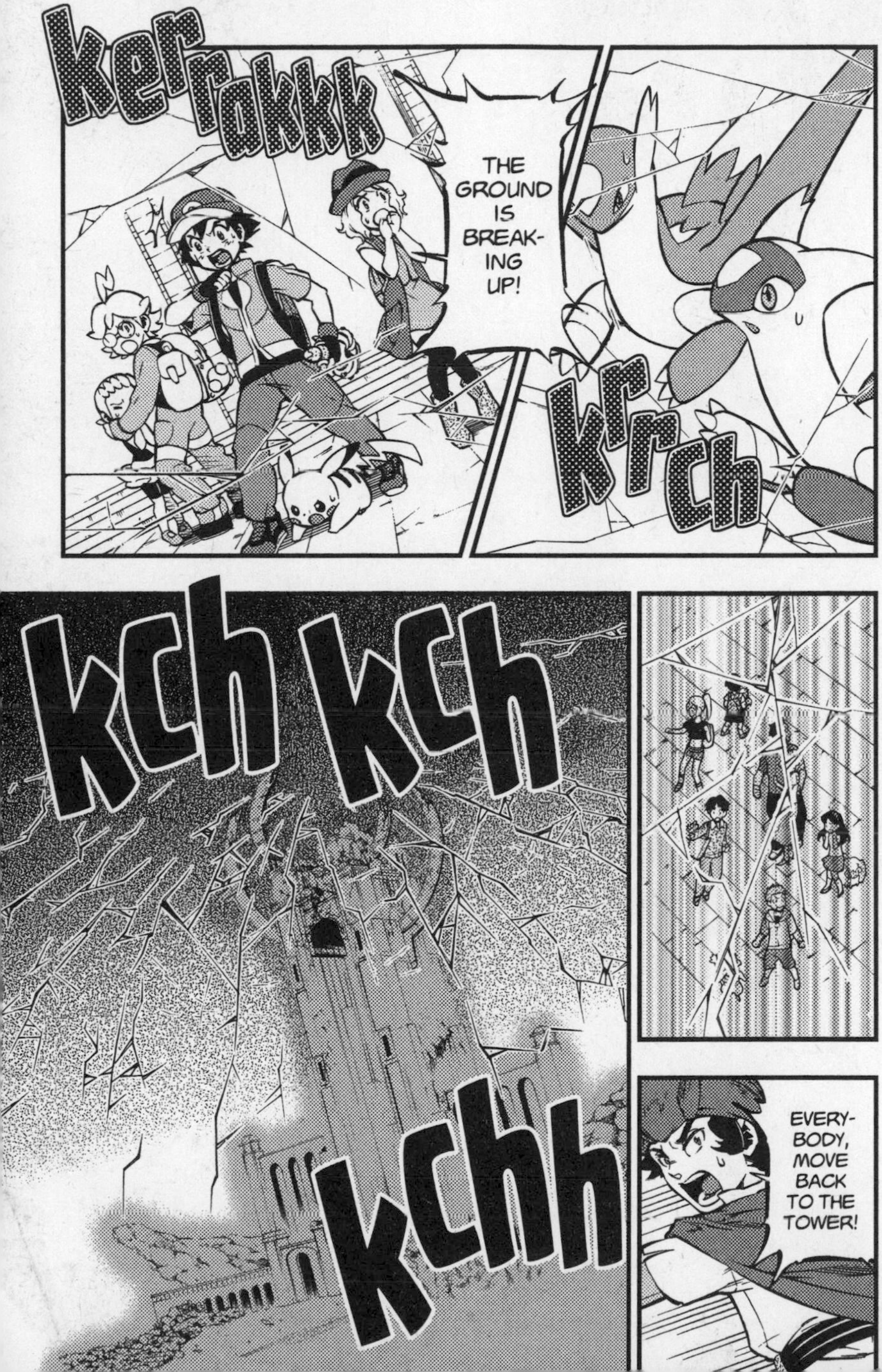
krrch
kerrakkk
THE GROUND IS BREAK-ING UP!
EVERY-BODY, MOVE BACK TO THE TOWER!
kch kch
kchh

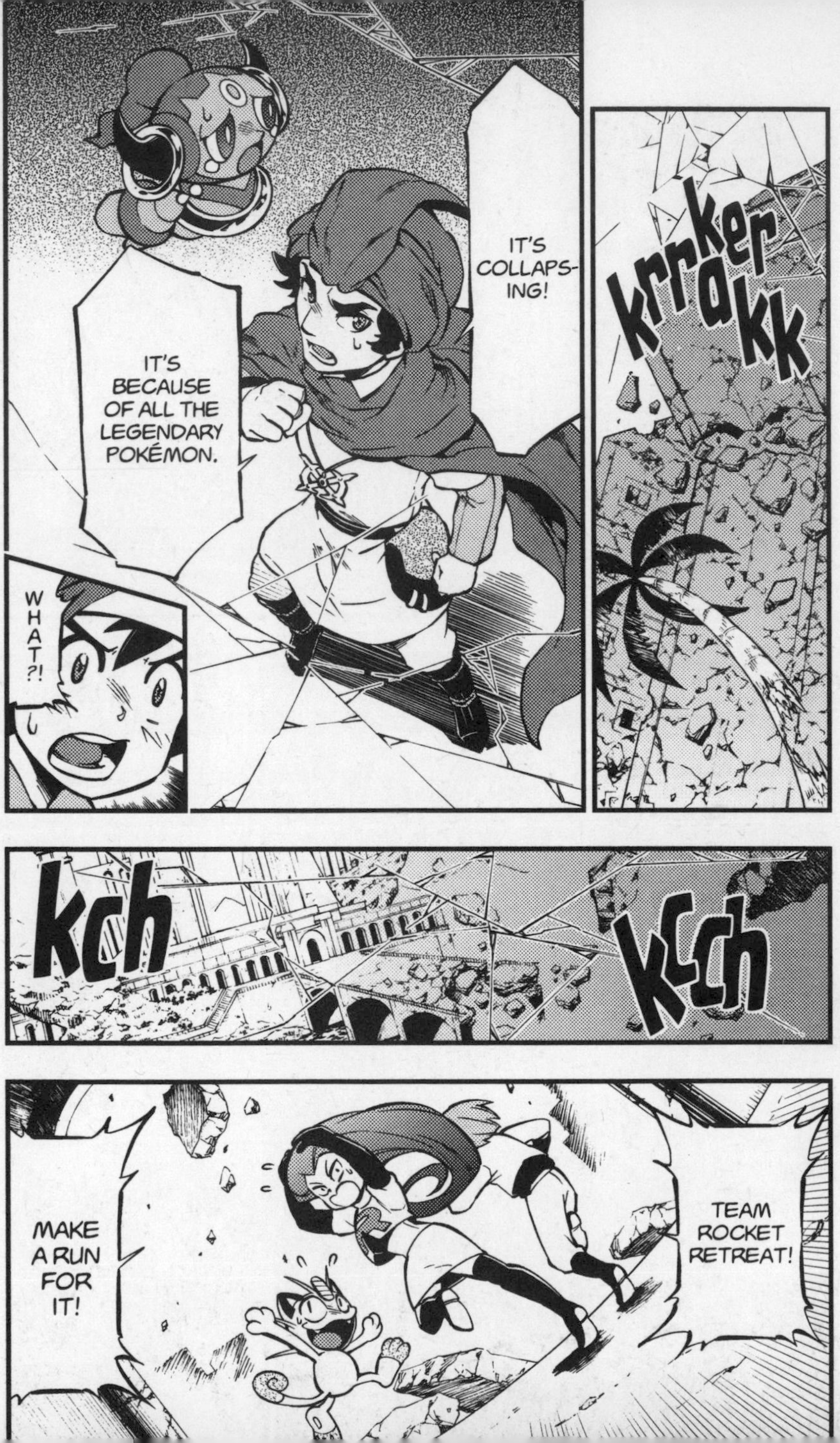
krrkerakk
IT'S COLLAPSING!
IT'S BECAUSE OF ALL THE LEGENDARY POKÉMON.
WHAT?!
kcch
kch
TEAM ROCKET RETREAT!
MAKE A RUN FOR IT!

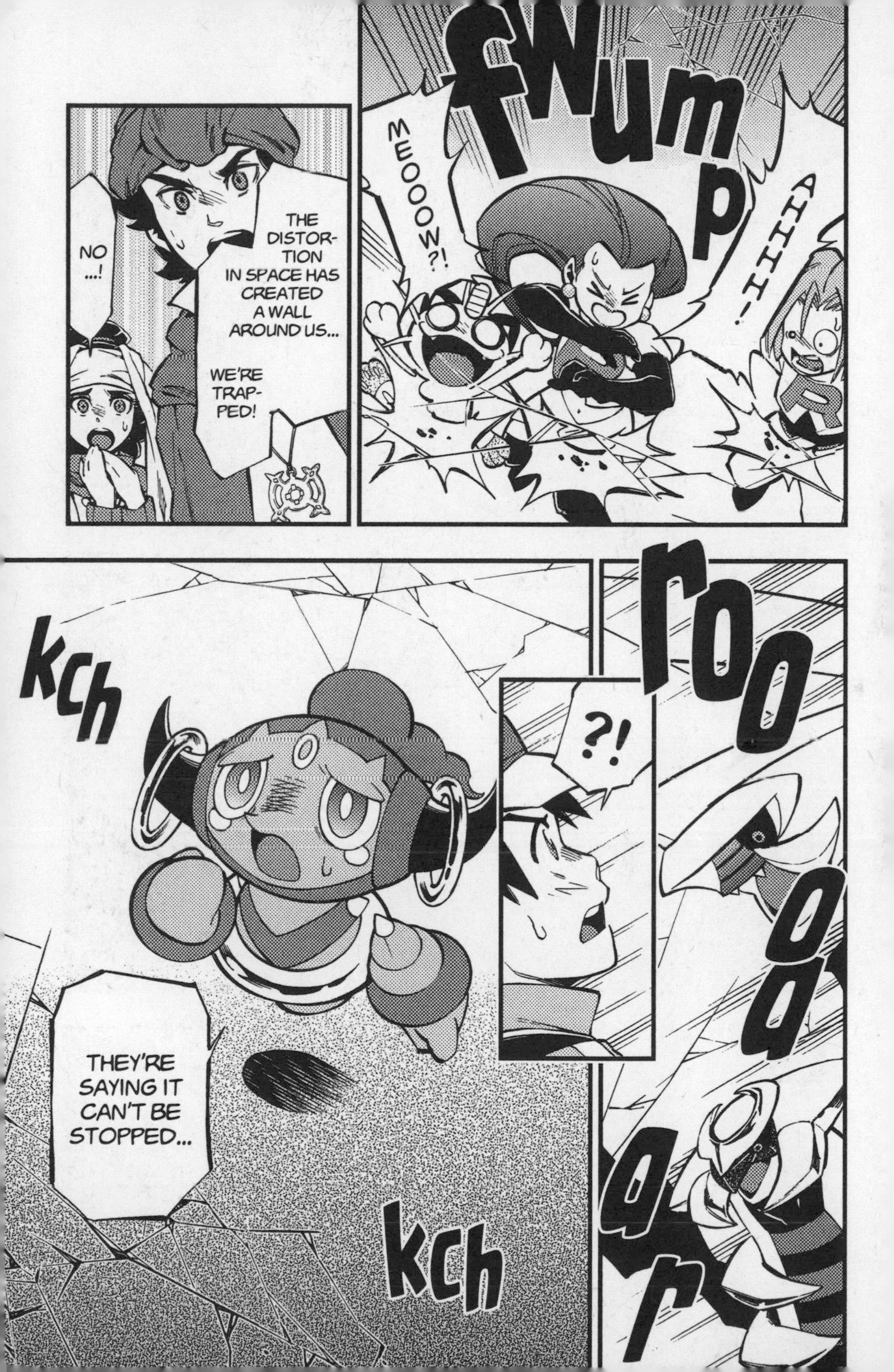
fWump
AHHHH!
MEOOOOW?!
THE DISTORTION IN SPACE HAS CREATED A WALL AROUND US...
NO ...!
WE'RE TRAPPED!
rooaar
?!
kch
THEY'RE SAYING IT CAN'T BE STOPPED...
kch

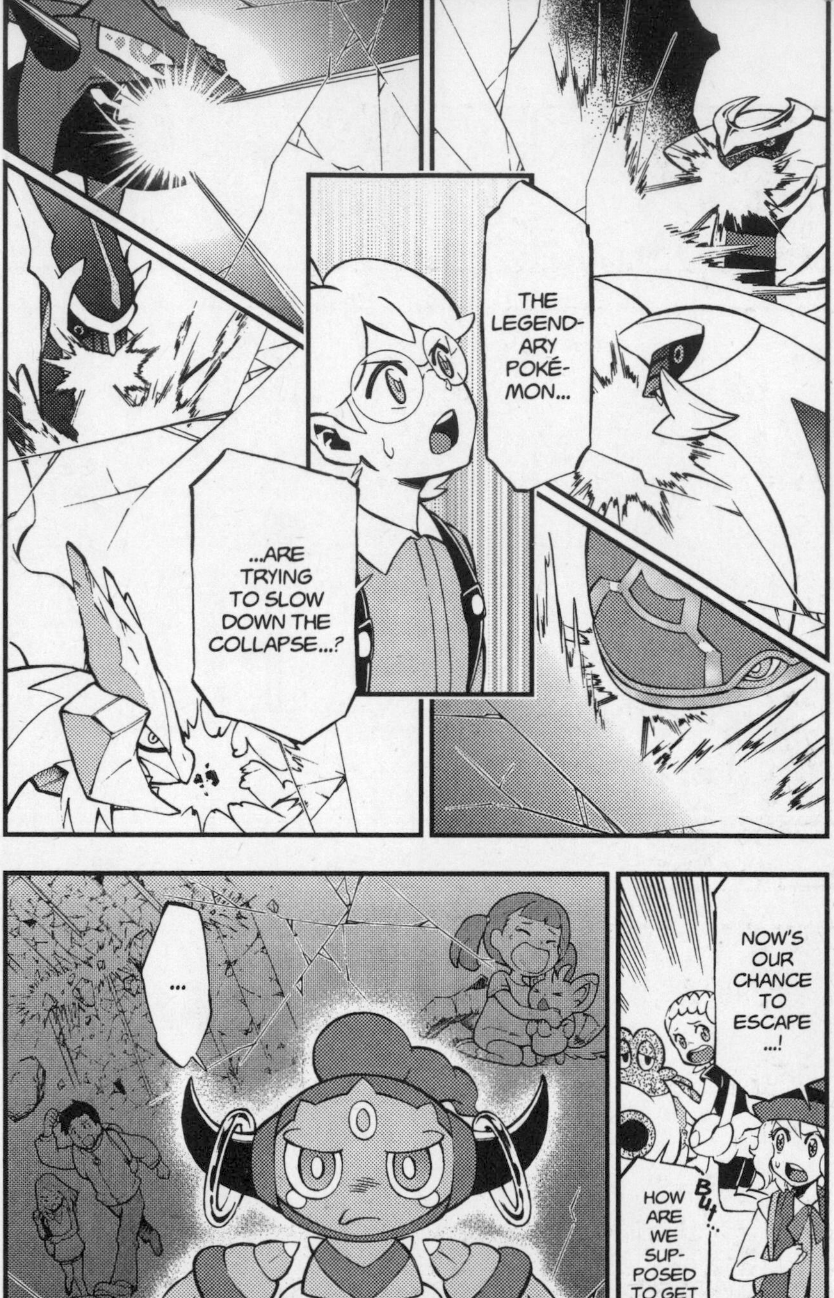
THE LEGENDARY POKÉMON...
...ARE TRYING TO SLOW DOWN THE COLLAPSE...?
NOW'S OUR CHANCE TO ESCAPE...!
But...
HOW ARE WE SUPPOSED TO GET OUT?!
...

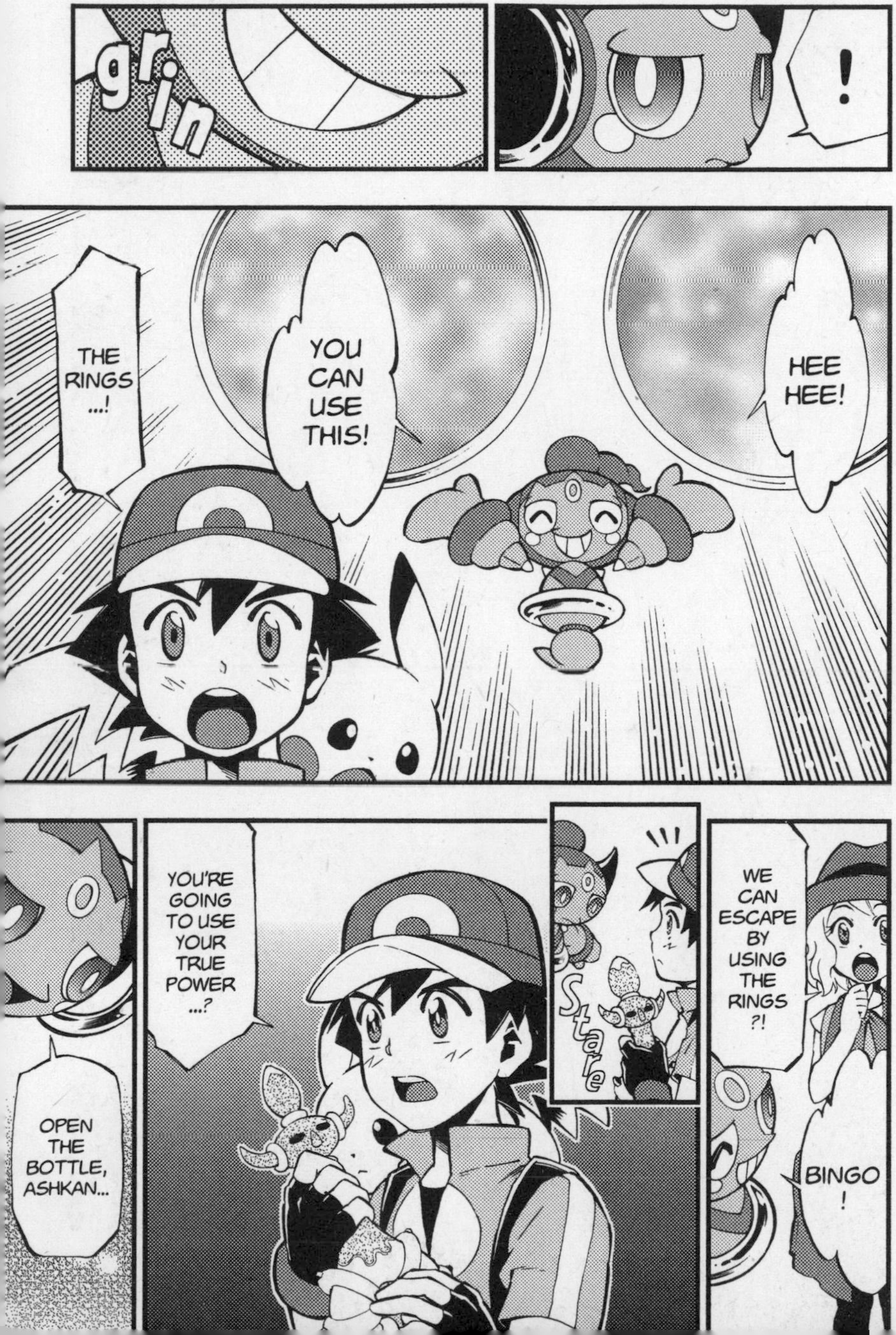
!
grin
HEE HEE!
YOU CAN USE THIS!
THE RINGS ...!
WE CAN ESCAPE BY USING THE RINGS ?!
BINGO !
stare
YOU'RE GOING TO USE YOUR TRUE POWER ...?
OPEN THE BOTTLE, ASHKAN...

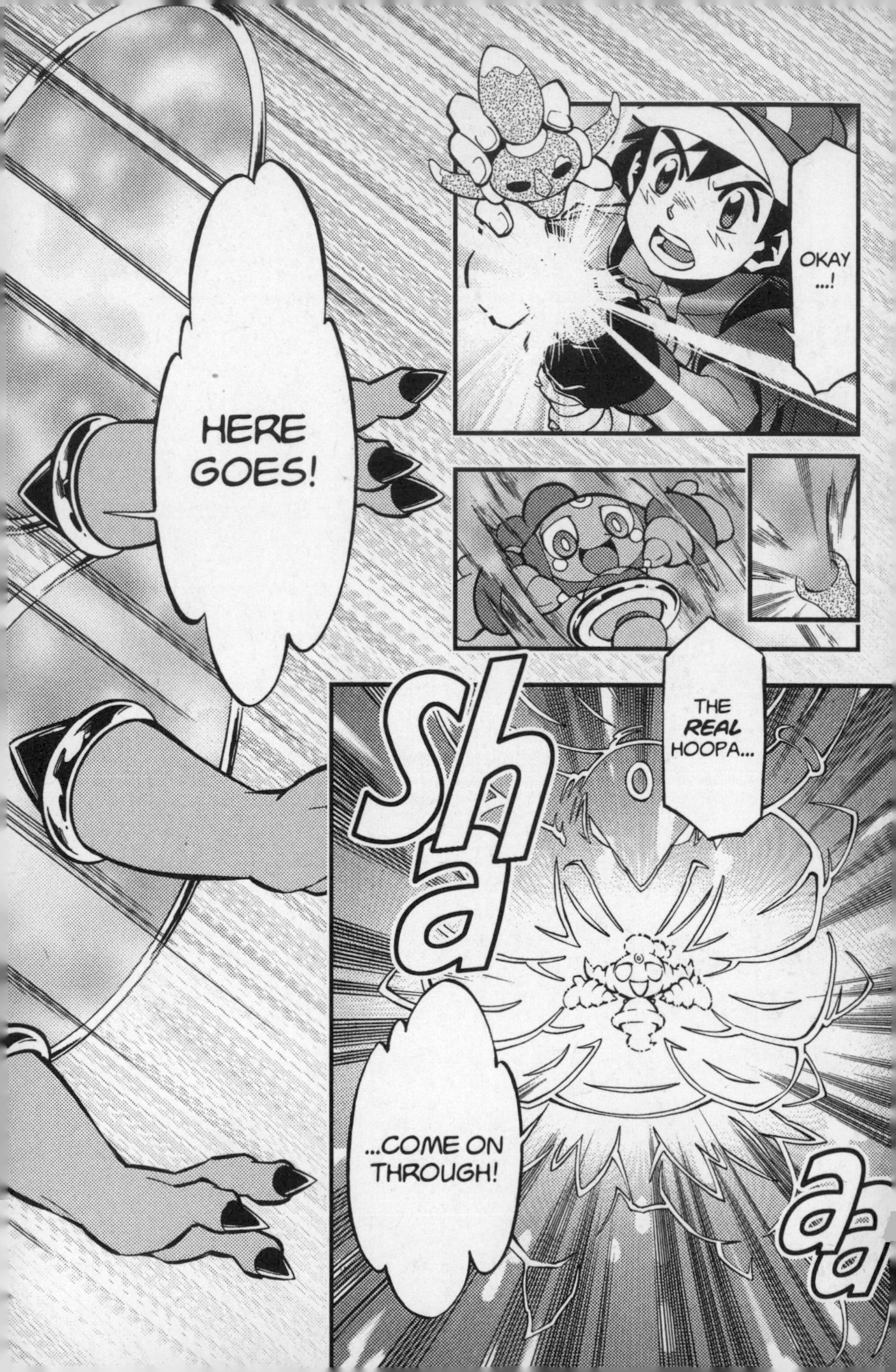
OKAY ...!
THE REAL HOOPA...
Sha
...COME ON THROUGH!
aa
HERE GOES!

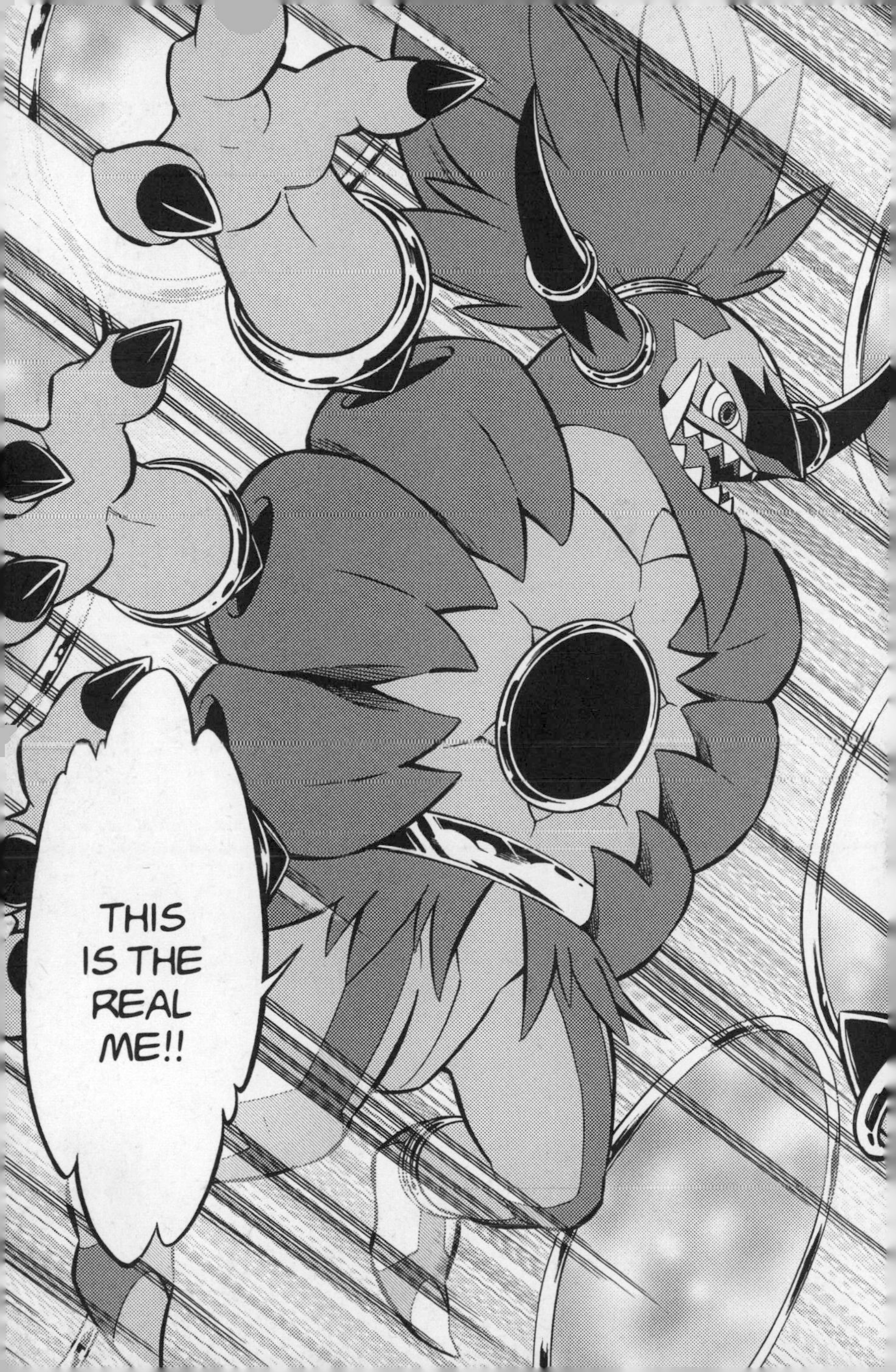
THIS IS THE REAL ME!!

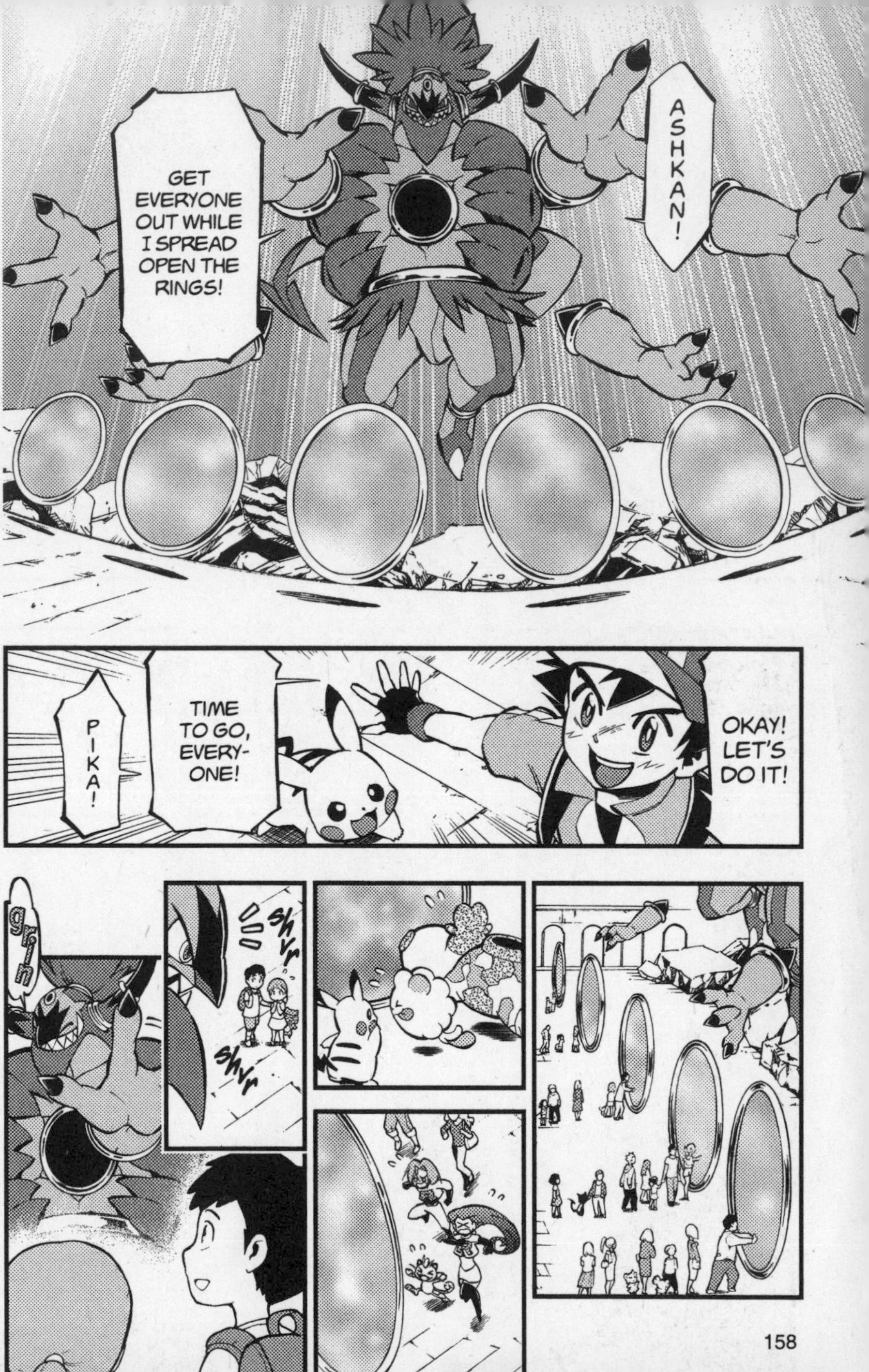
ASHKAN!
GET EVERYONE OUT WHILE I SPREAD OPEN THE RINGS!
OKAY! LET'S DO IT!
TIME TO GO, EVERY-ONE!
PIKA!
shvr
shvr
grrh

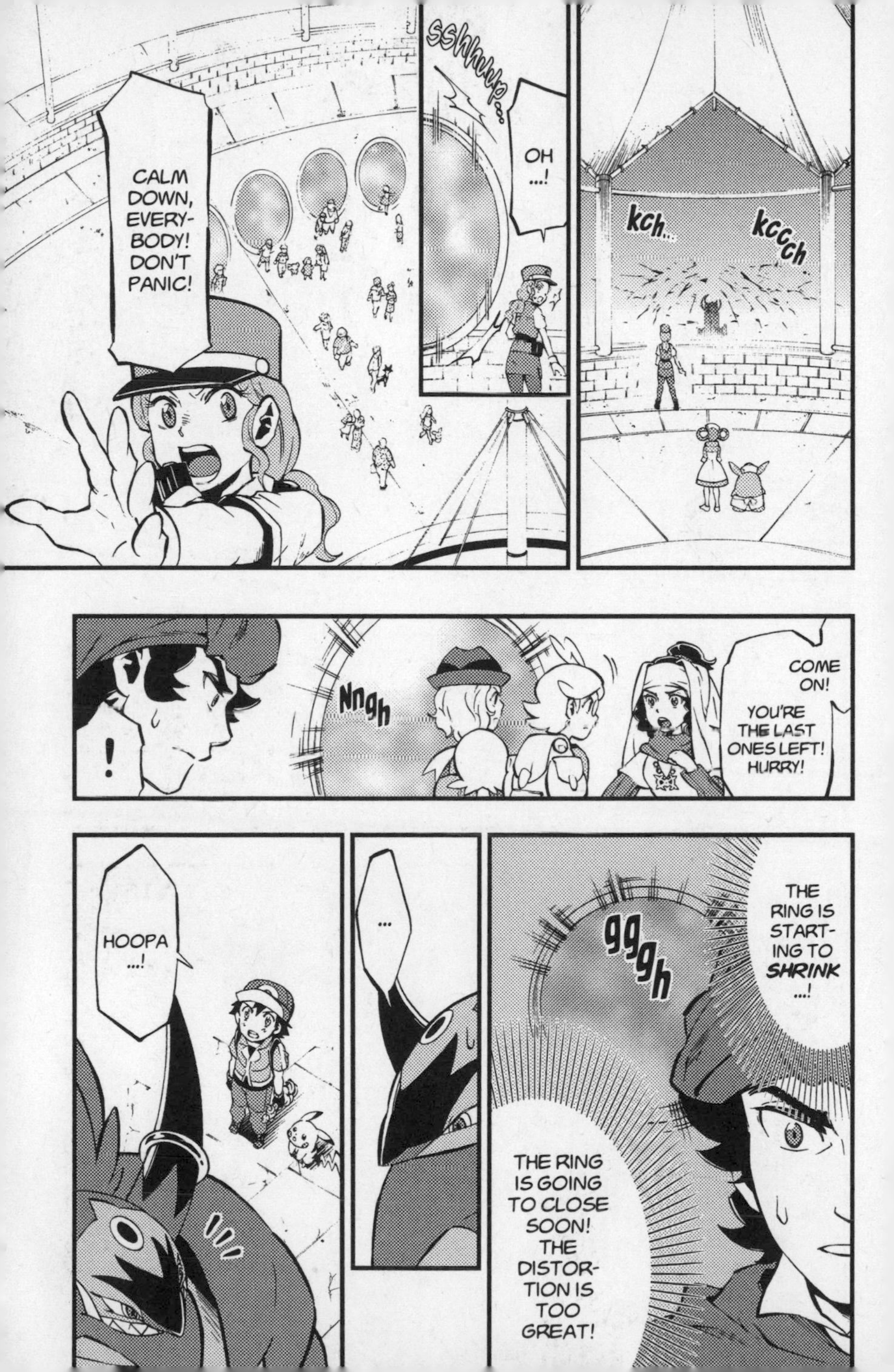
kch...
kccch
sshhuup...
OH ...!
CALM DOWN, EVERY-BODY! DON'T PANIC!
COME ON! YOU'RE THE LAST ONES LEFT! HURRY!
Nngh
!
THE RING IS START-ING TO SHRINK ...!
gggh
THE RING IS GOING TO CLOSE SOON! THE DISTOR-TION IS TOO GREAT!
...
HOOPA ...!

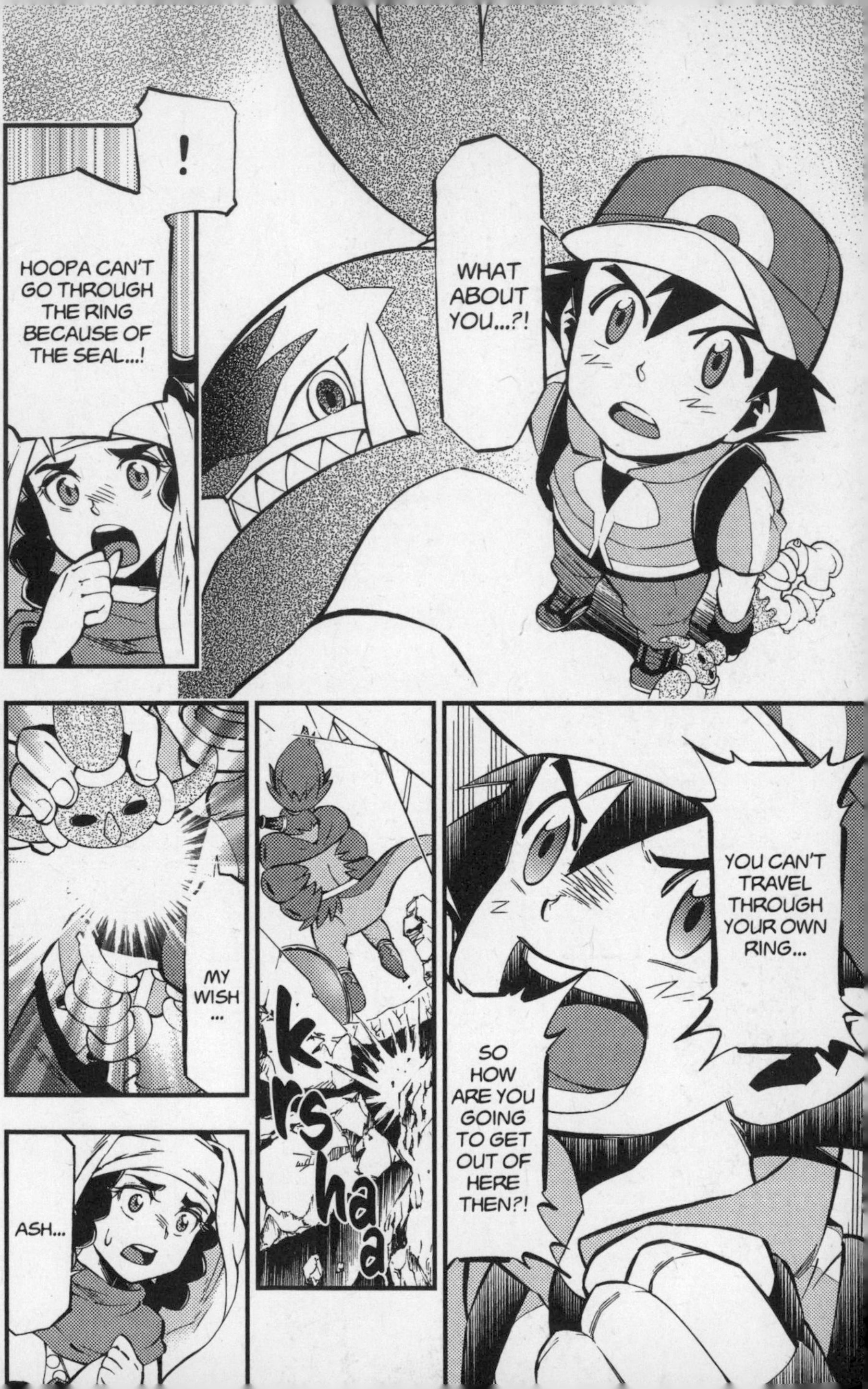
WHAT ABOUT YOU...?!
!
HOOPA CAN'T GO THROUGH THE RING BECAUSE OF THE SEAL...!
YOU CAN'T TRAVEL THROUGH YOUR OWN RING...
SO HOW ARE YOU GOING TO GET OUT OF HERE THEN?!
krshaa
MY WISH ...
ASH...

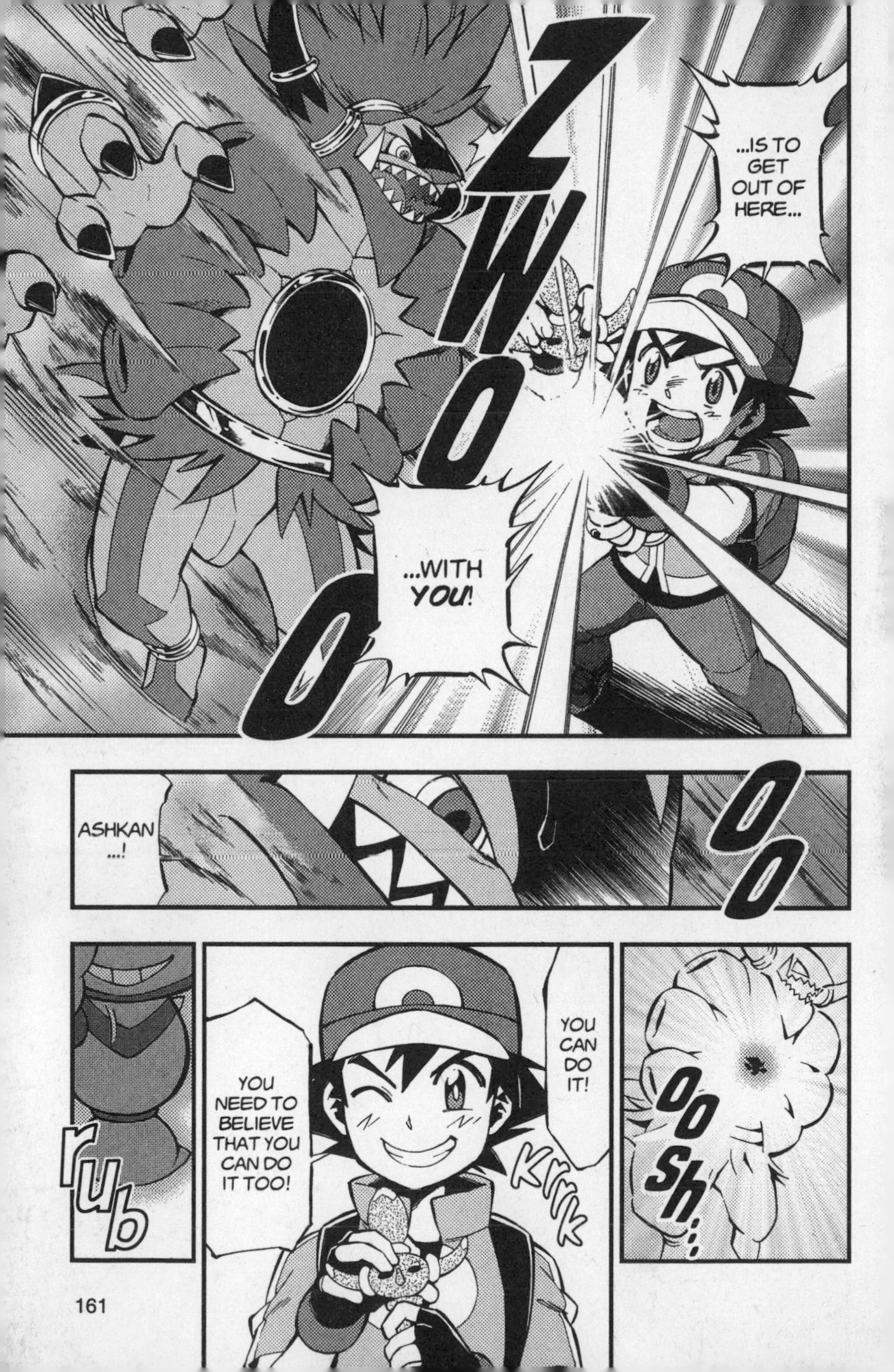
...IS TO GET OUT OF HERE...
ZWOOO
...WITH YOU!
OO
ASHKAN ...!
OOSH...
YOU CAN DO IT!
YOU NEED TO BELIEVE THAT YOU CAN DO IT TOO!
Krrrk
rub

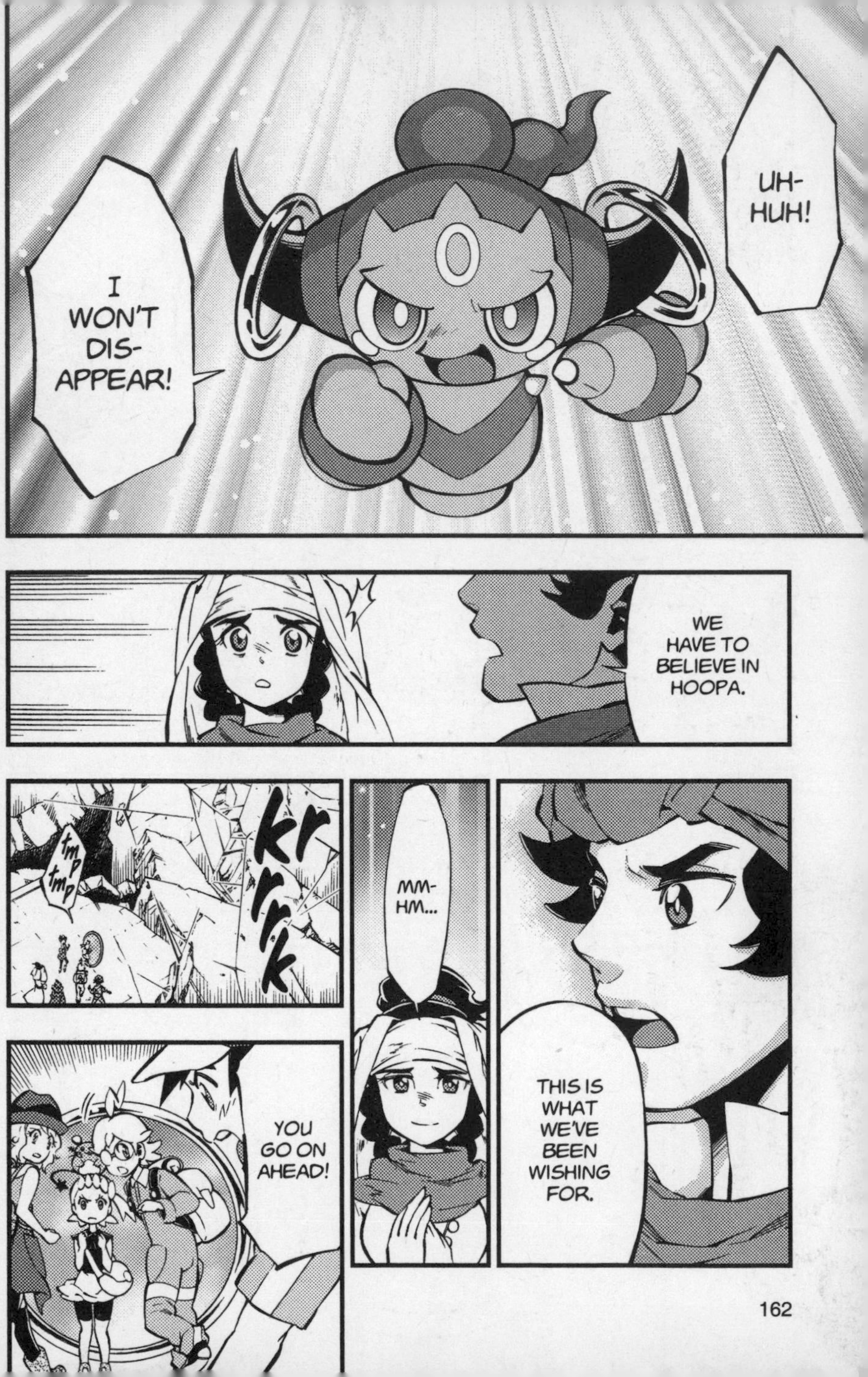
UH-HUH!
I WON'T DIS-APPEAR!
WE HAVE TO BELIEVE IN HOOPA.
THIS IS WHAT WE'VE BEEN WISHING FOR.
MM-HM...
krrrk
tmp tmp
YOU GO ON AHEAD!

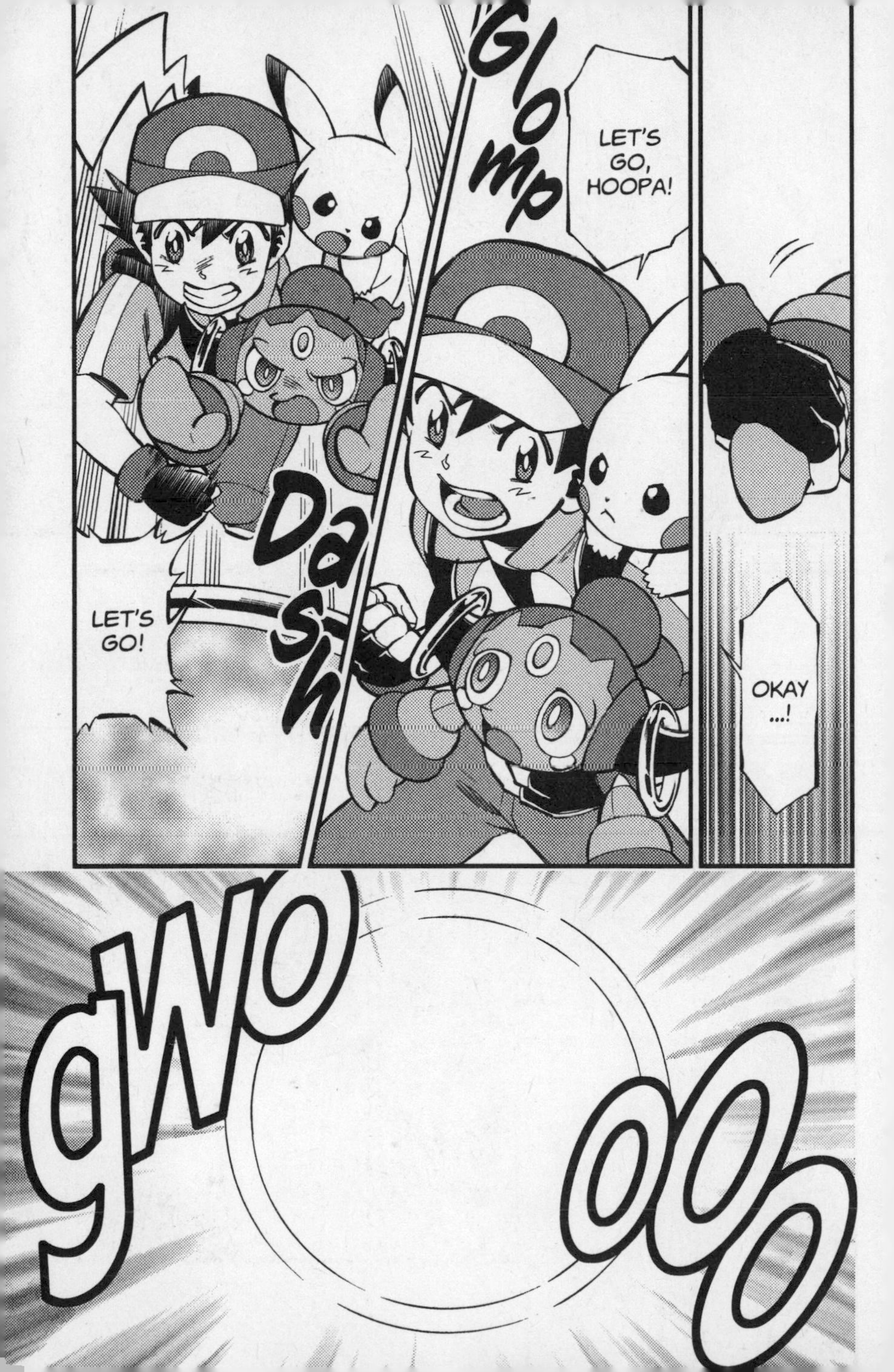
OKAY ...!
Glomp
LET'S GO, HOOPA!
Dash
LET'S GO!
gwoooo

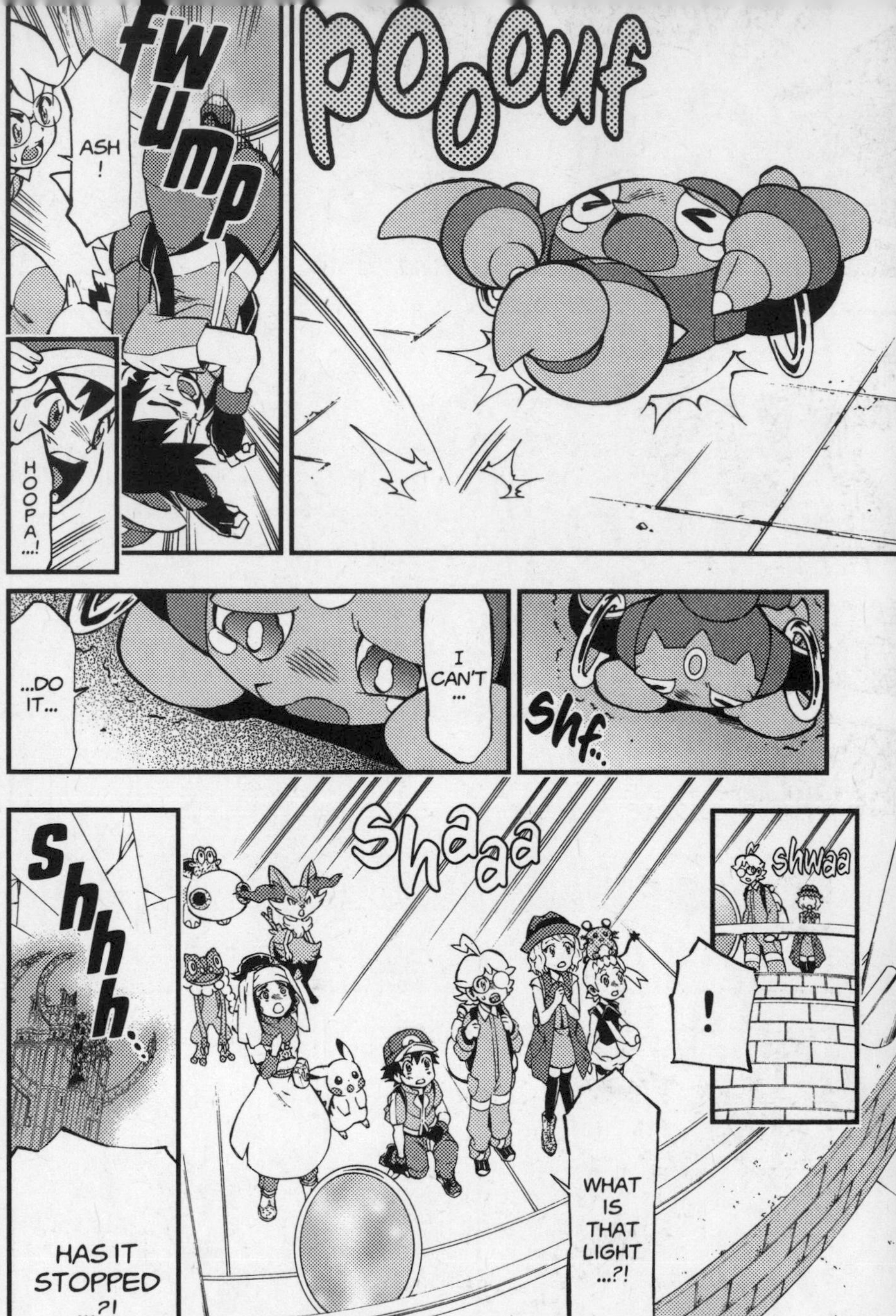
POOOOUF
ASH!
FWUMP
HOOPA...!
SHF..
I CAN'T...
...DO IT...
SHWAA
!
SHAAA
WHAT IS THAT LIGHT...?!
SHHH..
HAS IT STOPPED...?!

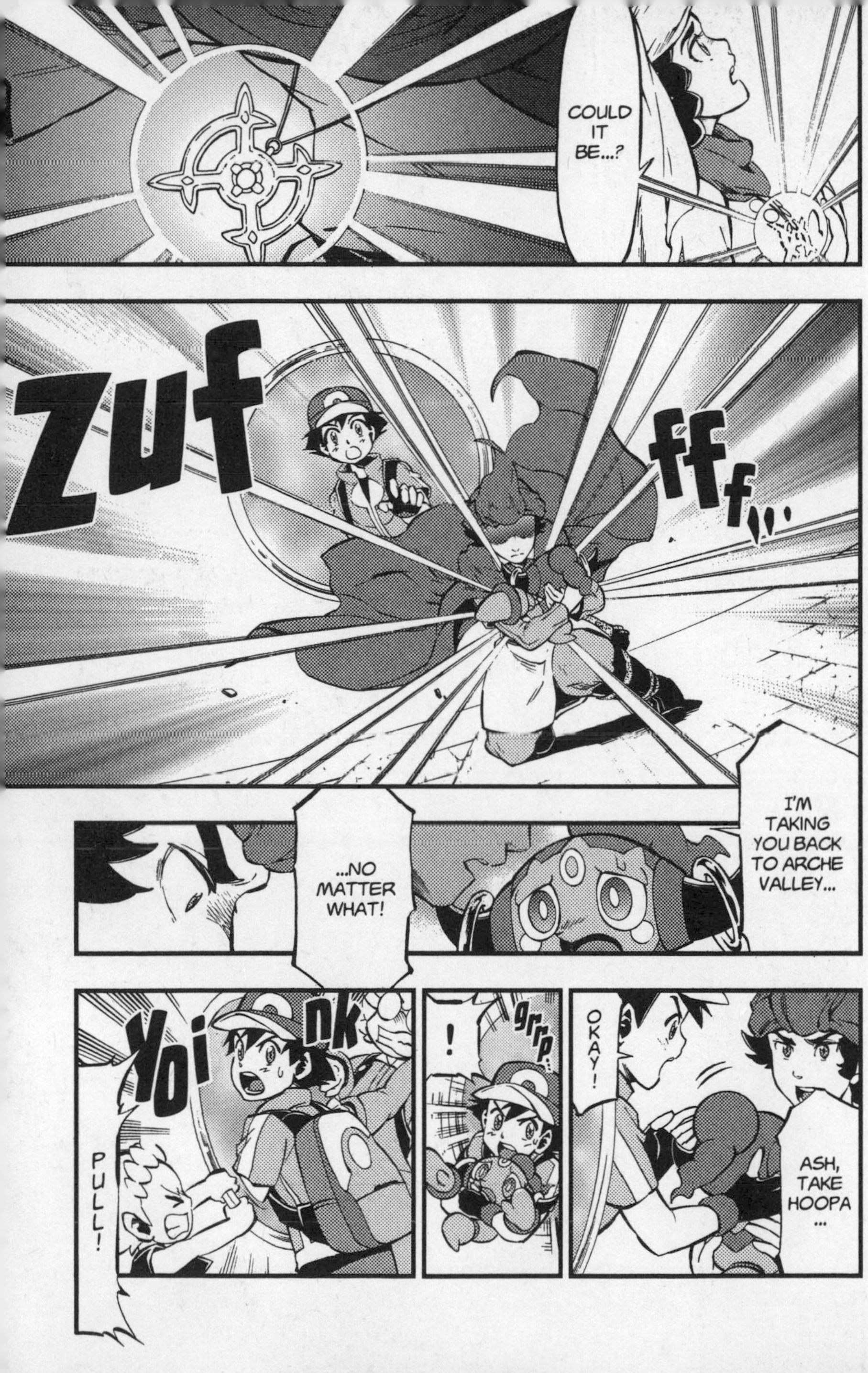
COULD IT BE...?
Zuf
fff...
I'M TAKING YOU BACK TO ARCHE VALLEY...
...NO MATTER WHAT!
ASH, TAKE HOOPA ...
OKAY!
!
grrp...
Yoink
PULL!

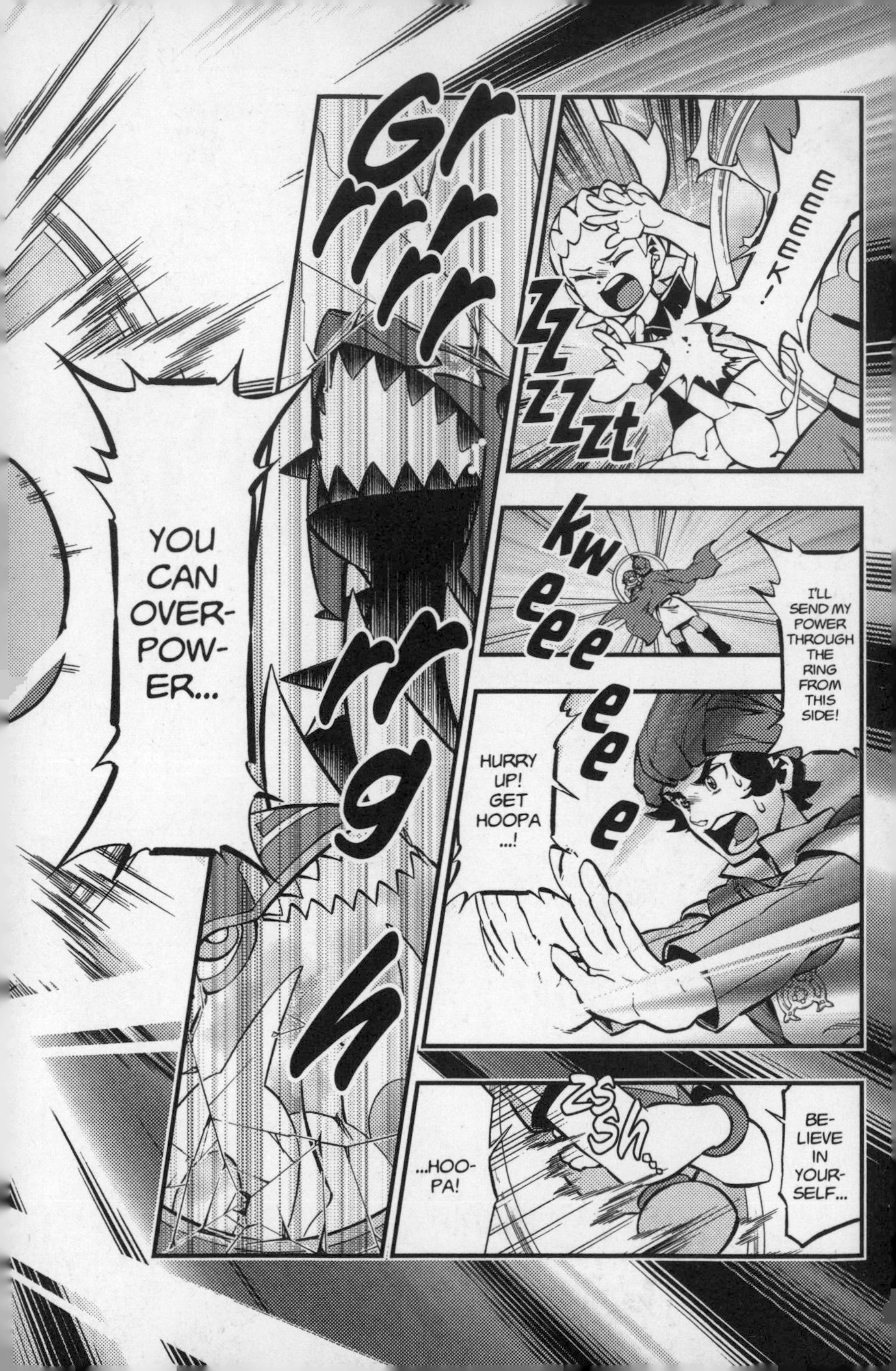
EEEEEK!
ZZZZZzt
kweeeeeee
I'LL SEND MY POWER THROUGH THE RING FROM THIS SIDE!
HURRY UP! GET HOOPA ...!
BE-LIEVE IN YOUR-SELF...
ZSSh...
...HOO-PA!
Grrrrrrrgh
YOU CAN OVER-POW-ER...

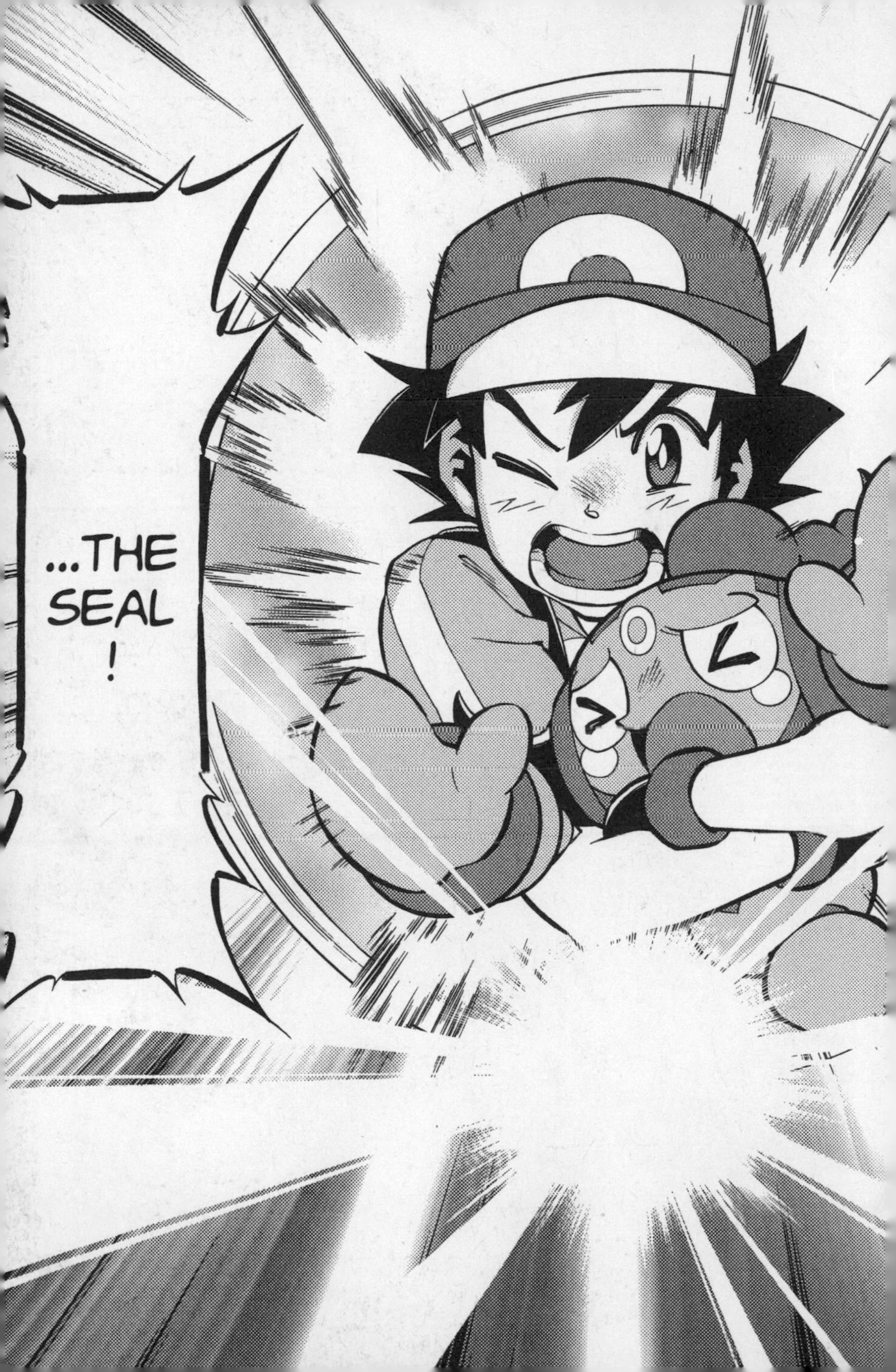
...THE SEAL !

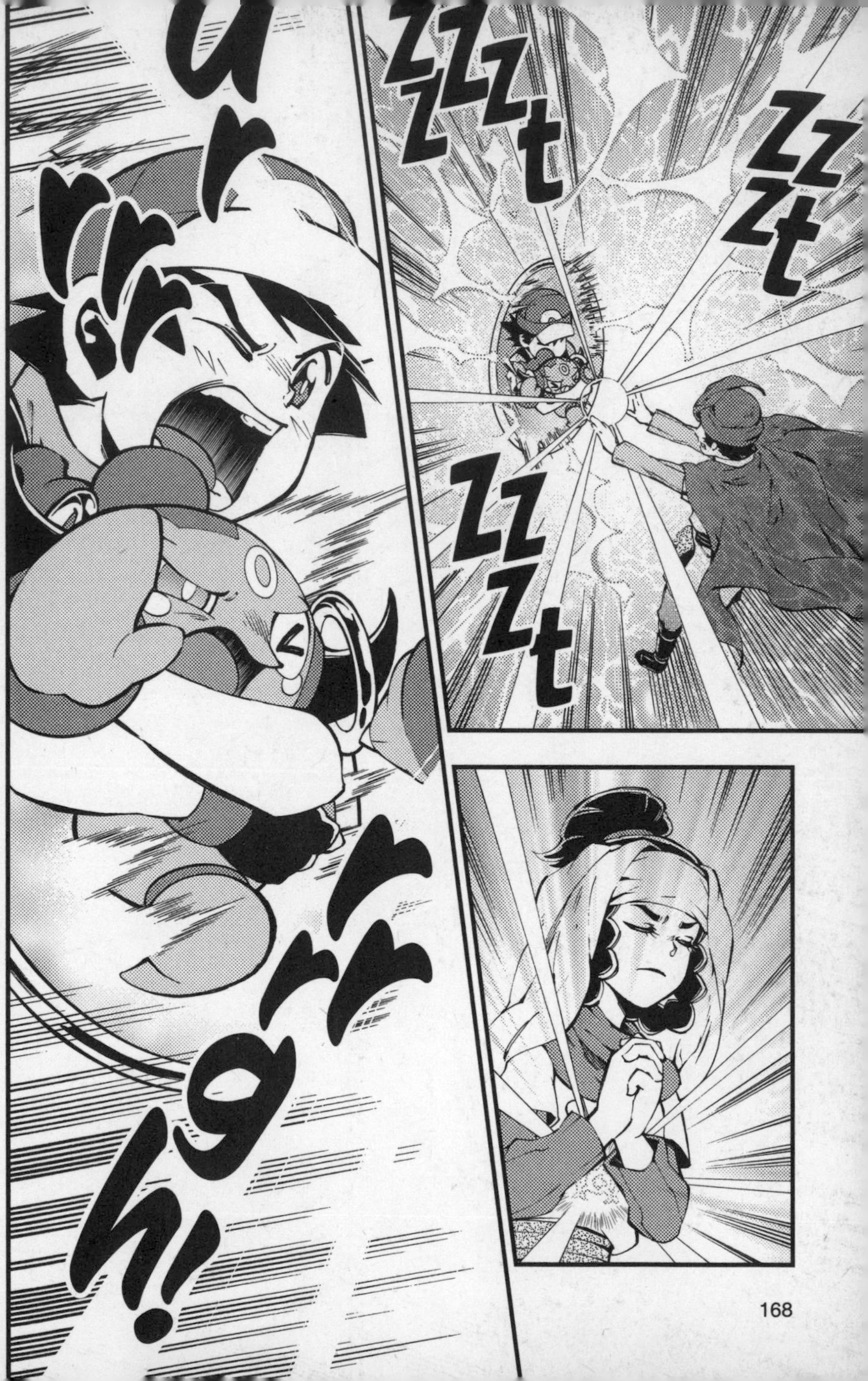
ZZZZt
ZZZt
ZZZt
Urrrrgh!!

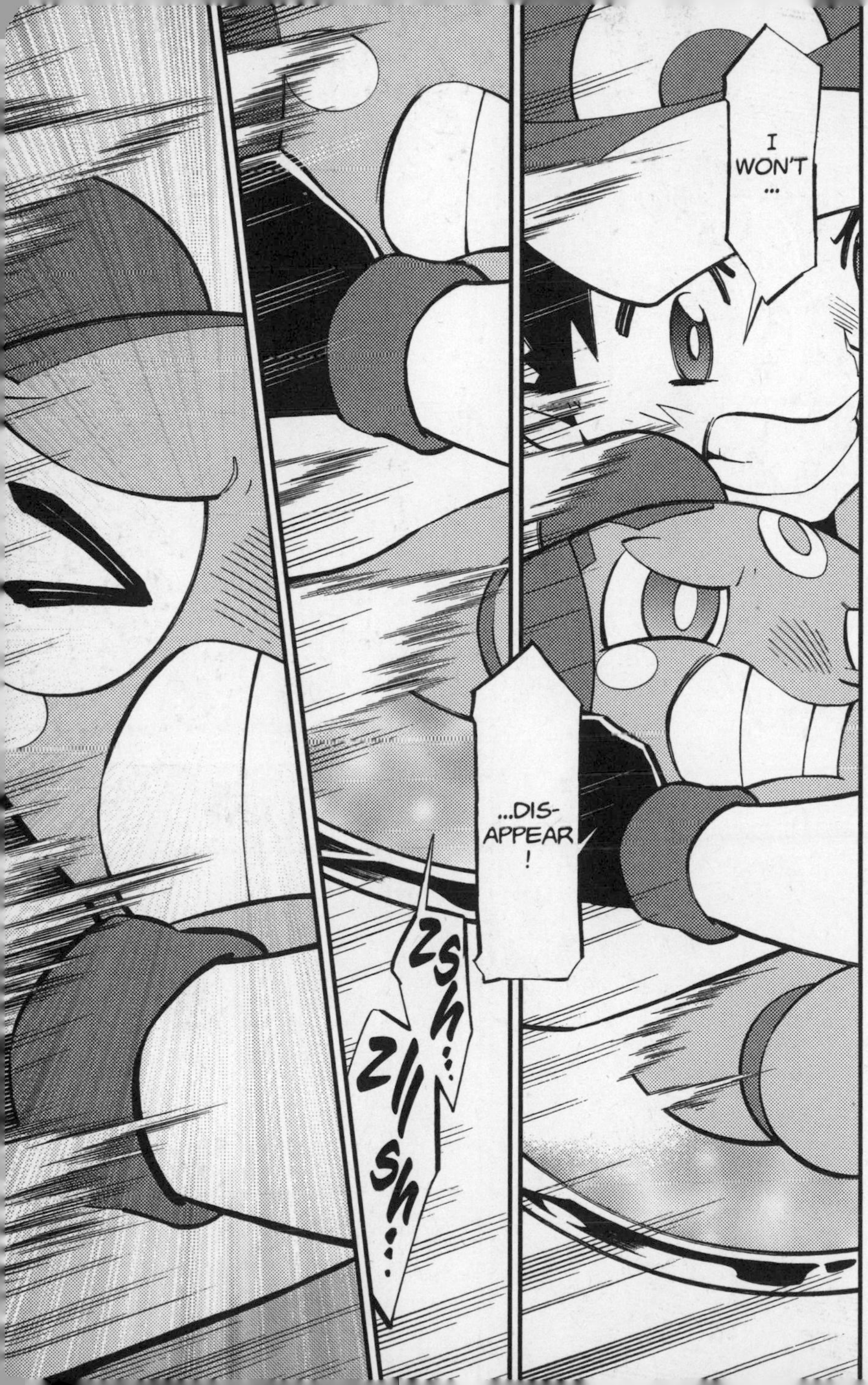
I WON'T ...
...DIS- APPEAR !
ZSH...
ZIISH...

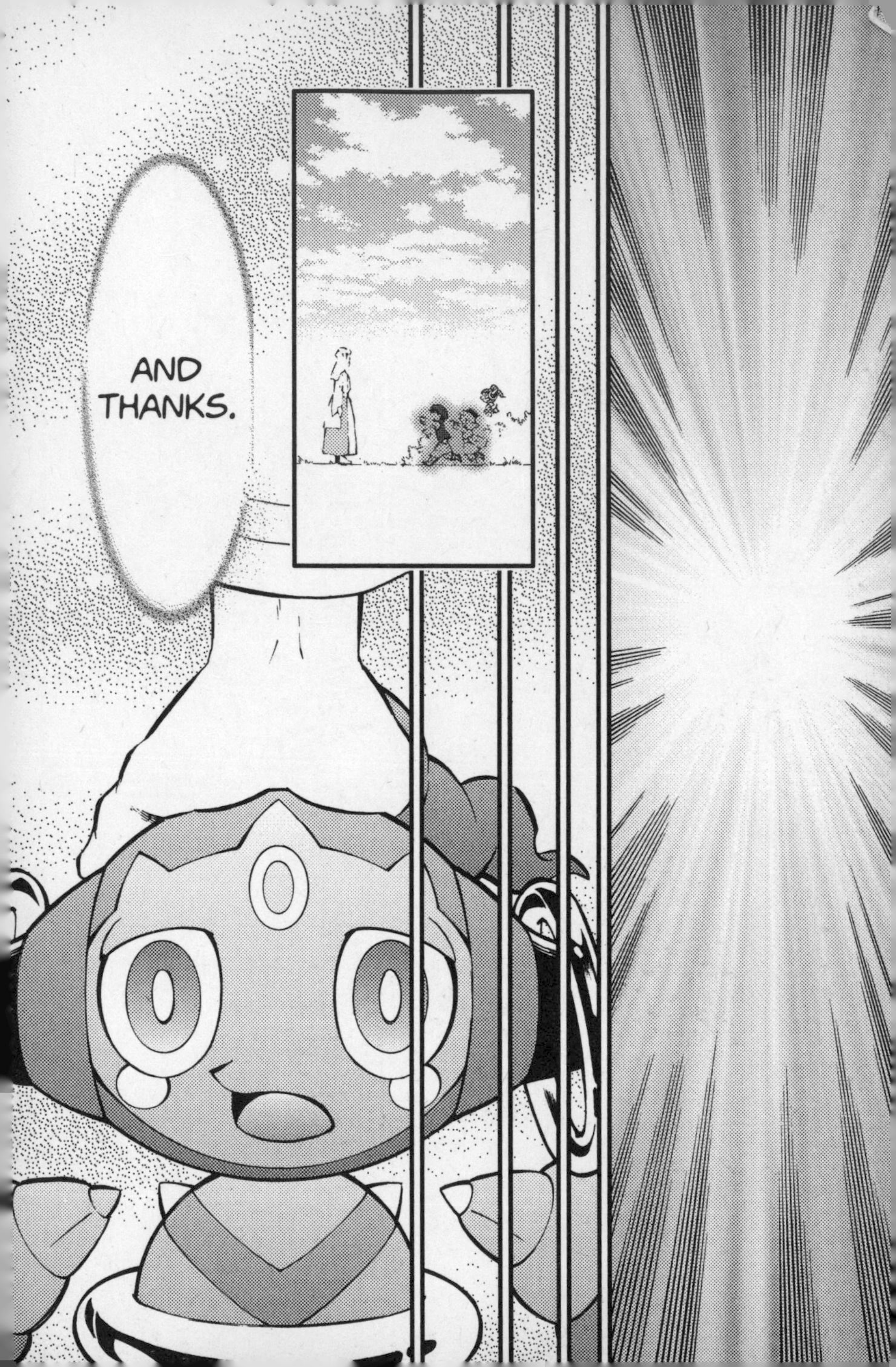
AND THANKS.

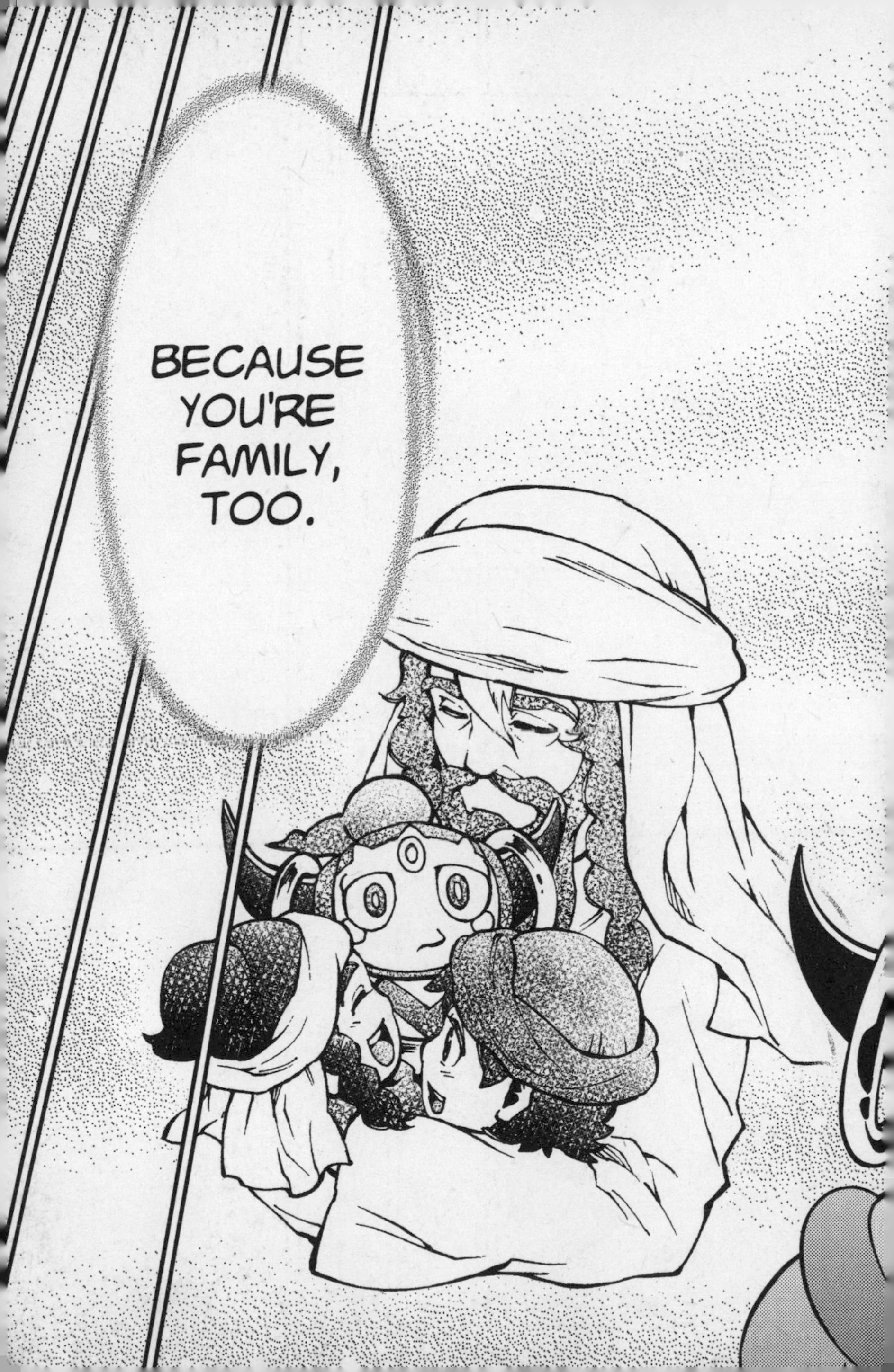
BECAUSE YOU'RE FAMILY, TOO.

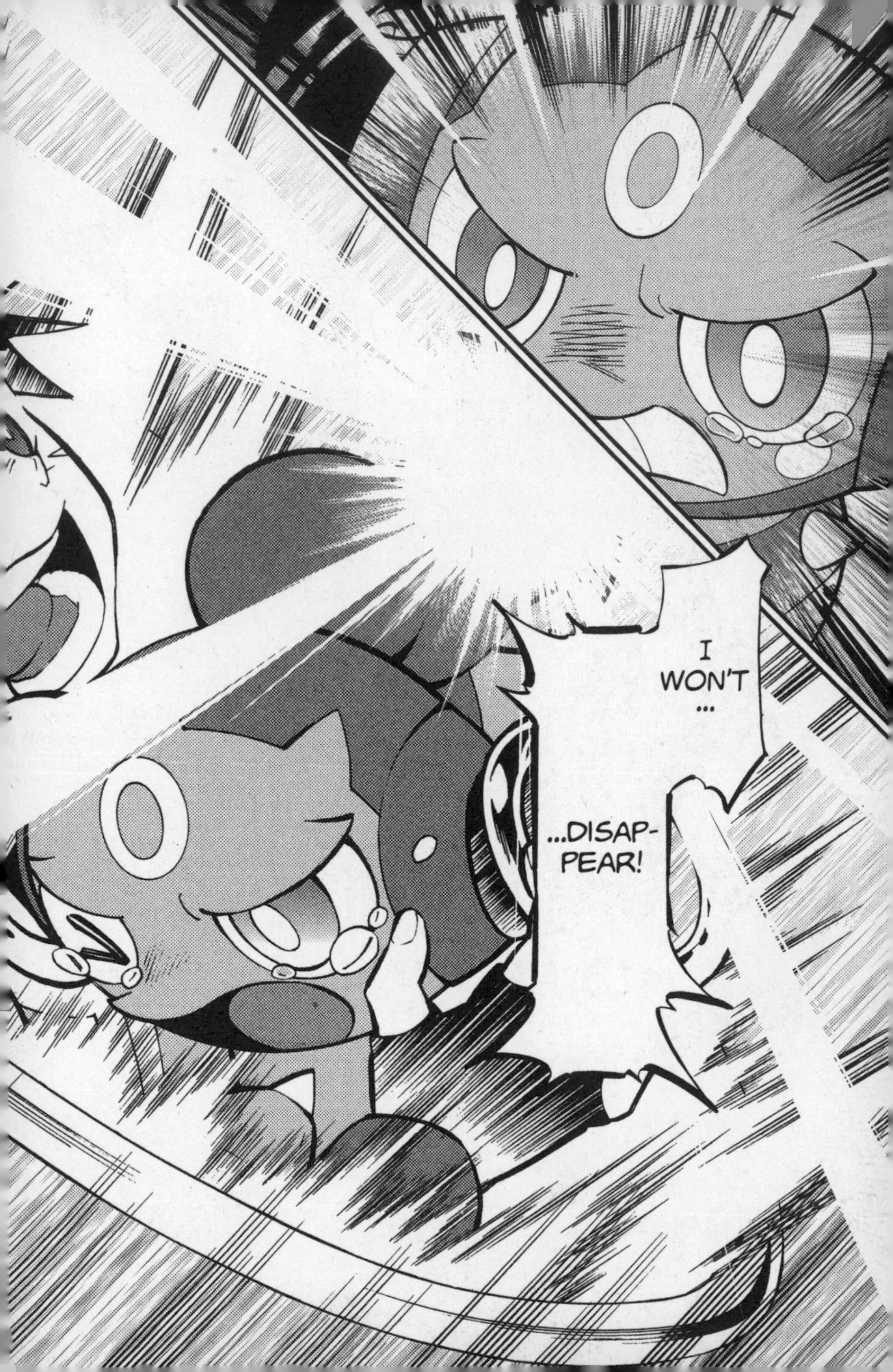
I WON'T ...
...DISAP-PEAR!

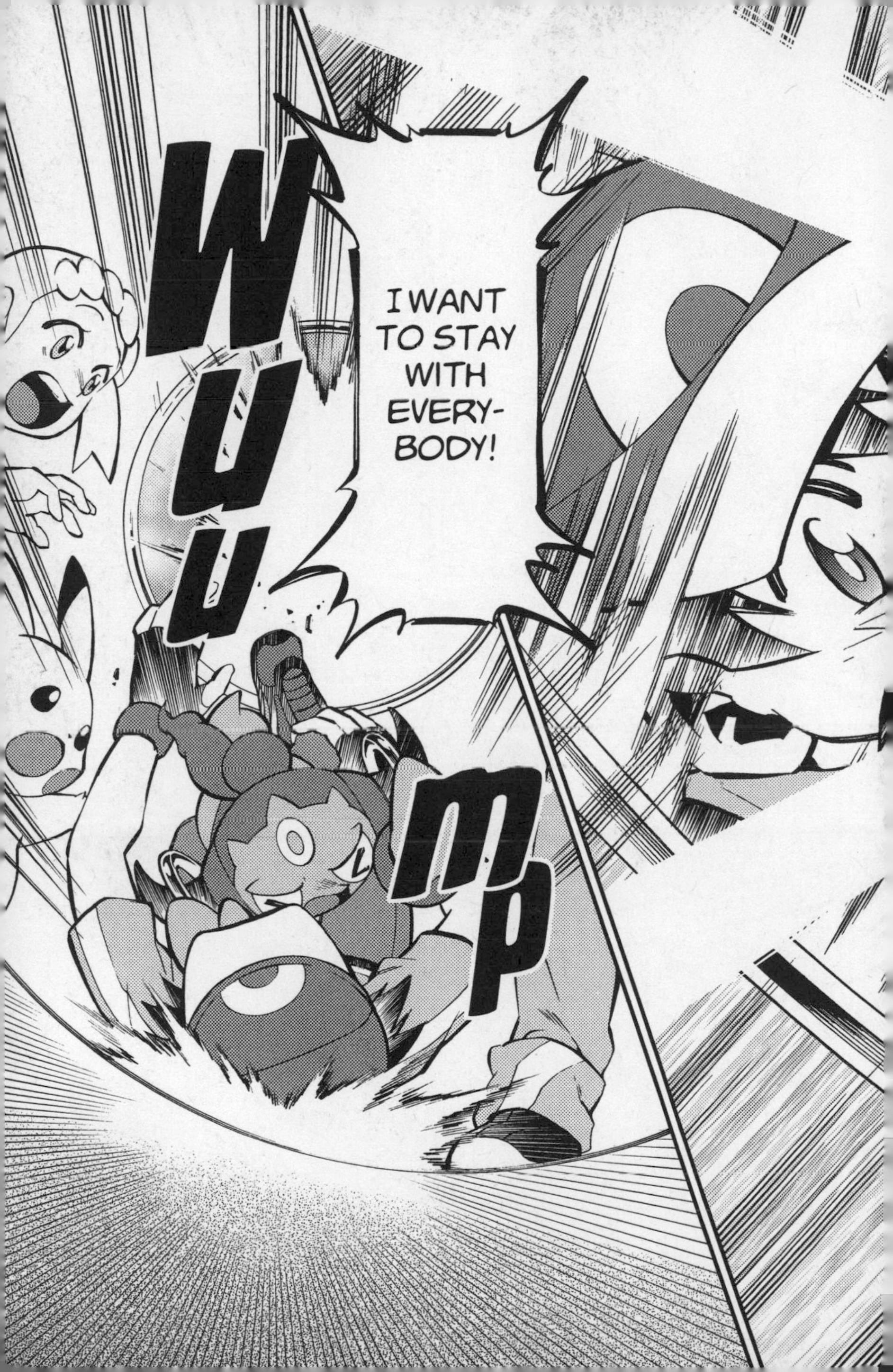
I WANT TO STAY WITH EVERY-BODY!
WUUU
MP

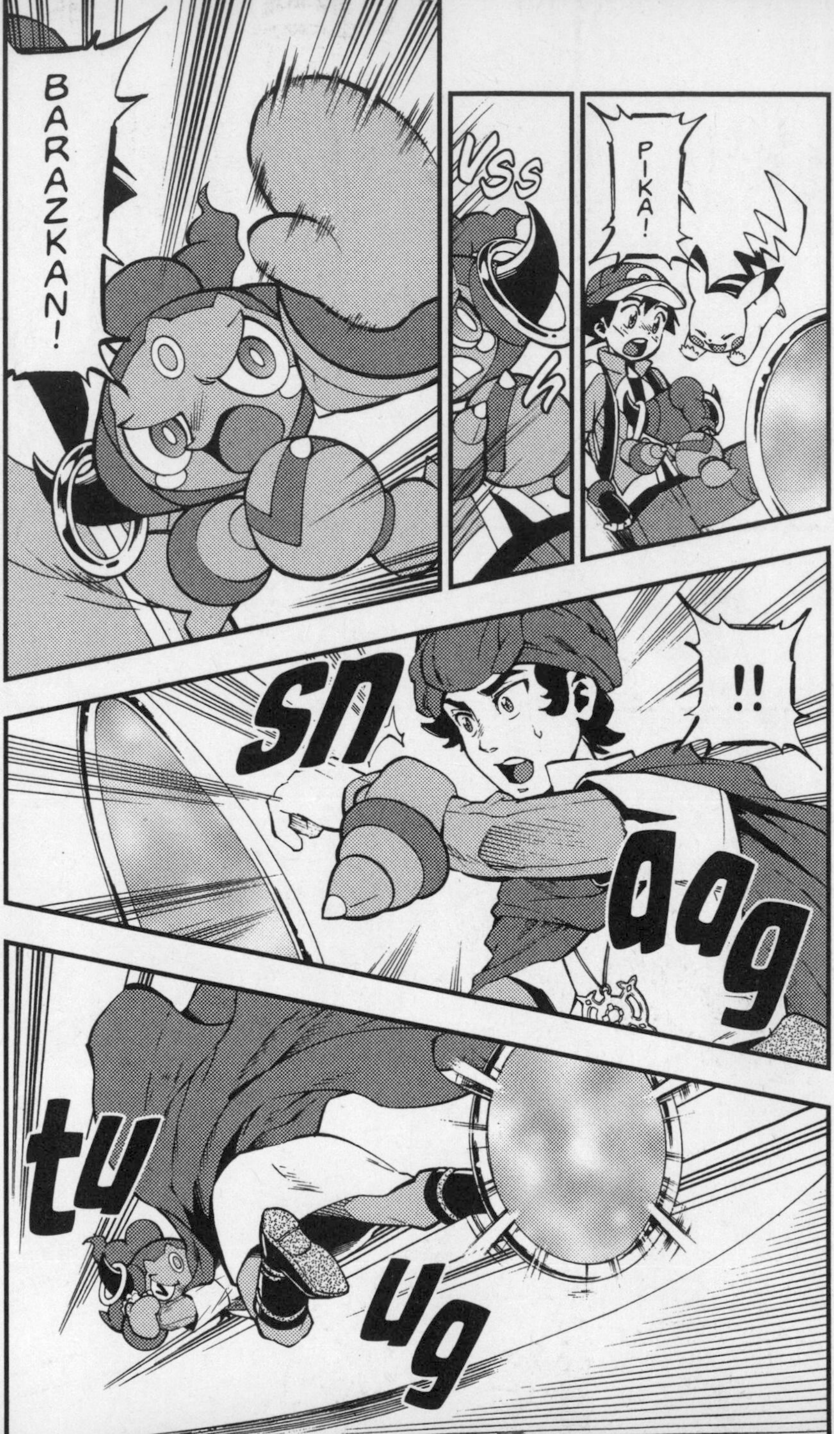

PIKA!
VSS
BARAZKAN!
!!
sn
aag
tu
ug

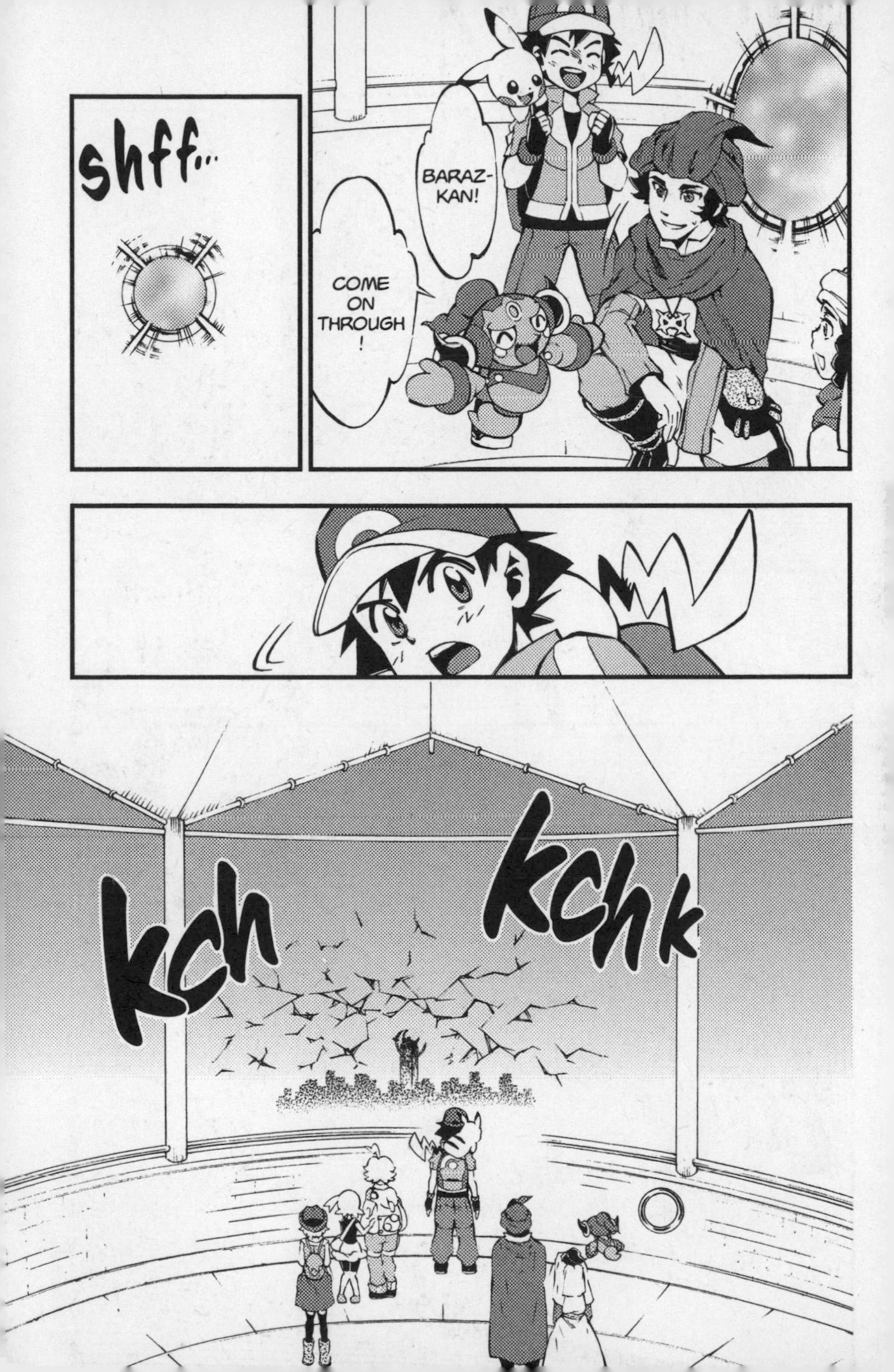
BARAZ-KAN!
COME ON THROUGH!
shff...
kchk
kch

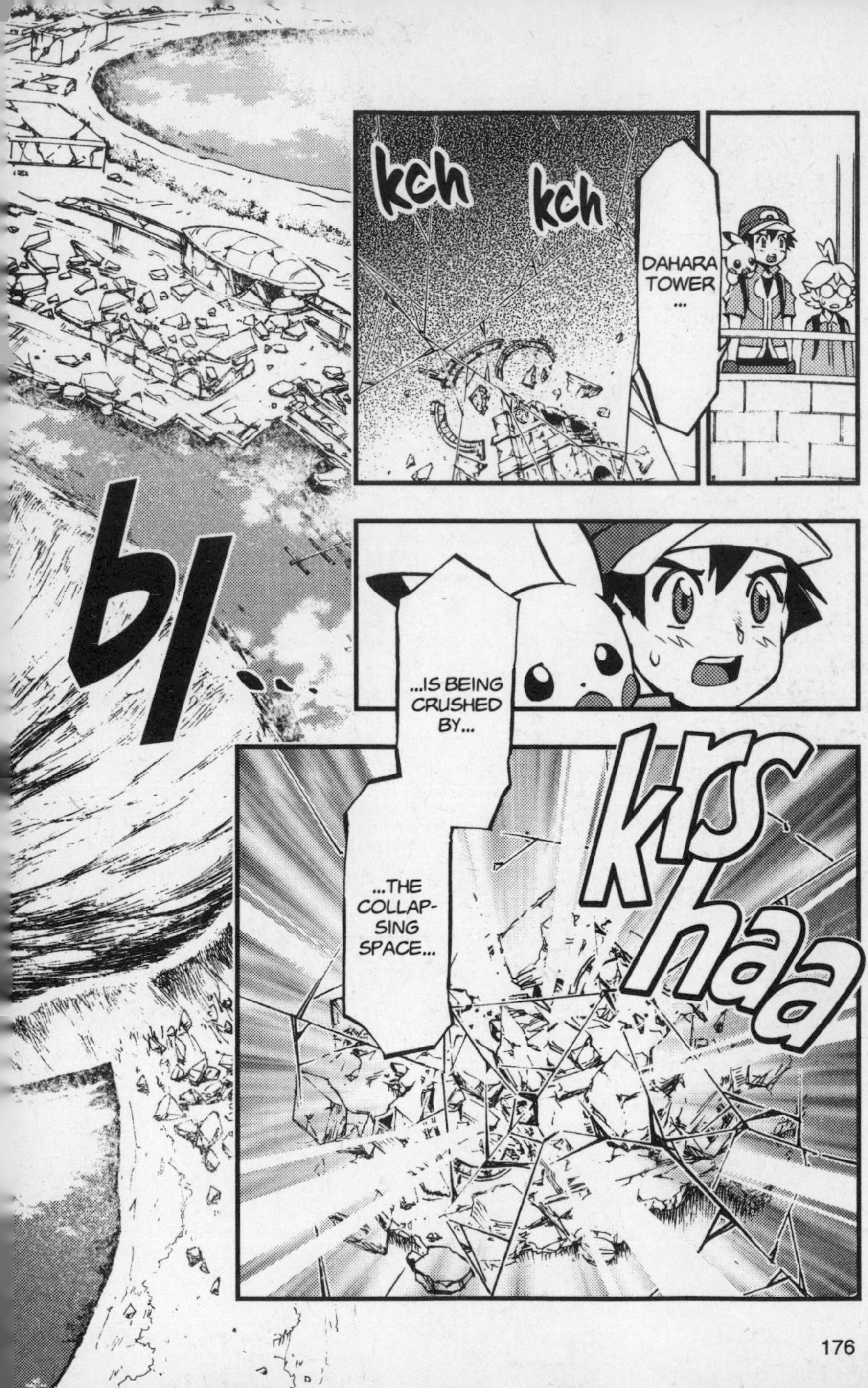
DAHARA TOWER ...
kch kch
...IS BEING CRUSHED BY...
...THE COLLAPSING SPACE...
krs haa
bi

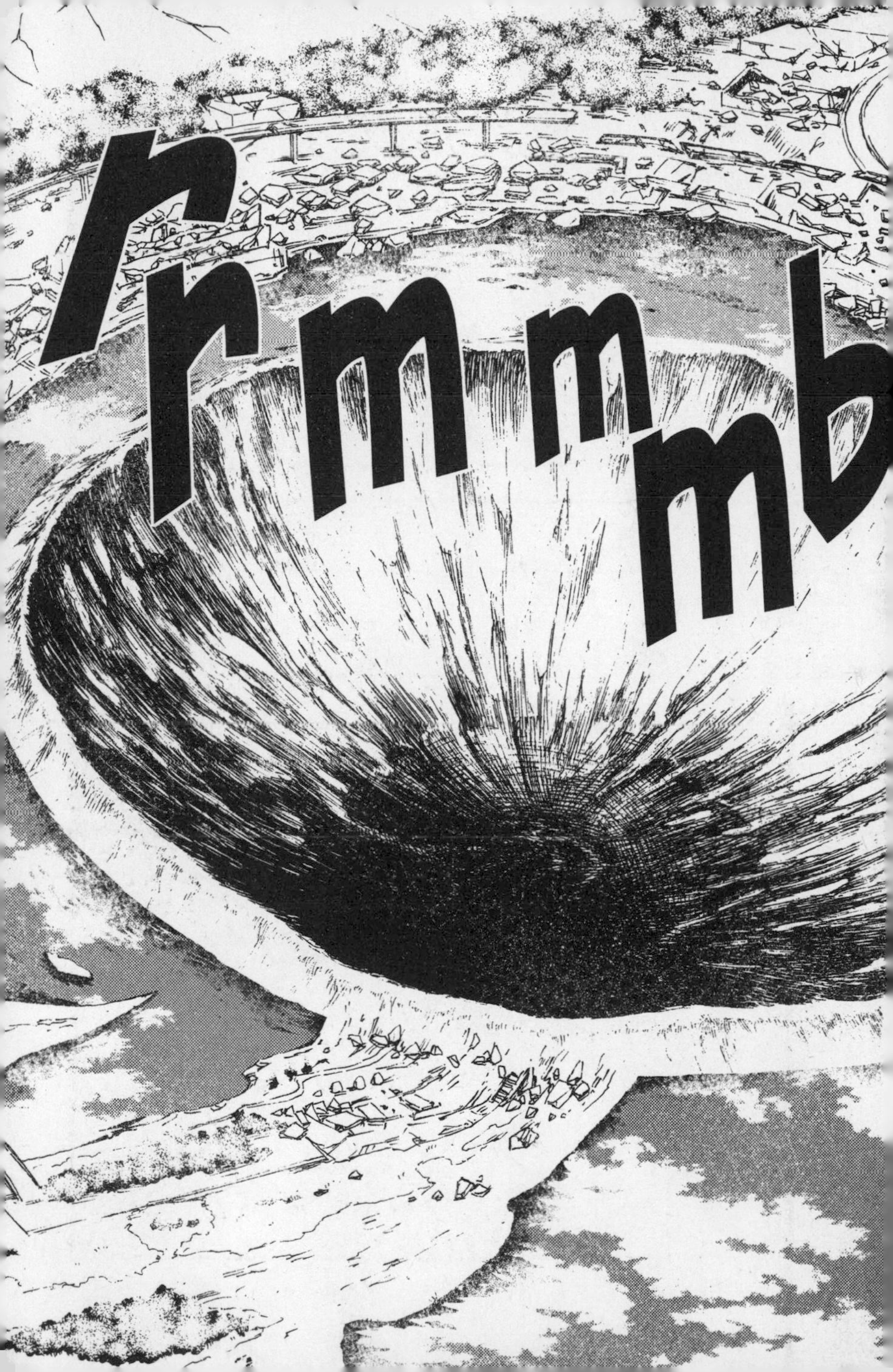
Rrmmmb

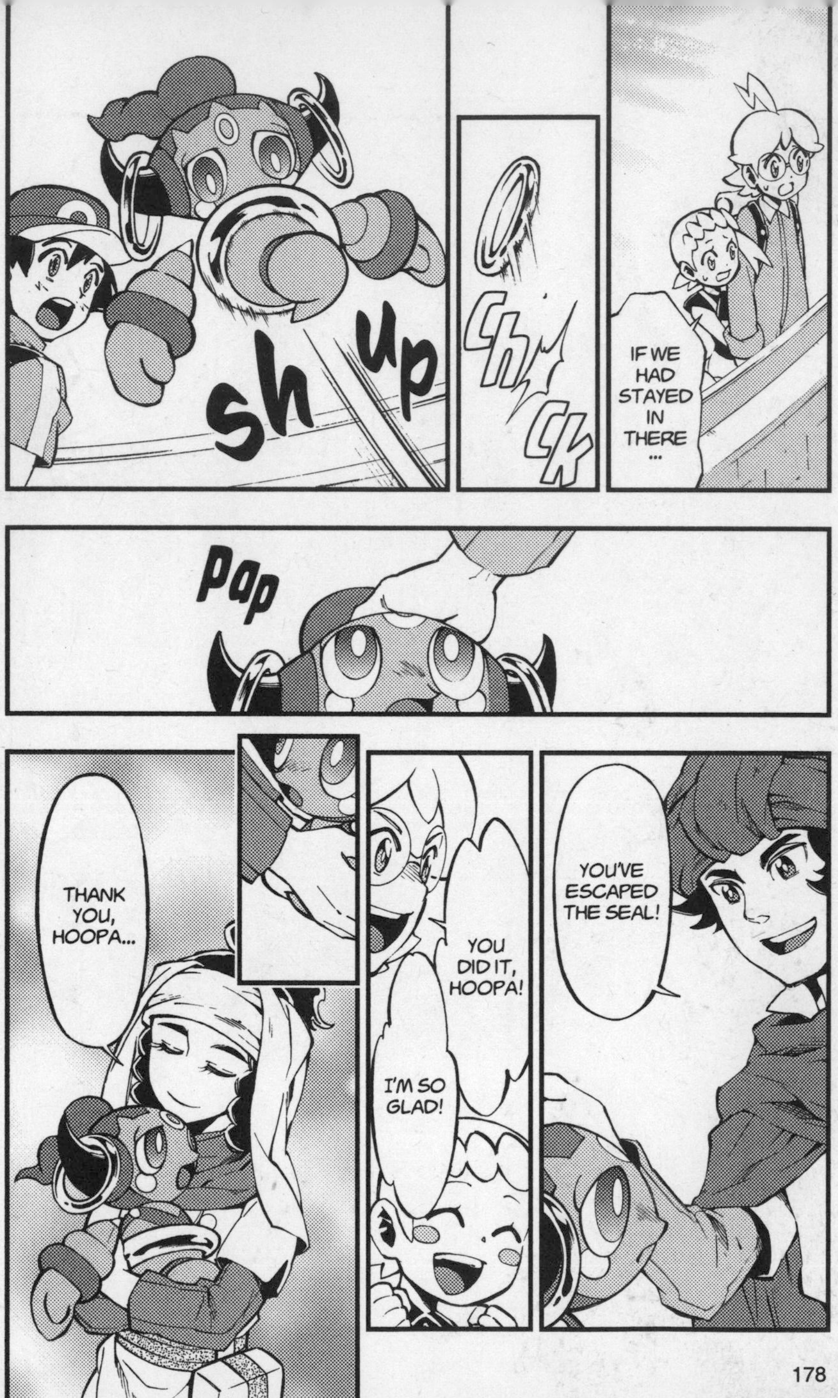
IF WE HAD STAYED IN THERE ...
Chck
shup
pap
YOU'VE ESCAPED THE SEAL!
YOU DID IT, HOOPA!
I'M SO GLAD!
THANK YOU, HOOPA...

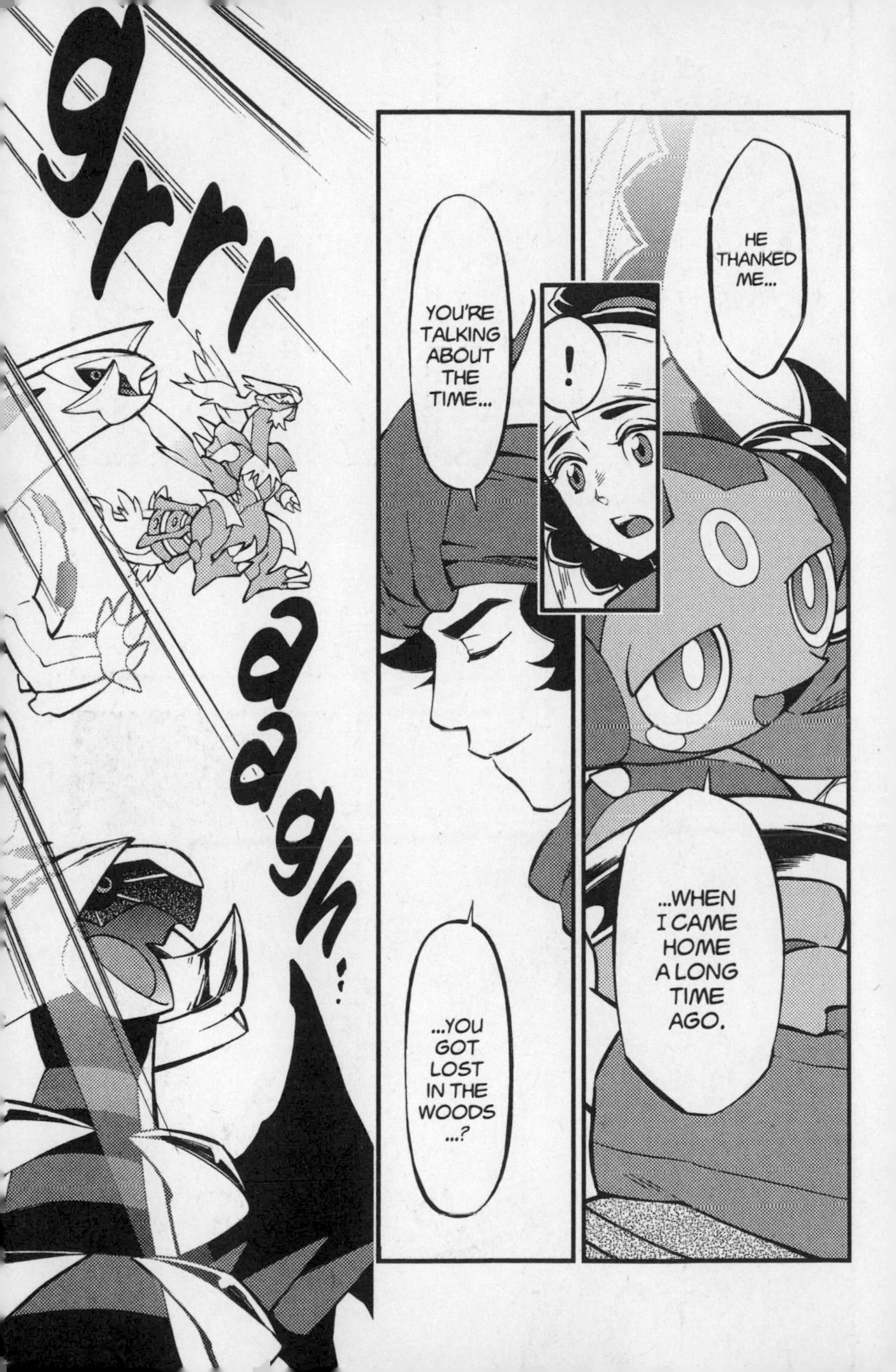
HE THANKED ME...
...WHEN I CAME HOME A LONG TIME AGO.
!
YOU'RE TALKING ABOUT THE TIME...
...YOU GOT LOST IN THE WOODS ...?
grrr
aagh..

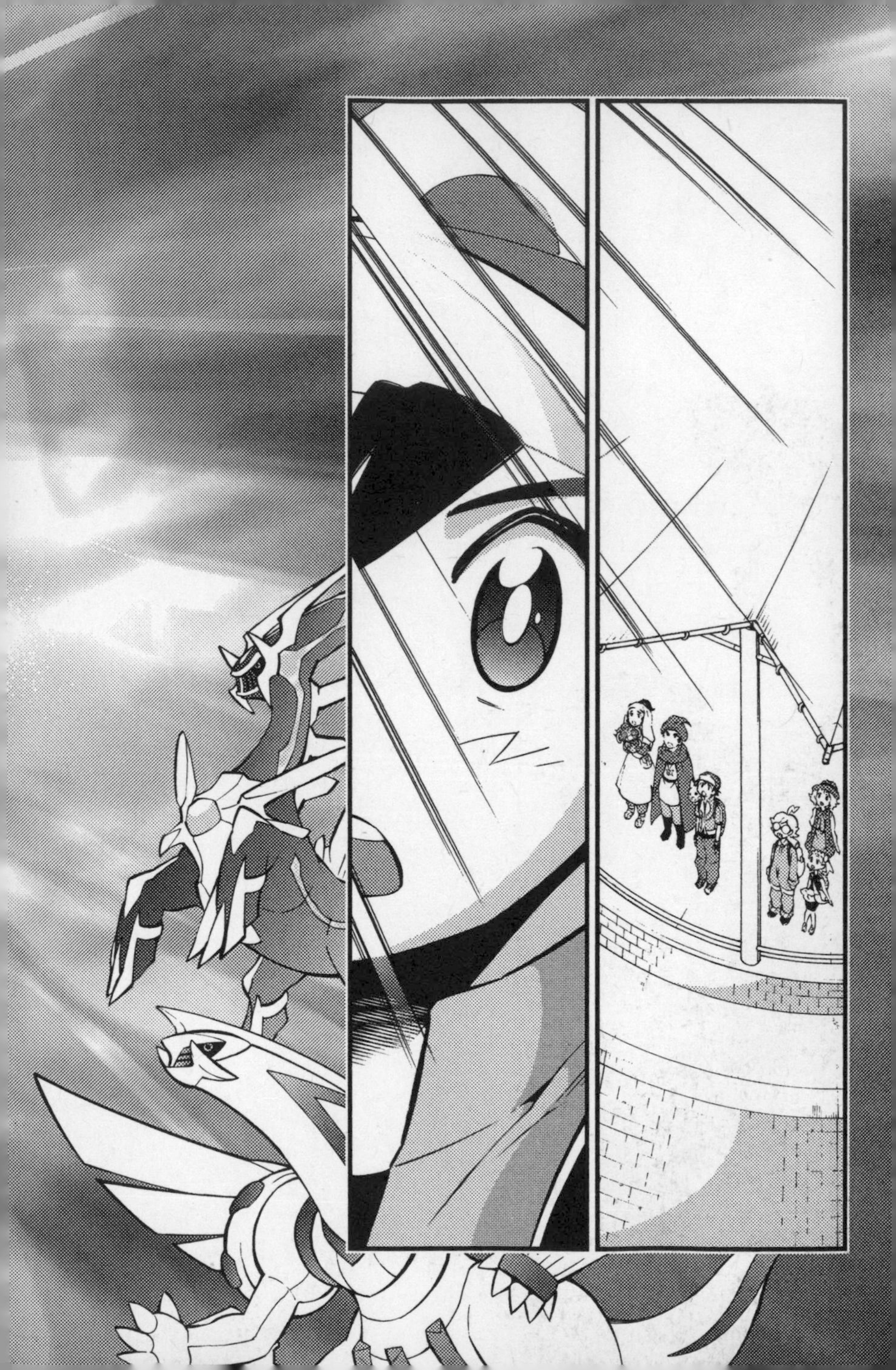

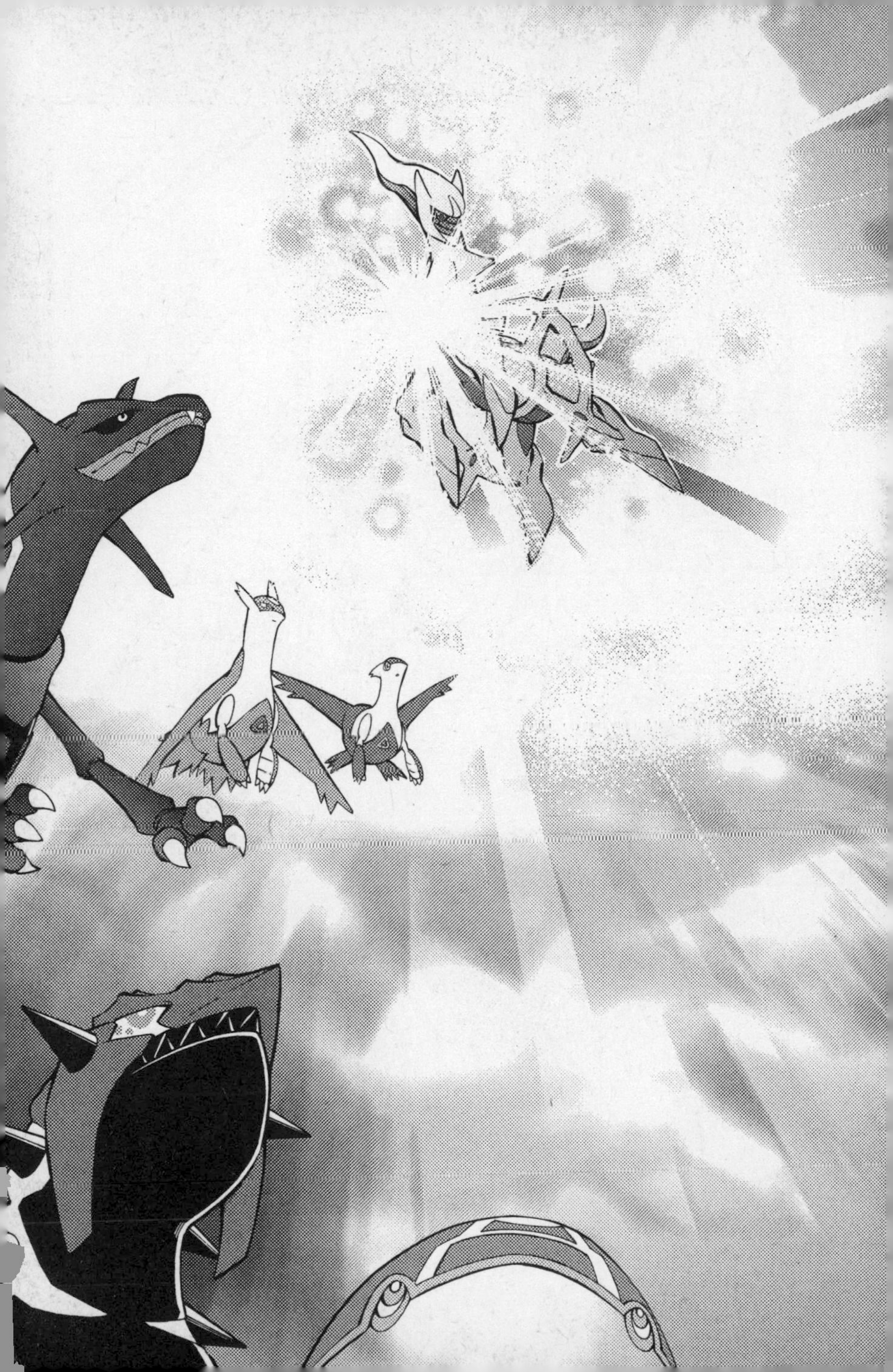

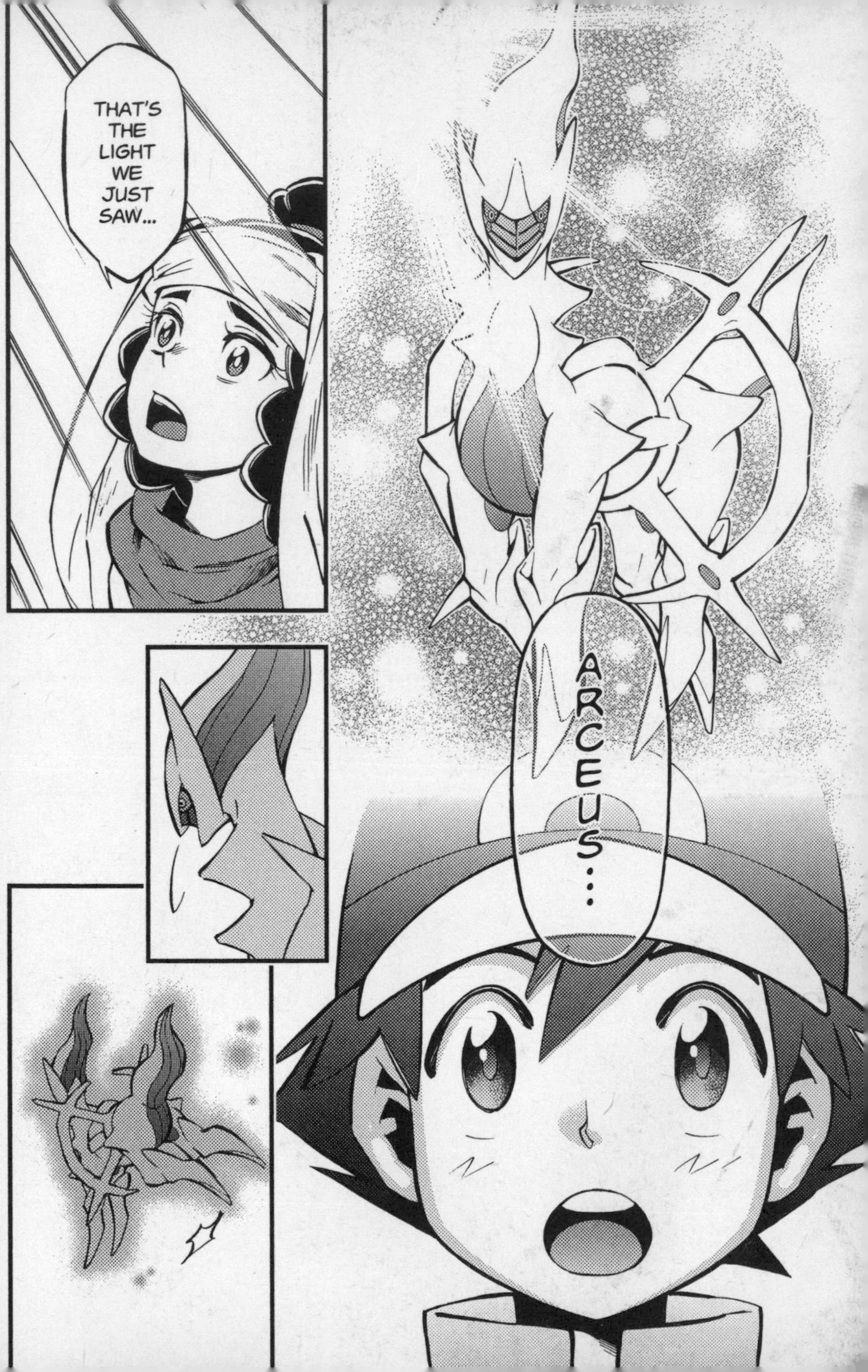
ARCEUS...
THAT'S THE LIGHT WE JUST SAW...

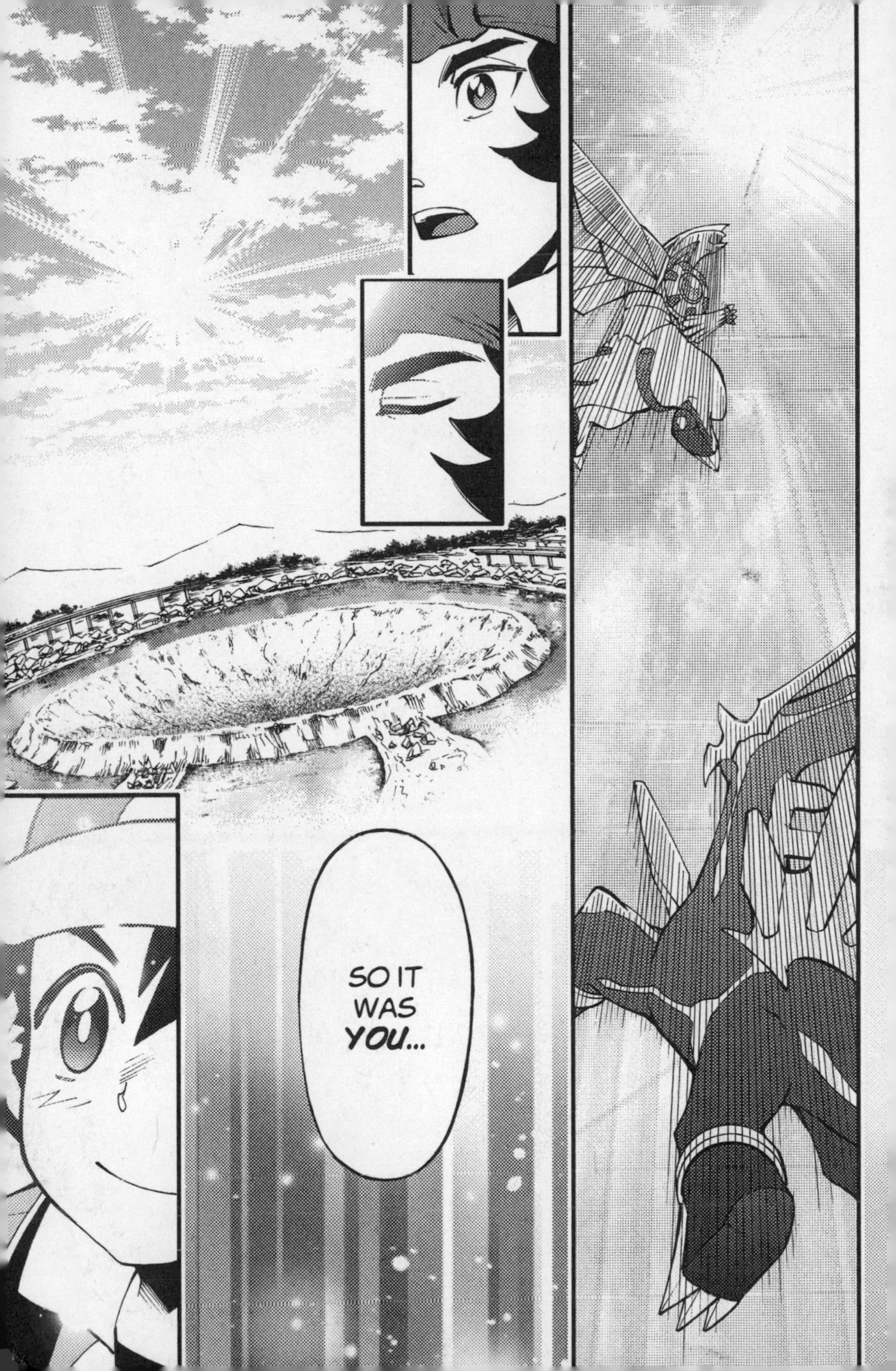
SO IT WAS YOU...

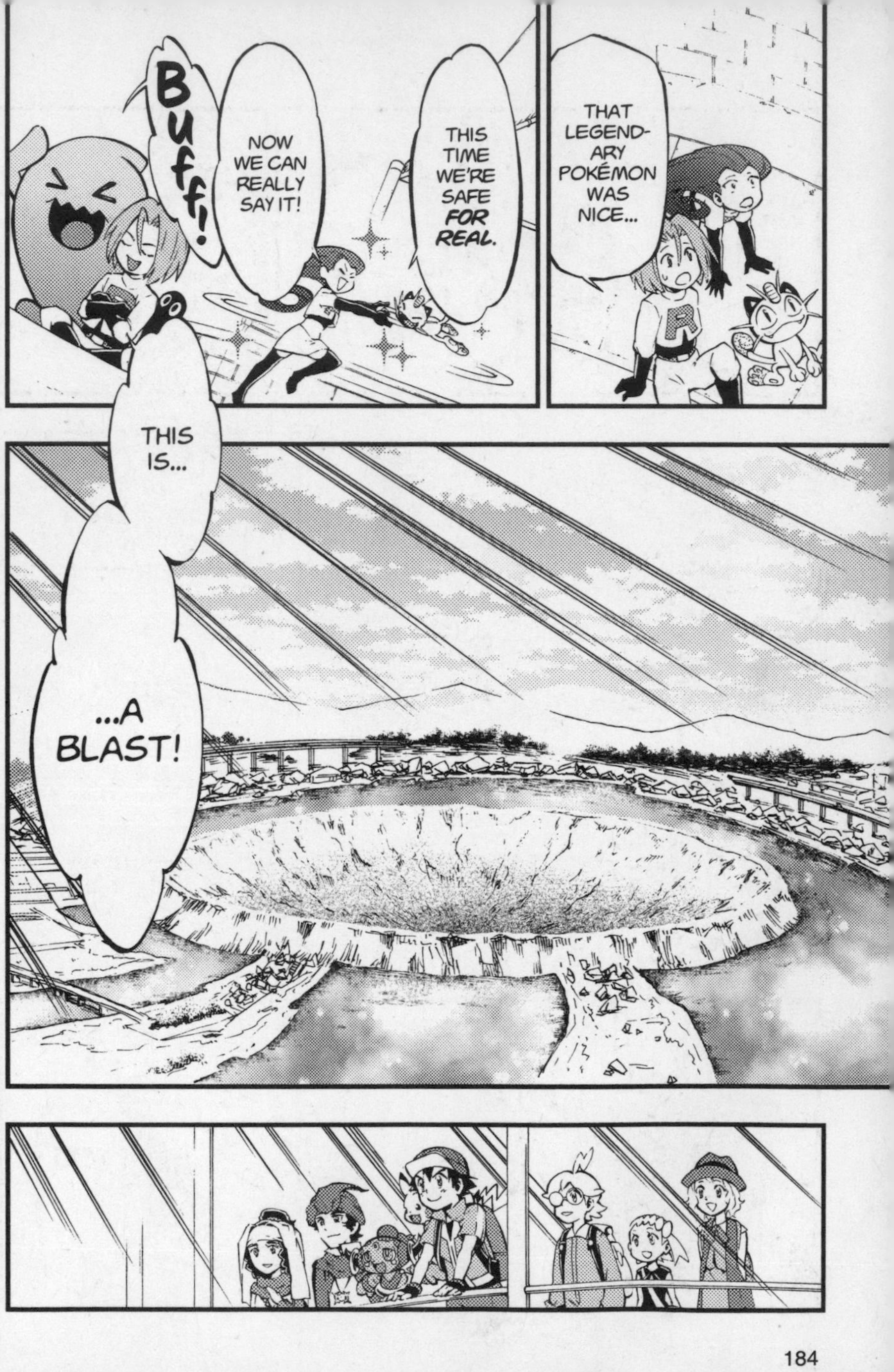
THAT LEGENDARY POKÉMON WAS NICE...
THIS TIME WE'RE SAFE *FOR REAL.*
NOW WE CAN REALLY SAY IT!
Buff!
THIS IS...
...A BLAST!

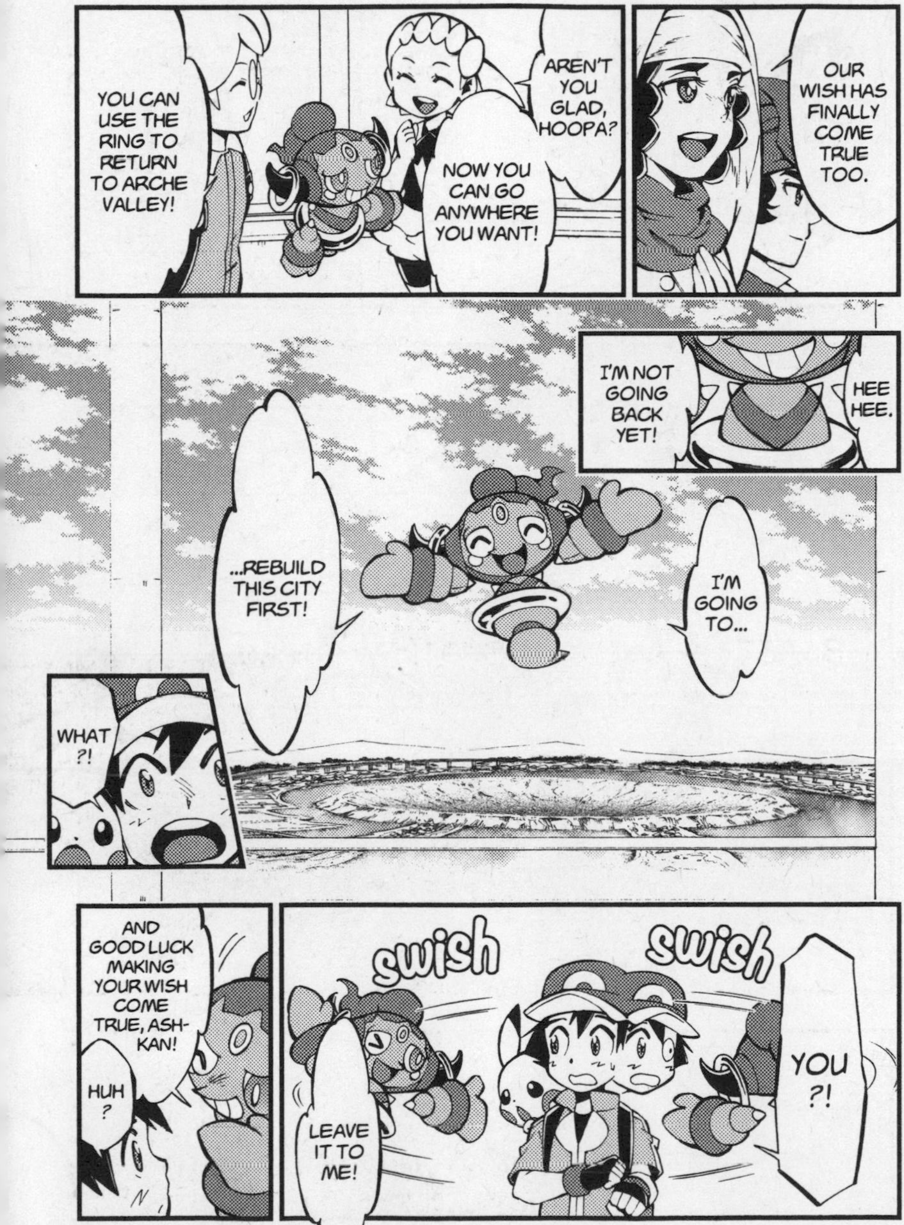
OUR WISH HAS FINALLY COME TRUE TOO.
AREN'T YOU GLAD, HOOPA?
NOW YOU CAN GO ANYWHERE YOU WANT!
YOU CAN USE THE RING TO RETURN TO ARCHE VALLEY!
HEE HEE.
I'M NOT GOING BACK YET!
I'M GOING TO...
...REBUILD THIS CITY FIRST!
WHAT ?!
swish
swish
YOU ?!
LEAVE IT TO ME!
AND GOOD LUCK MAKING YOUR WISH COME TRUE, ASH-KAN!
HUH ?

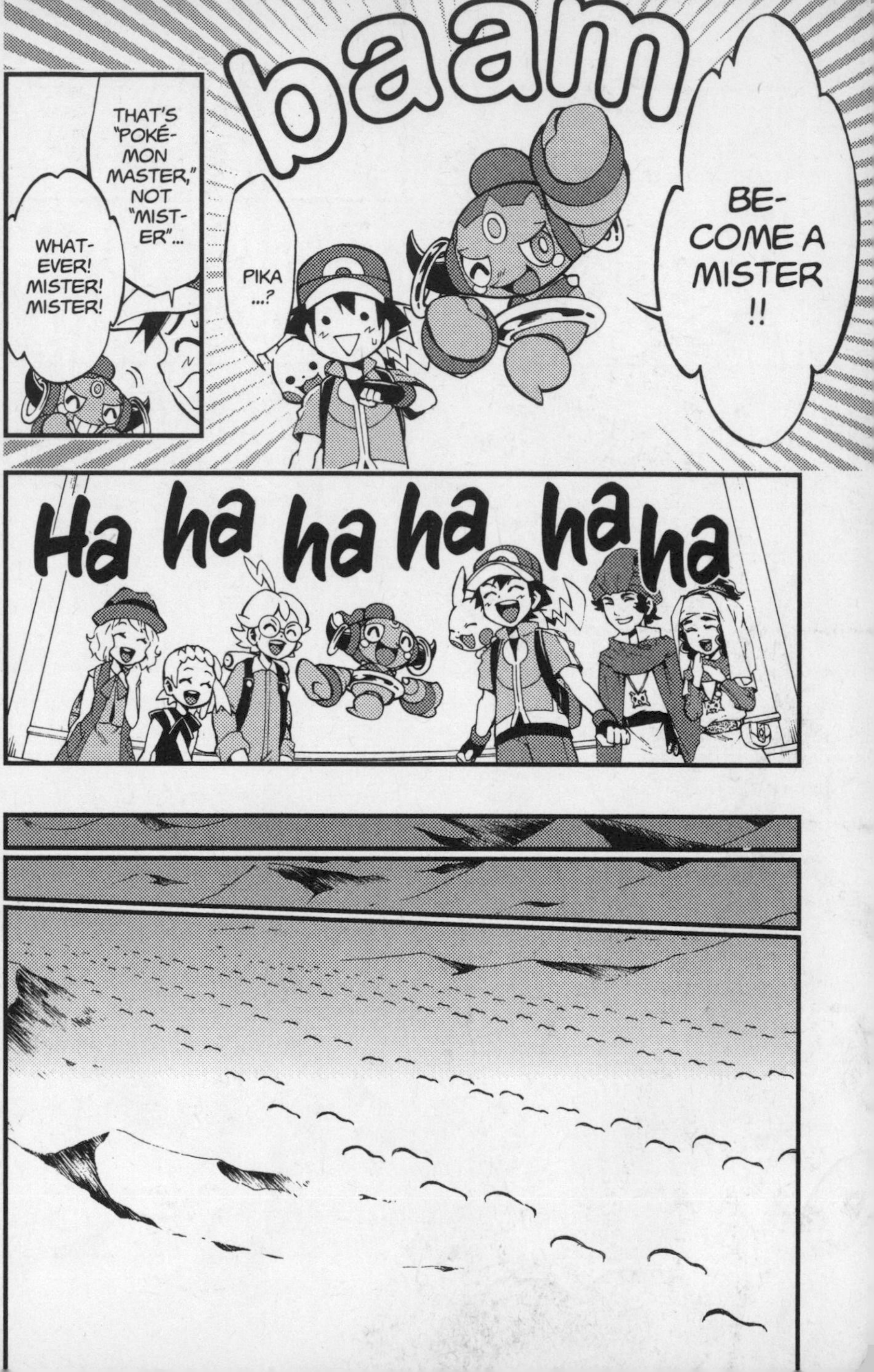
BE-COME A MISTER !!
baam
PIKA ...?
THAT'S "POKÉ-MON MASTER," NOT "MIST-ER"...
WHAT-EVER! MISTER! MISTER!
Ha ha ha ha ha ha

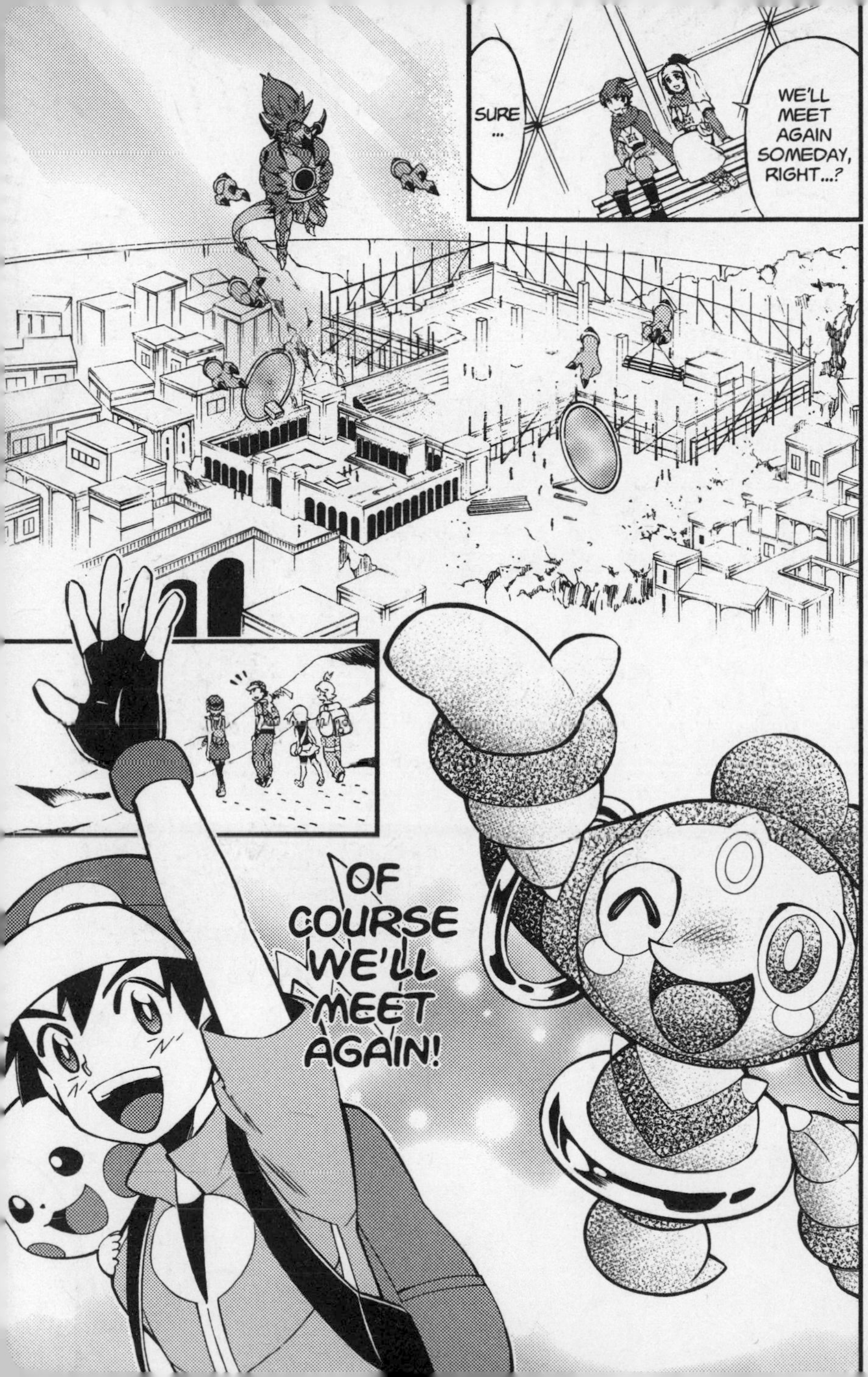
WE'LL MEET AGAIN SOMEDAY, RIGHT...?
SURE...
OF COURSE WE'LL MEET AGAIN!

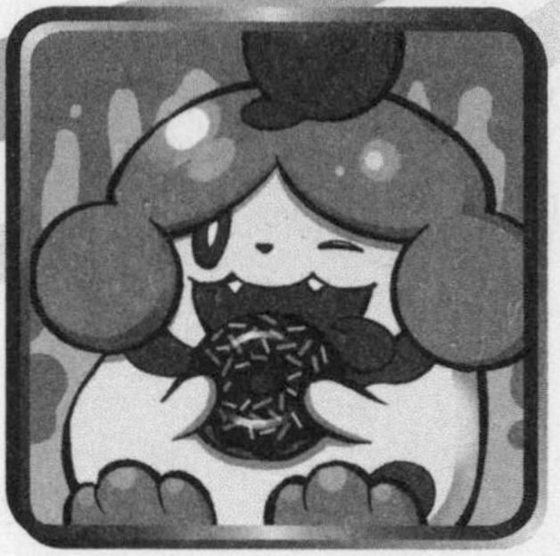

GIN KAMIMURA

I've loooooooved Pokémon ever since I was a child. It's a dream come true to get to work on a Pokémon manga! I'd like to thank all the people involved who supported me until the graphic novel came out, as well as my family. Thank you very, very much!

STORY AND ART BY
Gin Kamimura

©2016 The Pokémon Company International.
©1998–2015 PIKACHU PROJECT.
©1995–2016 Nintendo/Creatures Inc./GAME FREAK inc.
TM, ®, and character names are trademarks of Nintendo.
POKÉMON THE MOVIE XY RING NO CHOMAJIN HOOPA
by Gin KAMIMURA
© 2015 Gin KAMIMURA
All rights reserved.
Original Japanese edition published by SHOGAKUKAN.
English translation rights in the United States of America, Canada, the United Kingdom,
Ireland, Australia and New Zealand arranged with SHOGAKUKAN.

Original Japanese Edition Design: Plus One

TRANSLATION **Tetsuichiro Miyaki**
ENGLISH ADAPTATION **Bryant Turnage**
TOUCH-UP & LETTERING **Susan Daigle-Leach**
DESIGN **Shawn Carrico**
EDITOR **Annette Roman**

Printed in the U.S.A.

Published by VIZ Media, LLC
P.O. Box 77010
San Francisco, CA 94107

10 9 8 7 6 5 4 3
First printing, March 2016
Third printing, November 2016

Pokémon
BLACK & WHITE

STORY & ART BY **SANTA HARUKAZE**

YOUR FAVORITE POKÉMON FROM THE UNOVA REGION LIKE YOU'VE NEVER SEEN THEM BEFORE!

Available now!

A pocket-sized book brick jam-packed with four-panel comic strips featuring all the Pokémon Black and White characters, Pokémon vital statistics, trivia, puzzles, and fun quizzes!

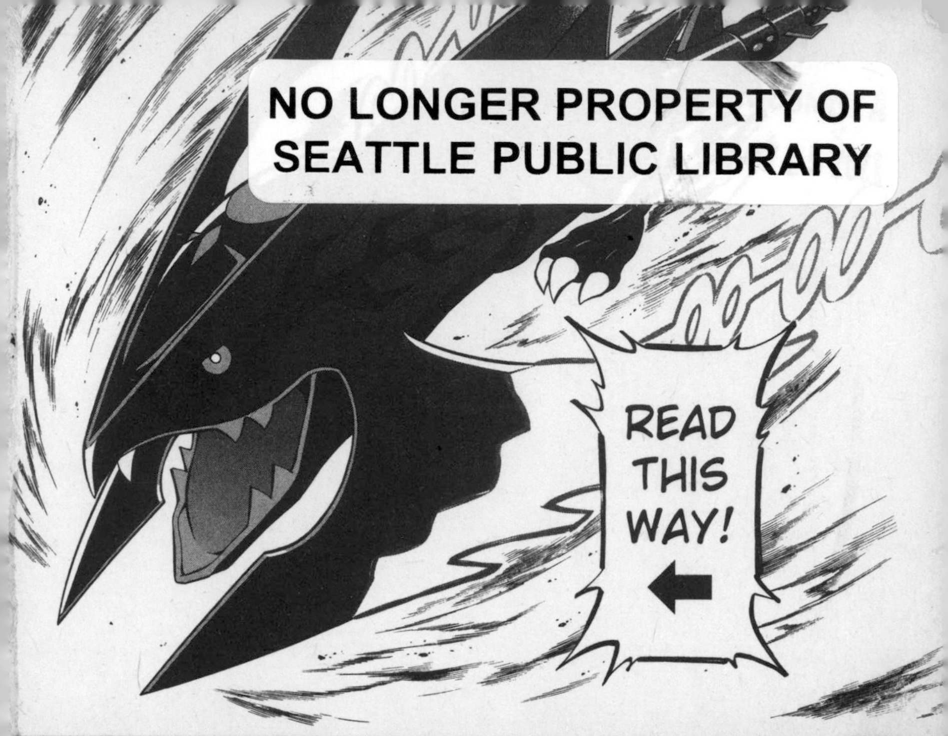
READ
THIS
WAY!

WE'LL SHOW YOU HOW TO READ THIS GRAPHIC NOVEL!

To properly enjoy this Perfect Square graphic novel, please turn it around and begin reading from right to left.

This book has been printed in the original Japanese format in order to keep the placement of the original artwork.

Have fun with it!

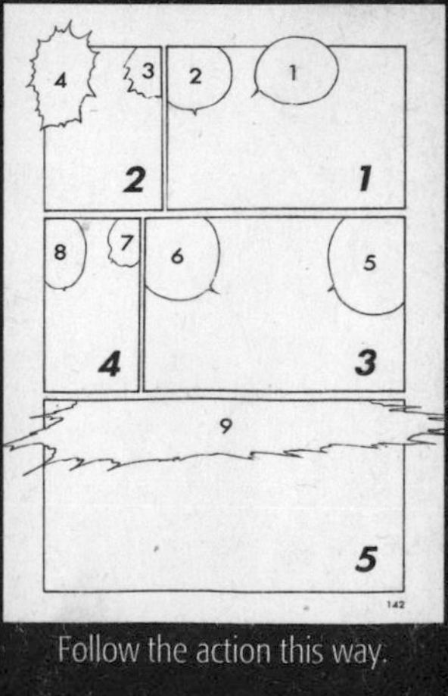
1
2
3
4
1
2
5
6
7
8
3
4
9
5
142

Follow the action this way.